Copse and Codgers

by

John Kemp

Copyright @ 2015 John Kemp

All rights reserved.

ISBN-13 978-1518605215

ISBN-10 1518605214

This paperback version of **Copse and Codgers**

Is produced by "Createspace"

It is available from Amazon and other booksellers.

An electronic version is

Published by Amazon's "Kindle".

By the same Author:

"Caring for Shirley"

Also available in e-book and paperback versions.

See website at: caringforshirley.co.uk

Copse and Codgers

John Kemp

CHAPTER 1

My day starts with a bang. Not a cosmological big bang, you understand, but enough to wake me in a sudden panic as the bed gives a lurch to starboard and I feel a cold current of damp air on my face. I am out of bed and searching for my life jacket on top of the wardrobe before I remember that I have been retired for twenty years and am no longer a sailor plying the seven seas. Reassured that I am not on a sinking ship, I pull myself together and take stock of the situation. I still feel a chill wind swirling around my ankles, although the floor seems firm enough.

There is a perfectly normal morning daylight trickling in through my bedroom window, but it is accompanied by the highly unusual sight of the upper trunk and branches of an aged oak tree. The force-eight gale which was clearly responsible for this unwelcome visitation is whistling in through the shattered window and rapidly covering my bed with leaves and lighter debris. I shiver in the blast of freezing air and take a look at the clock on my bedside table.

The time is eight-thirty, - still the early hours of the morning for a senior citizen like myself, who had long concluded that rising early was for larks and those unfortunate beings whose work requires them to do so. That had been me once, I reflect. I had never had a problem with turning to at midnight for the twelve to four watch, but I had always struggled to leave a comfortable, warm bunk at four a.m. for the four to eight watch.

I bring my thoughts back to the present and to the immediate calamity. I find my dressing gown and slippers, and make my way up-wind to inspect the damage. There are shards of glass on the carpet and the wind is moist and boisterous like the harbinger of the south-west monsoon in early June as it works up the determination to blow implacably across the Bay of Bengal for the next few months. The tree on the other hand, seems to have made itself comfortable in the side of my house and does not appear likely to shift and cause further destruction.

I stuff some cushions into the gaps between the tree and the much distressed window frame, which calms the mini whirlwind that was disporting itself inside my bedroom. Then I shake the leaves off my bed-cover and sweep up the worst of the broken glass and other litter from my floor. There seems nothing more to be done immediately, so I totter downstairs to make myself a restorative pot of coffee. Having filled the kettle and exhorted it to boil in double-quick time, I notice what appears to be the rear half of my cat, Barnacle, standing against the door to the garden. On closer inspection, I see that he has his front-end through the cat-flap while his less attractive back-end remains in the kitchen. He is no doubt surveying the fallen tree with conflicting responses of intense curiosity and equally intense caution, as is his habit when confronted by anything new,

I move over to the door and Barnacle immediately withdraws his head so that the whole cat is back in the kitchen with me. He stares at me reproachfully, as if it is my fault that his garden has been given an unwelcome makeover during the course of the night.

"It's not my doing," I assure him. "It's an act of God."

I take down the jar containing his salmon-stick treats, and offer him one. He accepts gracefully and rubs his whiskers against my leg. I can tell he still thinks the fallen tree is my fault, but he is signalling that he forgives me.

"Don't look at me like that, Barney." I advise him. "Take it up with higher authority if you want to make a formal complaint."

I fall to wondering whether cats have their own God or whether they share ours. I remember that the Ancient Egyptians worshipped cat deities, so perhaps it is the other way around and we share theirs.

I take a grip on myself. I have a feeling that my mind is tending to wander off onto side-tracks like this with increasing frequency. It must be a sign of increasing maturity, I tell myself. Lateral thinking is supposed to be a good thing, isn't it?

I decide I had better take a look at the situation in the garden, so I put on an old coat over my dressing gown, and open the kitchen door with exaggerated caution in case a gust of wind wrenches it from my grasp and blows it off its hinges. My first impression is that it is only blowing a moderate gale. The old tree had withstood many more violent storms than this in its long life. Perhaps it had been an especially strong gust of wind that did for it. A passing tornado, perhaps.

There is something sad about the sight that meets my eyes. The tree had been like a sentinel, standing to attention at the side of the house for as long as I could remember. Now it has abandoned its post and is leaning wearily against the side of the house. 'I've done my duty for a hundred years,' it seems to be saying, 'You don't begrudge me a hard-earned rest now, do you?'

"At ease, soldier," I tell it, as I walk over to pat its trunk, "You did a solid job for a long time, but, if you were going to give up, you might have toppled the other way, clear of my house."

At the base of the tree there is a hole in the ground where the roots have been snapped off and dragged upwards as the trunk had keeled over. Nevertheless, the situation seems to be stable and I decide that no further movement is likely. Accordingly, I take myself back into the warm kitchen, make the coffee and put a couple of croissants in the oven to warm up. It seems best to start the day with a simple breakfast. Plenty of marmalade on the croissants, I promise myself.

Feeling more settled after my fix of caffeine and calories, I reflect that the fallen tree is not all bad news. Barnacle is sitting on his personal chair at the table looking at me with an unwavering stare. I know he is expecting that, if he keeps it up long enough, I will give him another treat, but it is convenient to imagine that he would like me to talk to him.

"Listen, Barney," I begin, "You remember when the neighbours complained that the roots of our oak tree were interfering with their drains?"

Barnacle's gaze doesn't falter so I can assume he is taking note of what I am saying.

"Then, when I notified the Council that I was going to have it cut down, what did they do?"

Barnacle remains transfixed.

"I'll tell you what they did, Barney. They slapped a preservation order on it."

If the cat is surprised by this revelation, he doesn't show it, but he does reach out a paw and touch me gently on the knee as though he is commiserating. I know this is just his way of reminding me that I have a hungry cat in the house, but I prefer to retain my illusions.

"So there I was," I continue, "Between the devil and the muddy green sea. The neighbours threatening to sue me if I left the tree standing and the Council prepared to take me to court if I cut it down."

Barnacle mews in sympathy, or possibly to let me know that his hunger is becoming physically painful.

"That tree crashing through our bedroom window is inconvenient, I grant you, but it could be the answer to a major problem," I pronounce, little knowing that it was simply the start of what would prove to be a legion of even greater problems.

Cats are traditionally patient animals, but Barnacle is swinging his tail slowly, but ominously, from side to side to remind me that there are, nevertheless, limits. He has been a good listener to my diatribe and I reach for his tin of treats and reward him suitably. He accepts this as no more than his due and stalks off with the air of a cat that has done his duty and feels more than justified in finding a warm spot for his mid- morning nap.

Deprived of my audience, I decide it is time for action. The first thing, I tell myself, is to phone the insurance company so they can instigate the necessary action to remove the tree from my house and repair the damage. I am old enough to remember a time when this would have been easy, but technology has now become more sophisticated. An immediate problem is to find my way through a morass of instructions from automated voices, telling me to press keys with this number or that number depending on the nature of my enquiry. It doesn't help that none of the offered options mentions an uninvited tree entering a chap's bedroom at an unsociably early hour of the morning.

It takes forever before I find myself actually speaking to a human being. She is a young lady of few words, and these advise me that I have called entirely the wrong number. She provides me with an alternative, invites me to have a nice day, and leaves me to flounder once again through enough numbers to complete a dozen Sudoku puzzles. Eventually, I come across another human voice. A young man this time. I give him my policy number and explain the nature of my problem, but he totally fails to take on board the urgency of the situation.

"There have been other trees blown down by last night's gales," he tells me. "And some property damage to roofs and chimneys. We will send an assessor to inspect the damage as soon as possible, but there is no chance that he will have time to attend today"

I explain that the damage has made my bedroom uninhabitable and that I am a person of –well - mature years, living on my own, but this cuts no ice.

"Is there a threat to life?" he asks, "Or danger of further damage occurring?"

I have to admit that neither of the above apply, but I emphasise that I, personally, am being put to considerable inconvenience. Also that it is impossible to keep the house warm with something like a force-ten storm blowing in through the broken window. Exaggerating the wind speed by a couple of notches on the Beaufort scale seems a reasonable ploy in the circumstances.

"If there is some immediate danger to the public," he allows, "I am able to authorise emergency action, but I do not believe that applies in your case."

"I'm a member of the public," I tell him. "So you have a duty to protect me."

"No," he argues. "For the present purpose, you and I are parties to an insurance agreement. A member of the public might become involved as a third party, - but not you."

"So what are you going to do about it?" I demand. "I want that tree removed, my house repaired and the garden reinstated. And I want it done soon."

"Of course, sir," he says, soothingly. "As soon as our assessor has reported, we will arrange for the tree to be removed and the window repaired and any broken brickwork reinstated. And, since I see from your policy that you are a senior, I will try to make sure he comes to inspect the damage tomorrow."

He speaks as though he is granting me an inestimable favour when it seems to me he is doing no more than his job, but I do manage to thank him, albeit grudgingly. We say our farewells reasonably politely and hang up.

On reflection, I found this telephonic episode unsatisfying for at least two reasons. Firstly, I did not enjoy my battle with an indiscriminate technology that coerces a chap to choose numbered buttons based on a series of questions, none of which apply to his particular matter of interest. Secondly, there was the frustration of not having a counter to thump when trying to get sensible answers from a remote operative. Also I had the feeling that it might be a long time before anything was actually going to be done. Perhaps I should stir things up.

Barnacle is in cat dreamland by this time, and there is no way I am going to wake him up to discuss the situation. No-one should harbour the impression that I am incapable of independent thought and, sure enough, after a few moments of contemplation, I hit upon a course of action. I will eschew what might prove to be another unsatisfactory telephone exercise and make a personal visit to the Town Hall.

Unlike the insurance company, I have no contract with the Council, so I am a *bona fide* member of the public and it follows that they have a duty of care for my well-being. I will report the accident and demand that they take emergency action to make my house habitable again. At eighty-four years old, I see myself as little more than a well- rounded middle age, but I *am* a pensioner and it does sometimes pay to play the "poor old codger" card.

CHAPTER 2

I am about to leave on this mission when there is a knock on my front door. I open it to reveal a young lady with a smart tablet in her hand. I look at her suspiciously. I suppose she is the latest manifestation of the cold callers that used to appear with clip-boards at the ready, before electronic communications took over the world.

"I don't need any double-glazing," I tell her, as I begin to close the door again. She is not so easily dismissed and steps forward into the doorway so I cannot completely shut the door without doing her some physical injury.

"I don't need a new kitchen, either," I growl, "But you might need new fingers if you don't remove them from the door jamb."

My, we are pugnacious," she says, calmly. "As a matter of fact I am not selling anything. I am a reporter from the *Daily Recorder* and I'm investigating the damage caused by last night's storm. I would like to write a piece about your fallen tree."

I am somewhat mollified by this information because it seems to me that a paragraph or two in the local press might help to provoke some action from my insurance company and, perhaps by the Council also.

"I apologise for the misunderstanding," I gush. "Please do come in, Miss…?"

She offers me her hand. "Felicity Wright," she tells me, "But do call me Felicity."

"I'm William," I respond. With equal courtesy. "William Selsey." I stand aside, prepared to usher Felicity into the kitchen, but she steps backwards instead.

"I'd like to photograph the damage, from the outside, first," she says. "If that is alright with you."

"Absolutely fine," I say, "But I thought you people brought specialist photographers with you."

"Not any more for local papers like the *Recorder*," she explains as I conduct her to the side of the house where the damage had occurred. "It is tough to stay afloat these days with so much competition for advertising and fewer people buying the paper. They can't even afford to employ a full-time reporter. I have to work freelance, and I only get paid for what the editor chooses to print."

I notice that she is not carrying a camera, but it seems that the tablet can double as both a reporter's notebook and a camera. Felicity, meanwhile, appears to be impressed by the size of the tree and the extent of the damage.

Barnacle, who likes to keep abreast of what is going on, has joined us. He proceeds to explore the mass of broken branches and stands stock still when he reaches the top and is silhouetted against the sky as though posing for the photo-shot of a lifetime.

"What sort of tree is this?" asks Felicity, as she changes the angle of her tablet for her next picture.

"It is, or rather was, a venerable old oak," I inform her.

"Oak, eh?" she remarks, with a satisfaction that I feel is inappropriate.

"Well it might be OK for you," I reply huffily, "But it is a pain in the bum for me."

"I meant oak as in oak tree," she says hastily, "Not OK as in highly satisfactory, - although it is true that for newspaper work it could not be a better species. It would not have the same ring to it if I reported a fallen birch tree or, worse still, a sycamore."

"Stricken oak crashes into house! Miraculous escape for elderly pensioner," she murmurs to herself as she enters this information into her tablet.

I am not too pleased at the "elderly", although I have already decided that my age might be a useful weapon for prompting action by the insurance company. Nevertheless, it is one thing admitting ones age to a faceless corporation and quite another admitting it to a personable young lady. I can't let it pass unchallenged.

"What do you mean by elderly?" I demand.

"Over fifty qualifies," she assures me. "And it helps our readers identify. It is mostly old people who read newspapers these days."

"It's only old people who can still read anything at all, especially if it has long words like miraculous" I say sourly as we move indoors to continue the interview, leaving Barnacle to extend his exploration of the debris.

"You weren't hurt, then?" she asks.

I detect a feeling that she is disappointed that I have received no major injury, but she notes a minute bloodstain on my handkerchief and demands an explanation. She writes busily into her tablet as I explain that I sustained an insignificant scratch when I was clearing up the shards from the broken window.

"Slumbering senior wounded by flying glass," she recites to herself. "Did you have to go to the A and E at the hospital?" she continues, "Ambulance, police and firemen in attendance with sirens sounding?"

"Nothing like that," I tell her. "No-one has been near me," and (I hold up my thumb), "I certainly wasn't going to call the medics for a little nick like this. There are sure to have been more important emergencies after a storm like last night."

Felicity returns to her tablet. "Heroic victim refuses medical treatment," she continues.

"Here, steady on," I protest. "That is way over the top."

"Good copy, though," she says, smugly. "That's what matters."

"What about the truth?" I ask. "Doesn't that matter?"

Felicity stares at me in wonder. "Have you not been living in the real world?" she asks. "What *have* you been doing all your life?"

"I was a sailor until I retired," I tell her. "Just a short while ago." I add, hastily.

"Ah!" she says. "That explains it. You have enjoyed a sheltered life, away at sea with all your jolly-jack shipmates. No wonder you are so innocent and other-worldly."

I protest that I have come across plenty of scoundrels in many parts of the world and that even some of my own shipmates were as abrasive as shark-skin, and as dangerous as when the skin still had a shark inside it. But Felicity waves away my arguments. She presses a few keys on her electronic tablet. "There, that's filed my copy." She says with satisfaction. She puts her tablet into a capacious shoulder bag and makes for the door.

"Thanks for your hospitality," she says, "But I must be on my way. There is a protest meeting scheduled for the Town Hall this morning, and I need to be on the spot to cover it."

I explain that I am about to visit the Council Offices myself, and offer to give her a lift.

"I have my trusty bicycle," she tells me, "And it is best if I go under my own steam. It doesn't do for a reporter to be beholden to anyone for anything."

We shake hands again as I see her out of the front door. She walks to the gate and I notice that she glances towards my distinctive red Volvo. She retrieves her bicycle from where it has been leaning against my garden wall and gives me a cheerful wave as she rides off towards the town centre.

What a pleasant young lady, I think to myself, - but then I never was a good judge of character.

CHAPTER 3

I busy myself, checking that Barnacle has ample food and water in his dishes, put on my coat, and depart on my own mission. I walk across to my Volvo which, fortunately, has been standing safely in its driveway on the opposite side of the house to the stricken tree. As I drive into town, I work myself into a suitable frame of mind for demanding my rights at the Council Offices. I think of all the local taxes I pay to meet the cost of roads that are mostly used by other people, schools that benefit those who have been rash enough to have children, and a police-force whose salaries should really be paid for by the criminals they are employed to catch. This puts me into a moderately aggrieved mood, such that I feel more than justified in demanding a service that is of benefit to me for a change.

All goes well until, as I approach the Town Hall, I find more and more people in the street. The crowds build up and, eventually, in front of the building itself, groups of citizens spill off the pavements and into the road.

I bring the car to a halt and look around to see what the cause of all this excitement might be. I realise that I have become caught up in the protest meeting that Felicity was telling me about, and the subject of the protest is blazoned on banners and placards that are brandished by the more vociferous members of the crowd. "Save our Ancient Woodland" reads an informative example. "When it's Gone, it's Gone Forever," proclaims another, less specifically.

"Council Traitors" says a third, clearly not shrinking from allocating blame where it believes blame is due. And there are many more.

The crush around my car is such that I have to remain stationary. Some of the crowd glare at me suspiciously as though I have no right to be on the road, but most are concentrating on the Town Hall where a sparse blue line of four valiant policemen are preventing the protest leaders from forcing their way into the building.

As I watch, a tall, striking looking girl with long, jet-black hair is leading the charge. I notice that she is wearing a rucksack on her back, which allows her to keep her arms free to carry a placard on a stick which she wields like a medieval battle-axe. Trailing some way behind her and providing what seems to be reluctant support, is a well set up young man with a demeanour and appearance such that he could easily be mistaken for her pet mastiff.

A burly policeman confronts the young lady, seizes the placard that she has been waving dangerously, and attempts to wrest it from her grasp. As they wrestle, she brings up her knee in a most un-ladylike movement and the policeman, to balance things up, lets out a highly ladylike scream at least an octave above what one would expect from his macho appearance. He doubles up with both hands to his groin and even at a distance of fifty metres, I find myself wincing in sympathy.

The placard falls to the ground and the crowd falls silent for a handful of seconds, while the two principal actors remain frozen. Protest, even rowdy protest, is one thing, I think to myself. Assaulting a police officer in the execution of his duty is quite another.

As if she has just realized this, the young lady turns and takes flight with the policeman, still under a considerable handicap, hobbling after her. Her mastiff supporter, with a distinct lack of gallantry, follows but as a poor third. The crowd, having found their voice again, shout encouragement for the girl. More usefully, from her point of view, they move apart to allow her to pass and then close up again to impede the progress of the already handicapped policeman. As a consequence , the young lady has built up a useful lead by the time she reaches my position, but she is out of breath and the PC's performance is improving as his pain begins to subside. The young lady looks back to see him grimly following in her wake. Then, she grasps the passenger door of my car, hauls it open and flings herself in. I turn to protest on behalf of my old Volvo which isn't accustomed to such blatant hijacking attempts, but she has already collapsed her long and slender frame into the confined space of the foot-well. It is an incredible feat, like a dolphin squeezing itself into a lobster pot.

"Drive!" orders a muffled voice from somewhere in the depths below my dashboard. "We need to get out of here fast."

I don't much care for the way she says *we*, which seems to implicate me in her criminal activities, and I am about to object that the crowd is too dense for me to drive anywhere, when a clear path opens up as if by magic. Someway back, the policeman is beginning to make better progress through the mass of protesters and, still following him, doggedly but not too closely, is the pet mastiff. Felicity, the reporter has bobbed up from nowhere and is an equal third alongside the mastiff. She seems to be explaining something to him. I decide that a smooth getaway might save trying to answer a great many embarrassing questions.

I begin to move off just as the policeman reaches the car and, for a moment, we are face to face and eye to eye as he peers in through the windscreen. He sees no-one in the passenger seat and darts across the front of the car to continue his search amongst the crowd. As I gather speed, I glance in my mirror. He has come to a standstill, clearly puzzled by the complete disappearance of his quarry. My last glimpse is of him looking directly at the accelerating Volvo and then the protesters close in behind us and he is lost from view.

"You can come up for air, now," I tell my passenger as we clear the last of the crowd and find ourselves on an open road.

It is obviously a more challenging exercise for the young lady to extract herself from the foot-well than it was to fold herself into it. Or perhaps it is just that there is less urgency in the situation. She disentangles her legs, and arms from around her neck and expands to fill the available space as the universe is supposed to have done in the first few nanoseconds of its existence. To my surprise, I find that her hair has turned from black to a golden blonde and has become much shorter. She catches my askance look and smiles.

"It would be bad news if I were to be recognised as an aggressive activist," she tells me. "Daddy is a magistrate and he would gate me if I were to be found out." At the same time, she is endeavouring to stuff a luxuriant black wig into her rucksack.

"I am surprised that an independent girl like you would allow her father to restrict her freedom," I say.

"It's a matter of economics," she replies, cheerfully. "He would stop my allowance if he found out. Then I wouldn't be able to run my car, - I would have to find a regular job, and that really would restrict my freedom. I'd have no time for lobbying to protect the environment or to save the world."

"Young people have no principles these days," I grumble. "Sponging off your dad like that."

"Makes sense," she says, comfortably. "Anyway, it's not just young people. George Bernard Shaw was always recommending people to cling to their mothers' apron strings if they wanted to make anything of themselves, - and that from his own personal experience. Would he be old enough for you?"

This response takes me momentarily back-to-wind so I do my usual trick of changing the subject. She sounds suspiciously like an English graduate and not someone with whom I wish to bandy literary allusions.

"What do you mean by jumping, uninvited, into my car?" I demand. "Especially after what you did to that poor policeman."

She has the grace to look contrite. "Yes, it was a bit extreme," she agrees," But he did provoke me."

"And now you are on the run from the law," I say.

"So are you," she replies. "You have helped me escape, so you are an accomplice after the fact. Ten years hard labour, I should think, for aiding and abetting someone who has assaulted a police officer. The courts come down hard on grievous bodily harm."

I don't like the turn this conversation is taking.

"You can't shop me without implicating yourself," I remind her.

"Of course not," she agrees, "We are in this together, you and I."

"Oh, no we aren't," I tell her forcefully. "You are going to get out of this car very soon and, after that, I do not expect to ever see you again."

She looks at me reproachfully. "I don't see that it will work like that," she says. "If the law were to catch up with me, I would have to tell them everything, wouldn't I? - Especially how you volunteered to drive my getaway car."

The atmosphere in the car sudden feels much colder. Bound for New York across the North Atlantic in winter, there is a rapid and disconcerting drop in temperature as a ship crosses the narrow boundary between the warm Gulf Stream and the icy Labrador Current. That's exactly how it feels now. Up until this moment I had thought I was sitting next to a delightful, if over-idealistic, young woman. With a few words, she has turned into Lady Macbeth.

"You wouldn't drop me in it like that," I splutter.

"Of course not," she replies sweetly. "It won't be necessary. We are partners in crime, aren't we? All for one and one for all, sort of thing."

"Listen, Miss – er," I begin, but she cuts me short.

"Diana," she says. "Diana Hunter. And you are?"

"William Selsey," I say, grudgingly.

"Selsey Bill, no less," she laughs, clapping her hands.

"My parents had a lot to answer for," I grumble, embarrassed as always by their lack of foresight.

She leans across and kisses my cheek. "You are a lovely old man, Bill. So quaint. I really am hugely grateful to you for rescuing me."

"I didn't rescue you," I point out, doing my best not to be mollified. "You took it upon yourself. You leapt into my car uninvited and now I would like you to leap out of my life. Just tell me where to drop you off." The top of Beachy Head would do nicely, I think to myself.

"Keep going north on this road," she tells me. "The best thing would be for you to take me home. I can't do much more today."

"You've done more than enough already, if you ask me," I complain, "And I suppose that young man who was supporting you has remained behind to create more mayhem."

For the first time, Diana's cool and confident manner deserts her, and her face darkens. "Buster Crump! That spineless weasel." She snaps. "He'd run for cover if he thought there was mayhem within a million miles. Where was he when I needed him?"

I have no idea who Buster Crump might be, but it is clear he is closely involved with Diana. I already feel some sympathy for the poor chap.

"He was probably not expecting you to be so aggressive to that policeman," I suggest. "I am sure he would have been shocked by what you did."

"Not half as shocked as the policeman," giggles Diana. I can see that her heinous action is not likely to prey on her mind and spoil her sleep like a similar lapse did for the real Lady Macbeth.

"You are a hard-hearted woman, Diana Hunter," I tell her.

"You are too free with your compliments, sir," she replies, having recovered her poise. "Now, take the next right and then the second left, if you please"

As I follow the instructions, she returns to her rucksack, extracts a plain black top and pulls it over her head. It effectively covers the white tee-shirt which had the words *Hands off our Heritage* across the front and the more ominous *Death to Developers* on the back.

"Make yourself at home," I growl. "I'll concentrate on my driving while you change your jeans if you like." But she is impervious to sarcasm.

"Jeans are universal," she smiles. "You can wear them anywhere so they can stay where they are. They are non- incriminating."

We are entering an up-market area of the town, where large detached houses are set well apart in extensive gardens. Following Diana's further directions, I eventually make a left turn into a wide, gravel driveway leading to an unlovely but expensive looking mock-Tudor residence. Ahead of us is a green, four-by-four Range-Rover from which a thick-set character in a late-Victorian tweed outfit is removing a bag of golf clubs out of the open hatch.

As we crunch to a halt, he places the bag carefully on the ground, selects a number ten iron, and balances it, thoughtfully, in his hands as he comes across to meet us. He is a large man, in all directions and I can see at once, from his manner and the look on his face, where his daughter's aggressive trait has come from.

In my time at sea, I came across a few bully-mates and sadistic bo'suns, so I am not intimidated. In such cases it only encourages them to allow them the unchallenged initiative, so I get out of the car and advance to meet him as he bears down on me. As a result, he has to stop before he had expected and this does, momentarily, takes the wind out of his sails. I had noticed that Diana had been struggling to pull something else from her rucksack, but she soon follows me out of the car.

Diana smiles as her father comes to a halt. He is red-faced and breathing heavily, so she is able to get in the first word.

"Daddy, this is my friend, Bill Selsey. Bill, this is my father, Major Henry Hunter."

I offer the Major my hand, but he is concentrating on Diana.

"And where have you been, young lady?" he demands. "On my way back from the links I saw a lot of rabble rousers causing a disturbance outside the Town Hall. I hope you weren't mixed up with that."

"Only on the fringe, Daddy dear," says Diana soothingly. "As soon as I saw there might be something disagreeable going on, I came straight home. Bill, here, kindly gave me a lift."

It occurs to me that Lady Macbeth could have usefully taken lessons from Diana as to how a blatant lie can be pitched as a kind if half-truth.

The Major is sceptical, probably from long experience of 'butter wouldn't melt in my mouth' stories that his daughter has served up for him over the years. But, instead of interrogating her further, he turns on me.

"You sir!" he accuses. "You have been leading my daughter astray. Enticing her to become criminally involved with your so called protest movement. You should know better at your age. If you were a younger man I would treat you to a good thrashing." He wields the golf club as though he can hardly restrain himself.

He glares at me and I glare back at him until he gives in and looks away. No-one beats me at that game because I have had hours of staring out practice with Barnacle. And Barnacle is world class. In a contest between him and Lord Kitchener's World War One recruiting poster it would be Kitchener who dropped his eyes first.

"I have nothing to do with those protesters who are, for all I know, still besieging the Town Hall," I tell him, "And I certainly would not encourage your daughter, or anyone else, to join them."

"Ha!" he cries, triumphantly. "Then how do you explain that slogan on your car?"

I turn around and, sure enough, there is a poster stuck across the inside of my windscreen carrying the words, *Save our Ancient Woodlands.*

So that is what had delayed Diana in following me out of the car, I realise. In dismay, I look at her for support, but she is pretending to blow her nose and has her face buried in her handkerchief. I suspect it is to hide a laugh. Is there no end to her perfidy, I ask myself? As a villainess, she long ago left Lady Macbeth struggling in her wake.

My only option seems to be an orderly retreat.

"You have me wrong, Major Hunter," I tell him with what little dignity remains in my locker. "However, I do not have the time to waste trading pleasantries with you. I have more important matters to attend to."

"Just keep away from my daughter, Portland," he threatens as I regain my car. "It will be the worse for you if I catch you or any of your criminal friends attempting to influence her again."

There seems nothing to be gained by dallying to put him right about my name and it occurs to me that there might be some advantage in allowing him to associate me with the wrong headland, so I tear the offending sticker off my windscreen, put my car into reverse and remove myself from Hunter territory with an intense feeling of relief. It is a close run thing as to whether I am happier to have put clear water between myself and the Major or between myself and his daughter.

    I drive home in a pensive frame of mind. My life appears to have suddenly become complicated, and I am none too pleased to find the comfortable routine of my retired days so rudely interrupted. For one thing, I have had no lunch yet and I am looking forward to enjoying a quiet sandwich and a beer. I hope that this will set a relaxed tone for the remainder of the day. I have always been an unreasonable optimist.

CHAPTER 4

The lunch very nearly goes according to plan. Barnacle and I sit amiably at the table. We each have our own plate and I share a few scraps of corned beef with him but I still have a mouthful of crumbs when there is an urgent hammering on my front door. I obviously have a visitor who has no time for the niceties of pressing buttons to operate the gentler chimes of my door bell. Barnacle scuttles off and hides under a chair while I, cursing quietly under my breath, swallow the last of my sandwich and stride grumpily to discover who is disturbing our meal.

On opening the door, I am confronted by Diana's mastiff-like follower who I now know to be one Buster Crump. The first thing I notice is that closer inspection does not enhance his appearance as compared with when I last saw him in the distance outside the Town Hall. He has the build of a Rugby player and his face looks as though it has been too frequently trodden on by studded boots.

I think back to my own Rugby-playing days when, as a scrum-half, my main concern had been to feed the ball as rapidly as possible to the fly-half or centre three-quarters who actually enjoyed being jumped upon by eighty-kilogram wing forwards of the build of Buster Crump. Strictly speaking, I could not legally be tackled after I had passed the ball, but I was not always quick enough to prevent a couple of man-mountains, propelled by an unstoppable momentum, from collapsing on top of me. In such cases, my tactic was to feign death and hope they would not feel it necessary to break my legs or otherwise reduce my mobility before they cantered off on a further mission of intimidation in another part of the field.

I am brought back from these pleasurable reminiscences by a series of bellows from the young man on my doorstep. It takes me a few minutes before I realise that he is attempting to address me in English. His words are distorted by a barely suppressed emotion, but I concentrate hard and discover that I can just make out what he is saying.

"So it's you," he growls, looking me up and down contemptuously. I agree that it is indeed me that he is addressing, but this seems to enrage him even more.

He eyes my red Volvo in the driveway.

"You drive a red Volvo," he accuses.

His statements so far do not seem to be matters of dispute. And they certainly do nothing to explain his pugnacious manner. I feel the need for further explanation. "So what?" I ask.

"And you have a tree fallen on your house," he adds.

I see little necessity for this remark either, because it is perfectly obvious to any passer-by that there is a tree lodged in the side of my house. Despite my normally placid nature, I am beginning to feel annoyed with this oddball on my doorstep making a series of self-evident observations.

"Do you have some reason for jumping up and down on my door-step?" I ask him.

"Felicity Wright told me where to find you," he mutters.

I put a black mark against Felicity's name in my mental notebook, and continue trying to get some sense out of my visitor. "Do you have a point to make?" I demand, "Or is this your idea of a social call?"

"Darn right, I have a point to make," shouts the Crump person. "What do you mean by enticing my girl-friend into your car, you grubby little man? I know your sort, you are the same generation as those old TV celebrity perverts we keep hearing about. You think you can get away with anything."

I hold up a placating hand. "Just hold it right there young man," I tell him. "You have entirely grasped the wrong end of the stick."

"Don't try that smooth talk on me," he snarls. "I saw you attempting to abduct Diana with my own eyes. You had better tell me what you have done with her or I'll take what's left of your house apart until I find her. I suppose you are planning to get her drunk now."

With that, he forces his way past me and strides towards the kitchen, causing Barnacle to withdraw further under a chair. Crump hurries on, looking to the right and left as though he might find Diana bound and gagged in a dark corner. I follow close behind and he comes to a halt by the kitchen table. He inspects the two plates and the remains of my lunch.

"So, you have recently been feeding her here," he pronounces, like Sherlock Holmes identifying a piece of vital evidence in the curious case of the disappearing protest marcher. He sniffs the few scraps of cat-food that are left on Barnacle's plate.

"That smells strange to me," he growls, accusingly. "You have drugged it haven't you?"

Barnacle is peering out from his hiding place, his eyes wide with fright, so I can't depend on him to set the record straight. Clearly it is time I took charge of the situation.

"Look here, Mr Crump, which I understand is your name, I can set your mind at rest. Miss Hunter is now safely at home with her dear father."

I expect Crump to immediately crumple on the receipt of this information, but he is wilfully determined to misunderstand my role in the recent events.

"She managed to escape then," he cries. "I should have known a pathetic old crock like you would never have been able to hold her."

"It was never my intention to have her in my car for longer than was absolutely necessary," I tell him, coldly. "She leapt into my vehicle, uninvited, and I was only too pleased to decant her at the earliest possible opportunity at the feet of the unspeakable Major Hunter himself."

For some reason, my final words cause a marked change in Buster Crump's demeanour, and I am pretty sure this is due to my implied criticism of Major Hunter as a person. Whatever the case, Buster's aggression rapidly fades, and his new attitude reminds me of a previously disgruntled dog that has just been offered a bone. If he really were a mastiff, he would be wagging his tail.

"Yes, he is a possessive old bastard, isn't he," says Buster. "He has forbidden Diana to have anything to do with me, you know."

I am taken aback by the sudden change in attitude which allows him to confide this information. However, it is a welcome development, and I feel I should encourage it.

"I am sorry to hear that," I tell him. "I would have thought that you and Diana deserve one another completely."

On the basis of his talent for misinterpretation, I am fairly sure he will take this ambiguous remark as a compliment, and so he does.

"That I just how we feel," he confides. "We are absolutely made for each other."

Right on, I think to myself but, at this stage, I decide I have to put him right on what appears to be another misapprehension. I try to break it gently. "After I had rescued her from the arm of the law, she appeared somewhat disenchanted by what she saw as your lack of support."

Buster looked concerned. "What was I supposed to do?" he asked. "It wouldn't have helped if I had been arrested myself."

"Don't ask me," I tell him. "I am just alerting you to the probability that you may not be welcomed with open arms when you next meet Diana Hunter. In fact she expressed views about the desirability of never meeting you again which are currently coincident with those of her father."

"Look here," he pleads, in an awful, ingratiating manner that one associates more with spaniels than with mastiffs, "You will have to help us get together again. You seem like a good sort. Perhaps you could arrange for Diana and me to meet here, at your place. Her father need not know and I am sure I can explain everything to her if we can get together on our own."

All his belligerence has melted away and he is maintaining his spaniel impersonation by looking at me with sad, hang-dog eyes. But I am not to be seduced into an exercise that I am sure could only end in tears,- especially since some of them would probably be my own.

"The last thing I want to do is to have any further contact with Diana Hunter," I tell him, forcefully. "And there is no way I would ever invite her into my home. I am sorry, about your situation, but it is something you will have to sort out on your own."

I can see he is disappointed, and a flash of his earlier hostility returns. "Alright," he says, "I'll do that. At least I can be sure you will never have her in your car again and be tempted to molest her."

"Take it easy," I advise him. "At my age I am well past any interest in such things"

As I escort him out of the house, I continue to emphasise my determination not to become involved, but I, nevertheless, wish him the best of luck as he lets himself out of my front gate, and mounts a magnificent motorcycle which is adorned with more glittering accessories than a duchess at an embassy ball. He revs it up to a deafening roar, lets in the clutch and bombs off down the road.

I am feeling pleased with myself when I return to the comfort of my kitchen. I have successfully avoided any further involvement in what, I believe, could have become a complex and worrisome situation.

Barnacle, whose instinct for self-preservation only occasionally overcomes his normal nosiness, decides that the coast is clear and re-joins me at the table.

"Well Barney," I tell him, with my usual misplaced optimism, "We can look forward to some peace and quiet at last."

CHAPTER 5

In fact, we have barely ten minutes in which to wind down. Then there is a peal from the door-bell. As I go to answer it, I muse that this promises to be a more civilized caller than the Neanderthal Buster Crump. On opening the door I do, indeed, find myself face to face with a large, but well proportioned, middle aged lady. A pleasant, motherly looking woman will make a welcome change to the canine Crump, I tell myself.

"Good afternoon," she greets me, "My name is Wendy Fyler and I am the planning officer for the Town Council."

"Oh, do come in Ms Fyler," I say, "It is most kind of you to come out to see me, I was intending to call at your offices this morning to ask for advice and, perhaps some practical help, in sorting out my tree problem."

Barnacle pads across to greet her and to see what might be in it for himself, but she shoos him away without so much as a pat on the head. He struts off disdainfully to his current sleeping spot. Then, he curls up, shuts his eyes pointedly, and takes no further interest in the proceedings. Not for the first time, I envy the way he can handle situations that displease him.

I offer the Fyler person a cup of tea, but she declines with a curtness that seems to me unnecessary. She does, however, accept a seat opposite to mine at the kitchen table, from which position she fixes me with an appraising look.

"We would certainly like to investigate the circumstances surrounding the fall of this tree," she says.

"Ah! Getting to the root of the matter," I grin. She returns grin with grim. For her, this is not a happening to be treated lightly.

"You find this amusing," she accuses.

It is true that I have an unfortunate habit of chuckling at my own corny jokes, but I feel that even Queen Victoria might have smiled politely at this one. Not so Madam Fyler, who is thoroughly disapproving.

"Could your amusement be because you wanted that tree felled despite the preservation order we had placed on it?" She demands.

I don't much like her tone of voice. "It certainly solves the problem of its roots encroaching into my neighbour's drains," I agree. "But I am not at all pleased that it has fallen this way and damaged my house."

"A miscalculation on your part, then," she suggests. "You meant it to fall the other way into your back garden."

I stare at her aghast. "Are you accusing me of deliberately causing the tree to fall?" I ask.

"It does seem a most convenient coincidence, does it not?" she replies. "That tree had survived for a hundred years or more, and it toppled over in a fresh breeze a few weeks after we tried to protect it with a preservation order."

"More than a fresh breeze," I protest. "It was gusting up to force nine last night. My insurance company tell me that there is widespread damage to property. It is not just my tree."

"That is as may be," she accepts, grudgingly. "Meanwhile, I would like to inspect the fallen tree and the damage it has caused."

I escort her into the garden, where she looks keenly at the base of the tree and the exposed, broken roots. The trunk is at a forty-five degree angle, so some of the splintered roots are way above the ground.

"These could easily have been hacked through with a sharp implement to make the tree unstable," she observes.

"There can be no evidence of that for the simple reason that I did no such thing," I protest. "You can't go around accusing people of misdemeanours for no reason at all."

By this time she has moved across the garden to peer into my shed. With an air of triumph, she reaches in and brings out a large felling axe. I have a wood-burning stove in my living room, so I need the axe for splitting the logs that I use for fuel. I explain this to her, but she tells me that the fact that I have a legitimate use for the axe is irrelevant.

"The devil barber, Sweeney Todd cut his victims throats with a razor," she sneers. "And the fact that he used the razor to shave himself in the morning was no defence whatsoever."

She lifts the axe on high with two hands as though it is an Olympic medal and she has just won gold. "Motive, opportunity, and now means," she gloats. "It is all adding up, isn't it?"

"Only in your warped mind," I snap. "You are letting your prejudices overcome your reason. My only involvement in this affair is as an innocent victim. The falling tree was clearly an act of God. Why don't you trot along to the church and make a complaint there?"

The Fyler responds to this suggestion with a scowl. She is quite unmoved by my protestations and, after making some notes in a pocket book, she walks over to the gate.

"I have seen enough here," she pronounces, as she opens the gate to leave. "You will be hearing from us officially in due course."

"Hey! Wait a minute," I cry. "Aren't you going to arrange for help remove the tree, clear the debris and make my home safe? I thought that is what you had come for."

She stops in her tracks and looks at me ominously. "So," she says. "You think the house might be unsafe, do you?"

I realize, too late, that I may have made a wrong move because her face contorts into a kind of gratified smile like a prospector who has found a new seam of gold in what he had thought was a worked out mine. Right on cue, the tree gives a tremor and settles a little further into the side of my house, dislodging a brick as it does so. It falls, harmlessly into a rose- bed and lies there grinning at us.

"Yes, indeed," says Madam Fyler. "I can see now that the state of your house is a danger to the public. I am obliged to report this matter and, in due course, you can expect a formal order from the Council to make your premises safe or face prosecution."

She treats herself to a smug smile, like a lioness who finds that a tethered goat has been left out for her supper.

"Hold on," I say. "The public aren't going to be throwing a party on my flower beds, and people using the road are well out of harm's way." I conveniently forbear to mention that. only a few hours earlier, I had been arguing with the insurance company that I should, myself, be considered as a member of the public. It doesn't do to be too rigid in maintaining a position, I tell myself.

"Just comply with the terms of the order when you receive it," advises the Fyler, "And make sure your insurance is satisfactory. You *are* insured with a reputable company, I assume."

"Of course I am insured. With the Eversure Group as a matter of fact. Old established and reliable." I say this with a confidence I do not entirely feel. It is true I have a property policy with them, but I remind myself to check what the small print says about public liability cover.

Madam Fyler makes another note in her pocket-book and marches off to where her car is parked by the roadside. The gruesome smile is still lurking around the corners of her lips, suggesting that she is enjoying some private joke. Whatever it is, I wouldn't expect it to make me laugh.

"I will be in touch again when my report has been processed," is her parting shot.

So that's it, I think to myself as I return, disconsolately, to my kitchen. No help at all offered by the Council in return for all the local taxes they squeeze out of me. Just a whole raft of additional harassment that I could well do without.

And as for Wendy Fyler, herself, she is yet another of the clever, manipulative women that that have suddenly arrived to complicated my life. Whatever happened to the dumb, but kind-hearted, blondes that the world was once full of, I wonder, nostalgically.

CHAPTER 6

With the unfriendly stranger out of the way, Barnacle feels no need to maintain his studied detachment. He opens his eyes and strolls over to rub his jowls up against my leg as I come in through the doorway. I bend down to scratch him under his chin and he rewards me with an appreciative purr. Barnacle is a great companion, but the fact has to be faced that he doesn't actually say very much. Of course, that is sometimes his most endearing trait, but right now I feel the need for a chat with someone who is more conversationally responsive. At the same time, it occurs to me that staying at home leaves me prey to a succession of uninvited visitors, all seemingly determined to cause me anguish. I can empathise with that tethered goat.

 I go upstairs and gaze out of the window of my spare bedroom at the rear of the house. At the bottom of my back garden is a tall fence but, from my high vantage point, I can see over this to an extensive area of public allotments which are rented by the Town Council to amateur gardeners for cultivating and growing a variety of health-giving vegetables.

 Mostly, although with mixed success, the plots are used for this purpose. In some cases, the plot owners are growing marrows and runner beans that are destined to win prizes at the annual produce show, but others are obviously losing their perennial battle with the weeds and the myriad pests that assault their crops. Many are furnished with nondescript sheds or makeshift glass-houses. But one plot stands out as obsessively tidy in that the soil is raked smooth with not a weed spoiling its pristine appearance. Not a vegetable either, for that matter. Also, it is equipped with easily the most impressive shed of all and I notice a wisp of light grey smoke issuing from its stove-pipe chimney.

"Excellent news," I tell Barnacle. "Either they have elected a new Pope or our friend Shorty is in residence."

I check that Barnacle's dishes are topped up with cat comestibles, although I know this is unimportant because he will find a warm spot to sleep in while I am out. Then I throw on a coat, exit from the back door and jog down the garden to a gate in the fence which gives direct access to the allotments.

As I follow a path between the plots towards Shorty's shed, I reflect on his background. Many years ago, when Britain still possessed a large merchant fleet, Shorty had been employed on Purple Funnel ships. As a consequence, he assumes he is a cut above every other British sailor and especially superior to the likes of an old tanker-man such as myself. His tendency to look down on us lesser beings is helped by the physical stature that earned him his nickname, Shorty. He is as tall and thin as a wooden top-mast.

Shorty's wife, Mary, like many sailors' spouses, had been left to run the home and make all the necessary decisions involved while her husband was away at sea for many months at a time. As a consequence, she had developed an independent frame of mind and had built up a wide circle of friends who had supported her during his absences. She had also, as a matter of necessity, organised her house and domestic arrangements in a way that exactly suited her own requirements. She had coped with, and even enjoyed, Shorty disrupting this well ordered life-style during his infrequent periods of leave, but she was in no way prepared to put up with a retired Shorty, permanently under her feet.

The solution had been Shorty's idea as much as hers. After breakfasting together, he saunters off to the comfort and comradeship of his shed on the allotments. He might read the paper with his feet on the table (forbidden in the house). Then enjoy a pie or a sandwich with a beer for lunch, often with me or one of the other allotment holders for company. He might take a nap in the afternoon, rake over his already pristine allotment to make sure nothing green was daring to show its face, perhaps stroll around to chat to some of the more productive allotment holders and then return home for supper where he could discuss their separate day's happenings with Mary.

It was a pattern that allowed Mary to have the house free for most of the day to entertain her friends or, if she preferred, to meet up with them for recreational shopping or other excursions. Most importantly, I think to myself as I approach Shorty's shed, the arrangement works. They are both enjoying their retirement.

I knock on the door of the shed and let myself in without waiting for an answer. Shorty, who had been dozing in an arm-chair, looks pointedly at his watch and greets me with his usual condescension.

"Late again," he comments. "What kept you? It is nearly four bells. The Sun was over the yard-arm hours ago. It just shows you were never in the liner trade where proper time-keeping was a way of life."

I explain that a series of unforeseen incidents has thrown my day into disarray.

"We never experienced unforeseen incidents in Purple Funnel," he claims, snuffily. "Everything that could possibly happen was anticipated and provided for."

"I know all that," I say as I sink into an easy chair opposite to his. "Head office had already made the decisions for you. It saved you having to think for yourselves."

"We could use our initiative if necessary," he says, defensively.

"If you call opening the standing orders at the right page initiative, I agree with you," I say.

Shorty grins, "Grab yourself a beer and tell me about these incidents you haven't been able to handle," he says.

I take a can from Shorty's ice-box and swallow a calming mouthful as I collect my thoughts.

Then I explain about the fallen tree, my conversation with the insurance man, the interview with Felicity Wright, the involvement with the protest meeting and my subsequent encounters with

Diana Hunter and her overbearing father, the belligerent Buster Crump and the malevolent Wendy Fyler.

"You have gone miles off course this time," pronounces Shorty, after listening attentively to my story. "You are adrift amongst uncharted rocks in shark-infested waters by the sound of it."

"Situations that are not covered by standing orders," I agree. "Not even Purple Funnel standing orders."

"Our ships never went off course in the first place, nor did we find ourselves in uncharted waters," he tells me, "But, if we had done so, we would have been able to improvise."

"Well, do some serious improvising now, old friend," I tell him. "I could certainly use a few words of sage advice. What do you think I should be doing?"

For a few moments, Shorty strikes a pose reminiscent of Rodin's 'Thinker', with his brow as convoluted as a double carrick-bend. Then he pronounces judgement.

"There is a lot to think about, but you should concentrate on one thing at a time. It doesn't do to overtax the minds of you tramp-ship operators."

"I was in tankers, not tramp-ships," I correct him.

"The same thing, only oilier," he says, dismissively. "So let's make a check-list for you."

He fishes out a spiral-bound note-book and a pen from a drawer of his work-bench.

This strikes me as one of his better ideas. "That might actually be useful," I say, encouragingly.

"You should deal with the tree first," he advises, writing busily. "Make sure the bedroom is weather-tight and then clear it of debris until it is all ship-shape and Bristol fashion."

"I've done the first part of that," I tell him.

"It's got to be squirrel-tight and bird-tight as well," he warns, as he continues to scribble away with his ball-point. "Squirrels can be destructive beasts, and you don't want to find the room full of starlings in the morning."

"You needn't write all this down," I tell him. "I'm not senile. I can still remember things."

"Is that right?" says Shorty, smiling sardonically and without bothering to look up. "So where are your reading glasses, then?"

"Er – Back in the house. On the kitchen table," I tell him with a confidence I don't feel. "I left in a hurry. I expect the cat distracted me."

"They are hanging round your neck," says Shorty. I reach down and, sure enough, they are there, suspended by their cord.

"Just a momentary lapse," I bluster. "It doesn't mean anything."

"It means you need written orders." says Shorty. "They are what made Purple Funnel the most prestigious cargo line in the world."

"The most self-regarding cargo line, more like," I grumble, but I know I have been out-manoeuvred. "Carry on, then," I tell him. "Do it your way if you must."

"Next item. Make up your bed in another room," says Shorty, briskly. "You don't know what creepy crawlies will come out from amongst the oak leaves and acorns during the night." He continues scribbling furiously.

"And then what?" I ask.

"Get on to the insurance company again," he says. "Tell them it is a matter of life and death to have the tree removed, the house damage repaired and the window replaced."

"I don't believe it is that urgent," I protest. "There's no real danger."

"You'll never get anything done if you admit that," says Shorty. "Explain that you are a frail old man and that, if a draught from the broken window causes pneumonia, it could see you off in a matter of days."

"I'm only middle aged," I object, but Shorty will have none of it.

"Middle aged if you expect to live until you are a hundred and sixty," says Shorty. "From where I am sitting we are both elderly."

"I've been called quaint as well as elderly already today, so I suppose once more wouldn't hurt," I concede.

"Then," he continues, "There is the mental anguish which, for an old codger who is losing his marbles, could be the final pallet of cargo that overloads the ship."

This is too much, "Of course I am not losing my marbles," I object. "My brain is as good as it ever was - well, perhaps a bit slower, and I might occasionally lose track of my glasses, but there is nothing wrong with my mind."

"So why have you started carrying that notebook in your top pocket?" asks Shorty.

This touches a sensitive spot. I use the notebook to record things that might otherwise slip my mind. Items of shopping, appointments, names of people I meet, Telephone numbers, including my own.

"OK, I might have become a little forgetful," I admit, "But that doesn't make me stupid. Albert Einstein was forgetful, which was a good thing because it cleared his head of preconceived ideas."

"I must say you are being over-defensive about all this," observes Shorty. "That's a bad sign if you ask me. I'll tell you what, let's just tell the insurance company that you are vulnerable."

"I am not vulnerable, either," I grumble. "I keep a heavy-duty marline spike under the mattress. I'd soon see off a burglar, or any other midnight prowler."

"That shows you are anxious, keeping a weapon on hand" says Shorty, still writing industriously. "Why don't we make it vulnerable *and* anxious? Or does apprehensive sound better?"

"Alright," I capitulate, "You've made your point. I have to play the sad little old man, even though I am fit, feisty and in my prime."

"Now you have got it," says Shorty unfeelingly. "Act the doddery pensioner. The insurance assessor will only need to take a look at you to believe it." He continues writing out his impromptu instruction manual and then he looks up. "OK," he says. "Finished that. Now let's move on. What's next?"

"What about the Council?" I ask. "They are suggesting that I might have sabotaged the tree so it would be blown over by the first fresh breeze, just because I wanted it down and I couldn't have had it felled legally because of their preservation order."

"Put them on the back foot," advises Shorty. "Write to them and point out that they recklessly made a preservation order on a tree that was in a weakened condition and dangerously near a property occupied by an elderly, vulnerable and apprehensive pensioner."

"Not quaint, then?" I ask, but Shorty is as impervious to sarcasm as Diana Hunter, and he takes my remark seriously.

"Definitely not," he pronounces. He looks me up and down, "Of course it's not a bad description of you if one is limited to a single word. But I think it is not the right word for this purpose." He turns over to a new page in his notepad and continues writing. He is way out of line in the way he describes me personally, but the general notion of taking the initiative in my dealings with the Council strikes me as sound.

"Alright," I say. "But the Council is only one of my problems. What should I be doing about Felicity Wright, the reporter?"

"You definitely need to keep her on-side," counsels Shorty. "You might need the local press as a lever if there is a dispute with the Council, or with your insurance company for that matter."

"Isn't that a dangerous game, trying to use the local press for my own purposes?" I ask.

"Now you are doing your apprehensive thing," claims Shorty

"Just being sensible," I protest. "We could be navigating into dangerous waters if we become too involved with the press. They are interested in selling papers, not in campaigns to help individuals. Suppose they were to pick up Buster Crump's suspicion that I go around trying to kidnap young ladies?"

"You worry too much," says Shorty. "I am making it an action that you should cultivate this Felicity Wright and feed her selected information to help your case with the Council and your claim with the insurance company. However, now you mention the bold Buster Crump, we need to think about how you are going to deal with him."

"I would prefer not to deal with him at all," I mutter. "I managed to persuade him that I did no more than save Diana from being collared by the constabulary and, then deliver her safely to her father's tender care, but Buster strikes me as a box of fireworks past its use by date, – fundamentally unstable and liable to explode without warning."

"Leaving him alone is exactly what I would recommend," says Shorty. "I recognise the type although, of course, we didn't get any of them on Purple Funnel ships."

"What type is that then?" I ask.

"Blokes that jump to wildly improbable conclusions in the face of blatantly obvious evidence to the contrary," says Shorty. "Fancy him thinking that someone who could only cope with driving tank ships would have the initiative to abduct a personable young lady from under the eyes of the police."

I am stung by this assessment of my capabilities. "Here! Hold on," I cry.

But he continues, undeterred. "Anyone in their right mind could see that you are too old and quaint to take on anything so ambitious."

"You are quite wrong about that," I protest, "But, in any case you are wandering off the point."

"Ah, yes," agreed Shorty. "Let's get back to Buster Crump."

"Crazy people can be dangerous," I point out. "I'm not sure forgetting about him will cause him to forget about me."

"Your apprehension is kicking in again," says Shorty. "The standard cure for that is a couple of vallium tablets or, better still, a stiffer drink than this beer." He reaches up to a cupboard at the end of his shed and fetches down a bottle of single malt whisky and a couple of glasses. He pours two generous tots and we relax in our chairs as the late afternoon sunshine beams in through the window and lights the interior with a mellow glow. After a sip of the magic liquid, our personal interiors feel much the same.

Shorty adds a few more notes to his pad. Then he reads it through carefully, makes one or two additions and underlines what he considers are vital sections. Finally he signs and dates it, tears off the relevant pages and hands them to me with the air of Moses presenting the ten commandments to the children of Israel.

"Treat these as the preliminary standing orders for your coming voyage," he says. "We may need to produce addendums as you proceed but, at least, these will set you off in the right direction."

I have not been uniformly pleased with Shorty's analysis of my problems and how to deal with them, but it was useful to talk about them and, in his own way, he has gone to considerable trouble on my behalf. I am properly grateful to him.

Shorty, meanwhile, has decided that we have discussed my predicament for quite long enough and that he has done his duty by pointing me in the right direction for a solution. Perhaps he also feels that I was not entirely convinced when he has explained that Purple Funnel regulations provided for every possible eventuality. He takes another sip of his whisky and begins.

"I sailed with a captain once, on the old *Purple Emperor*," he reminisces. "His night order book contained instructions on what to do in case the ship was invaded by hoards of little green aliens."

I lean back in my chair and accept the inevitable. The whisky bottle is still half full and I can see this session is going on for a couple of hours. I hope Shorty's wife is not expecting him home for an early supper.

It is nearly 1900 by the time Shorty finally concludes his story-telling. He looks at his watch in alarm and springs to his feet. "It's liver and bacon tonight," he says. "Mary will keel-haul me if I am late."

I pick up the now empty whisky bottle and take it with me as we leave the shed and set off towards our respective homes. It might save Shorty an awkward moment of explanation, although I know Mary is perfectly happy for him to share a drink or two with his friends. It is a small price for her to pay to enjoy a Shorty-free house for most of the day.

CHAPTER 7

As I walk home, I think back to my discussion with Shorty, and I do feel more settled after sharing my problems. Of course, he talks complete nonsense much of the time. Purple Funnel crews were never confused because there was a company rule which told them what to do in any conceivable situation, although that does not mean the rules were always right, or even sensible. Nevertheless, Shorty's simplistic reading of my complex problems does allow me to face whatever tomorrow might bring with more confidence. There is a pronounced spring in my step as I march up my garden path and I even give the stricken tree a consoling pat in passing.

"I'm sure it wasn't your fault, old chap," I say.

Barnacle is waiting for me in the kitchen with his 'what's for supper' look in his eyes. I sling a potato into the microwave and, when it is partly baked, I fill it with cheddar cheese and a handful of chopped ham, and return it to cook for another few minutes. I find a bottle of Australian Shiraz in a cupboard and take a sachet of mackerel cat-food from a shelf. I am planning a relaxing evening for Barney and me, watching some undemanding television entertainment. Of course, once he has eaten his supper, Barney usually watches TV with his eyes shut, so I don't need to take account of his preferences in selecting a programme. I decide that my best option is a detective drama.

It starts in promising style with an imaginative murder that is so wildly improbable that I believe it must be the beginning of a pleasantly escapist romp. Exactly what I need in my present mood.

Unfortunately, it soon turns into something much darker. The main suspect is an innocent man who is harassed by a police team led by the pathologically introspective Inspector Morose. Not only do they try to goad the poor suspect into a confession, but he is also hounded by the dead man's vengeful family and, as the story unfolds, even his own friends turn against him.

In the face of all this persecution, he crumbles into a self-pitying wreck. "Pull yourself together man," I shout at him. "You will be cleared in the final ten minutes of the programme when Morose has his flash of inspiration and collars the real murderer. You've only got to keep going for another half an hour."

The wimp does nothing of the sort and, before long he is feeling so abandoned and unloved that he is torn between jumping off a cliff or throwing himself under a train. Soon afterwards, Inspector Morose does have his eureka moment, apprehends the real murderer and rushes off to break the good news to the hero and to apologise for giving him such a hard time. Inevitably, he arrives just too late. Our hero had passed on the cliff and the train, but had taken an overdose of drugs instead. As he goes down for the third time in the arms of the distraught Inspector, he manages to croak out, "I told you it wasn't me."

This has turned out to be nothing like the escapist fare I'd had in mind when I switched on, and it reflected my own situation to an uncomfortable degree. The hero being attacked from all sides until he was beaten into the ground. I had expected to watch an absorbing and, hopefully, mildly amusing who-dunnit which would take me out of myself, and here I am feeling more down in the dumps than ever. I could, of course, stay tuned and watch the news, but even I am not optimistic enough to expect anything but the usual dismal tidings about the parlous state of the world.

I give up on the television and return to the kitchen where Barnacle opens one eye at a time, stretches to twice his normal length, gives a yawn the size of an open cargo hatch, and pads across the floor to greet me. He rubs his tom-cat jowls against my leg as though he is telling me that I can depend on his continued affection however hostile the world might become. I know this display of apparent sympathy will only last until I put some fresh food out for him, but it is welcome nevertheless.

I regain a little of my customary good humour as I open a new packet of cat food, but I am still somewhat out of sorts as I fill Barnacle's dish and then take myself upstairs to prepare for bed.

I act on Shorty's advice to collect my sheets, pillows and duvet from the room that suffered the arboreal invasion, and bunk up for the night in my guest bedroom. It is at the front of the house and it says much for my unsettled state of mind that, although I know there are no trees on that side, I nevertheless peer out of the window to make absolutely certain. There is a lamp-post in the street not far away, but it looks sturdy enough to stand anything the weather might throw at it but then, I tell myself, so did the oak tree.

With so much churning around in my mind I find it difficult to sleep and, when I find myself wondering whether lamp posts can have preservation orders attached to them, I decide that some kind of calming medication might be useful if I am to have a good night's rest. I return downstairs and mix myself a hot rum toddy. Three parts rum, one part lemon and a spoonful of honey, - or was it supposed to be the other way around? As I drain the glass, I can feel it having a beneficial effect, so it seems best to repeat the dose. I am surprised at how rapidly the rum bottle becomes depleted as a result of this treatment but, eventually, I begin to feel quite unworried by the day's events and the only remaining challenge is to negotiate the suddenly treacherous staircase as I make my way up to bed.

My last thought as I settle down for the night is that, at least, tomorrow cannot possibly be as taxing as today has been. Didn't I say earlier that I have this tendency to be unreasonably optimistic!

CHAPTER 8

The next morning, I wake up with my head spinning like a radar scanner. Sitting up too suddenly causes the bed to pitch and roll as though I am sailing across the Bay of Biscay in October. With exaggerated care, I swing my legs from under the duvet and place my feet gingerly on the floor. The bed gives one final heave and then subsides to its normal passive state. I remain in a sitting position until I have reoriented myself sufficiently to be able to cope with a new day. As the synapses in my brain reorganise themselves, I become capable of rational thought, and factors like cause and effect begin to make sense. This prompts me to wonder whether I had been wise to drink so many rum toddies yesterday evening, especially after an earlier session of whisky drinking with Shorty.

"Mind you," I tell Barnacle who is sitting in the bedroom doorway watching me with a worried look on his face. "They did have the required effect. I think it would not have disturbed my sleep if a whole forest of trees had fallen on the house during the night."

Be that as it may, I am still feeling somewhat befuddled and unsteady on my feet as I stand up to make a start on whatever the new day might bring. I have never before noticed the absence of grab rails to assist my transfer to the bathroom but, this morning, it seems to be an unfortunate omission. Shaving, showering and dressing are too complicated processes to be undertaken immediately, so I splash some cold water on my face, shrug myself into a dressing-gown, and start an ultra-cautious descent of the stairs to the kitchen.

Barnacle dances down the stairs ahead of me, making light work of a descent that seems to me fraught with danger but, mercifully, I make it safely into the kitchen. Barnacle runs to stand by his empty milk saucer and turns his head to stare at me meaningfully. He has lost his worried look now that he believes I have become capable of fixing his breakfast, but he is over optimistic. With my whirling brain, there is no way I am prepared to do anything so reckless as bending down to replenish his food bowl. For me, making coffee is the immediate priority and that, like making toast, is an automatic procedure that I do not even have to think about.

I gather my wits sufficiently to drink two mugs of strong, black coffee which, supported by a couple of paracetamol tablets, I hope will bring me back onto an even keel. I also manage to locate a jar of marmalade which, spread thickly on my toast, will have to suffice for breakfast. This seems to work, at least to a certain extent, and I feel sufficiently on top of the situation to embark on the tricky exercise of bending down to fill Barnacle's dishes. As is his usual style, he attacks these with gusto, but omits to say thank you. I am beginning to wonder whether I am sufficiently recovered to make another attempt at the stairs, perhaps, even to try a shave and get dressed, when the door-bell peals.

I run through a few sailors' curses under my breath as I hurry to open the front door, where I find Felicity Wright standing on the doorstep, tablet at the ready. She takes in my dishevelled appearance at a glance and looks immediately concerned.

"For Heaven's sake, William, you look like the wreck of the Hesperus," she exclaims. "Whatever has happened to you? Have you been mugged?"

She seems disappointed when I deny any such occurrence. Not being mugged or otherwise assaulted constitutes an absence of news and is unwelcome information for a young news-hound.

"Is this what you usually look like in the mornings?" she asks, as I stand aside and usher her into the kitchen. "Yesterday you seemed much as one would expect from the normal wear and tear of life since the swinging thirties."

I ignore this unfeeling reference to my age, and I recognise that she is being sardonic about the swinging thirties. Most of her generation believe that society only began to swing in the era of their teens despite being told by their parents that it was the swinging sixties that started it all. What would she know about swing and the thirties anyway? She probably thinks that Glen Miller is a Scottish valley and that Duke Ellington was an alphabetically truncated descendent of the other Duke who won the Battle of Waterloo. This doesn't seem the right time to enlighten her and, in any case I feel I could use a little sympathy.

"Yes, I do feel somewhat under the weather," I admit, making a pathetic attempt at a brave smile. " It was probably something I ate."

Felicity looks me up and down and notes the stubble on my face and the dark bags under my eyes. "More like something you drank," She observes. "You old people should be more careful."

As we make our way into the kitchen, she holds my arm to steady me. It is quite unnecessary of course, but I find it somehow comforting all the same. We sit down at the table and Barnacle prises himself out of his own chair and comes to greet Felicity. He is rewarded by a scratch behind his ear which he accepts gracefully. Then, having confirmed that her i-pad is not edible, he takes himself back to his personal resting place.

Mindful of Shorty's advice to make an ally of the press, I offer Felicity a cup of tea or coffee, but she declines on the grounds that she has not long had breakfast.

"So, what brings you here again?" I ask, at the same time wondering what information I might feed her to my best advantage. "I can't tell you much more about the tree, but I am hoping there will be helpful responses from the Council and my insurance company."

Felicity frowns. "The tree is one of the things I wanted to talk to you about," she says. "It has been hinted that its fall might not have been a complete accident. Would you care to comment?"

This accusation takes me completely back-to-wind. "What are you suggesting?" I croak. "Who has been spreading scurrilous rumours like that?"

"I have my sources," she says, "But you will appreciate that they have to remain anonymous."

"It must have been that woman, Wendy Fyler, from the Council," I say. "No-one else has ever suggested such a thing."

"I have no intention of confirming or denying that," says Felicity, "But it is true that the Council Offices do tend to leak like a selective sieve. Stuff they want to spread around seems to fall unto my lap, which has the effect of concentrating my interest on the items that don't fall through. Reporters dislike feeling they are being manipulated, and we react against it."

Is she warning me off, I wonder, or is her objection to being used directed only to the likes of Madam Fyler?

"You don't tap into telephone conversations, then?" I ask.

"I'm an arts graduate," says Felicity. "I don't have the technological background to do that kind of thing, even if I were prepared to risk it. Perhaps if someone produces a suitable app for my tablet one day -----"

"Well, I am glad you disregard leaks that come your way too easily," I say. "Especially this rubbish about me wanting the tree to fall down."

"But it was convenient for you, wasn't it?" says Felicity. "According to the Council records you made an application to have it felled about a year ago."

"I'm surprised you have had time for that kind of research," I say, eyeing the clock. "The Council offices have not long been open."

"As a matter of fact, a copy of your letter of application appeared on my desk this morning," she acknowledged.

"How convenient," I suggest.

"Yes, indeed," agrees Felicity, "But it means it is true, nonetheless."

"I have never denied it," I point out. "And, if you delve further into the Council records you'll find that they slapped a preservation order on the tree within a week of my application to have it cut down."

"So it was well timed from your point of view that it happened to fall down in yesterday's blow," says Felicity.

"It's a weight off my mind, certainly," I agree, "Because the neighbours were complaining that its roots were damaging their drains. But the fact is that I did nothing whatever to make the tree more likely to fall."

"You have the benefit of the doubt for now," is Felicity's judgement, "But, if there is smoke, one tends to expect fire, so I'll be keeping an open mind. After all, it would make a lovely headline, wouldn't it? Pensioner falls foul of his own sabotage."

"You are letting your imagination run away with you, young lady," I tell her. "And, if you take my advice you will ignore these snippets of misinformation that are so conveniently fed to you by some malignant Council mole."

"OK," agrees Felicity, amiably, "Let's talk about something else that might, or might not, be related. How come you just happened to be at the right spot to spirit away the leader of the protest meeting outside the Town Hall yesterday afternoon? Would you care to comment on that?"

She has dropped this one on me with all the subtlety of casting a twenty-eight pound deep-sea lead. I suppose I should have expected something of the sort, but it is still a shock to realise that my involvement had been observed and that I had been identified. I try to bluster, but without any real hope of success.

"What! Me?" I say. "Whatever gives you the idea that I was even present at that gathering of maniacal mobsters?"

"Felicity smiles sweetly and waves her tablet. "Only the fact that I saw someone who looked very much like a disguised Ms Hunter dive into your car after assaulting a policeman, and I have a photograph of your red Volvo heading for the sticks with her on board."

"There are lots of red Volvos," I protest, weakly.

"Yes, but only one carrying your registration plate," says Felicity "It is easy to read on the photo when I zoom in."

A curse on modern technology, I think to myself, as I realise I have no-where to run. "So, what are you going to do?" I ask. "Publish and be damned?"

"Tempting," says Felicity. "But I have a feeling in my bones that there is a much bigger story to be uncovered. A major conspiracy perhaps. If you can tell me about that, I might not need to publish anything about your part in yesterday's criminal attack on our valiant police force."

I am beginning to revise my opinion of Felicity. During our previous meeting, she had come across as a thoroughly pleasant young woman, and here she is putting pressure on me in a way that is veering towards blackmail.

"What conspiracy is this?" I ask, beginning to feel out of my depth with no sign of a life-jacket.

"Come, come," says Felicity, and it suddenly dawns on me how toothy her smile is. "You handled that getaway like a professional. You aren't going to tell me it wasn't all planned beforehand."

"I give you my word," I say. "Before yesterday, I had never set eyes on the girl who leapt aboard my car. And how do you know her name? She was heavily disguised while she was protesting."

"So she was," agreed Felicity, "But the presence of Buster Crump nearby gave me a clue. I suspected a wig and, once I had her picture on my tablet it was easy enough to change the hair colour and style. Then I recognised her at once. She often pops up at local society do's and, in any case, we were at school together."

"Are you going to let on?" I ask, curiously. "She will be in deep trouble with her father if he gets to know about it, - not to mention the police."

Felicity looks thoughtful. "I think you are both in similarly precarious situations," she says. "I'll hold fire for the time being, but only if you help me to uncover the big story."

"This so called conspiracy," I say.

"Exactly that," agrees Felicity. "So let us start with what *you* can tell me."

"Absolutely nothing," I tell her. "Two days ago I was leading a peaceful existence without the least expectation that it would be shattered in the aftermath of a falling tree. I did not know you or Diana Hunter or Buster Crump or Wendy Fyler. I'd had absolutely no contact with any of these crazy protesters and I still don't know what it is they are so hot-under-the-collar about."

Felicity looks at me thoughtfully, as though she is weighing up the truthfulness of my words. "I'm not sure I am doing the right thing, but I am prepared to allow you the benefit of the doubt," she says at length.

"Well, thank goodness for that," I say, "I was beginning to feel persecuted by the population of the whole town".

"That doesn't mean you are completely off the hook," she warns me. "It might, or might not be true that you were not involved with any of these people until yesterday, but you are certainly involved with them now, and I mean to find out what is going on."

"Well I am keeping my head down from now on, and I don't intend to have anything to do with this protest crowd ever again."

Felicity becomes thoughtful again. "My problem is that I need you as an insider so you can investigate this conspiracy for me. If you can't do that, I'll have no big story to report and I will have to revert to my low-level story about the gang of vicious terrorists who carried out that dastardly assault on a police officer doing his duty."

To say I am dismayed would be the understatement of the year. Hitherto, the young women I had met in the market place of life had mostly seemed perfectly sound citizens, each adding their two penny-worth towards the common good. And now, in as many days, I find myself beset by two clones of Lady MacBeth. Or perhaps mutations. Even Lady MacBeth did not go beyond incitement to murder. Surely she would never have stooped to anything so low as blackmail.

"You are a dangerous woman, Felicity Wright," I tell her. "This is naked coercion."

"That is not a nice thing to say," admonishes Felicity, "And I am sure you don't mean it. An upright member of the public like yourself will surely jump at the opportunity to help expose a fraudulent conspiracy."

Despite her placatory words, I know she has the upper hand, and she knows that I know it. "Alright," I mutter, "I'll do what I can to help you, but don't expect too much. I am a complete outsider. I don't even know what this conspiracy is supposed to be about. Something to do with ancient woodlands, I suppose."

"The ancient woodlands concerned in the protest are in Hangman's Copse, about five miles to the west of the town centre." Felicity looks at me appraisingly. "Are you sure you don't already know this?"

"Keel-haul me if I tell a lie, this is all news to me," I assure her.

"Very well," she continues, "The Copse is owned by Major Hunter, no less, and he goes there every so often to blast away with a shot-gun at any pigeons, rabbits or any other wild-life that happens to annoy him , - human trespassers not excepted. But they are not managed woodlands for raising game or anything like that, which is why they are of particular interest to conservationists. Apart from the Major shredding the leaves with lead pellets from time to time, the trees have been left to themselves for as long as records exist."

"And now someone wants to develop the Copse, I suppose," I chip in, to show that I have been keeping up with Felicity's story.

"Exactly that," she says, looking at me sharply. "Perhaps you know about it already."

"Certainly not," I say hurriedly. "Just a logical deduction, given that there was an organised protest against it. But please tell me more."

"That's as maybe," she says, suspiciously. "Well we know about the proposed development because of a brief notice that appeared in my paper. It simply stated that an application for outline permission to develop the site could be viewed at the Council Offices. This turned out to be a sketchy plan for six hundred houses to be built on the site, with just a few token trees left from the original copse."

"So was it the Major who applied for this planning permission?" I ask.

"No," says Felicity. "The application was from a private company called Verdant Heritage but, because it is not a public company, we have been able to find little about it."

"It seems likely that the Major is involved then?" I ask.

"It's a possibility," agrees Felicity, "But when I phoned him for comment, he denied all knowledge of Verdant Heritage, or any plans for developing Hangman's Copse. Very forcibly, in fact."

I could imagine that from my own encounter with the Major.

"You are up against a brick wall, then," I comment.

"For the time being," agrees Felicity, "But there is something fishy going on and I intend to find out what. Why the secrecy if it is all above board?"

"Alright," I say, "If any inside information comes my way, you will be the first to know about it." I decide to play my old codger card. "But I am a very old man, well past my use-by date, so you won't expect me to go running around the town with my nose to the ground like a geriatric James Bond."

Felicity gives me a hard stare. "You looked active enough when you were driving that get-away car," she says. "So I shall expect more of you than sitting comfortably at home waiting for things to happen."

This sounds ominous to me, especially since I am thinking that sitting around and waiting for things to happen would be the best thing for me to do.

"I don't see what other help I could be to you," I say.

"Let's start with an easy one, then," says Felicity. "On Saturday there is a fund-raising fête for the 'Save Hangman's Copse Action Group.' I suggest you attend that and keep your eyes and ears open for any clues as to what might be going on behind the scenes."

"Fêtes are not my scene," I protest. "And surely it would be better for you to go in person rather than rely on a second-hand report from me."

"Oh, I shall be there. Don't worry about that," says Felicity, "But people tend to clam up when they see a newspaper reporter, whereas an apparently harmless old codger doddering around the place with a vacant look on his face would be practically invisible."

I don't much like any of this, especially her description of how she thinks I will appear. "Well, perhaps I could look in and act the part for half an hour," I agree, grudgingly.

"Cheer up," says Felicity, "You'll enjoy yourself. You might win a goldfish or a coconut."

I look at her sourly. "Never mind all that," I growl. "Just tell me the time and the place."

"It will be from two o'clock on Saturday afternoon at number four, Laburnum Avenue." She tells me.

"Wait a minute," I object, "That is in the same street as Major Hunter's House."

"Just two doors away," confirms Felicity. "It belongs to a Mrs Emma Gooding. She is a comfortably off widow and she happens to be the Chair of the 'Save Hangman's Copse Action Group'. You will get on well with her. She has a soft spot for pensioners. If you go there looking hungry I expect she'll offer you a bowl of potato soup."

"*She* might have a soft spot or two, but I am sure the Major doesn't, " I object, "And I would prefer not to be in the same street as him."

Felicity looks at me severely. "Don't become all faint-hearted on me, William," she warns. "You have an urgent interest in helping me to get to the bottom of this conspiracy, remember."

"OK! OK! I get the message," I tell her.

Felicity rises. "And don't you forget it," she admonishes, as she picks up her tablet and makes for the door.

It is with relief that I see her out and watch her cycle off to put the screws on some other unfortunate member of the public. As I return to the kitchen, it occurs to me that I have not done very well in getting the press on my side as specified in Shorty's list of actions. Or any of the other actions for that matter.

CHAPTER 9

With the house clear of reporters, I make my way upstairs to the bathroom, and treat myself to a shower and a shave. I slip into some clean clothes and begin to feel more like my usual self. Another coffee and, I tell myself, I will feel able to face the world again. I return to the kitchen, switch on the kettle and spoon some ground coffee into the cafetiere but, before the water boils, the doorbell peals again.

I look at the clock and see that it is only ten-thirty, and I have already been sorely tried by a self-serving reporter. The last thing I need is further aggravation, but I have developed a bad feeling about today. It has not started well and I fear the downward trend might continue. It does nothing to allay my fear when I open the door and find myself confronted by a smiling Diana Hunter. It looks to me like the smile on the face of a boa-constrictor as it contemplates a cow prior to trapping it in a few coils and swallowing it whole.

"What do you want?" I demand, rudely. "I wasn't expecting to see you ever again."

"Don't be like that, partner," she says, "We got on so well together, yesterday, and I wanted to thank you again for rescuing me with such gallantry."

"OK," I tell her. "You have said thank you. Now beat it. I can recognise trouble when it turns up on my doorstep."

"Aren't you going to invite me in?" asks Diana. "I am in desperate need of advice, and I think older people are so wise."

"Don't give me all that stuff," I snarl. "Oblige me by making a one hundred and eighty degree turn and sailing out of my life."

"But I need your help for my campaign to save the ancient woodlands," she pleads, speaking more loudly than the situation requires. "If I blunder on by myself I just know the police will catch me doing something outrageous. Then yesterday's events would all come out and we would both go to prison."

It strikes me that it would not be good policy to continue this conversation on the doorstep because neighbours have notoriously long ears.

"You had better come in," I say, grudgingly. "We need to come to an understanding about this, and fast."

"Oh, I absolutely agree," says Diana as she follows me into the kitchen. She spots the cafetiere. "Why, you are about to make coffee. How marvellous. Please let me do it"

She waves away my protests and busies herself with the preparation. Barnacle strolls in through his cat-flap to see what is going on and immediately trots across to make friends with the new arrival.

"Ooh," she greets him. "You are a Maine Coon, aren't you? Big and butch, and the nearest thing we have to a native wild-cat."

Barnacle gives the lie to any idea that he might be a wild-cat by rolling over on his back and inviting Diana to scratch his expansive tummy, and she duly obliges.

"His name is Barnacle," I say, irritably.

"Well, Barnacle, you are much friendlier than your master," she tells him. "And I have only called in because he seems so kind and I was sure he would like to help me."

"Let's get this straight before you come out with any more threats," I say. "I do not wish to become involved in your campaign and I am not going to be influenced by what might happen if it became known that I was kind enough to give you a lift in my car yesterday. You know as well as I do that I had nothing at all to do with the protest meeting."

Diana places two mugs on the table and pours coffee into them. "Of course, Bill," she says, easily. "You and I know that, but we have to think about what other people might believe."

"They can believe what they like," I reply, warmly, "But it was you who assaulted the policeman. If they were to catch up with us, you would face prosecution whereas I, as a simple bystander caught up in the action, would be let off with, at most, a caution."

Diana looks thoughtful. "Unfortunately, if we were caught, we would be brought up before a magistrate who would be either Daddy or one of his chums. And Daddy thinks that you're the ringleader in this and that you have been leading me astray. I have a feeling he might want to make an example of you."

"I am sure you would make it clear that I had nothing to do with leading you astray, or anywhere else for that matter," I say.

Diana pours the coffee and takes a sip. "I don't believe I would be strong enough to say anything like that," she says, regretfully. "I am sure I would be so overwhelmed by all the trappings of a court of law that I wouldn't be capable of doing anything but sob quietly into my handkerchief."

I suddenly feel the need of a gulp of strong coffee myself. I can feel the trap closing around me. You might have heard the saying that lightning never strikes twice in the same place, but I can tell you it is absolute nonsense. It is not more than an hour since I was coerced by exactly the same threat into an undertaking that all my instincts told me could lead only to trouble. And here I am being caught again.

What is it with young women these days I ask myself? Are they all like villainesses from Shakespearian tragedies? Felicity and Diana seem to be so devoid of any form of conscience that It occurs to me they might be psychopaths, in which case it might be safest to humour them.

"Alright," I hear myself saying. "I'll be willing to help you in some small way, but I am sure I will not be able to do much. I am a little old man, both physically and mentally frail. It takes me so much effort to get out of bed and make breakfast in the morning that I immediately need a lie-down until lunchtime."

It says much about my state of mind that I feel I have no option but to play the age card but, if I am hoping it will soften up Lady Macbeth II, I am sorely disappointed.

"You look good for another eighty years to me," she says, dismissively. "In any case, it will do you good to have a useful project to keep your brain active."

I rise to the bait. "I'm not senile yet," I tell her. "There's nothing wrong with my brain."

"I'm pleased to hear that," she smiles, sweetly. "Just a moment ago you were claiming to be mentally frail."

So, I have been outwitted again. "I can't stand clever people," I tell her, seeking refuge in the depth of my coffee cup.

"Seriously," she says, "It will make you feel good to help prevent an ecological disaster and to preserve some of our natural heritage for future generations."

"Oh, yes?" I say, cynically.

"Certainly , yes," she replies, firmly. "And, in any case I would only ask you for a very small service, which would put you to absolutely no inconvenience whatsoever."

It comes to me that I am beset by mixed feelings. On the one hand common sense tells me that I should have as little involvement in Diana's plans as possible but, on the other hand, I feel hurt that she believes I am only capable of making a trivial contribution. At times like this, I don't even understand myself, so what hope is there that I might understand what makes people like Diana and Felicity tick.

"Very well," I say, glumly. "What exactly is it you would like me to do?"

"I take it you know what yesterday's protest was all about," begins Diana.

I explain that Felicity Wright has given me some background, but that is all I know. And I didn't even know that much yesterday, so perhaps she could fill in some details. "What is it between you and your Dad, for a start?" I ask. "Felicity told me that Hangman's Copse belongs to him so, if you want to save it from development, can't you just persuade him not to sell it?"

Diana smiles, ruefully. "You have met Daddy," she says. "How easy is it to persuade him of anything, do you think? In any case, when I try to broach the subject he denies having any intention to sell his woodland at all."

"So who has applied for planning permission to develop the copse for housing?" I ask. "Surely, as the owner, your father must have something to do with it."

"That application by Verdant Heritage is why we started the protest movement," explains Diana, "But we haven't been able to find out who owns the company. When we attempted to trace the owners, we simply came up against faceless nominees with addresses in solicitors' offices."

"So you have nothing solid to engage with," I say, "Like trying to catch a jellyfish with a fish hook."

"Well the Council is the one concrete target we have," says Diana. "Hence the protest yesterday. We need to make sure that the application is turned down."

"I must say you made your presence felt," I quip.

"True," she agrees, without so much as a blush. "But we have to keep up the pressure."

She is looking at me appraisingly, as a peckish spider might view a fly trapped in a corner of its web, and I have a horrible awareness that I am being considered for an active part in whatever scheme she has in mind.

"You have something up your sleeve," I accuse, with all too obvious dismay.

"Yes," she says, "But don't look so alarmed, yours will only be a passive and very simple role."

"I'll believe that when you tell me about it," I reply, warily.

"The thing is," she explains, "Ancient woodland is worth preserving in its own right. It is woodland that has been in existence since before 1600 and so, by definition, it is irreplaceable."

"Is that not enough to keep it from being destroyed, then?" I ask.

"No," she tells me, emphatically. "Such woodlands are still being cut down for projects like new roads or urban development. We need something more."

"Like what?" I ask.

"Like the discovery that Hangman's Copse is home to some endangered species of plant, bird or, better still, an iconic animal."

"Is there anything of that kind in the Copse, then?" I ask.

"I don't know," says Diana, "But, if there is not, there soon will be. Do you know anything about dormice?"

I have to admit that this is a gap in my experience. A sailor's life did not offer a chap many opportunities for meeting dormice. We would sometimes have rats on-board, and cockroaches by the thousand, but never a dormouse.

"Well, never mind," says Diana. "You will find them easy enough to look after."

I look at her in disbelief. "What do you mean?" I quaver. "I can't have dormice in the house. The only things I know about them are from reading Alice in Wonderland when I was about six. Don't they live in teapots or something?"

"You needn't worry," says Diana in a reassuring voice that suggests to me that I really do have to worry. "I will leave you with full instructions about their keep."

"And what about Barnacle?" I ask. "How are we going to convince him that they are not for his lunch?"

"You worry too much," Diana tells me. "The dormice will be in a closely barred cage. There will be no way that Barnacle can get at them."

It occurs to me that dormice are probably 'protected' animals and that there is likely to be some regulation against keeping such wildlife as pets in cages. My brief acquaintance with Diana leads me to believe that she would have no compunction about inviting me to break the law.

"It is all above board," she assures me. "These will be rescued dormice, and we are planning to release them into their natural habitat. We are the good guys in this exercise."

I am still far from happy at the idea of hosting dormice, but I realise that Diana could easily have asked me to do something more onerous. Nevertheless, I make one more effort to divert her.

"Why can't you look after these dormice in your own home?" I ask.

She gives a savage laugh. "What do you think would happen if Daddy found them?" She demands. "He can't see any sort of wildlife in Hangman's Copse without a compulsion to fill it with lead shot, so how do you think he would react if he discovered a cage full of furry animals under the kitchen table?"

I give in with the best grace I can muster. "And how long would I be expected to offer my hospitality to these rodent guests?" I enquire.

"Oh, just a few days until I can organise their transfer to Hangman's Copse," she says, airily. "Of course, I will also have to arrange for a photographer, and perhaps the press, to be in attendance. The presence of dormice in the woodland must be witnessed and recorded beyond question."

This timing sounds uncomfortably vague to me. The shorter their stay in my house the better I shall be pleased.

"Well, don't hurry to bring them here," I tell her, "I need time to get used to the idea of running a B&B for rodents."

"I'm taking delivery of them tomorrow," she tells me. "That will be plenty of time for you. I'll bring them round to your place in the morning."

"Are you sure there aren't any dormice in Hangman's Copse already?" I say, in a last, forlorn attempt at putting Diana off. "If there are, it would save us from going to all this trouble. For all we know, the woods might be as alive with dormice as those hills were with Julie Andrews's music."

"They might be," Diana concedes, "And there are very likely, equally endangered Barbastelle bats, but they are both nocturnal and very difficult to find. Any animal that showed itself during the day would long since have been blasted to oblivion by Daddy's shotgun."

Diana looks at her watch. "Oh dear, is that the time?" she says. "Well thanks for the coffee, Bill, and for your kind offer to provide a foster home for my orphan dormice."

I have no idea how she can interpret my reluctant submission to her blackmail as a "kind offer" but I let it go.

As I usher her to the door, I remember that Buster Crump had asked me to help heal the breach that had opened up between him and Diana as a result of yesterday's events.

"Buster Crump came to see me yesterday afternoon," I tell her. "He was most concerned that I might have abducted you and driven you off to a fate worse than death."

"Ha!" she replies, caustically. "Well I would be ecstatic if someone were to carry him off to a fate worse than death."
Clearly, if I am to help the poor chap, I need to make his case more persuasively. "I believe he came here in case you need rescuing." I explain. "Like your own, personal white knight."

"Ridiculous," she snorts. "He wouldn't dare to rescue me from a chicken house in case the hens ate him alive like they do with the other worms."

I decide this is a lost cause. She puts her nose in the air and I see her off the premises with a heartfelt sigh. Perhaps I can look forward to a little peace and quiet for the rest of the morning, I think to myself but, of course, it is not to be. I have barely cleared away and washed the coffee mugs when the doorbell sounds again.

CHAPTER 10

This time it is the assessor from my insurance company and, for a change, it is someone I am really pleased to see. He is a soberly dressed and courteous man and he wastes no time in getting down to business.

At his request, I take him firstly upstairs to inspect the wreckage of my bedroom. I am pleased that he notes the damage on a proper clip-board, rather than on some kind of electronic device, but he is a man of few words and makes no verbal comment. Then I conduct him into the garden to view the stricken oak. He examines the exposed and broken roots with particular interest, which seems to me a little odd. Then he hrrmphs a few times as if to warn me that he is about to break some holy vow of silence and utter a few words. It has been a long wait and I do not like what I hear when he does start to speak.

"We have to consider all eventualities," he begins, "Including the possibility that the tree might have been interfered with so it would be more prone to falling down."

I look at him in surprise and not a little annoyance. "What on earth put that idea in your head?" I ask.

He tells me that he received a routine call from the Council earlier in the day and that a Miss Fyler had explained about the tree's protected status and my application to have it felled, and had hinted that it might have been more than a coincidence that it was blown down in not much more than a moderate gale.

"That wretched Fyler woman had no business spreading unfounded rumours like that to everyone," I explode, much put out by this uncalled for example of busy-bodying.

"Some of the white scars on those broken roots do look as though they might have been caused by hacking with an axe," he observes.

"They are white because they are newly broken by the falling tree," I tell him, forcefully. "And there is no way you are going to wriggle out of paying my claim because of a vindictive old witch in the Town Hall."

"Alright. Alright." He says soothingly. "I am not saying that we are influenced by her speculation, but you will appreciate that we in the insurance business do sometimes have to deal with fraudulent claims, so we have to be extremely careful."

"Do you really think for a moment that I would have encouraged that tree to fall into my bedroom?" I demand. "It might have killed me."

"Well, Mr Selsey, that is certainly a point we will take into account," he allows, as if he were granting me a great personal favour. "On the other hand, for a huge old tree near the house like this one, it would have cost you over a thousand pounds to have had it safely felled by a tree surgeon. We have come across people causing trees to fall as if by accident and then expecting us to pay for whatever damage resulted. They don't realise that it is not always possible to anticipate which way a tree will topple."

This is becoming too much. I feel as if I am being picked on and assailed from all directions like a lone Manchester United supporter on a ship where the rest of the crew had signed on in Liverpool. It is not something one should take lying down. The assessor is not a big man and it is with some difficulty that I resist the temptation to grasp him by the lapels of his jacket and give him a good shaking.

"Will you please get it into your head and onto your clip-board that I have done nothing whatever to weaken that tree." I shout. "It has fallen because of its age and a gale of wind, and I expect the tree to be removed. and my house to be repaired as a matter of urgency, and at your expense."

Too late, it comes to me that I am not doing a good job of playing the frail and vulnerable old pensioner that Shorty recommended. In fact the poor assessor looks somewhat alarmed by my demeanour. However, he is made of stern stuff and is only moderately conciliatory.

"I am making a note of your statement," he says, "And it will be contained in my report. But you should be aware that we are only responsible for extracting the tree from your house and making the necessary repairs to the building. Removal of the actual tree from your premises will be to your account. It is your house that is insured with us, and not the tree."

"Well thank you for not very much," I retort, more rudely than I intend, "And be sure I will check the small print of my policy to satisfy myself what is and what is not covered."

"We recommend that our customers do that *before* they sign the agreement," he says, mildly, "But many people don't bother."

He hands me a long envelope. "Now, if you would be kind enough to complete the claims form and send it to us as soon as possible, I can assure you that your case will be give every proper consideration."

At this late stage, it dawns on me that this is a person that I need on my side and that I was, perhaps, unwise to give him such a hard time.

"I am sure I can rely on you to make a fair and impartial assessment," I tell him. "Now, can I offer you a cup of tea or coffee? Or, perhaps, something stronger?"

"In the ordinary way, that would be most pleasant," he says, with exaggerated politeness. "But, as you will expect after a storm, I have a very busy day ahead of me. Your case was given priority because (he consults his clip-board) you are considered to be aged and , perhaps, infirm." He pauses and looks at me appraisingly. It is clear that he thinks I might be old but that I am certainly not his idea of infirm.

I ignore whatever his level gaze might be implying and wish him every success with the remainder of his engagements. We shake hands and he removes himself from my presence with more haste than seems strictly necessary. He does pause to shut my garden gate but then he wastes no more time in reaching his car and driving off to explain to some of his company's other clients why their payouts may not meet their expectations.

CHAPTER 11

I return to my kitchen and sort out some cat food for Barnacle. Then I find a couple of pork pies and a six-pack of beer in the fridge, stow them in a bag, and set off to find sanctuary in Shorty's hut on the allotments. I move at more than my usual retired person's amble to make sure I am clear of the house before any more callers can add further irritations to my day. I find Shorty sitting with his feet up on the table, reading the morning paper. He looks up and smiles appreciatively when he sees what I am carrying.

"Have you seen the paper today?" he asks.

I throw myself down into the vacant chair and glare at him. "I have had people bugging me all the morning," I tell him. "I've not enjoyed a moment's peace since I woke up. How do you think I have had time to read a paper?"

"Like that was it?" remarks Shorty in a voice that I feel is somehow lacking in sympathy.

I open the beers and put the pies on the table

"Let me take a swig of this sanity saver," I say, as I open a can, "And I'll tell you exactly how it was."

"You'd better check this headline first," advises Shorty, holding up the paper and reading aloud: "PLUCKY PENSIONER SURVIVES STORM-STRUCK OAK".

I nearly choke into my beer. "That girl's has gone alliteratively mad," I splutter. "What is her editor thinking of to allow a sentence like that?"

"He's thinking of his circulation," says Shorty, drily, "Although, come to think about it, he can't be too bothered about that because he has also printed a picture of you."

I snatch the paper away from him and, sure enough, there is a shot of me standing by the fallen tree with a worried look on my face which I am sure Shorty will describe as apprehensive. I hadn't noticed Felicity take this particular shot, but she had been waving her tablet around as she was talking so she could easily have done so. Beneath the picture is a caption: "TREE CRUSHES HOUSE - OAP WILLIAM SELSEY WOUNDED".

Felicity is stretching the truth, somewhat, I decide, but that is to be expected, and I am not altogether displeased at becoming headline news.

Shorty breaks into my train of thought. "The article goes on say that, although you were injured by flying glass, you bravely declined hospital treatment. " He pauses to look up at me. "Where are all these wounds, then?" he asks.

"She is exaggerating, of course," I explain, holding up a thumb. It is the merest nick from when I was sweeping up the room. Nothing to do with flying glass. But that is the least of my worries, I have much more serious problems with Felicity Wright."

"I'm impressed," exclaims Shorty in mock alarm. "Woman trouble at your age! Should I commiserate or congratulate you?"

"It's not just one woman," I complain. "It's two of them."

"Now that definitely is over the top," leers Shorty. "You might be able to ride out a problem with one woman, but when it is two you should consider leaving the country. Australia might be far enough."

"This is no joking matter," I tell him.

"Of course not," agrees Shorty, trying, without much success to supress a grin. "What have you been up to, you old dog? And am I going to have to visit you in jail?"

I sip my beer, gloomily. "The answer to your first question is, nothing. And the answer to your second question is, quite probably."

Shorty takes a long pull at his beer and a bite out of his pork pie. "You had better tell me all about it," he invites, through a mouthful of pastry crumbs.

He listens, attentively as I relate the morning's happenings. I tell him the whole story and, to give him his due, he manages to avoid smiling for most of the time. I explain how I am being blackmailed by Felicity Wright, out-manoeuvred by Diana Hunter and treated as a potential fraudster by a nameless man from the insurance company.

At the end of my tale of woe, Shorty absent-mindedly opens another can of beer and then delivers his verdict.

"The longer you stay here, the more desperate your situation is becoming," he pronounces. "Normally, I would recommend that you should slip your anchor and go to visit your sister in Barnstable for a week or so until the storm has passed. That would be nearly as good as Australia. But, of course, you can't do that until the tree has been dealt with and your house has been repaired."

"Well that has established what I can't do," I say, grumpily. "Have you got any ideas that might actually help? What do you suggest I *should* do?"

"As little as possible, if you ask me," he says. "Keep your head down and out of everyone's way until things blow over, and avoid becoming involved in other people's affairs. Particularly, keep away from your two girl-friends."

"They aren't my girl-friends, and I don't want anything to do with them," I say, forcibly. "I'll be happy if I see them as rarely as Sir William Hamilton saw his lady wife when Horatio Nelson was in the offing."

"Batten down the hatches, then," says Shorty. "Repel all boarders."

"That is exactly what I would like to do," I complain, "And it is exactly what the whole world seems intent on preventing me doing. I am expecting a consignment of dormice to arrive on my doorstep tomorrow. How do I avoid becoming involved with them?"

"You can't possibly be worried about a couple of dormice," says Shorty. "We used to regularly carry live cattle in Purple Funnel. We thought nothing of loading a dozen testosterone-charged bulls in the 'tween decks. You tanker-men had it too easy, just filling your ship up with oil at a loading port and squirting it out again at your discharge port."

"There was more to it than that," I protest.

"Not much," says Shorty, dismissively. "You should have had to deal with general cargoes like those we had in the liner trade. And keep to a tight schedule as well. If you had experienced our problems you wouldn't be panicking about having a few innocuous little rodents lodging with you overnight."

Shorty takes another pull from his can of beer and goes into reminiscent mode. "We picked up an elephant in Bombay once," he says. "Had to build a kind of outsize stable on deck for it and stow a ton of hay in the fo'c'sle. Now that would have exercised our minds if there hadn't been a section in the company's manual telling us exactly how to go about it."

He pauses for effect and the turns to me. "No one has asked you to look after an elephant, have they?"

"It's not the size that matters," I growl. "It is the fact that I am being coerced into something that I would prefer not to do, and which I have a feeling is verging on the illegal."

"So, it's all in your mind," says Shorty. "OK, these girls are leaning on you which, understandably, you don't like, but what they are actually asking you to do is not at all a big deal. Or, at least it wouldn't be for a Purple Funnel sailor,"

It goes against the grain to accept that there might be something in Shorty's analysis, but I have to agree that it contains an element of truth. If I am honest with myself, I can admit that I am becoming interested in Felicity's theory that there is some conspiracy to be investigated and in Diana's linked crusade to save an area of ancient woodland. It is just that I don't like the feeling that I am being pushed into it rather than taking an interest because I happen to want to. I explain as much to Shorty, but he has an answer for that too.

"Just think of it as being patronising, and indulging their dear little feminine wiles," he advises. "That way, it puts you in the driving seat."

"Oh, of course, I forgot that you are an expert on female psychology," I say, sarcastically.

"I like to think, diplomacy, rather than psychology," says Shorty, unmoved by the sceptical edge in my comment, "We used to carry up to twelve passengers on most Purple Funnel ships and the memsahibs amongst them could be extremely demanding. The trick was to make a grand gesture of letting them have their way in small things and then to play down the few occasions when we had to draw the line on important matters."

"Alright," I say, grudgingly, "Suppose, for the sake of argument, we accept that. How would it work in my case?"

"Well," says Shorty. "Since you ask me, you seem to be doing the right thing so far by exaggerating the trivial things. You are making a great fuss about attending a garden fête, and an even greater song and dance about looking after a few mice for a couple of days. Elephants, now, might have really been a challenge."

"OK, OK," I tell him. "There's no need to go on about elephants."

"Or tigers," says Shorty. "We had to take a pair of Bengals from Calcutta to Sydney Zoo once." He rolls up his sleeve. "See here, I've still got the scars."

I happen to know that Shorty collected those scars when he had misplaced a bottle-opener and had unwisely tried to remove the crown-cork from a bottle of Guinness with his clasp knife. However, we have a tacit agreement that we don't spoil each-others old sailor stories by questioning elements that grow more and more unlikely with the passing years. One of the afflictions of old age is that one forgets many details of the episodes that have contributed to a long and eventful life. But nature, as is often the case, provides compensation and our imagination can easily fill the gaps. It would be sad if we allowed cold logic to interfere with this rich vein of entertainment. On the other hand, right now I need to keep Shorty concentrating on present business.

"Never mind about your Noah's Ark stories," I tell him. "I accept that I might be exaggerating my difficulties with Felicity and Diana, but the man from the insurance and Wendy Fyler from the Council are still bugging me with their innuendos that I might have been somehow to blame for the tree keeling over."

"Don't worry about it, old mate," says Shorty comfortably. "In this country, you're innocent until proven guilty. If you didn't do it, there is no way they can prove you did. Remind that Council woman that they were putting property and the public at risk by making a preservation order on a dodgy tree. And next time you see the insurance man, don't forget to tell him that you hold the Council responsible for not allowing you to cut down a dangerous tree. It could get Ms Fyler off your back if she thinks the insurance company might try to recover their costs from the Council."

As usual, talking things through with Shorty gives me a fresh angle on my problems and I can view them from a more manageable perspective. Not everyone is out to get me. In Shorty, I have at least one person on my side. Two, if you count Barnacle.

It is late afternoon by this time, so we turn-to and clear the lunch table. I put the empty beer-cans in my bag for recycling and I walk slowly back to my house where I intend to potter around in relative peace until supper time.

I have no idea why I believe this is likely to happen.

CHAPTER 12

I enter the kitchen to find Barnacle taking his afternoon sleep, which he schedules almost immediately after his morning snooze and a short while before his evening nap. He lifts a heavy eyelid to make sure it is me and then allows it to slowly fall again. I check the answer phone and find a message to call Wendy Fyler. When I get through, I make an attempt to seize the initiative and berate her for suggesting to the insurance company that I might have sabotaged the tree to make it more vulnerable to being uprooted.

"There's no smoke without fire," she responds, tritely.

"You had no business spreading rumours like that on no evidence whatsoever," I tell her. "Making false accusations could be actionable."

"I made no accusations," she says, unperturbed. "I merely passed on a few facts. Firstly, that you had applied to have the tree felled, secondly that we had placed a preservation order on it, thirdly that you have a huge axe in your shed, and finally, that the tree did fall down. Any construction the insurance company puts on those facts is entirely a matter for them."

"You were clearly implying something more, just by choosing to tell them those particular facts," I complain. "And I would like to know why you took it upon yourself to make contact with my insurance company at all. It is no business of the Council to interfere in what is a private business arrangement between my insurance company and me."

"I told them nothing they could not have easily found out for themselves," she points out.

"I am sure that is true," I say, "But why would you bother? That's what I want to know. Is this some kind of personal vendetta?"

She becomes a little more conciliatory, but it is only a little.

"I think you are becoming a touch paranoid about this." She warns. "Providing useful information to the public and to local commercial interests is one of the functions of a Council. In any case, that is not what I wanted to speak to you about."

"Well you are making that clear enough," I tell her.

"No," she says. "What I need to tell you is that, in the light of my report on yesterday's visit, it has been confirmed that the tree, in its present state, may not be stable and it therefore represents a danger to the public. This is your responsibility and it needs to be made safe as a matter of urgency."

"Now you are talking absolute bilge," I tell her. "The tree is leaning against my house and there is no way it can fall any further. Even if it did, it is nowhere near the road or the pavement. It is no threat to anyone except me and my cat."

As our conversation proceeds, it is clear that I am to be held responsible for injury to anyone who might enter my premises, a friend, the postman or even a burglar, and I am being threatened by a hefty fine if I do not take immediate steps to have the site made safe. I point out that her own action in raising doubts with the insurance company might have the effect of delaying remedial work but she dismisses this out of hand as a possible mitigation of my liability. Her final shot, before ringing off is to inform me that a formal notice demanding that my premises should be made safe will arrive in the post tomorrow and that, in the meantime, I should assume that the notice will commence from the time of her phone call.

I decide that I should take another look at the tree and the damaged house while there is still daylight. I give the trunk a good heave-ho this way and that, but it is firmly wedged into the broken masonry and it does not give an inch. It wouldn't shift if it was hit by a China Sea tsunami, I tell myself. I have not the slightest fear that there is any further risk of injury to a member of the public, or to myself for that matter. On the other hand, I *am* worried about the notice to make the situation safe despite my belief that it is already perfectly secure. There is more than meets the eye in Ms Fyler's actions, I feel. She has brushed aside my accusations that she has been going beyond the normal limits of her job, but she has not answered any of them.

I occupy myself by picking up some of the fallen masonry and stacking it neatly against the side of the house. Some of the bricks are nearly whole and I think about how I might make use of them around the flower beds. Then I collect some of the broken twigs and branches from the tree and stow them on my bonfire site which I have at the bottom of the garden, well away from the house. I know there is little point in these tasks before the tree is lifted away from the house, but the activity is preferable to sitting around feeling sorry for myself.

After twenty minutes or so, Barnacle slips out of his cat-flap and sits solemnly watching me for a while. Then he jumps onto the tree-trunk and walks up it all the way to the window, where he pauses to peer into my bedroom. It has to be said that he is not being a great deal of help, but it is nice of him to take an interest. The physical exercise has had a therapeutic effect and I feel more at ease by the time I decide to call it a day and return indoors.

Back in the kitchen, I am looking in the fridge and wondering what I might find there for supper, when the phone rings. I would have jumped a fathom into the air if my head had not come into painful contact with the underside of an overhead cupboard. So much for my supposed calmer state of mind, I tell myself, as I rub the developing bump on my cranium. I reach for the handset with some diffidence because, on current form, it seems unlikely that it will be the source of any good news. In fact, it is a pleasantly deep and friendly voice that greets me, as comforting as a bowl of hearty onion soup on a cold winter's day.

"Hello," it says. "Am I speaking to Mr William Selsey?"

A couple of days ago, I would have been reassured on hearing such warm tones, but recent experiences had made me cynical beyond recognition. Confidence tricksters speak that way, don't they? That's how they convince their victims to invest their life savings in a company that is proposing to use the Ponzi process to manufacture fairy dust.

"This is William Selsey speaking." I admit, cautiously.

"Good evening, Mr Selsey," says the voice. "I apologise for calling you so late in the day, but I do believe I may be in a position to help you."

This sounds ominously like one of those cold-callers preparing to talk me into some kind of scam, except that he isn't urging me not to hang up, and he isn't immediately going into a long, previously rehearsed, spiel about how he can make a thousand pounds for me next week if I will just send him a cheque for twenty pounds today. I decide to give him a chance.

"And why would you think I am in need of any help. Mr ......?" I ask.

"Ah. Well, I am Councillor Oliver Crump," he explains, in his mellow tones. "And I am aware that you have a problem with a fallen tree. Such accidents can be highly stressful, especially for older people, but I am sure I can assist in sorting it all out."

I explain to him that Ms Fyler, for the Council, is not being at all helpful in sorting it all out, at which he gives a jolly laugh and tells me that she can sometimes be over-zealous and ultra-careful but I am not to worry. He is sure he can placate her. He is, after all, the Chairman of the Planning Committee, and Wendy Fyler, as planning officer, reports to him.

"It would help if she would rescind the safety order she is threatening me with," I say. "I don't like the possibility of a fine hanging over my head, and the insurance company seem to be dragging their feet. In any case the tree looks perfectly safe to me."

"I'll tell you what," says Oliver Crump. "Why don't I come round to have a look at the situation tomorrow morning at, say, nine o'clock? Then we can decide on a way forward that will put your mind at rest."

Nine o'clock is early-ish in what I think of as a normal day, but I am not about to quibble when someone is offering the possibility of helpful action.

"Nine o'clock will be fine," I tell him, and then a thought comes into my mind. "I met a Buster Crump the other day. Would he be a relation of yours?"

"Yes, of course," says Oliver. "He is my son, but still a bit of a gadabout, I'm afraid. As yet, he has shown no interest in my business or Council activities."

"That's young people for you," I commiserate. "Well, thanks for your call, Mr Crump, I look forward to meeting you."

"And I you," he replies, affably. "I'll see you tomorrow and, in the meantime, don't you worry about a thing."

As I replace the telephone, my first reaction is one of relief that I have actually been talking to someone who is prepared to be helpful – even friendly. It is only after further reflection that my newly acquired cynicism kicks in. Could it be that Oliver Crump is just a bit too cooperative and plausible to be true?

I decide there is no point in letting things get on top of me, and that the best thing will be to forget about it all for the evening. Tomorrow I will simply deal with things as they come.

I find nothing I fancy for supper in the fridge, so I send out for a pizza and settle down with a purring Barnacle on my lap for an evening of non-demanding television. After yesterday's melancholy experience, I zip through the alternative channels until I find a promising comedy. It revolves around a middle aged chap who spends his time trying to help others but, due to misunderstandings, or sometimes just bad luck, he creates more problems than he solves. His cascading mishaps are often funny, but the central theme of a well-meaning bloke finding himself tumbling deeper and deeper into trouble feels too close to home for comfort, and there is a wryness about my laughs.

On the positive side, I am sufficiently entertained that I do not drink so much as yesterday evening. As I put myself to bed, I look forward to starting tomorrow with a clear head and making some progress in getting my life back to normal.

It is always good to think positively, I tell myself, even when all the evidence suggests otherwise.

CHAPTER 13

I feel that virtue has been rewarded when I wake up with clear head in the morning. I cut things fine, but I am showered, shaved and breakfasted by the time Oliver Crump arrives on my doorstep soon after nine o'clock.

I conduct him around the side of the house to where he can inspect the damage caused by the tree. He tuts, tuts sympathetically and wonders, out-loud, whether my old home is really worth saving. He says that the best thing might be to knock the place down completely and replace it with a modern and more convenient new house.

I explain that I cannot afford to undertake a major project like that, so he offers to help me by buying my house, as it is, including the tree damage, for its full market price.

"You older people have done your bit for the country," he says. "People of your generation should be looking at ways to make your retirement more secure and comfortable , and we younger people should be helping however we can."

"But I am very attached to the house," I tell him. "I like it here and I have no plans for selling."

"It is entirely up to you, of course," he replies. "But ownership of a substantial property like this becomes a real hassle when incidents of this kind occur. You might like to consider moving into a nice retirement apartment more suited to your age and capabilities. None of us are getting any younger."

"I am not ready for an old-person's home yet." I say, frostily.

"No. Of course not," he agrees, hastily. "But you don't need all the responsibility that comes with this sort of place, either. Like the public liability created by the damaged state of your property as Ms Fyler has advised you."

I turn to him in surprise. "When we last spoke on the phone yesterday evening, I thought you said you could get Ms Fyler off my back."

"And so I did, Mr Selsey," he says, placatingly. "And I have already let it be known that the draft Public Safety Order needs further consideration, which means that you will not be receiving it today. However, these things take a little while to arrange. In the meantime, why don't you consider my offer. It might turn out that the fallen tree was a happy accident, triggering a decision that should be made sooner rather than later. It so happens that I have built a development of retirement properties nearer the town centre. They provide residents with complete independence but with a warden on site in case of emergency. I am sure one could be offered to you at a very favourable price."

"Very well, I will give the matter some thought," I say, to get him to change tack rather than with any intention of seriously considering his offer. He smiles and puts a friendly arm around my shoulder.

"Please do that, Mr Selsey," he says, "And by all means discuss my suggestion with your friends and advisers. I'll keep in touch and I'll continue to pull a few strings, and we will soon bring this affair to a satisfactory conclusion."

Hmm. Does that mean satisfactory for me or satisfactory for him, I wonder as he takes his leave along my garden path and out into the street where he has left his Jaguar. Having passed through the gate, who should he meet but Felicity Wright on her way in.

Oh no! It is going to be another of those mornings, I tell myself. Oliver Crump, pointedly it seems to me, does not stand back or hold the gate open for Felicity. As he stumps past her, they exchange frosty greetings, and he has driven off in his car without so much as a look back by the time she has come up to me at my front door. She lets me have it with both barrels straight away.

"I don't need to be clairvoyant to sense an atmosphere of double-crossing conspiracy here," she begins. "What were you doing conniving with that warthog, Crump, if you aren't up to no good?"

I protest my innocence of even being aware of a conspiracy, let alone involvement in one, but she is not easily put off. She accuses me of sleeping with the enemy, running with both the hare and the hounds, and other metaphors for treacherous behaviour that can be conjured up so readily on the electronic tablets used by journalists. What is my game, she demands. And is there some kind of link between my friendship with Oliver Crump and my interest in the fate of Hangman's Copse?

I tell her, emphatically, that I have no interest in Hangman's Copse other than that which she and Diana Hunter have forced upon me, and that I had never met Oliver Crump until this morning. Felicity curls her lip and looks at me with all too obvious disbelief. "So what were you two old crows hatching up just now?" she demands.

"The bloke just came to view the damage to my house, in his capacity as Chairman of the Council's Planning Committee," I explain. "What is more, he has made an offer to buy my house as it stands, damage and all. This has nothing to do with Hangman's Copse, neither it, nor ancient woodland, were even mentioned. He says he just wants to help me."

"Help himself, more likely." says Felicity, darkly. "There is always an angle with Oliver Crump. What is the old villain up to this time? And why his interest in you and your house?"

"I don't know but, if it's any consolation to you, I also have a feeling that he is too good to be true," I say. "He even claims he can get Wendy Fyler to back off on her latest attempt to crucify me."

"Ah!" says Felicity. "That will be the Public Safety Order that is to be served on you shortly. As a matter of fact, that is why I came to talk to you. Would you care to make a comment?"

"I would like to make lots of comments," I tell her. "None of them printable in your paper. But I have not received it as yet, and Crump tells me he has, at least, delayed its delivery."

"You are obviously aware of its contents though?" says Felicity.

"Of course I am, the Fyler person phoned me yesterday afternoon to taunt me about it. More to the point, how do you know about it?"

"A first draft of it mysteriously appeared on my desk this morning," explains Felicity. "I told you we often receive selective leaks from the Council offices."

"You also said that you were not keen on following up deliberate leaks," I remind her. "You said it's the information that is not leaked that is more interesting."

"A good general rule, that," agrees Felicity, "But I look at each case on its merits. So tell me how you intend to react on this one?"

"I think the Fyler is being deliberately awkward," I say. "That tree is firmly wedged in position. It would not shift any further in an earthquake and, in any case, it is far enough from the road so there is no possible danger to passers-by."

"So you are not going to do anything," notes Felicity.

"Certainly not before the written notice arrives," I tell her. "And I hope the insurance people will remove the tree and start repairing my house very soon."

"Would you agree that you are being harassed by the Council, then?" asks Felicity, electronic pad at the ready to record my answer.

I decide that I need to be cautious in what I say to a newshound but, on the other hand, as Shorty suggested, it is useful to have the press on my side. "Harassed might be too strong a word," I say, carefully. "But they are certainly being unhelpful to a long-suffering ratepayer."

"OK," says Felicity, putting her tablet away in her bag. "That's all I need for now. But there is something going on that I have yet to work out."

"What sort of something?" I ask.

"The way Wendy and Oliver are working on you, for a start," says Felicity, thoughtfully. "They are playing hard-cop, soft-cop, if you ask me. But what are they hoping to achieve? As Council Planning

Officer, she is secretary to Oliver Crump's Planning Committee, you know."

"Very cosy," I agree. "I can see I shall have to watch my step with those two."

"And I shall be watching my step with all three of you," promises Felicity. "I am still not entirely sure how you fit into all this although, for the time being, you are being given the benefit of the doubt."

"Thanks a lot for your touching trust," I say, sarcastically. "You are the one coercing me to work for you."

"I'm glad you remember that," says Felicity, cheerfully. "And I am sure you will do your best for me at Saturday's fête."

She gathers up her things, gives Barnacle a pat on the head and takes her leave. As I close the door behind her, I heave a sigh of relief.

"Two callers already," I complain to Barnacle, "And we are only half way through the first watch. If you were a dog, I'd take you for a walk in the park just to get out of the house before anyone else arrives to bug me."

Barnacle is following every word with rapt attention. He is probably trying to detect if any of the noises I am making might be are related to food for felines, like the mouth-watering sound of a foil sachet being opened, but I prefer to interpret his gaze as telling me that he has no intention of apologising for being a cat and that I may take a walk on my own whenever I feel like it, and see if he cares.

I decide to do just that, and I am reaching for my coat when the doorbell rings again. Clearly, I should have got out of the house when I had the chance instead of pausing for an asymmetrical conversation with my cat. The sigh of relief I hove a few minutes ago unheaves itself in the form of a groan. Where are these people all coming from? I peer out of the window, half expecting to see some kind of conveyor belt in the street delivering a new person to disturb my peace, every hour, on the hour.

CHAPTER 14

I grumble away to myself as I wander off to open my front door, and it does nothing to improve my mood when I find Diana Hunter standing there. I was hoping she might have been abducted by aliens overnight and taken for a long holiday to Venus or some equally remote location. She is holding a large cage covered by a sheet of what looks like old curtain material.

If I am not pleased to see her, it appears that the feeling is mutual because she immediately begins to give me a hard time. It seems that she had met Felicity in the street outside my house and Felicity had mentioned seeing Olive Crump leaving my premises.

"So!" she begins, "You have been entertaining the unspeakable Oliver Crump. And what obnoxious schemes have you two lovebirds been hatching up?"

I feel that I had enough of being harangued on this topic by Felicity Wright and I have no intention of putting up with more of the same from Diana Hunter.

"If you talked to Felicity, I am sure she would have told you that Crump came to see me on a matter entirely unrelated to your crusade to save Hangman's Copse, or any other ancient woodland."

"Well yes," concedes Diana. "She did say you half convinced her that he only came to offer help with your fallen tree."

"He offered to buy the house as it stands," I tell her. "To take it and all its related problems off my hands."

"Just like that?" says Diana.

"Just like that." I agree.

"Don't have anything to do with him, that's my advice," says Diana. "It's bound to be some kind of scam."

"I don't wish to sell my house to Crump or to anyone else," I tell her, "But he is extremely persuasive. What is more, Wendy Fyler from the Council is causing me a great deal of aggravation and, at her instigation, the insurance company has become wary about accepting my claim."

Diana looks thoughtful. "So the Fyler woman is giving you a headache and that Crump bounder is offering to cure it. Why am I not surprised?"

"Don't ask me," I tell her. "Why are you not surprised?"

"Because," says Diana, "The two of them are as thick as yesterday's custard. Chairman and Secretary of the Planning Committee, - and then some," she adds, darkly.

"I accept that I am not as well versed as you on the seamier aspects of human relationships," I say, "But I can't see what they hope to achieve."

"Neither can I, for the moment," agrees Diana, "But, whatever it is, there must be the prospect of piles of money for Oliver Crump and perhaps ten percent for Wendy Fyler. That's what makes them tick."

While we have been talking, the covered cage has been resting on the kitchen table where Diana had put it when she came in. This has become a source of considerable interest to the third occupant of the room. He is standing on his chair with his front paws on the table, stretching his body and his neck to their fullest extent and sniffing appreciatively as he picks up the scent of what he imagines might be an unusual, but very acceptable, supper.

"I'll bear in mind what you say," I tell Diana, as I make a grab at Barnacle and remove his paws from the table. "And I suppose you have the dormice in this cage," I add, gloomily. "I was hoping it would be a few days before this invasion of rodents."

"Right in one," confirms Diana, cheerfully. "I'll have to get the photography organised, and then we can release them into Hangman's Copse. There are only four of them and you shouldn't have to keep them for more than a week."

I am aghast. "A week is a long time to be on tenterhooks," I croak. "Can't we get rid of the little beasts this afternoon?"

"Certainly not," replies Diana. "This has got to be a properly coordinated operation. We need convincing photographic and eye-witness evidence that dormice are endemic to the Copse."

"But we don't know that they are endemic," I protest. "I don't like the idea of attempting to falsify evidence. It all sounds very dodgy to me."

"There might be some dormice there," says Diana, defensively. "Being nocturnal, they are hard to spot and Daddy, with his shot-gun, doesn't exactly encourage many visitors to the Copse."

"You are planning to deliberately mislead the public, Miss Hunter," I tell her. "It is no wonder you are so quick to detect conspiracies by other people wherever you look. You have a very devious mind,"

"It's a talent," she agrees. "It comes from long experience of having to outwit Daddy whenever I need to do something of which he disapproves. And he disapproves of nearly everything."

"This is all very well, but I don't want any part of it" I complain, "Even supposing I am not doing anything illegal by looking after these precious rodents for a few days, there is the question of what care they need. What am I supposed to feed them on?"

"You do tend to worry a lot," says Diana, soothingly. "They need a change of water every day and they like nuts, berries and other fruit as well as the buds of young leaves and the odd insect. They won't expect you to read them a bed-time story every morning."

She reaches into her back-pack and brings out two plastic containers. "This will be enough to get you started. Don't forget they will be most active at night so make sure their food dishes are topped up every evening."

"And what about their droppings?" I ask "Are the house-trained?"

"Just use your common sense, says Diana. "Change the litter in the bottom of the cage if it becomes smelly. Barnacle will not mind if you use some of his."

I glance to where Barnacle is sitting on his chair with his eyes fixed to the cage and licking his lips.

"Barnacle wouldn't mind eating them for breakfast," I point out.

"They will be perfectly safe in their cage," Diana assures me. "The bars on mouse cages are very closely spaced. If a mouse can't get out, there is no way a cat can get a paw in."

"Alright, I say, wearily. "You win. You have an answer for everything."

Diana claps me on the shoulder. "That's the spirit," she says. "They won't be the least bit of trouble to you, and doesn't it feel really good to be helping to protect our heritage?"

I manage a wan smile and she accepts this as a signal that I am happy with the task she has set me.

"Well, thanks a lot, Bill," she says. "I must be off. Things to do, you know. I'll be in touch when it's time for the next stage."

She scratches Barnacle behind his ears, tells him that the dormice might look small and tempting but they taste absolutely foul, and then makes for the door. As a parting shot, she reminds me that Oliver Crump is thoroughly bad news and that the less I have to do with him the better it will be for my health and my bank-balance.

A few minutes later, and she has shot off in her bijou roadster and left me staring blankly at a cloth-covered cage of unwelcome guests. I sit like that for a while, as rigid as a deep-frozen frog, and without a single useful thought entering my head. Then I pull myself together and decide that the quicker I vacate the premises the less chance that the conveyor belt will deposit yet another visitor on my doorstep. I make up a couple of sandwiches, grab a six-pack of beer from the fridge and throw some cat-food at Barnacle. As a last thought, I lift a corner of the cage cover and am reassured that the dormice are curled up together and fast asleep in a box of hay. Then, wasting no more time, I set course for Shorty's shed.

CHAPTER 15

I move more quickly than is sensible for an octogenarian and arrive, hot and flustered, to find Shorty quietly reading the paper. He is pleased with the provisions I have brought with me and sets out plates and glasses on his table.

"Your story has been relegated to the inside pages today," he tells me, indicating a short paragraph on page two.

"TREE IN HOUSE 'ACCIDENT'. REMEDIAL ACTION DELAYED", I read. I am pleased that I am no longer front page news, but I don't like the inverted commas Felicity has put around the word 'accident', and I say as much to Shorty.

"She's just trying to stir things up without saying anything that might be libellous. Reporters are experts at that. One of the first things they learn on a course in journalism is the thousand and one ways you can use the word 'allegedly'.

"That's one of your snippets of wisdom 'that everyone knows,' isn't it?" says Shorty, drily, but I ignore him.

"She is suggesting doubt where there isn't any," I grumble.

"Well never mind that now," he urges. "I have something more important to show you."

He turns to a column headed COUNCIL AFFAIRS. It is set in small type at the back of the paper where not many people are likely to read it. Half way down the column is a short paragraph reporting that the Planning Committee had briefly discussed an agenda item, proposed by the Chairman, to look into the future of the allotments. The matter had been referred to a sub-committee for detailed consideration and report.

"That would be Councillor Oliver Crump then," I point out. "He is the Chairman of the Planning Committee."

"What is he up to?" demands Shorty, and he goes on to explain that the allotments cannot be developed for housing or industrial use because there is no access apart from a narrow driveway that is not wide enough to be used by service vehicles for refuse collection or for emergencies such as fire or ambulance.

While he is telling me this, some cogs in my head begin to mesh and rotate. If my home were to be demolished, the plot of land on which it stands could be used to provide a wide access road and the whole allotment area of several hectares could then be used for residential housing. What is more, my house is one of the few that has a wide enough plot for such a purpose.

I pass on the fruits of this brainwork to Shorty and tell him that, only this morning, I received a pressing offer to buy my house from that same Oliver Crump, and it's ten-to-one he will appoint himself Chairman of the sub-committee that is to consider the future of the allotments.

Shorty looks a worried man, as well he might be with the continued existence of his beloved shed in doubt. To his credit, it takes him only a few moments thought before coming up with a plan of action and he tells me that he will call an emergency meeting of the Allotment-Holders Association so that pre-emptive action can be taken to scupper any possible development of the site. Meanwhile, he exhorts me not to sell my house, and especially not to Oliver Crump.

I explain to Shorty that I have already been warned not to become involved with Oliver Crump by two people but, since the two people were the nefarious Felicity Wright and unprincipled Diana Hunter, it was like being warned by a couple of sharks not to go near a salt-water crocodile.

We look at each other glumly. At least I am not now the only one beset by problems, I muse, Shorty and his fellow allotment holders are also threatened by an impending catastrophe. It is a sad reflection on human nature that this thought actually makes me feel more cheerful.

"There is only one thing for it at this stage," says Shorty, glancing towards the six-pack.

"Open the beer," I agree. I operate on the ring-pulls and we both take a long draught of the cool restorative. We sit back in silence for a few minutes to allow the elixir to work its magic.

"So, how has your day been, otherwise?" asks Shorty at length.

As we munch our sandwiches and continue to deplete our stock of beer, I tell Shorty about the visits of Felicity Wright and Diana Hunter.

"They both had a go at me for entertaining Oliver Crump," I say. "They seem to be obsessed by the idea that some kind of conspiracy is being hatched and half believe that I may, somehow, be part of it. They certainly have Crump marked as a key figure, so anyone who has a contact with him is automatically a suspect."

"Did they mention anything about the allotments?" asks Shorty.

"Nothing at all," I reply. "They keep banging on about Hangman's Copse, that's all."

"So why did they come this morning?" asks Shorty.

"The same reason anyone seems to call these days," I say, morosely. "Just to bring me more problems. Felicity half believes that I might have somehow encouraged that tree to fall and she is still leaning on me to do some snooping for her at Saturday's fête."

"And Diana Hunter?" prompts Shorty.

"Even more demanding," I tell him. "She delivered a cage full of dormice and I've no idea how to look after them or how long I will have to keep them."

"It could be worse," says Shorty, with a distinct lack of sympathy. "It could have been elephants. Did I ever tell you about the elephant we carried once?"

"Yes, you did," I snarl. "And the lions and the tigers, and a consignment of Yetis too, for all I know."

"Alright," says Shorty. "No need to get shirty. I'm just trying to help you achieve a sense of proportion."

We each take a calming drink of our beer and sit quietly for a space before speaking again.

"You are right," I concede. "The worst that can happen is that the little beasts fall sick and expire, in which case it wouldn't be my fault. If I had wanted to become a zoo keeper I would never have gone to sea."

"That's the attitude," applauds Shorty. "But I'm sure the dormice will be fine for the few days you have them."

"I'll be happier when they are out of my house," I say, "But I have to agree it is no big deal."

"And then you will be able to put our plan into action by keeping your head down and avoiding involvement in their schemes," says Shorty.

"This remark jolts me into remembering that the dormice are not my only problem and that there is still the ordeal of attending Saturday's fête hanging over me. I explain to Shorty that there is not much chance of keeping my head down there.

Shorty, for once is sympathetic to my plight. Garden parties, fund-raising fêtes, bring and buy sales, are the stuff of nightmares to the likes of Shorty and me. We are un-nerved by the compulsion to be unnaturally polite to everyone, the pressure to buy items we don't want, and a complete absence of a drink stronger than tea or lemonade. It is like being stranded in some middle-eastern souk.

"Well, it does seem Felicity has you over a barrel." Shorty commiserates. "So best to go along, make a quick circuit of the stalls, and exit as soon as possible."

"My thoughts exactly," I agree.

As always, I feel more settled after chatting to Shorty or, perhaps, the cans of beer helped. Whatever the case, as I take my leave and walk back to my house, I think about his anxiety concerning the future of the allotments and his exhortations not to sell my home and especially not to Oliver Crump. And Shorty is the one who has been telling me that I worry too much, I think to myself.

CHAPTER 16

Back in my kitchen, I lift the cover of the cage holding the dormice and I am pleased to see that they are all curled up in their bed of hay and apparently fast asleep. I have to push Barnacle away as he takes the opportunity to inspect the contents of the cage, and I explain to him that they are guests in the house and are to be treated with proper respect.

Then I telephone the insurance company who assure me that they have arranged for a local contractor to remove the tree from my house tomorrow morning. Their assessor will be in attendance.
Well, at least something is going right for me, I think to myself, and I am receptive when Barnacle rubs his whiskers against my leg and treats me with his "what's for supper" look. It is a timely reminder because not only is my stock of cat-food running low, if one excludes the dormice, but there is not much in the fridge for my own supper either.

I decide to drive to the supermarket for provisions, so I scribble a few items on the back of an envelope, throw a couple of shopping bags in the Volvo, and set off. After half a mile or so, the thought suddenly pops into my head that I am being followed. Over the next couple of miles, I realise that there is a motor bike tailing me but keeping a few car-lengths astern. Could it be a policeman? If Felicity was able to identify me from the episode at the protest meeting, perhaps the police could too. I make a right-angled turn to starboard into the supermarket car park and find a vacant parking bay. Sure enough, a motor-bike roars in and pulls up alongside my car.

Astride it, and not looking happy, is Buster Crump. He dismounts and approaches pugnaciously. He is still wearing his Judge Dredd motor-cycle helmet, for all the world as though there is something in his head that is worth protecting. I attempt to ignore him and start off towards the supermarket entrance, but he brings me up 'all standing' with a scream of rage.

"Hold it right there, Selsey," he yells, having obviously spent too much of his childhood watching Clint Eastward in old spaghetti westerns. "You and I need to talk."

I turn square on to him and give him like for like. "You gotta problem, mister?" I growl.

"You bet I've gotta problem," he explodes. "And so will you have, Selsey, by the time I've finished with you."

I decide that this confrontational, tough guy, talk has gone on long enough and, in any case, at my age I need to take life quietly and conserve what little is left of my supply of testosterone.

"Would you please come to the point and explain why you have followed me and are now behaving so aggressively?" I say.

Buster looks dangerously close to exploding, but he controls himself sufficiently to explain what is on his mind. "You told me you were going to have nothing more to do with Diana Hunter," he says, accusingly. "And now I hear you have inveigled her into you house not once, but twice. You are a deceiver and a liar, sir."

I raise a defensive hand. "Hold on, young man," I say, "You are completely misjudging what happened."

Buster is taking great gulps of air like a weight-lifter preparing to break a world record, but I suspect he has other things in mind to break. "There is no way she would have gone into your house willingly," he grunts. "You must have forced her in some way. Did you blackmail her by threatening to shop her to the police?"

This is too much. How could he read the situation so completely the wrong way round? Usually when someone tells me that the whole world misunderstands them, I can see that the whole world probably has good cause to do so but, for once, I am experiencing what it feels like. And Buster continues to dish it out.

"What evil practices have you been inflicting on her?" he demands, grasping me roughly by the shoulder.

"Look here," I gasp. "Before you go any further. Please get it into your head that Diana came to my house uninvited and, indeed, unwelcome. In any case, how do you imagine an old bloke like me could force unwanted attention on a well set up young woman like Diana?"

For some reason, the second part of my plea penetrates the red mist and lodges in what passes for Buster's brain. He paused for a moment, relinquishes his hold on my shoulder and looks me up and down.

"Yes, you do look a decrepit old wimp," he concedes. "So what was it all about? And you had better make it convincing."

With the immediate danger to my person averted, I marshal my thoughts and explain to Buster that Diana had come to my house seeking help with her campaign to save Hangman's Copse. I go lightly over her heinous use of blackmail to obtain my cooperation because I am sure it will make him angry again if I criticise the love of his life.

I wonder whether or not to mention the dormice, but my story sounds thin without them and I have a premonition that Buster might grab my neck rather than my shoulder if he becomes suspicious again. My instinct for self-preservation overcomes my feeling that the dormice should remain confidential, so I explain their place in Diana's plan and why she has lodged the little rodents with me. I am relieved when this proves to be the clincher.

"Yes," he says. "That is just the kind of stroke Diana would think of. Isn't she brilliant?"

Devious, rather than brilliant is the word that comes to my mind for Diana, but I decide not to mention this. I agree that she is, indeed, a smart girl, but then I remember her reaction when I tried to bring Buster's virtues to her attention at our last meeting. I explain to him that Diana's response when I mentioned his name was, to say the least, discouraging, and he becomes immediately despondent.

"I need to do something dramatic to regain her trust," he laments. "Perhaps I could take over caring for the dormice."

Much as I would like to see the back of the dormice, I am sure this would be a recipe for disaster. Disaster for the dormice, disaster for Buster, and probably disaster for me too."

"Not the dormice," I tell him. "But just keep a low profile for the time being, and I am sure an opportunity to get back into her good books will arise."

Thoughts of his fall from grace with Diana have drained all the belligerence out of Buster and he stands downcast and forlorn for a few moments. I am almost feeling sorry for him when a query comes into my head.

"How did you find out about Diana coming to my house," I ask, curiously.

He looks up, glumly. "It was Felicity Wright," he tells me.

Not for the first time I wish Felicity Wright would stop shaking other people's trees to see if any fruit would fall into her lap.

"And she told you that for no reason?" I ask.

"Well she did get me to promise that I would let her know if Dad and Major Hunter have any secret meetings," admitted Buster. "Although I don't know why she thinks they might. I always thought they didn't like each other."

That's my Felicity, I think to myself. She never misses a trick.

Having placated Buster, I don't feel like sticking around to give him a comforting pat on the head in case he reverts to his angry mastiff persona and bites my hand off. I wish him the best of luck in repairing his relationship with Diana, watch him with relief as he remounts his bike and rides off, and then resume my progress towards the supermarket.

After all the hassle of the past few two days, it is somehow comforting to be doing something simple, straightforward and undemanding like shopping for food and drink.

CHAPTER 17

I am not in the mood to tackle extensive cooking when I return home, so I buy a couple of ready cooked meals and a few packs of beer for myself, plus enough food to feed a dozen cats for a month. I pick up some pork pies for tomorrow's lunch and, as an afterthought, I add a packet of chopped nuts for the dormice.

While paying for my modest purchases at the checkout, I hear the sound of a police siren in the distance. It rapidly grows louder until, eventually, it cuts off in mid-shriek. Then, as I am walking towards the supermarket exit with my plastic bags, two policemen burst in through the doors. I recognise the younger as the one who had been assaulted by Diana and had attempted, despite an all-too obvious handicap, to chase her.

He takes one look at me and then grabs my arm, none too gently. "It's alright, Sarge," he calls to his colleague, "I've got the culprit."

Fortunately for me, the supermarket manager comes bouncing across the foyer to meet the policemen. "No! No! constable," he cries. "I have the person who was stealing our goods in my office with our security operative."

He separates me from the constable and, not having a brush to hand, he dusts me down with a nervous laugh. " This is one of our most valued customers," he says to the policemen, and, abjectly to me, "I do apologise, sir."

The constable had been reluctant to release me, and he now regards me with deep suspicion. "I've seen your face before," he growls. "We are trained to remember faces. Especially criminal faces."

I protest that I am not, and never have been, a criminal, but he remains unconvinced although clearly unable to recall the precise context in which he had seen me on a previous occasion.

"Perhaps you have two shop-lifters," suggests the constable to the manager. "We ought to search this person thoroughly before we release him."

"Definitely not," says the manager, "We have the utmost respect for our customers and cannot possibly harass them like that without evidence of wrongdoing."

"Nor can we, constable, as you well know," adds the sergeant, "Though we would be within our rights to ask him to show us what is in his bag."

"Not even that, sergeant, if you please," urges the manager. "I have a business to run, and it will do us no good if we earn a reputation for gratuitously insulting our customers. Meanwhile, we have a real thief, caught red-handed, who is in need of your attention."

He takes the sergeant by the arm and leads him off to make an easy arrest that will add a positive item to the local crime statistics. The constable takes another troubled look at me and follows them with obvious reluctance.

I decide that a rapid exit is my best move in case the constable does remember where and when he last saw me. I make good time to the car and return home, but I have found the whole episode unsettling.

I had been looking forward to a quiet evening and, back in my familiar and comfortable kitchen, I do begin to relax. I start by dispensing food to the animals. The nocturnal dormice wake sleepily from their slumber and tuck into the nuts. Barnacle, like Cassius eying up Caesar, takes a mean and hungry look at the dormice, but settles for his cat-food as a poor substitute.

I put my own supper in the oven and break out one of the beers. I park myself in my favourite chair and flick though a few television stations. They are mostly cooked up show pieces for celebrity chefs, terminally depressing medical dramas, grit-filled police stories or carefully staged 'reality' shows. None of these appeal to me in my present mood and I settle for a repeat of a repeat of a repeat of a nineteen-thirties mystery featuring the pear-shaped Swiss detective, Monsieur Poire.

I know I am on safe ground here, and that the sleuth will use his famous clockwork mind to solve a case that has baffled the worthy but unimaginative Inspector Plugg who, as usual, with be suspecting quite the wrong person for two or three villainously contrived murders.

Sad to relate, this does not work out as well as I had expected. Right on cue, Plugg does pursue an innocent man for the first two murders and, for various reasons, everyone else gives the poor chap a hard time. Even the urbane Poire despises him as a weakling although he, alone, does not believe he is a murderer. And he is vindicated when, with half an hour to go, the innocent chap is, himself, the victim of a gruesome killing.

This comes as an unwelcome surprise, not only to Inspector Plugg, but also to me. After two days as a kind of scapegoat to all and sundry, I had identified with the suspect and am not at all pleased when he is so heartlessly killed off.

"He was a weak little man," sneers Poire, as Plugg bemoans the loss of his prime suspect. "He foolishly allowed himself to be manipulated by a more astute criminal mind. I have little sympathy for him."

I am so disgusted by this contemptuous treatment of a perfectly ordinary chap who had done nothing but try to keep out of trouble, that I switch off the TV and go in search of consolation. This has been far too much of a let-down to be fixed by an extra can of beer, so I broach a single-malt whisky that I have been keeping at the back of the kitchen cupboard for just such an emergency.

After a few sips, I feel more relaxed. I notice that Barnacle's dish is empty and, as a consequence, he is giving me his full attention. This is an opportunity not to be missed.

"If you had been a ship's cat, Barny," I begin, "You would remember what it is like sailing the Caribbean Sea in the summer.

Blue skies, puff-ball clouds and the north-east trade winds keeping the temperatures wonderfully warm, but not oppressive. Some would say it's the most perfect sea the world has to offer.

Barnacle's great yellow eyes are fixed on my face and I suspect he is making a supreme effort to pick out anything in my speech that might relate to food.

"Then, Barney," I continue, "The very next day, we could be hit by a hurricane. Thunderous black clouds from horizon to horizon, except that you can't see the horizon for the rain. It is like being under the Niagara Falls. The winds are so strong you can hardly breathe and the waves are like the Himalayas have taken up break dancing. Well that just about sums up what has happened to me. My comfortable and well-ordered life has become storm-struck overnight, and I am being buffeted and beaten from all directions."

Barnacle turns his head to stare at his empty plate and then turns it back to focus on me again. "When are you going to get to the bit about cat food?" he seems to be asking.

"Alright, Barney," I say. "Thanks for listening." I drain my whisky glass and rise to replenish his dish from a packet of tuna. It is time for us both to turn in.

Caribbean hurricanes don't normally stick around for more than twenty-four hours, I remind myself. Our standard procedure was to heave-to with the wind on the port bow and ride out the storm. The next day we might well be heading out into the sunshine again, with just a few items of storm damage to clear up.

So surely, tomorrow, I can expect my problems to blow away and I can look forward to fine weather and smooth sailing. Of course, I do recognise that my natural optimism sometimes verges on the irrational. If I were to fall over the side of my ship into a shoal of great white sharks, I would probably find myself hoping they were all vegetarians.

CHAPTER 18

The next day starts earlier than usual. As a pensioner, I never see much point in getting out of my bunk too soon when the chill, damp air carries all kinds of risks for those reckless enough to venture forth. This morning, I am awakened by the clunking, clanging and roaring of heavy plant at eight-thirty. It sounds as though some tone-deaf operative is conducting Beethoven's fifth with an orchestra of bull-dozers

I peep out of the window and am surprised to discover that so much noise is being generated by nothing more than a cherry-picker and a giant mobile crane manoeuvring themselves into position in the garden at the front of my house. I hastily dress and go downstairs to find out what is happening. The insurance assessor is there, and so is Wendy Fyler from the Council. I don't trust people who are out and about in the early morning when they do not have to be. Is it their consciences that curtail their sleep? I certainly feel uneasy about the conspiratorial fashion in which these two are talking together.

I hurry across to join them, and they break off their conversation with an abruptness that adds to my suspicions. They turn to watch the workmen as I arrive at their elbows. I complain to the assessor about the lack of notice for this work, but he reminds me that he had told me yesterday that the tree would be extracted from my house today. It seems pointless to explain that, for me, a new day doesn't begin until ten o'clock in the morning, so we all stand and observe the developing drama in silence.

Two of the workmen are manoeuvring the cherry-picker into position and then one of them clambers aboard the extended platform with a chain-saw in his hands. He uses this to cut off the outlying boughs and branches so that what remains is mostly the tree trunk and a few of its major divisions. When this stage is completed, the cherry-picker turns and I see the name of the contractor painted on its side: OLIVER CRUMP & CO.

The debris from the tree is left where it has fallen, and then the crane moves in. It lowers a huge fabric sling to a point three-quarters of the way up the tree and the man on the cherry-picker makes it fast around the trunk. He waves a hand at the crane-driver and the hoist slowly takes the strain.

Nothing happens for a long minute of tension and then, with a splintering crack, the trunk tears itself away from the house taking much of the window frame with it. A dozen or so bricks are also dislodged and fall into a heap onto my rose-bed.

"I thought you might like to make that one into a rockery, Guv," shouts the crane-driver cheerfully. He then swings his crane around through ninety degrees and lowers the tree-trunk until it is lying in my garden right across the front of the house.

There is a desultory clapping from a small group of sightseers who have gathered in the street to watch the proceedings. The crane driver stands up in his cab and gives an extravagant bow to acknowledge the applause and some wag in the crown shouts "Encore! Encore!" But I am not looking at the crane driver.

I have spotted Felicity Wright among the spectators and I notice that she has been using her tablet to photograph the proceedings. Further down the road I see a Jaguar parked at the kerb with Oliver Crump standing beside it. He is looking pleased with himself.

Felicity has also spotted Oliver Crump and starts to walk towards him. Quickly, but smoothly, Oliver slides into his car and drives off before she can accost him. Sensible chap, I think to myself.

Meanwhile, the crane backs out of my driveway, and is followed by the cherry-picker. The drivers secure their vehicles and are clearly preparing to make their departure. I turn to the insurance assessor.

"You can't leave my garden in that state," I complain. "The tree-trunk is lying across the front of my house and all those broken branches are in a tangled heap with fallen bricks and window frame. It's like the shattered main-mast which fell on the deck of HMS Victory amid the litter of destruction at the Battle of Trafalgar."

"I am sorry about that," he replies, "And I agree that it was bad luck for Lord Nelson to lose both his mainmast and his life in the same engagement, but I can only repeat that it is the house you had insured with us and not the tree. In due course, we will clear away the fallen masonry and the window frame, but what remains of that oak is of no concern to us now it has been successfully disengaged from the building."

The workmen set up steel posts to fence off the front garden and stretch tape between them, printed with the words, DANGER. DO NOT ENTER. Then, with a 'that's a job well done' look on their faces, they climb into their vehicles and drive off down the road.

"Of course," the assessor tells me consolingly, "We are organising the repair of the damage to your house and we will fit a new window."

"Also by Oliver Crump, I suppose," I comment, grumpily.

The assessor consults his clip-board. "As a matter of fact, yes," he agrees. "His company submitted the lowest estimate and could do the work immediately."

"I wonder why that was?" I mutter, half to myself, and then, more loudly. "I still think you should remove the tree and the debris completely."

"Perhaps you should consider including your garden and its contents in your domestic insurance when it comes up for renewal," suggests the assessor, amiably. Then he turns to look at Wendy Fyler who has come across to join us. He raises his eyebrows so far that they could be advertising a MacDonald's burger-bar. "I believe the site is secure and the tree is no longer a threat to public safety."

She frowns as though she is disappointed at this pronouncement. "That is probably the case," she agrees, grudgingly. "The tree can stay where it is for now."

She turns to me and I see that her face is contorted as though she has bitten into a Stilton cheese that is past its use-by date. She obviously has something distasteful to say. Fortunately, it turns out to be distasteful to her rather than distasteful to me. "In view of this prompt action by you insurers, the Council is rescinding the order to make your site safe and it will not now be issued. However (and she stares hard at me) the tree will have to be removed and tidied up if the neighbours complain."

"Well thanks for some good news," I exclaim, while wondering if Oliver Crump had a hand in this. I turn to the assessor, "And I am glad that your company has accepted liability for the damage to my property."

The assessor raises a dismissive hand. "We have not formally accepted liability," he explains. "We decided to make the site safe in order to protect our own interests, but we could still send you the bill if we believe the event was not entirely accidental."

I catch Wendy Fyler smirking behind her hand when she hears this. I am beginning to suspect that there is more behind her malevolence than simple, over-the-top officiousness. I surprise myself by making a mental note to ask Felicity's opinion. I wonder if this means I am allowing myself to become involved in her conspiracy hunt.

Wendy Fyler has, meanwhile, been looking for new problems. "This wall needs urgent attention," she says. "Falling bricks could still cause injury to members of the public."

"The builders will be here shortly to fix that," says the assessor. "And the public will be safe provided they observe the fenced off area."

"I am reasonably reassured," says Wendy. "Now, perhaps, we should take a closer look at those tree roots to see if there is any evidence that they were deliberately weakened. Also, there is a large axe in Mr Selsey's shed that I would like to show you."

That woman really has it in for me, I think to myself as they move away, talking confidentially to one another in a way that I find unsettling. Looking around, I see that the sightseers are dispersing, but Felicity is crossing the road and clearly wishes to speak to me.

"That seemed to go well," she comments, brightly, "And I see that it was your friend, Oliver Crump, whose firm did the work."

"He's not my friend," I tell her. "He has been retained by the insurance company and not by me. What is more, although I can't put a finger on it, I feel I am somehow being stitched up, as thoroughly as a prize winning sampler at a sewing bee, by a combination of the insurance company, Oliver Crump & Co and that Fyler woman."

"Can I quote you on that?" asks Felicity.

"No you can't," I snarl, "But why are those people so intent on finding evidence that I might have tampered with the roots of the tree to make it more likely to fall down?"

"I remember you telling me that you did no such thing," muses Felicity, "But then you would say that, wouldn't you?"

"I told you I didn't do anything to the tree because it happens to be the truth," I yell. "But that gang of three seem to be colluding to try to prove otherwise. And putting the word 'accident' in quotes in your article in yesterday's paper was no help to me at all."

"Don't worry," says Felicity, soothingly. "I won't go into print with any wild and unsubstantiated accusations."

"Well, thanks for not very much," I tell her.

"I expect you are just being paranoid," comments Felicity. "Although, of course that doesn't necessarily mean there is no conspiracy. I fact, I am sure there is, but I don't believe you are as central to it as you appear to think."

"Well, at least we can agree that there are some dodgy dealings going on." I say. "There is a distinctly fishy smell about it all, like a chip-shop with a bust ventilation system."

"It is fair to assume that there is a plot of sorts," says Felicity, "But I have so far identified neither what the conspiracy is, nor who the key conspirators are. And I have to say that, despite your protestations of innocence, you are not entirely in the clear."

I have had enough of people getting at me, so I decide to change the subject. "There was a notice in your paper, yesterday, about an application to develop those allotments at the back of my house," I say in as offhand a manner as I can manage.

She is instantly alert, and I can see her reporter's nose twitching like a pig scenting truffles in the undergrowth of an oak wood.

"What!" she exclaims. "The allotments have nothing to do with Hangman's Copse. Why did you bring that up?"

"Just an idle thought," I tell her. "Do you know who is behind the application?"

"I don't know anything about it at all," she admits. "The sub-editor looks after routine news releases of that sort. But I don't see any connection."

"There isn't one with the insurance company," I say.

"Which leaves the Crump and Fyler duo," she murmurs. "I wonder why you think that?"

Then another thought strikes her. "You wouldn't be trying to divert my suspicions away from your crafty little self, would you, Mr Selsey?"

"Why don't you decide, Miss Wright?" I reply, and we stand eye to eye for a protracted thirty seconds until we both break into a smile.

At this point, the assessor and Wendy Fyler return from their examination of the tree, and Felicity immediately transfers her attention to them.

"Have you any news for me?" she asks, brightly. "What is your verdict? Have you found any evidence of foul play. Are you giving Mr Selsey a red card?"

"There is nothing I could possibly discuss with the press," says the assessor, primly.

"No comment from me, either," snaps the Fyler.

"Of course there was no foul play," I bark. "I am being set up."

Felicity regards us sceptically, as though we are three children, with brown smears on our faces, denying ever going near that box of chocolates. "My reporter's nose tells me there is a story here," she says at last. "Well, I don't mind spinning it out – it will be good journalism to keep my readers in suspense while the story unfolds, and it will do, I can promise you. Perhaps it would be better if, later on, you each tell me your own version so you will appear in the best light when all is revealed."

Not for the first time, it occurs to me that this Felicity Wright is a remarkably smooth operator. Meanwhile, she hands us each a business card.

"Just so you don't forget my phone number," she says. "And bear in mind that you are likely to be happier to see your own words in print rather than something I might dream up."

With that last warning, she wanders off to take further photographs of the torn roots of the fallen tree before returning to her bicycle and riding away. She has a smile on her face like that of a gardener who has planted seeds in his vegetable patch and is anticipating a bumper crop of parsnips.

"Lord save us from reporters," says the assessor, as he finishes writing some notes on his clipboard.

"I take it that you are recording a complete absence of any evidence that the stability of the tree was compromised." I say.

The assessor shrugs his shoulders and makes no comment, but Wendy Fyler chimes in. "There was nothing to show that the roots were not tampered with, either," she points out. "Some of the places where the roots are broken could easily have been weakened by chopping at them with that axe of yours."

"You are talking absolute bilge again," I object. "You can't accuse someone of wrongdoing because of a lack of evidence that they behaved properly."

I remember Shorty's advice that I should be more assertive and put her on the back foot. "That tree blew down because it was in a dangerous state. It could have fallen across the pavement and hurt a passing pedestrian. It should have been felled long ago as a matter of public safety. Your preservation order prevented that being done and was clearly a dereliction of duty by the Council. You were lucky it fell on my house and not on some passing mother with a pram full of children."

I am pleased to see that my diatribe does, indeed take the wind out of the Fyler sails but, although obviously disconcerted, she attempts to retreat in good order.

"Bluff and bluster won't help you if you did sabotage that tree," she tells me, and the assessor nods in agreement. But I still have a shot in my locker.

"If you had not placed that ill-considered preservation order on the tree, I would have had it cut down safely and it wouldn't have caused any damage to my house. That could make the Council responsible for the repairs, if my insurers are looking to recover their costs."

I am pleased to see that this causes the assessor to look up, sharply. He doesn't make any comment but he does make an additional entry on his clip board. The Fyler notices this also. The normal grim look on her face notches up several points on the grimness scale and she starts to say something but then thinks better of it. Although thoroughly steamed up and crosser than an oven full of buns on Easter morning, she relapses into a malignant silence.

Great, I think to myself. It is about time I had something to smile about.

Meanwhile, the assessor is keeping his head down, shuffling his papers and stowing them in his briefcase.

"I'll be visiting again tomorrow," he promises, "To check that work is starting on repairing the window and the wall. We don't want to leave it in a delicate state for longer than is necessary."

He nods a polite farewell to Wendy Fyler and to me, and walks briskly to his car as though he is relieved to get out from under before either of us give him more problems, or a loose brick falls on his head. Wendy Fyler, meanwhile, fixes me with the kind of stare I get from Barnacle when he feels he is being made to wait too long for his breakfast.

"Alright, Mr Selsey," she says, "You are lucky that the prompt action by your insurance company has given you some breathing space, but don't imagine that this is the end of the matter. And remember that your house remains in a dangerous condition and you are responsible for any risk to the public until it is properly rebuilt to our satisfaction."

She omits a parting nod, friendly or otherwise, and strides off, I suppose to return to her lair at the Town Hall so she can re-marshal her forces and plan the next stage of her campaign for harassing me.

The morning has been stressful and I feel the need to get out of a house that everyone seems to think is about to collapse into the street. I leave some fresh food tor Barnacle and the dormice as compensation for leaving them in such a dangerous situation, but none of them give me a thank-you. The dormice are fast asleep and Barnacle only manages to regard me with one eye for perhaps ten seconds before burying his face in his tail again.

"Don't stay awake worrying about me," I tell them as I raid the fridge for four cans of beer and a couple of pork pies. In view of their indifference, I don't feel a need to shut the door quietly as I set off to Shorty's shed for lunch and a consultation.

CHAPTER 19

"I see you have hit the headlines again," Shorty greets me as I enter his shed and collapse into one of his battered but hugely comfortable easy-chairs.

I place the provisions on the table and take the newspaper he is offering. There is a picture of my house with the caption, "DANGER HOME – STILL NO ACTION?"

The addition of the question mark, I decide, is another example of Felicity's talent for creating an element of doubt in what should be a perfectly straightforward statement. The headline is followed by a discussion as to whether the parlous state of the structure constitutes a threat to passing members of the public, and there is a broad hint that questions need to be answered about the cause and the extent of the damage.

"Well, she has gone off at half-cock this time," I tell Shorty. "Her message has been overtaken by events already. The tree has been removed from its uninvited intrusion into my bedroom and the contractors will start work on repairing the brickwork tomorrow."

"Yes, I noticed all the activity outside your house as I came past this morning," says Shorty, as he opens two of the beer cans and finds a knife to operate on the pork-pies.

I bring him up to date on all the morning's happenings and he congratulates me on taking the battle to Wendy Fyler. On the other hand, he seems to think that I am still too worried about the situation.

"If the assessor and Miss Fyler had any grounds for suspecting that you had sabotaged the tree, they would have made an accusation in the hope that you would be provoked into saying or doing something stupid," he counsels.

"I realise that," I say, "But they never let up. Especially the Fyler woman. She gets right under my skin"

"I can see that," says Shorty. "It's a pity you never sailed on proper liners. You would have developed a way of maintaining a professional calm in spite of all the provocations of managing mixed cargoes consigned to many different ports and the consequent fraught dealings with shippers, freight forwarders, stevedores and surveyors."

"I am perfectly calm and collected," I assure him, with an irritability that belies my words. "But I am, through no fault of my own, caught up in a situation that I don't like and don't fully understand."

"Let's work on that, then," suggests Shorty. "The first thing will be to put what we know into a logical order so we can consider the implications in a calm and measured way."

I take a mouthful of beer and cut a chunk off my pork-pie as I think about this idea. How would Monsieur Poire, or even Inspector Plugg, approach the matter, I wonder.

"I know," I cry, "We need an incident room, like all the best TV detectives have."

"What, here you mean?" asks Shorty, looking around his shed at the gleaming garden tools, most of which have never been used, clipped neatly in their places. There is even an almost pristine notice board with only a gardeners' calendar in one corner and menus for the local Chinese and pizza take-aways on the other side.

"Just what we need," I exclaim, removing these items and stowing them away in a drawer. "And there is plenty of unused shelf-space and hooks for displaying any items of evidence we might come across."

"Well do make yourself at home," comments Shorty. "Don't mind me. It is only my shed."

But I can tell that this is only a token protest and that he is nearly as keen as I am to get started. "Paper? Drawing pins?" I ask. "Marker pens? Computer?"

"Negative to all those," says Shorty, trying desperately to create the impression that he is not particularly interested but is willing to go along with my ideas to indulge me.

"I'll pay a visit to the stationers this afternoon," I tell him, through a mouthful of pastry crumbs. "And I can bring my lap-top back with me tomorrow."

"Don't forget to buy a deerstalker hat and a curly meerschaum pipe," Shorty tells me, but this is only because he doesn't want me to think that he is taking my idea seriously.

As a matter of fact, I have always fancied a deerstalker hat but I have, so far, jibbed at actually buying one because I felt it would be overdramatic and ostentatious. For the present, I do not intend to encourage Shorty in his comic suggestions, so I don't give him the satisfaction of an answer.

We sit back in our chairs to finish our lunch. We are relaxed and self-satisfied that we have identified a satisfactory way forward and made an important decision. We enjoy the comfortable, job-well-done-let's-have-a-beer feeling that Jack Kennedy and Nikita Kruschev must have experienced in 1962 when they agreed it would be best not to start a nuclear war after all.

"One thing we do suspect," says Shorty, reflectively, "Is that Oliver Crump is offering to buy your house because it would be a key to developing the allotment site."

"Yes, indeed," I agree. "And, if Felicity and Diana are to be believed, he is in cahoots with Wendy Fyler, which would explain why she is doing her best to push me into selling."

"I shall hint as much to the emergency meeting of the allotment holders," says Shorty. "I've called it for tomorrow evening. Come along if you like. We need all the publicity we can get."

"In that case, you should invite Felicity Wright," I tell him. "I have already put the thought in her head that Crump's offer to buy my house may be something to do with access to the allotment site."

"Has she heard anything about it?" asks Shorty. "I'd very much like to know what is behind that Council agenda item."

"When I suggested a possible connection, it came as completely new to her, unless she is a remarkably good actress," I say. "But, knowing Felicity, she could well be following it up right now." I fish her card out of my top pocket and pass it to Shorty. "There is her mobile number."

It is in a more cheerful frame of mind that I return to my home with the empties. Barnacle wakes up and wanders across to greet me as I enter the kitchen, but I do not intend to dally. A peek under the cover of their cage shows the dormice still sleeping. There is nothing to delay me, and I am soon driving into town to purchase incident room supplies from the stationers.

I buy a large layout pad, marker pens in four colours, sticky notelets and plenty of blue-tack. I notice that the shop also sells magnifying glasses, but I reject these as over-dramatic. A magnifying glass would be in the same bracket as a deerstalker hat and a meerschaum pipe.

I leave the shop well satisfied with my purchases. Then the thought occurs to me that I might as well gather some useful background information while I am out and about. I know roughly where Hangman's Copse is, and I am interested to see the ancient woodland that Diana and her friends have become so worked up about.

When I have driven about five miles out of town, I stop and consult my road map. Soon afterwards, I make a turn to port onto a narrow secondary road, little better than a single track in places. After another mile or two, the open farm-land ceases abruptly and the lane plunges into dark and unkempt woodland, so gloomy that I have to switch on my headlights.

There is little doubt that I have found Hangman's Copse. It certainly looks ancient enough, although neglected rather than old is the adjective that first springs to mind. The trees are too close together, some are dying and others are dead, lying at drunken angles but prevented from falling to the ground by their still surviving neighbours.

Beneath the canopy of leaves the dim light is only sufficient to support moss and a few ferns in the dampness. I can easily believe that this woodland has been uncared for since well before 1600. It looks as though no-one has ever bothered with it other than a witch or two, or perhaps a few none-too-choosey woodland sprites. However, I can well believe it might harbour species of plants or animals that have not been seen by man since the stone ages. And, quite possibly, even dormice.

The copse has a forlorn, barbed wire fence around the perimeter which looks as though it is desperately trying to hold the mass of vegetation together but wondering whether it is worth the continued effort.

"I wouldn't bother, if I were you. Let the trees escape and find some decent sunlight," I catch myself muttering.

I immediately start wondering whether I have just lost another of my decreasing store of marbles. Lots of people talk to cats, I tell myself, and it is not too outrageous to talk to trees, fallen or not, but talking to a barbed wire fence might be enough to earn me a one-way ticket to the funny-farm.

While my mind is occupied by this speculation, I nearly overshoot a gated entrance into the depth of the wood. At this point, the fence is set well back from the road and a green land-rover is parked on a grassed area in front of the gate. The gate, which has seen better times, bears a notice declaring that the woods are private property, followed by the warning, DANGER KEEP OUT. I notice that a chain and padlock are provided to secure the gate, but it has been undone and the gate is partially open.

Not many people would drive a green Range Rover *and* have a key to allow them to enter the Copse, I surmise, so I deduce that the Major is visiting his property, and I wonder what for. I would prefer not to have another confrontation with him, so I drive a few hundred metres along the road until I find a suitable, off-road parking spot, and then I walk back to the gate. I lean comfortably on it, and consider the pros and cons of following the muddy track that leads into the Copse beyond the gate. There is little wind and I can see no movement anywhere. I am content to stay quietly where I am for the time being, but my reverie is rudely interrupted by two loud cracks in quick succession. I become temporarily airborne, like a startled flying fish, and my feet are already in sprinting mode by the time they hit the ground.

I take a grip on my scattered senses and realise that the Major had not actually been shooting at me. The sound had come from much deeper in the trees. I turn back to peer as far as I can into the woods but there is nothing to be seen. I regain my composure and it occurs to me that firing both barrels of his shotgun would have been extravagant overkill for a pigeon or a rabbit so I wonder whether he is after something more substantial. I half remember that there is some law against discharging a fire-arm within fifty feet of a public highway, which doesn't seem enough to me, bearing in mind that a short-tempered old soldier who dislikes me is stalking the woods with a shot-gun.

I am still wondering what he might have been shooting at when I spot a movement among the trees. I duck behind the gate and squint through the bars, expecting to see the Major striding out with a few brace of lead-filled pigeons and rabbits over his shoulder. To my surprise, it is an old lady, dressed in black that shuffles along the track.

She is carrying a wicker basket but she does not appear to be bearing arms, so I straighten up and, as she approaches, I hold the gate open for her.

"Thankee, young sir," she quavers. "You are a real old fashioned gentleman."

"Not many of us left," I say, as she passes through.

"Just as well, if you ask me," she replies. "I like old-fashioned gentlemen but I never trust 'em. They'll walk on the outside to protect a lady from the carriages when they escort you down the lane, but its only to make it easier to nudge you into the ditch if it serves their purpose."

"That is very cynical of you," I remonstrate, but she has her answer ready.

"'Tain't that I'm cynical," she tells me. "It's experience. That's what it is."

It occurs to me that there might be a reason for her poor opinion of gentlemen. "Has Major Hunter just been shooting at you?" I ask. "I heard two shots just now."

"No. No. He dursant attempt to harm me," she says. "He don't understand women, and folks is afraid of what they don't understand."

This lady is overdoing the old witch-in-the-woods routine, I begin to suspect. Coming out with antiquated words like "thankee" and "dursent", when she means thank you and daren't but I decide to let her carry on without making a challenge.

"So, what is he doing in the woods then?" I ask.

"What he allus does," she tells me. "A-killin' my little animal friends."

"I don't believe the farmers think of the rabbits and pigeons as friends," I say, mildly.

"The farmers have a reason," she says. "The Major don't. And it ain't just vermin. He'll have a go at anything that moves. I've known him use both barrels to bring down a butterfly."

This sounds far-fetched to me, but I am beginning to feel that this woman could be a useful source of information. "You don't like the Major much, I take it?"

"We puts up with each other," she replies. "He don't like me much, either, but he lets me use the Copse to pick up bits of this and that to take home and sell."

"Well, it's kind of him to let you do that on his property for nothing," I say.

"'Tain't for nothin'," she retorts with a wicked gleam in her eye. "In return, he hopes I won't make him come out in warts or turn him into a toad."

I wonder about her ability to manipulate warts because she has several on her own face, including one on the tip of her nose that particularly catches the eye. Perhaps she is cultivating them as a threat to the Major. I decide not to pursue the subject, and then our conversation is interrupted by two more cracks from deep within the woods.

"That sounds like another Red Admiral has bitten the dust," I say.

"He'll get his cumuppance one day," she mutters, and then, more brightly. "But I can't stand here all day talking about nothing. Things to do, you know."

"Cauldrons to boil," I suggest.

She regards me coldly. "There's matters you shouldn't joke about, young man," she warns.

"I'll walk along with you," I offer. "Carry your basket if you like. And I promise not to tip you into the ditch."

She looks at me suspiciously, and then makes a decision and hands me the basket.

"It is a mile down the road," she warns me.

"I parked my car just round the corner," I tell her. "I'll give you a lift."

"My old bones could do with a sit-down," she says. "And I don't s'pose you'll kidnap me. You wouldn't get many offers if you tried to sell me as a sex slave."

She lets out a throaty chuckle and I am at a loss as to how to reply. It would be ungallant to agree that she is too ugly to be saleable and, perhaps, upsetting if I suggested she could command a good price. The safest thing would be to change the subject. As we stroll towards the car, I take a peek into her basket and I see that it is full of horribly misshapen toadstools.

"I hope you know what you are doing with these things," I say. "They all look disgusting to me and I am sure some of them must be poisonous."

"Don't you worry," she tells me." There's three sorts there. One's delicious, one will make you sick but do no real harm, and the other contains enough toxins to kill a cow."

"So why don't you just collect the edible ones then?" I ask.

"Well, it's like this," she explains. "There's some folk I like, and there's some folk I don't like, and there's some folk I hate." She fixes me with a beady eye. "I ain't yet made up my mind about you, young man."

I think about this pronouncement as we continue our walk to the car, and decide that she is being deliberately enigmatic. Probably the toadstools are all perfectly safe to eat, - although I have to admit that I don't like the look of the lurid red ones with off-white spots on their crowns. I open the passenger door and see the old lady comfortably seated. Then I stow the mushrooms on the back seat and take my place at the wheel.

"About a mile, you said?" I ask.

"Just beyond the woods, on the right," she confirms. "It's a little cottage, all on its own and way back from the road."

We set off at a leisurely pace because I want to ask her some more questions about the Major and whether she knows about any plans to develop Hangman's Copse, but she is the first one to speak,

"What's your name, then, young man?" she asks.

"It's Bill," I tell her. "Bill Selsey."

She smiles at this, but gives no indication as to what is amusing her. "Mine's Peggy Morven," she tells me.

"OK Peggy," I say. "So what do you know about Hangman's Copse?"

"Ah! 'tis a dark and mysterious place," she says. "Dogs and people have been known to go into the woods and come out a few hours later raving mad. There was a vicar once, who went in to cast out the evil spirits and he was never seen again."

"Never mind all those old myths and legends," I say, irritably. "I'm not talking about tales invented by superstitious country-folk in the eighteenth century. I'm interested in what is happening at the present time. Do you know if anyone is planning to clear the trees and build houses on the site?"

"It don't do to talk about them old stories like that," warns Peggy. "There's more goes on in this world than you knows."

"Alright," I say, "I'll give you your mad dogs and disappearing clergymen if you'll tell me what is happening in the Copse right now."

"Well, there's been some goings on in the Copse right enough," she tells me. "There's been cars with big tyres that are half-way to being tractors churning up the paths, and young men with things like cameras on tripods, only I don't think they were cameras at all. And the blokes wore jackets with bright colours that showed up in the dark and frightened my animal friends."

Surveyors, no less, I tell myself. So someone is interested enough in the Copse to invest money in having the site properly investigated.

"And what was the Major doing while all this activity was taking place on his property?" I ask. "Why doesn't he take pot shots at these people like he does at anything else, saving your good self, that so much as moves in the woods?"

"Ah!" she says. "Well, I ain't never seen any sign of the Major while those young men have been tramping around in the woods. P'raps he don't know about them, and they goes there when they are sure he won't be around."

That seems unlikely to me. The Major must surely see traces of their activities and be aware of what is going on. However, by this time I have driven out of the trees and into more open countryside. Soon, I spot a small, thatched cottage behind high hedges on the right hand side.

"That's my place, there," says Peggy. "You can turn off the road and park in front of the house."

I follow her instructions and come to a halt on an area paved with ancient, moss-covered, stone slabs. A small porch provides protection for the cottage door, and a birch-broom leans against the side of the porch. This, I tell myself, is going too far. Quaint speech and black garments are bad enough, but to add a witches broom is way over the top. If I had known things would become this theatrical I would have bought that magnifying glass and a deer-stalker hat to complete my detective outfit.

"You know what, Peggy," I tell her, as I help her out of the car, "You are overdoing this wicked-witch-of the-west routine. "A birch-broom ready for take-off, indeed. The next thing you'll come up with is an evil looking black cat."

As if on cue, a scruffy, charcoal-grey cat, that might have been black in its younger days, puts his head round the corner of the cottage. He has a battered ear, and he glowers at me, balefully, from a single, yellow eye.

Peggy introduces him. "This is Horror," she says. "Short for Horatio."

I do not need to ask who he is named after because he is not only one eyed, but he has also lost one of his legs. Having decided that I am harmless, he lollops over to greet us on his three remaining limbs.

"He hates dogs," explains Peggy. "An' he made a mistake of picking a fight with two bull-terriers. It didn't end too good for the bull-terriers, neither."

I bend down to fondle Horror's good ear but he backs away and snarls at me. "I can see why you call your cat Horror," I say.

"He ain't always a cat," says, Peggy. "He's my familiar, so at night he changes into a bat and then, in the morning, when he goes into the woods, he changes into a toad. You had best be careful not to upset him."

"It would upset me, being called Horror," I say.

"Ah, well. I calls him Captain Blood when he's a bat and Warty when he's a toad. He don't seem to mind that."

"You will excuse me if I find all this a bit far-fetched," I murmur, "Although I have to admit that you put on a good show."

"Spend a night in the copse if you dare, Bill Selsey," she challenges, "And you'll soon change your tune. Captain Blood will come looking for you at midnight and you'll find Warty sharing your bed when you wake at dawn."

"You mean I might see a bat and a toad if I overnight in the Copse," I respond. "Surprise me with another prediction."

"You'll sing a different tune if you find yourself in the woods at midnight when the bats are on the wing," she cackles. "An' you'll know which one is Captain Blood alright when he swoops down on you."

"Too right," I agree. "If he's missing a leg, he'll be the one that's flying around in circles."

"You've got too ready a tongue in your head, young man," she says, "It don't do to scoff at things you don't understand, and one day it will get you into trouble." A sudden thought seems to strike her. "You ain't one of those blokes what gets his fun by a-killin' my animal friends, are you?"

"Certainly not," I protest. "I'm an old sailor. An ancient mariner if you like, so I usually only shoot albatrosses, but I might make an exception for a fairground witch."

"It ain't no use speakin' to you," says Peggy. "But I don't hold no malice. Why don't you come in for a nice cup of herb tea, or something stronger? I makes my own wine, an' the last batch has just finished fermenting."

I know better than to ask her where she finds the herbs for the tea or what she makes the wine from, although I have not the least doubt that she would enjoy telling me.

"I am sure you will not be offended if I decline," I tell her. "I have a feeling it might be too strong for me."

"I got some home-brewed acorn beer too," she says, hopefully.

"You are too kind, Peggy," I tell her, "But some other time. I have to get home to my own cat."

Mentioning Barnacle reminds me that I also have some dormice waiting for me, but I have more sense than to mention them.

"One last thing," I say. "Do you know if there are any specially rare animals or plants in the Copse?"

"They're all rare, if you asks me," says Peggy, "What with him banging off at anything that moves with his guns and those young men tramping everything that don't move with their big boots and their trucks."

"Well, thank you for answering all my questions, Peggy," I say as I climb back into my car. "You have been most helpful."

"Me and Horror likes the Copse as it is," she replies. "And bad luck to the Major or anyone else that wants to spoil it."

Well, that's something we can agree on, I think to myself as I reverse the car and drive back the way I had come. As I return through the woods, I notice that Major Hunter's Range Rover has gone, and I wonder what his role will be in the unfolding story. Clearly he enjoys using the Copse as a safety valve for all the frustrations of his work as a magistrate now that he is unable to have insolent youths transported to Botany Bay for crimes like, well, insolence. It is hard to believe that he would want to dispose of the Copse and lose the opportunity to blast a few squirrels out of the trees after sitting through a particularly irksome day in court.

On the other hand, it seems unlikely that he is unaware of the surveying activity that has been taking place in his property. There is plenty to mull over as I drive home. I am beginning to feel that I am caught up in a theatrical production involving a large and varied cast of players, but with only a fragmented idea of the plot or the roles of the actors.

Finding out who has written the script and who is responsible for the direction presents an interesting challenge. As my natural optimism reasserts itself, I feel sure that, as the actors play their parts, the ongoing drama will be resolved before too long. I seem to remember Hamlet saying something catchy about all the world being a stage. I cross my fingers and hope we can make a better job of a happy ending than William Shakespeare managed for the Prince of Denmark.

CHAPTER 20

My journey home is plain sailing for which, bearing in mind recent events, I am truly grateful. It is early evening and so I stop off at my local fish shop to buy haddock and chips for my supper. The shop owner, one Charlie Spratt, greets me in his ever cheerful manner.

"Hello, Mr Selsey," "I've saved a special for you today, the piece of cod that passeth all understanding."

"That sounds heavenly, Charlie," I reply, "But I'll have my usual large haddock if you don't mind."

Charlie is a serial gossip and, while my fillet is frying, I ask him, with what I hope is well-staged nonchalance, if he has heard any rumours about the future of the allotments.

"Ho, yes," Charlie tells me, "I should say so. Your friend, Shorty Smith, has called a meeting of the allotment holders for tomorrow evening at the Church Hall. That has set the cat among the pigeons good and proper. People become very attached to their vegetable patches you know."

"Yes, I do know," I say, "But what about before today? Was there any talk then about the future of the allotments?"

He swishes a basket full of chips around in the boiling oil to give himself time to think before he replies. "Nothing as such," he says, "But old Jim Barnes who has the plot next to your friend's did tell me that a stranger came poking round the allotments about a week ago. Jim noticed him 'specially because the bloke carried a briefcase and most people on the allotments carry bags of fertiliser or push wheelbarrows full of compost."

"Jim didn't speak to him I suppose?" I ask, hopefully.

"No, he didn't," replies Charlie. "But he did wonder if the bloke was up to no good. They've had trouble with people stealing their veggies, you know. Anyway, Jim made a note of the name on the side of the brief-case ……" His voice trails off.

"And now you've forgotten it?" I prompt.

"Give me a minute, sir," says Charlie, turning away to serve another customer.

I am happy to give him time while I savour the ambience of his establishment. For those of us brought up in the early post-WW2 years, the pervasive chip-shop smell has the same potency for stimulating the taste-buds as the aroma of roasting coffee. Within a few minutes, Charlie is back with me. He rescues my haddock from the bubbling oil, wraps it in paper with a generous helping of chips, and places it on the warm counter-top.

"That name on the brief-case," he says. "It was a firm of solicitors. Sommat like Cash and Carry. Can't remember better than that, I'm afraid."

"Many thanks, Charlie," I say, as I pay for my supper.

"And why are you so interested in all this, sir, if you don't mind me asking?" asks Charlie.

"The allotments are at the bottom of my garden," I tell him. "I don't want to see a block of flats go up there. And I don't want to see Shorty lose his allotment. Keep your ear to the ground, will you Charlie?"

"Don't I always," grins Charlie, as he turns back to his sizzling vats. "Enjoy your supper, sir."

I drive home quickly and, as I approach my front door, a large cat emerges from the shadow of a shrub and walks across the garden to meet me. His nose is pointing towards the sky and his nostrils are twitching as though he is attempting to locate a drift of falling star-dust. In reality, of course, he is interested in the less exotic but, from his point of view, more desirable, aroma of fried fish.

He follows me into the kitchen and remains in close attendance as I put our supper in the oven to keep warm. I add a plate and then take my time to freshen up and make myself comfortable. Barnacle is in two minds as to whether he should follow me as I move around the house or whether a better strategy would be to remain by the oven. In the end, he compromises by oscillating backwards and forwards until I finally recover the fish and chips from the oven, grab a can of best bitter from the fridge, and take my usual place at the table. At this, point, he jumps up onto his chair, and rests a gentle paw on my arm to ensure that I am aware of his presence.

I slice off ten percent of the fish and transfer it to his dish, whereupon he emits a loud purr and sets about it as though he had not eaten for a fortnight.

I take a more leisurely approach and am only half way through my meal when the telephone rings. Dammit, I think to myself. Just what I need as I am relaxing with my cat at the end of another challenging day.

I pick up the handset and I immediately recognise the deep brown, soothing tones of Oliver Crump. I move around to replace my supper in the oven and the remains of my beer in the fridge as we talk.

"Hello, Mr Crump," I say. "What can I do for you this evening?"

"Do please call me Oliver," he coos. "I don't like to stand on ceremony."

I'd better go along with this, I think to myself. I need to be on good terms with him if I am to find out that he is up to. Keep your friends close and your enemies closer. Isn't that what they say?

"Very well, Oliver," I agree. "How can I help you?"

"I believe it is more a case of me helping you, Bill," he says. "I expect you are pleased that the Council is no longer proceeding with the Public Safety Order."

"Indeed I am," I respond. "Although I believe that was mainly because my insurers got cold feet and authorised the removal of the tree in case *they* might be held responsible for injuries to the public."

"A related, but separate issue, I think," says Oliver, smoothly. "It would take more than that to deflect Wendy Fyler from what she sees as her duty, but a word from me might have done the trick."

"Well, thank you for that, Oliver," I say, with my best shot at sounding grateful.

"And I was able to make my workmen available to do the job immediately," he added. "It was at some inconvenience, but I could see you might have had to wait for a week or more for the insurance company to find another contractor."

"That was, again, most kind of you," I say. "It has certainly put my mind at rest to have had the tree removed from my bedroom and to know that work is in hand to repair the damaged wall."

"My men will be with you first thing in the morning," promises Oliver. "We will do our best, but it will take several days to have the material delivered and put your house to rights again."

"You are very reassuring," I gush. "It makes such a change to talk to someone who is prepared to be helpful. I have had so many dealings with the other sort over the past few days."

"It's all part of the service, Bill," says Oliver, easily. "Now, I wonder whether you have given any further thought to my offer to buy your house as it stands? No questions asked."

"Well, it's going to get properly repaired now," I explain, "So there is no reason for me to sell it. Barney and I are perfectly happy here."

"Barney?" asks Oliver, "I thought you lived alone. Ah, yes, I remember. Your faithful cat."

"It's not a good thing to live alone," I tell him. "You can become too self-centred. There's not much chance of that with Barney around."

"You will forgive me, Bill," says Oliver, "But, at your age, I believe you would be better off if you had more social contact with human beings. You have a large house to look after and you don't need so many rooms just for you and Barney."

This remark hits me in a vulnerable spot. I have a large, comfortable kitchen and it is true enough that Barney and I spend most of the day there. We transfer to my bedroom at night, where Barney sleeps on the foot of my bed and, from time to time, I make necessary visits to the bathroom, but we wouldn't miss it if the other three-quarters of the house were to disappear overnight.

"We like it here," I mutter, defensively and, probably, unconvincingly.

"Don't forget my offer of a place in a warden-assisted apartment, Bill," says Oliver. His voice has deepened and is oozing reassurance. "I know I have said this before, but I believe society owes you older people a safe, secure and comfortable retirement,"

Sure, you do, if there is something in it for yourself, I think to myself, but I am not about to show any open cynicism.

"What about Barnacle?" I ask. "I imagine he would not be welcome."

"True enough, pets are usually discouraged," accepts Oliver, "But I am sure we could make an exception for him. A nice, ground floor flat with a small garden, and he could be the happiest cat in the county."

"I am most grateful for your help so far, Oliver, but I'll need time to think about all this," I say. "You have given me a great deal to consider."

"Of course, Bill," he assures me. Each word is bubble-wrapped with concern for my well-being. "There is absolutely no pressure. Look, I'll come around tomorrow afternoon to make sure my men are making a satisfactory start on the repairs. We can continue our little chat then."

"I look forward to that," I murmur and then, in as offhand a manner as I can manage, "By the way, Oliver, if I were to sell you my house we would need to put our solicitors I touch with each other. Do you use a local firm?"

I hear Oliver make a quick intake of breath, and I wonder if I have alarmed him but, when he replies, he is his usual, urbane self. "We are getting a little ahead of ourselves, aren't we, Bill, but no harm in telling you at this early stage. I use Messrs Case and Carey. They have offices in the High Street."

"You are absolutely right, Oliver," I say. "I *am* getting ahead of myself. Forget I asked. The way I feel at the moment, I would be very reluctant to sell."

"Don't worry about a thing, Bill," says Oliver, "His voice dripping with solicitude. "I understand that it is often difficult for older people to make decisions."

"There is so much to think about," I bleat in my most plaintive manner. I even manage to add a quaver to my voice and I wonder, since we are both clearly putting on an act, who is actually kidding whom.

"Sleep on it, Bill," advises Oliver. "We'll talk again tomorrow."

"Good night, Oliver," I tell him. "And thanks for your help."

"My pleasure, Bill," he responds, and I am thankful to hear the click as he hangs up his phone. I am not sure how long I could have kept that up.

"So, what am I to make of that, Barney?" I say as I retrieve my supper from the oven and my beer from the fridge. "Do you reckon he is above board, or is it all just so much Oliver oil?"

Barney has resumed his place next to me and stares pointedly at his empty dish. There is nothing for it but to give him ten percent of my remaining fish. I do some rapid mental arithmetic. "This means that you are having fifteen percent of the original fillet," I tell him, but he sticks his face in his allotted portion with no hint of gratitude.

"I think we can agree that it was all Oliver oil, don't you?" I say, through a mouthful of chips. "I'll accept no answer as meaning yes."

Barney seems to have forgotten that he has already eaten his standard allowance and is attacking his bonus with single-minded gusto. Predictably, he makes no reply.

"And what a clever master you have to discover the name of his solicitors. Case and Carey. Less than a biscuit toss in terms of spelling from what Charlie remembered as Cash and Carry."

Barnacle has cleared his plate by this time and sits solemnly watching me as I finish mine at a more civilised pace. His stare is unblinking but, in my view, he has had more than enough human food so he gets no more.

"That Oliver is still urging me to sell our house to him you know, Barney. And he's pushing hard. All that stuff about not wanting to put any pressure on me is so much hogwash."

I can feel Barney's gaze faltering as he begins to accept that there will be no more hand-outs coming his way.

"We are finding more pieces of the jig-saw every day," I continue. "We know Oliver Crump has set up a Council Sub-Committee to consider the future of the allotments, We know his solicitor has been checking out the site, and we are pretty sure the reason he wants to buy our house is to provide access for its development. Case nearly proven, I suggest, M'lud."

But Barnacle is replete with food and does what any feline will do in the circumstances. He curls up in his chair, buries his head in his tail, shuts his eyes firmly and is soon in cat dreamland.

Clearly I have lost my audience for the rest of the evening. In any case, I tell myself as I wash the dishes and tidy up, I have done enough serious thinking for one day, it is time to switch on the TV and switch off my brain.

I open a fresh can of beer and relax in the easy chair I have set up by the kitchen stove. A flip though the available channels leads me to what promises to be a mindless action film entitled "The Long Pursuit". It turns out to be a comfortably, undemanding choice in that it follows the pattern of classic chase movies from Robert Donat remaining the perfect gentleman as he is hounded across Scottish moors in Hitchcock's "Thirty-Nine Steps", through a worried looking Harrison Ford running for his life as "The Fugitive", to Matt Damon's hyperactive performance in Robert Ludlam's "Bourne Trilogy", and many more in between.

In the perennial battle between the baddies and the goodies, the baddies think our hero is a goody and the goodies think our hero is a baddy, so he is being hunted remorselessly by both sides. It is formulaic but entertaining and it keeps me well amused for a couple of hours. The only thing I don't like is the ending, where the hero ends up in a safe haven with the love interest. However, the baddies don't all get their come-uppance and the goodies don't actually realise they have been mistaken about the hero. I suspect the production team were keeping their options open in case the film was a runaway success, thus providing the opportunity for a sequel. If that was the case, they were disappointed because it didn't hit the big-time on the silver screen and only reappears occasionally on secondary TV channels. It serves them right for not providing a proper ending, I decide. I like to see the hero, with whom I have been identifying, sail off into the sunset with the heroine, all their troubles behind them and not a cloud in the sky to cast a shadow over their future happiness.

I switch off the television and decide it is high time I gave the dormice some attention. Barnacle opens one eye as I provide our rodent guests with fresh water and dispense some of the dry food that Diana had left for them. They are scuttling around their cage and, as they have not long been awake, I suppose they think it is breakfast time. Whatever the case, they fall upon the food immediately and I decide that, since we are into their active hours, I should leave the cover off the cage. I am sure they would not be too happy if they were to see the huge face of a cat leering at them through the bars, so I take the cage into my dining room and place it on a table near a window. Take note, Oliver Crump, I think to myself, I do sometimes use rooms in my house other than the kitchen.

When I turn round, I see Barnacle in the door-way. I shoo him back into the kitchen and shut the dining room door. I make sure his dishes are replenished and then make for my bedroom with Barnacle hard on my heels.

"Things are looking up, Barney," I tell him. "Tomorrow should see the start of repairs to the house, and I am beginning to see some shape in the conspiracy that Felicity and Diana are always hinting at. I am definitely feeling more in control of my own destiny."

Barnacle give me a questioning look which makes me wonder whether I am being too upbeat or whether I should adopt a more cautious outlook. I revise my thoughts accordingly.

"The trouble with optimism," I tell him, "Is that it leaves a bloke open to disappointment. Do you think I should take up pessimism as a lifestyle choice? At least I would seldom be disappointed and, if things turn out well, there is the chance of being pleasantly surprised."

But Barnacle has already curled up at the foot of the bed with his oversized tail covering his ears. "Alright," I tell him. "I can take a hint. And it I not long before I join him.

CHAPTER 21

The next morning begins criminally early for me again, when I am woken by the clanging of steel poles. It is like being at a campanologists' party where all the bells are cracked. I peer out of my bedroom window and see that two scaffolders are noisily offloading the tools of their trade from the back of a lorry. Barnacle has already disappeared and I find him downstairs watching the proceedings from the safety of the kitchen window sill.

I look into the dining room to check that the dormice are all alive and squeaking. They are moving around their cage but without any great urgency, so it looks to me as though they are winding down towards their day-long bed-time. I take the cage into the kitchen with me, which leaves Barnacle torn between continuing to observe the scaffolders or coming across to sniff at the dormice. Being a cat, he takes the least tiring option and remains on the window sill, from which vantage point he can switch his attention from one scene of interest to the other.

I make a pot of coffee and fix myself a bowl of muesli. As an afterthought, I offer some of the muesli to the dormice and they devour it with evident enjoyment. One of my better ideas, I tell myself.

I complete my breakfast with toast and marmalade, by which time the dormice, replete with their supper, have formed a close-knit ensemble in their hay box and are fast asleep. I put the cover on their cage and take them back into the dining room so Barnacle won't be tempted to interrupt their slumber. Then I return upstairs for a shave and a splash, throw on a few clothes and am ready to face the scaffolders and discover what is going on. Barnacle elects to stay in the safety of the kitchen and leaves me to make my way into the garden.

There are two workmen whose names, I soon ascertain, are Chris and Fred. They have already made good progress in setting up a sound base for their lattice of poles and are not averse to pausing for a chat.

I am surprised to find they are not employed by Olive Crump. They are independent contractors. I ask them if they have come across any problems, but they tell me that the job is perfectly straightforward. It seems they often do work for Olive Crump & Co under sub-contract. They accept my offer of cups of tea but, before returning to the kitchen, I pause to ask a few questions.

"Have you ever been involved in a project for Verdant Heritage?" I ask. "Chris scratches his head with a spanner. "We did once," he tells me. "It was for a development of a new apartment block in Upper Bidsworth, wasn't it, Fred?"

"Ooh, ah," agrees Fred.

"That's about ten miles away, isn't it," I comment. "And were you working for Mr Crump then?"

"It's a couple of years ago," says Chris, "But, yes. we certainly were. He gives us a lot of work, don't he, Fred?"

"Yeah, lots," contributes Fred.

"So Verdant Heritage were the developers, but the building work was undertaken by Crump and Co?" I ask.

"That's right, Guv," says Chris. "They were retirement flats for the over–fifties if I remember right. Not what you'd call a lively town, Upper Bidsworth, but it has a big crematorium and a twenty-acre cemetery so it's a good place to die in."

"My oath," affirms Fred.

"It's a good earner for Verdant Heritage," says Chris, who has the wind in his sails and doesn't need any further prompting from me. "I've got an old Aunt lives there. They sells the flats cheap, but they make a hefty service charge and then they take forty percent of the selling price when people leave."

"Daylight robbery," offers Fred, encouraged by Chris's increasingly garrulous contribution to extend his own to four syllables.

"It's not a worry if you go out feet first, of course," continues Chris. "But it's obvious, the sooner residents falloff their perches, the better it is for the Company. They keep the stairs well polished, I shouldn't wonder."

"Too right," adds Fred, reverting to his more economical use of words.

I am grateful for all this background information and so, when I return to the kitchen to make their tea, I reach to the back of my cupboard and break out the special chocolate biscuits that I keep for just such occasions. I take them out to the scaffolders and, as they suspend their work once more, I take the opportunity for further investigation.

"What about Oliver Crump?" I ask.

"What about him?" asks Chris. "He is paying our wages for this job when it comes down to it."

"A trustworthy bloke then" I suggest.

"Straight as a corkscrew he is." says Chris, enigmatically.

"Right on," adds Fred, sipping has tea after ladling six spoonfuls of sugar into it.

"Do you have any new projects lined up for Crump & Co?" I ask.

"We dunno what we'll be doing tomorrow," says Chris, "Let alone next week."

"Not a clue," contributes Fred, extending himself, once more.
I am not sure whether they have been marvellously patient with me or whether they have welcomed the opportunity to stop work, but I decide that I ought not to persist any longer with my questions and that I should leave them to continue assembling their clamps, poles and couplers.

"I'm just off to the shops," I tell them. "I'll be back in time for lunch. Can I get you anything?"

"A caviar sandwich for me," says Chris. "Beluga if they've got it. And a nice bottle of Bollinger on ice."

"Yum, yum." Says Fred.

I don't relish the idea of another visit to the supermarket, although I know the chances of the police turning up again are remote. Instead, I take my custom to a small corner shop which is closer but, inevitably, somewhat more expensive. There are times, I tell myself, when it is worth paying a little extra.

I buy half a dozen assorted sandwiches and a case of twelve bottles of best bitter, and I add replacement chocolate biscuits to my basket. I need to be well provisioned if I am to be entertaining the building trade over the next few days. I pick up an oven-ready shepherd's pie for my own supper and a kilo bag of sugar in case I have to supply Fred with another cup of tea. One or two additional impulse buys complete my shopping needs and I am ready for my next port of call.

This is the local pet shop, where I breeze in and ask the young lady assistant for some food suitable for dormice. She looks at me suspiciously. "Are you keeping dormice as pets, sir?"

An alarm klaxon sounds in my head immediately. "Er, no, I say, I just want some mouse food, that's all."

"You just said dormice," she accuses. "You understand it is a criminal offence to keep protected wild animals in captivity without a licence, sir? I should be phoning the police and the RSPCA to report this matter."

This puts me in a panic. The last thing I want is another encounter with the police.

"They aren't dormice, they are just mice," I tell her. "Forget the dormice, I don't know what made me say that."

"You definitely said, dormice," persists the assistant. "Describe these animals to me."

"Well, er," I stutter. "They are small and sort of mousey colour, and they squeak."

The assistants hand hovers over the telephone for a few seconds.

"These mice are orphans," I say, quickly. "I am just taking care of them until they can be released into the wild."

"How do you know they are orphans?" she asks, dubiously. "Did they come knocking on your door to tell you they had lost their mummy and daddy.?" But I am relieved to see she has withdrawn his hand from the phone.

Then I have a flash of inspiration. "My cat ate their parents," I say.

"So you need food for some mice that are not dormice, and are orphans because you are not able to control your cat?" she queries.

"Exactly," I say, contritely. "So the least I can do is to feed the little beasts until they are big enough to fend for themselves in the wild."

"And how big do you think they will have to be to stand up to your cat?" she asks.

"They don't need to fight him, they just need to know when to run away," I tell her.

The assistant frowns. "I am not sure I believe any of this, sir," she says, dubiously. "But, against my better judgement, I am giving you the benefit of the doubt" She reaches up to a shelf and takes down a packet marked MOUSE DELIGHT and places it on the counter.

"I am most grateful, and so will the mice be," I tell her, as I pay for my purchase and remove myself from the shop as quickly as possible.

I hope the dormice are, indeed, grateful, I think to myself as I drive home, after the ordeal I have just been through on their behalf.

When I reach home, I find that Chris and Fred have made good progress and, by midday, they have their platforms, guard rails and ladders erected so as to provide safe access to the whole of the damaged section of wall. I take their lunch out and explain that Bollinger's new policy is to pack their champagne into brown beer bottles to comply with the European Union's safety regulations.

"Good oh," Says Fred, who accepts a bottle enthusiastically.

"He'll believe anything," explains Chris with a grin, as he opens his own bottle and takes a generous mouthful. "What's happened to the caviar?"

"It's out of season," I tell him. "Sturgeon don't produce eggs at this time of the year."

He selects a bacon and egg sandwich. "We'll have to slum it, then," he says.

I stay with them for a chat while they enjoy their lunch, but I decide not to return to the subject of Oliver Crump and his dubious connections. When they have finished, they thank me politely, pick up their tools, and surplus poles and connectors, stow them on the back of their lorry, and clatter off to their next assignment. There is no-one else in the offing, so it seems a good opportunity to visit Shorty.

I throw a couple of sandwiches and four bottles of beer into a bag, lodge the remaining beer and sandwiches in the fridge, and check that there is sufficient food in Barnacle's dish so he won't expire from hunger while I am out. I am half way to the door when I remember the purchases I made yesterday afternoon for setting up our incident room. With so much happening, I had almost forgotten about them. I add them to my bag and hot foot it to the allotments.

The weather is fine, and Shorty is taking advantage of it by spending some time on what he likes to think of as gardening. He is hoeing the already weed-free expanse of his plot and there is a rake to hand with which, when he has finished hoeing, he will meticulously level the surface as though he is preparing a championship standard croquet lawn without the grass or the hoops. He straightens his back as I approach, and is happy to be provided with an excuse to defer his horticultural activity.

"Ahoy there, Bill," he greets me. "Good to see you. Why don't we find a berth outside on this lovely day."

"I've got the bits and pieces for the incident room," I say, holding up the bag.

"Leave them in the shed," says Shorty. "I'll set them out later."

I do as he suggests and, when I return, he drops his hoe and leads the way to an area of uncultivated ground in the centre of the allotments. This is mainly laid out to grass and is provided with a number of wooden benches so the public can spend happy afternoons taking the air and watching the allotment holders at their labours. It is nothing more than a small piece of wasteland, but it has pretentions to be a mini-Hyde Park. There are a few shrubs and some larger trees, including a mature, spreading, walnut tree which shelters one of the benches. We make for this and sit for a while, enjoying the warmth of the sun on our backs. Then I reach down for the beer and we take a bottle each. I have a crown-cork opener on my Swiss Army knife so we are soon sampling the cool, refreshing liquid.

"I see you have the workmen in," says Shorty eventually.

"Just the scaffolders, so far," I reply. "I'm expecting the builders to turn up this afternoon and, probably, Oliver Crump in person. He was on the phone to me again, yesterday evening."

Shorty is immediately alert on hearing this. "Tell me about it," he says. "I've called the allotment holders meeting for this evening and I need all the ammunition I can get."

I bring Shorty up to date on Olive Crump's continued efforts to persuade me to sell my house to him while assuring me that it is because he has my own welfare at heart. I also relate what I discovered from Charlie in the fish and chip shop about a snooper that Jim Barnes had noticed sizing up the allotments. I am particularly pleased with myself as I tell Shorty how I was able to establish that Oliver Crump's lawyers are Messrs Case & Carey, which tallies with the name on the snooper's brief-case.

"It gives us a second link between Oliver Crump and the allotments," I say. "The first being the decision of his Planning Committee to consider the future of the allotments."

Shorty is sufficiently impressed that he almost treats me to an unqualified compliment, but he doesn't quite lose his composure.

"That was excellent work, Bill," he enthuses, "For someone who didn't ever make it to a proper liner company."

"You haven't heard it all, yet," I say, smugly.

As we make a start on our sandwiches, I go on to tell him about the conversation I had with the scaffolders, and especially the association I established between Verdant Heritage and Oliver Crump's company.

"It's a bit tenuous," complains Shorty, "And didn't you tell me that Verdant Heritage are behind the threat to Hangman's Copse? So why would they have anything to do with the allotments?"

"It's just a possibility, Shorty," I say, "But it hangs together. Verdant Heritage are linked to Oliver Crump, Oliver Crump is linked to the allotments, the allotments may be under threat of development and Verdant Heritage are into property development."

"Well, if you put it like that," says Shorty, "But that is a long chain with some highly suspect links in it."

"It is something for you to bear in mind," I tell him. "Keep a sharp lookout for any mention of Verdant Heritage at your meeting this evening."

"OK, so that's another useful piece of work on your part, Bill," he accepts. "Perhaps you missed your vocation. You might have made a great detective rather than a sailor who was only allowed to drive tankers."

I ignore the second of those statements because I understand how hard it is for a Purple Funnel man to accept that anyone else might be more advanced in their thinking.

"There is something else, Shorty," I say, and I tell him about my visit to Hangman's Copse and my encounter with the old would-be witch. He is particularly interested in learning that a team of surveyors had been working in the Copse, and agrees that it would be strange if they had been operating there without Major Hunter' knowledge and approval.

"Yet another piece of information that we can't, positively connect to anything else," he comments.

"And it doesn't have any obvious link to the allotments," I point out. "It's something to watch out for but, for the moment I think we should concentrate on this evening's meeting. I will definitely drop in?"

"The more people the better," says Shorty. "I've invited Felicity Wright to attend, as you suggested, and I also phoned the Town hall to ask if anyone from the Council would be prepared to make a statement."

"I'm sure it is a good move to get the press involved," I respond. "I think you will be lucky to get anyone from the Council at this short notice, but it will be interesting if they do agree to make a contribution."

Shorty shades his eyes with the back of his hand and stares towards my house. "I can see movement at the side of your house," he says, "It looks as though the builders have arrived."

I leave Shorty with two bottles of beer that we haven't yet touched. "I'll see you at the meeting this evening," I call, as I scoot off to see what is being done to my home.

CHAPTER 22

I arrive to find an empty skip being planted in a corner of my already cluttered front garden. I stand and watch as this is followed by an Oliver Crump & Co lorry which backs into my driveway and disgorges a small concrete mixer, a huge sack of sand, some bags of cement and a pallet load of bricks. The delivery vehicles drive away, leaving two workmen on site. They introduce themselves as Kevin and Sean, and they stand looking at me expectantly.

"Thirsty work, this," says Kevin, when he perceives that I do not have a grasp on the situation.

"What work is this?" I ask. "You haven't done anything, yet."

"We had to load all this stuff up at the depot," explains Sean.

"All that cement dust," adds Kevin. "Catches in your throat, it does."

"It'll probably see us off in a few years," offers Sean. "Builders don't have long lives you know."

"Yes, I can see why people might be tempted to kill them," I say. They regard me sadly, as they digest this comment.

"Alright," I say. "Would you like a cup of tea?"

"We thought you'd never ask, Guv," says Kevin, brightening at once.

"Five sugars for me and three for Kevin," adds Sean, helpfully.

They stand, weighing up the task in front of them as I go into the kitchen to fulfil their order. Barnacle is on the windowsill, peering worriedly through the curtains. I might have thought he hadn't moved since he took up station there when the scaffolders arrived except that I notice the food in his dish has been half eaten. I congratulate myself on observing this detail and making an appropriate deduction. I am clearly fitting well into my new persona as a detective. Perhaps even a great one, as Shorty grudgingly suggested.

I serve the teas to the new team, but they are only offered plain biscuits. They will have to perform outstandingly well to qualify for the chocolate variety, and they are not making the best of starts.

"We are going to remove all the damaged brickwork first," Kevin informs me. "We'll have to take it back to where the wall is still sound before we can start rebuilding."

"Skilled work, this is, Guv," Sean assures me, as he sips his tea. "It needs thinking about."

I assume these two reluctant workmen are employed by Crump & Co, so I am wary about asking questions about the Company and its doings. But I can't resist a gentle probe.

"What is the Company like to work for?" I ask.

"Well, it only employs highly skilled people," says Kevin.

"Like us," puts in Sean, in case I missed the implication.

"No complaints," continues Kevin, "They pays our wages every week, but Mr Crump can be a hard man to please."

"You mean he might be expecting you to start work on my house some time this afternoon."

They look at me reproachfully. "We are fast workers when we get going," Kevin assures me. "We just need refuelling before we start."

"Like those tennis champions who eat a banana between sets and then go back on court and smash the other bloke to bits," Sean explains.

"I don't have any bananas," I apologise, as I collect their empty mugs. "But I look forward to seeing you get your hands dirty."

"Oh, no," says Kevin, keen to keep the conversation going. "We don't have to do that any more. We have gloves and hard-hats and steel-tipped boots and safety harnesses."

"It's a tough and dangerous job, building, but we are better protected than we used to be," explains Sean.

It is clear to me that these two layabouts will do anything to postpone having to start any actual work.

"Oliver Crump phoned me yesterday evening," I say, casually. "He told me he was going to drop by this afternoon to check the progress on my house repair."

The effect is immediate.

"This has been time well spent, sorting out our work plan," says Kevin to Sean. "Are we ready to make a start?"

"Let's go for lift-off, captain," agrees Sean, who has obviously been watching too many science-fiction programmes.

They pull on their gloves, put on their hats, pick up their clump hammers and chisels, and climb the scaffolding in a remarkable surge of energy. If they could do that on a couple of biscuits, I wonder how they might have performed if I had been able to supply them with bananas. Swung up like monkeys, I suppose.

Reassured by their sudden outburst of banging and hammering, and the occasional thump of a dislodged brick falling amongst my roses, I return to my kitchen. Barnacle comes to greet me but with uncharacteristic coolness. I pick up the feeling that he is holding me responsible for all the noise and disturbance that has descended on his garden for most of the day.

"I'm sorry about all the din," I say, "But it is essential work if we are to have a seaworthy ship again."

Barnacle is unimpressed by my apology. He jumps up onto his chair and shuts his eyes firmly. At least he seems sufficiently reassured by my presence to take his standard afternoon nap.

Having had what was, for me, an early start to the day, it seems to me a good plan to join him. I make myself comfortable in my easy chair and allow my eyelids to droop. The sound of Kevin and Sean belabouring the brickwork of my stricken wall is muffled and almost soporific, although I don't expect to actually fall asleep. But it won't hurt to just relax for a while……..

After what seems only a few seconds, I hear the ringing of my door-bell. A glance at the clock tells me I have been asleep for forty minutes. I do my best to collect my thoughts as I rise and go to answer the door. It says much for my befuddled state of mind that I am surprised to see the urbane figure of Oliver Crump standing on my door-step.

"Hello, Bill," he says in his usual warm tones. "I'm not disturbing you at an awkward time, am I?"

I am sure it is perfectly obvious that I have just woken up, but I am not prepared to admit that.

"Of course not, Oliver," I say. "I have been catching up on my paper work, you know. Do come in."

"I'll be pleased to in just a few minutes," says Oliver, "But first, why don't we take a look at what progress my men have made."

He turns away, and I follow him into the garden where Kevin and Sean are making a great show of intense activity as they continue cutting away the damaged brickwork.

"How is it going, you two?" calls Oliver.

Kevin and Sean cease their hammering and look down in feigned surprise. "Oh It's you, Mr Crump," says Kevin. "We are doing alright, but we've had to take the brickwork back a long way to get to where it is solid."

"There is this long crack running all the way down from the corner of the window," adds Sean. "But another hour should see us clear of it."

"That's some crack," says Oliver, following Sean's pointing finger with his gaze. "It might well be structural and it goes almost down to the damp-course, doesn't it? Come here and look at this, will you, Kevin?"

Oliver has his back to me, but I catch Kevin giving a knowing nod as though Oliver might have winked at him.

"What do you make of that damp-course, Kevin?" asks Oliver, when Kevin has descended to join us at ground level.

Kevin pulls a disapproving face. "It is old and decayed, Mr Crump," says Kevin. "The whole thing needs replacing. Nothing to do with the accident though."

"I agree," says Oliver, turning towards me. "Bad news I'm afraid, Bill," he tells me. "This is an old house, perhaps built during World War One, when there was a shortage of materials. Your damp-course is decomposing and needs to be completely replaced. I'm surprised you haven't experienced damp problems."

I reach down and prod the damp-course with my finger. "It looks alright to me," I protest.

"You need a new one alright, Guv," says Kevin. He looks up at the wall. "If you ask me, you could do with a new house altogether. That brickwork came down much too easy for my liking."

Oliver looks sharply at Kevin and, if I were a fanciful person I might have construed this as warning him not to overdo it. Whatever the case, Kevin puts his hands in his pockets, stares into space and whistles quietly to himself.

"I think the best thing I can do is to test the wall for dampness," says Oliver. "I have a moisture meter in my car. I'll go and fetch it. You can come with me, Kevin, I've also brought a couple of new bolster chisels you might find useful for cutting into the wall."

They set off on their errand and I am left with Sean who is still on the scaffolding platform, hammer in hand, as though he can't wait to resume his demolition work."

"What do you think about that, Sean?" I ask him, but he declines to be drawn. "I dunno, Guv," he shrugs. "I just knock down walls or build them up again. I ain't paid to think."

He's not going to be helpful, I conclude, and I wonder whether I made the right decision in not breaking out the chocolate biscuits. A touch like that might just have softened him up.

Oliver and Kevin return, carrying a moisture meter and a large canvas bag respectively. Kevin climbs the ladder and hands the bag to Sean, while Oliver leads me indoors and deploys his meter. It is about the size of a flash-light, with a scale at the top and twin metal probes at the base.

He crouches down to obtain access to a section of the kitchen wall beneath a window, but he is hindered by Barnacle who creeps between his feet trying to discover what is going on. Oliver curses quietly to himself and I attempt to look over his shoulder to check the reading, but it is out of my line of sight. He grunts and straightens up leaving Barnacle sniffing around the skirting board to try to see if the object of Oliver's attention is of any interest to a cat.

"Hrmph," says Oliver. "Thirty percent wood moisture equivalent. That is over the top. Bad news for you, Bill, I'm afraid."

"It doesn't feel damp in here to me," I protest. "There is no mildew on the walls. The sugar and salt in my cupboard haven't become damp and lumpy."

But Oliver takes no notice at all. "Perhaps we should check the other rooms in the house while I'm here," he suggests. "Just to confirm the extent of the problem."

This remark brings me up with a jolt. I remember the cage of dormice in my dining room. It would be damaging if anyone else were to find out about them, and disastrous if that person happened to be Oliver Crump.

"No, I don't want to do that right now," I tell him, "I'm prepared to accept that there might be a damp problem, but I can only think about one thing at a time. Let's get the insurance work completed first and then we can conduct a proper investigation."

"It would be no trouble while I am here," says Oliver.

"No," I say firmly." I won't hear of it. Now, can I offer you a cup of tea, or would you like something stronger? Do take a seat,"

Oliver selects my favourite easy chair, but I am glad enough that he has given up so easily on his idea of making a tour of the house on a damp-finding expedition. I busy myself making both the tea and a decision on whether to offer my guest plain or chocolate biscuits.

"The cat's got the best seat in the house, as always," he remarks, gesturing towards Barnacle who is perched on his own chair, and inspecting our guest as he considers whether Oliver's arrival is good news or bad news. For cats that is.

"Barnacle is a cat of many talents," I say.

"Oliver looks around. "I think it is nice that you choose to do your entertaining in the kitchen," he observes. "Television as well, I see. Don't you use the rest of the house?"

I place two mugs of tea on the table, with sugar and milk to hand, Then I offer him a plate of plain biscuits.

"I like to have plenty of space," I say, defensively.

"It's a lot to look after," he says, "And there are many families that would love to live in a house this size. Of course, the damp might put them off, I suppose."

"I have never come across any dampness," I tell him.

"You were a sailor in your younger days, weren't you, Bill," points out Oliver. "You must be used to being surrounded by water. Perhaps you just don't notice it."

"Well, I don't need my sea-boots and oilskins indoors, I can tell you that," I say, warmly.

"Alright, Bill," says Oliver, placatingly. "I won't go on about it. But I hope you have given my offer to buy your house some consideration. You would have everything you need to make yourself and Barnacle comfortable in one of my flats, but without the responsibility and expense of maintaining an impractical old property like this."

"I am thinking about it," I assure him, "But Barnacle and I are set in our ways. We don't like change much."

"Fair enough," says Oliver. "Let's talk about work in progress. I hope you are happy with the way we have made a timely start. I have had to take men off another job, but I decided that this was more important."

"That's good of you, and much appreciated," I say, with all the sincerity of a chat-show host welcoming a rival he can't stand.

"My pleasure," replies Oliver. "Many of my developments are aimed at providing comfortable living and peace of mind for older people."

The uncharitable thought pops into my mind that he has worked out that pensioners often have more spare cash than younger people. I begin to feel uncomfortable with myself. I never used to be this cynical. But, looking on the bright side, he has given me an opening for a probe.

"That would be like Verdant Heritage, then," I suggest. "I believe they specialise in sheltered accommodation for the elderly."

Oliver appears to freeze for a second or two, and I feel sure I have found a chink in his armour of bonhomie. But he recovers smoothly.

"There are a number of firms working in this area," he tells me, placing his business card on the table and rising to leave.

"Won't you stay for more tea or another biscuit?" I ask.

He consults his watch. "I would love to continue our chat," he tells me, "But you will appreciate that I am a busy man. I will look in from time to time to see how the work is progressing, and do give me a ring if you have any worries at all."

"You are most kind, Oliver," I tell him. "And, thanks to you, I look forward to having the house ship-shape very soon."

At least my insincerity is consistent, I think to myself, but Oliver demonstrates that I am not the only one that can keep it up. He pauses on the step and puts a friendly arm round my shoulder.

"I have taken a liking to you, Bill," he confesses. "I don't spend this much time talking to everyone I meet during the course of my day"

"I understand that," I reply, "And I am most grateful. I am sure there are many more important calls on your time."

"So let me give you a piece of advice," he says, dropping his voice to a confidential, whisper. "That reporter, Felicity Wright. She is ambitious and is out to make a name for herself. For sure, she doesn't plan to spend her whole life working for a provincial paper. She'll cosy up to you when it suits her, but she'll sell you down the river without a thought if she scents a good story. Don't trust her an inch."

"Thanks for the warning, Oliver, I'll keep it in mind," I say.

He pats me on the back. "Good man," he says, as he makes off towards the Jaguar that has been patiently waiting for him by the kerbside. He gives me a comradely wave of his hand as he climbs into the car and drives off.

I look up at the side of the house where Kevin and Sean are continuing to remove the damaged brickwork. I can't help but notice that their rate of hammering decreases significantly once Oliver Crump's car is out of sight. I decide not to disrupt their labours by offering them another cup of tea and take myself back into the kitchen where Barnacle is sitting up in his chair and stretching.

"So, what are we to make of that, Barney?" I ask him. Barnacle slowly completes his stretching exercises and gives a gigantic yawn.

"If you are suggesting that Oliver Crump is covering the same old ground, I have to agree with you," I tell him. "He is obviously still keen to buy our house, but what about his reaction when I mentioned Verdant Heritage? Now that was something he definitely didn't want to talk about."

Our conversation is interrupted by a knock on the door. I open it and find Kevin and Sean standing there. "Can we use your toilet, please, Guv?" asks Kevin.

"It's been a long afternoon," puts in Sean.

"Second door on the right, down the corridor," I tell them, and Sean immediately sets off in the direction I have indicated.

Kevin shuffles from one foot to the other, and then brings a piece of wooden board from behind his back. It is blackened and covered on what look like cobwebs. "We thought you ought to see this, Guv," he tells me.

"Where did this come from?" I ask. "It looks disgusting."

"It was behind the damaged wall, underneath the window frame," explains Kevin.

"Well, I suppose you will be replacing it as part of the repair," I say. "Why show it to me?"

"It looks like dry rot, I'd say," Kevin tells me.

"You'd better burn it, then," I suggest.

"It's not as simple as that, Guv," says Kevin. "There might be more under the floor-boards.

I don't reply immediately, as the implications sink in and, in the meantime, Sean reappears and Kevin excuses himself.

"Did you see where this came from, Sean?" I ask, indicating the distressed board.

"In the wall, under the window, Guv," Sean assures me.

"Could you see if anywhere else was affected?" I persist, but Sean resorts to his professional builder's shrug. "You'll need to take all the floorboards up to do that," he tells me. "That'd be a big job."

At this stage, Kevin returns and resumes possession of the offending board. "We just thought we ought to tell you, Guv," he says. "We'll be getting along then, shall we?" He is not cut out for this kind of thing and is looking as shifty as the wind direction at the turn of the monsoon.

I agree that they should, indeed, be getting along, and taking their mouldy piece of wood with them, but they linger at the door looking pointedly at the remains of the hospitality I had been offering to Oliver Crump.

"Any chance of a cup of tea, Guv?" asks Kevin, at length.

"Very well," I say, wearily. "I'll bring it out to you."

They return to the garden, closely followed by Barnacle. Now that all the banging has stopped, his curiosity has got the better of his innate caution.

A few minutes later, I take their tea out to them. It is well laced with sugar to replace the extra calories they had expended during their unaccustomed rate of working while their boss was within earshot. They are sitting on the tree-trunk, making friends with Barnacle who has strolled over to see what they might have to offer. Kevin treats him to a scratch behind the ear, so he rolls onto his back, inviting Sean to do the same for his expansive tummy. Sean duly obliges. "He's a big cat, isn't he, Guv?" he observes.

"He's a Maine Coon," I explain. "In the world of domestic cats, they have the top spot, like Clydesdales do in the world of horses."

"They still pull brewery drays at county shows, and the Queen's golden coach on Royal occasions," says Kevin, knowledgeably.

"What?" says Sean. "Cats?"

"Yes, of course, cats," says Kevin. "Ain't you never seen them pulling the coach on television?"

Sean looks nonplussed and Barnacle, for whom petting is acceptable but second best to offers of food, decides to move on. Sean frowns at Kevin, and then appeals to me. "He's having me on, ain't he, Guv?" he says, plaintively.

"Don't worry about it, Sean," I advise. I consult my watch, pointedly. "You will be wanting to get back to work," I say.

"No hurry," replies Kevin, equably, as he sips his tea. "We'll easily finish cutting back the damaged brickwork this afternoon, but it will be too late to start mixing mortar to begin the rebuilding. We'll get going on that tomorrow."

It is clear that nothing short of Oliver Crump's return, will get these two lead-swingers back into action until they feel properly refreshed and rested, so I give up on them and go back indoors.

There is not a lot I can do until the meeting of Shorty's allotment holders, so I fire up my lap-top and Google a few phrases that I think might prove instructive.

I have in mind to try, 'keeping dormice', 'Hangman's Copse', 'Ancient Woodland', 'Oliver Crump & Co', 'Council Planning Committee' and 'Verdant Heritage'. As always when I am unwise enough to search the Web, I become entangled in the mesh and am side-tracked to sources of unreliable information and specious opinions on topics that have nothing to do with my original entries.

By the time I give up in disgust, having discovered nothing remotely useful, I find that a couple of hours have passed. Kevin and Sean have long since departed and I have a need for a quick sandwich if I am to catch the beginning of Shorty's meeting.

"I wonder whether any of the speakers will throw new light on what is going on," I say to Barnacle as we sit over our hurried meal. "I have a feeling I might just enjoy this event."

CHAPTER 23

It is a few minutes before seven o'clock when I arrive at the Church Hall. There are about fifty people, doing their best to fill a space that could easily take three-hundred. At one end, Shorty and his fellow allotment holders have deployed a table, set athwartships across the width of the hall. It is on a raised platform and is furnished with five chairs, which I assume are for the main speakers. On the table, in front of each of four of the chairs, is a notepad, a pen and a glass of water. The fifth place is provided with a lap-top computer.

Rows of seats, facing the platform are for the bulk of the attendees and, to one side, is a smaller table with a card marked 'PRESS' standing on it. I am pleased to see that Shorty has everything highly organised in true Purple Funnel style.

Some people have already taken their seats and I select one towards the rear of the hall. I am on a mission to observe and to listen, I tell myself, not to contribute.

I begin the first of these objectives by looking around to see who I might recognise among the attendees. I am pleased to see Felicity Wright taking her place at the PRESS table, and she waves a greeting to me as our eyes meet. Shorty is standing behind the centre chair at the top table and is trying to marshal his speakers into their places. One is a woman who has her back to me and, when she turns to take her chair, I am surprised to see that it is none other than Wendy Fyler. So the Council has responded positively to Shorty's invitation, I muse.

Two of the other places are taken by people that I recognise as being allotment holders although I do not know them particularly well. The seat with the lap-top, is occupied by a young lady that I do not remember having seen before. Shorty, having obviously appointed himself as chairman of the meeting, takes the centre chair and waits for a few minutes as the attendees in the main section of the hall settle themselves down and the hubbub of many different conversations subsides.

Shorty rises and bangs on the table to attract attention. He begins by welcoming everyone and explains that this is an extraordinary meeting of the Allotment Holders' Association, but that it is also an open meeting to which interested members of the public are welcome to contribute. He then tells us that he has convened this meeting because the Town Council's Planning Committee has decided to set up a Sub-Committee to consider the future of the allotments. Why, he asks, has this item been slipped through at the end of a busy Committee meeting? And why has no notice been given to allotment holders who might wish to have a say in a matter that affects them more than anyone else?

He then goes on to introduce the other allotment holders who will be speaking and also the young lap-top lady who is the daughter of one of the holders and who is currently attending a secretarial course at the local technical college. She has kindly agreed to record the minutes of the meeting. Shorty tells us that, after the main speakers have made their presentations, he will throw the meeting open and invite comments from the floor.

He then turns to Wendy Fyler. He introduces her as secretary of the Town Council's Planning Committee and says he is pleased that the Council have responded at short notice to his invitation to provide a speaker who will set out the official position. He hopes she will explain why the future of the allotments has suddenly become important enough to warrant the setting up of a special Sub-Committee and, at what stage it is intended that the views of the allotment holders would be considered.

"Ms Fyler," he announces, "You have the floor."

Wendy Fyler rises to what, I am sure, she feels is a hostile silence. She begins by reassuring the allotment holders that there is no intention, on the part of the Council, to exclude allotment holders or, indeed, any of the town rate-payers, from the deliberations of the Sub-Committee. It had not, yet, held its first meeting and all the stake-holders with an interest in the future of the allotment site will be invited to contribute their views.

There are mutterings from the audience as she completes this first statement, like "So you say," "Why the secrecy?" and the less specific, "Yah, boo." Whereupon, Shorty bangs on the table again and reminds us that there will be an opportunity for questions later.

"You have to understand," continues Wendy, "That, in this matter, there are stakeholders other than those of you who are lucky enough to enjoy a lease on an allotment. Not least is the ordinary rate-payer who, indirectly, subsidises the low rental we charge for the allotments. The Town Council has a duty of accountability for the way we use the money we collect from local tax-payers."

There are more mutterings as Wendy pauses for breath, but they are subdued, and Shorty only has to sweep the audience with a glare and they become settled enough for her to carry on.

"Your chairman has asked why the Sub-Committee has been formed," she continues. "I can tell you that it was as a result of a submission to the main Planning Committee suggesting that the Council could make more profitable use of the site occupied by the allotments."

This statement provokes a renewal of the louder mutterings.

"More profitable for whom?" asks a voice. "Who made the submission?" asks another. "Yah! Boo!" says a third, with commendable consistency.

Shorty rises to his full, imposing, height and raises a hand as though he is attempting to quell a mutiny on-board HMS Bounty, - fortunately with more success than was achieved by the ill-starred Captain Bligh.

"I do not need to tell you that these are difficult time, financially, for all of us," Wendy resumes, "The Council must therefore use its resources as efficiently as possible for the benefit of the majority of all rate-payers, and this could mean using the allotment site for some other purpose or, perhaps, selling it so that the proceeds can be used to improve the town's other amenities. The submission that I mentioned suggested that many of the allotments are ineffectively used. A number of them are neglected to the extent that they harbour weeds and pests that are detrimental to neighbouring gardens, and others are not used for growing vegetables for family consumption which is their prime purpose. One plot, I understand, is left completely barren."

This time, there are outcries rather than mutterings. "Rubbish", and "Who says so?" are shouted and the 'Yah, Boo' man, waxes in eloquence to contribute the more explicit, "Get her off the platform."

Shorty once more outdoes William Bligh in the matter of putting down mutinies. "Please," he says (a word that was not in Bligh's vocabulary). "Quieten down to allow Ms Fyler to finish. There will be an opportunity for questions later."

Sadly, this turns out not to be true.

"I am sorry to say that I will not be able to remain to answer your questions," she tells them. "The basis of the statement I have made was approved by the Chairman of the Planning Committee and I am not authorised to say anything further. You have to understand that I am simply an officer of the Council. It is the elected members that decide policy and make planning decisions.

This is a signal for further uproar which Shorty makes heavy weather of tackling. Wendy Fyler, meanwhile, is wearing her grim-but-self-satisfied look, and is coolly stowing her papers into her brief-case. She gives Shorty a curt nod and marches out of the Hall, apparently oblivious to the cat-calls and, it has to be said, a reversion to 'Yah, Boos' from the floor. With their target gone, the audience quietens and Shorty regains control of the meeting.

He tells us that he is as disappointed as anyone that Ms Fyler had not been prepared to answer questions but, at least, it was useful to know the present thinking in the Town Hall. He then goes on to introduce his other two speakers.

First up is Eileen Mulcher, one of the allotment holders. She makes a case that gardening provides valuable exercise, and the production of vegetables contributes to a healthy diet. As such, the allotments fulfil an important part of the Council's duty to provide recreational facilities for rate-payers and to promote public health and well-being. Furthermore, they are green oases which, like parks and other open spaces, enhance residential areas and prevent them degenerating into concrete deserts.

She reminds us that these allotments were created in World-War I and were revitalised during World War II, when home-grown food was vital for the country's survival. It is just as important now that people should be encouraged to grow their own, herbicide-free and pesticide-free produce. Council members, she reminds us, are elected servants of the public and, if they fail to maintain traditional and much loved public amenities, they should not expect to remain in their posts.

She sits down to warm applause and Shorty then introduces Ben Stamping, his second speaker, and also an allotment holder. He is a lawyer by profession and he goes into detail about the rights of his fellow allotment holders under the terms of the leases they have with the Council. He tells us that each agreement runs for a five-year period and, since they all started on the same date, the current five-year leases for the allotment holders all finish on the same date. That is in six month's time. Because the cultivation of an allotment is a long-term undertaking, there is an understanding that the Council will give several year's notice if leases are not to be renewed, but this is not a formal provision in the leases and could not be legally enforced.

This information is greeted by groans and low-level muttering, and the speaker then carries on to talk about the rights and duties of both the allotment holders and the Town Council.

Following the presentations by the speakers, Shorty takes comments and questions from the audience but neither he, nor his speakers are able to provide much in the way of answers. He winds up the meeting by proposing that a small working group should be formed to monitor any further developments from the Council or elsewhere, and especially to keep a watching brief on the deliberations of the Planning Committee and its Sub-Committees. Two members of the audience volunteer to serve on the working group alongside Shorty and his speakers. It is agreed that the working group will use its discretion to convene a further full meeting of the Allotment Holders Association as soon as that becomes desirable.

I sit at the back of the hall until the audience have all departed, and Shorty has dealt with all those people who wanted a private word with him before they left. I go up to him on the platform and congratulate him on his chairmanship, and for keeping the proceedings on course through distinctly choppy waters.

"I think you've earned yourself a beer or two," I tell him. "Shall we take ourselves to the *Black Horse*?"

"I like the idea of a beer," says Shorty, "But let's go to my shed rather than the pub. I've something I want to show you."

CHAPTER 24

There is no electrical supply to Shorty's shed, but he has installed very effective gas lighting served by a bottle of gas which also supplies his small cooker and a compact refrigerator. In the brilliant, white light of his two lamps, I see that he has been remarkably busy. The notice board is covered by newspaper clippings, not only those reporting the incident of the tree entering, uninvited, into my bedroom, but also a record of recent decisions by the Council's Planning Committee, including the setting up of the Sub-Committee to consider the allotment site. Other clippings cover Felicity's account of the 'Save Hangman's Copse' protesters besieging the Town-hall.

Taking centre-stage is the A1 layout pad that I had bought yesterday. It is set up on an artist's easel which I recognise as belonging to Shorty's wife who works off her intolerance of life's manifold irritations by painting aggressive landscapes in violent acrylic hues. If Shorty has 'borrowed' the easel without her knowledge, that would be just one more irritation to add to her list. I do not ask him about that because knowing, and not reporting it, would make me an accessory to the crime. In any case, my attention is fully occupied by what he has set out on the top sheet, using my black marker pen.

"You have certainly been busy," I tell him. "That is an amazing situation chart you have produced. If Inspector Plugg and M'sieu Poire had combined their expertise they could not have done better."

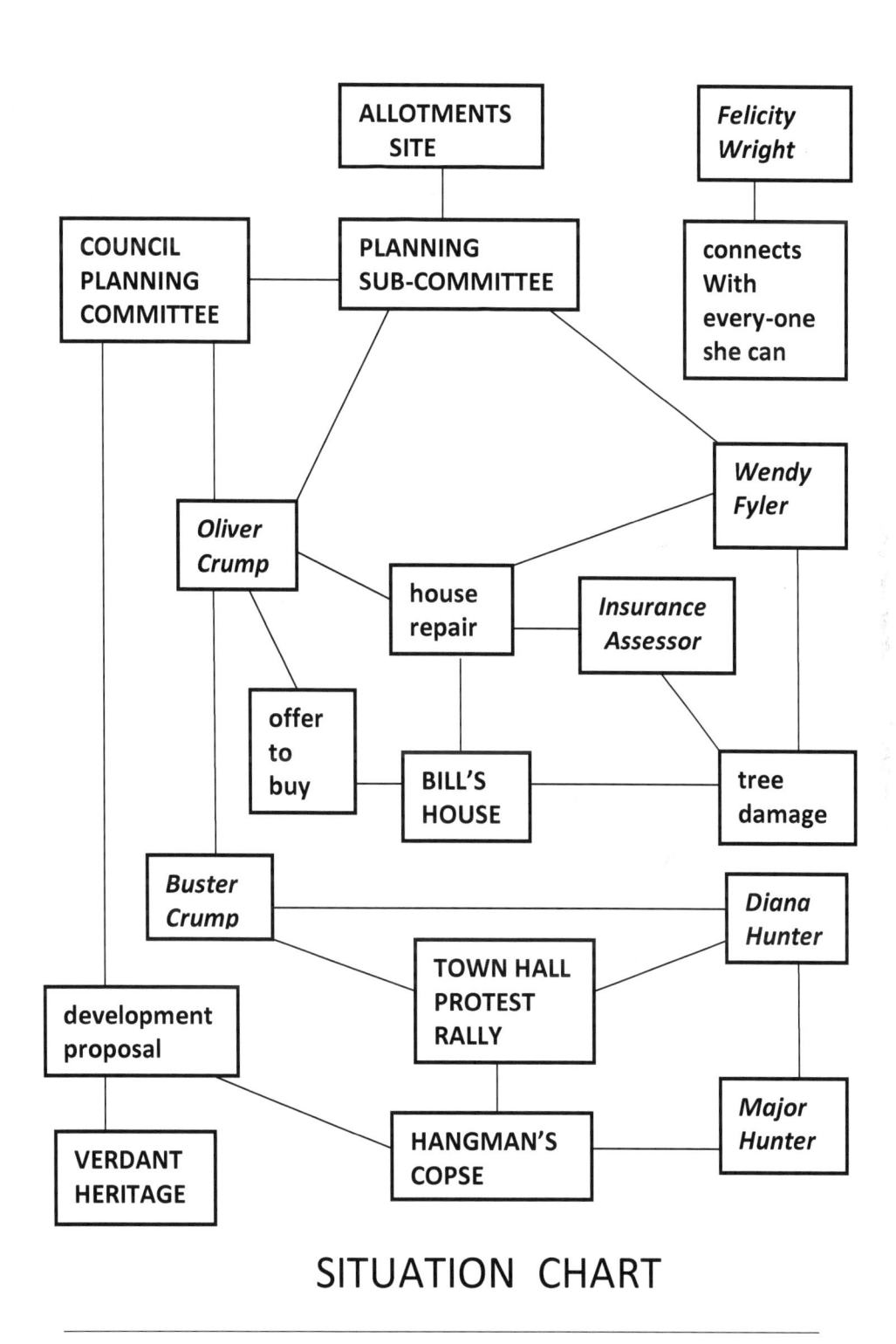

```
                    ┌─────────────┐              ┌──────────┐
                    │ ALLOTMENTS  │              │ Felicity │
                    │    SITE     │              │  Wright  │
                    └──────┬──────┘              └────┬─────┘
                           │                          │
  ┌───────────┐     ┌──────┴──────┐              ┌────┴─────┐
  │  COUNCIL  │     │   PLANNING  │              │ connects │
  │ PLANNING  ├─────┤ SUB-COMMITTEE│             │  With    │
  │ COMMITTEE │     │             │              │ every-one│
  └─────┬─────┘     └──────┬──────┘              │  she can │
        │                  │                     └──────────┘
        │                  │                ┌─────────┐
        │           ┌──────┴──┐             │  Wendy  │
        │           │ Oliver  ├─────────────┤  Fyler  │
        │           │  Crump  │             └────┬────┘
        │           └──┬───┬──┘                  │
        │              │   │  ┌──────┐  ┌──────────┐
        │              │   └──┤house ├──┤Insurance │
        │              │      │repair│  │ Assessor │
        │           ┌──┴──┐   └───┬──┘  └────┬─────┘
        │           │offer│       │          │
        │           │ to  │       │      ┌───┴───┐
        │           │ buy │   ┌───┴──┐   │ tree  │
        │           └──┬──┘   │BILL'S├───┤damage │
        │              └──────┤HOUSE │   └───────┘
        │                     └──────┘
        │     ┌────────┐                    ┌────────┐
        │     │ Buster ├────────────────────┤ Diana  │
        │     │ Crump  │                    │ Hunter │
        │     └────┬───┘                    └───┬────┘
  ┌──────────┐    │     ┌──────────┐            │
  │development│   └─────┤TOWN HALL ├────────────┤
  │ proposal │         │  PROTEST │            │
  └─────┬────┘         │   RALLY  │            │
        │              └─────┬────┘        ┌───┴────┐
        │                    │             │ Major  │
  ┌─────┴────┐         ┌─────┴────┐        │ Hunter │
  │ VERDANT  │         │HANGMAN'S ├────────┤        │
  │ HERITAGE │─────────┤  COPSE   │        └────────┘
  └──────────┘         └──────────┘
```

SITUATION CHART

"It took me two or three attempts before I got it right," admits Shorty, "But, for someone who was brought up making stowage plans for dozens of cargo parcels for as many different ports and, at the same time ensuring that the ship remained at all times stable and not overloaded, it wasn't too much of a challenge,"

"Talk me through it, then, Shorty," I say. "What is the rationale behind the different scripts?"

"It goes like this," he explains, "I use capital letters for places or other entities, the italics are people, and the lower case letters are for happenings. The lines, of course, indicate where we have established definite links between boxes."

"I notice you don't include me amongst the players that appear in your chart," I comment. "Or yourself for that matter."

"That is to prevent the chart becoming too complex and cluttered," he explains. "I think we can assume that you have connections with almost all the boxes, and we don't need a diagram to remind us of that."

"And I see that you have indicated that something similar applies to Felicity Wright," I comment, "I agree with that. If she has made no connection with any of those boxes, it will not be for want of trying."

Shorty has been breaking open a couple of beers while I have been talking. He offers one to me and takes a swig from his own.

"Let's get into problem solving mode, then," he suggests. "There are multiple connections between most of the boxes," I point out. "But Verdant Heritage is an outlier."

"So is the allotment site, in a way," says Shorty. "It would be useful if we could tie them both in more definitely."

"I can help you with the allotment site," I tell him, and I remind him about the law firm, Messrs Case and Carey sending a representative to check out the allotment site, and my discovery that they just happen, at least in other matters, to be acting for Oliver Crump.

"Hmm, you did well digging that out, Bill," says Shorty, thoughtfully. "It's not conclusive but, taken together with Crump's chairmanship of the Council's Allotments Sub-Committee and his offer to buy your house, I think we are justified in making a direct connection between him and the allotments."

"Felicity and Diana keep suggesting that there is more to the Crump/Fyler association than can be explained by the work they do together at the Council," I say.

"They are hardly the most reliable of witnesses though, are they?" demurs Shorty.

"True enough," I agree. "We probably shouldn't even put a dotted line connecting the Crump and Fyler boxes yet, but we should keep an eye on those two in case there is further evidence to connect them."

"What about Verdant Heritage, then?" asks Shorty. "Anything to report?"

"Nothing conclusive" I reply. "But I found out from the guys who are repairing my house that Crump & Co did some building work for Verdant Heritage a couple of years ago."

"So, another possible link," says Shorty, "But, I agree, not definite enough to make a firm connection."

"Perhaps a dotted line, though," I suggest. "Crump's firm must have had a proper contract with Verdant Heritage at that time."

"Fair enough," Shorty agrees, and he adds a pecked line to his chart. We contemplate the result in silence for a few minutes as we put in some more effort on our beer.

"The thing that shouts at you is the number of connections to Oliver Crump," I point out. "Five full lines and a pecked line so far, and the possibility of a future connection to Wendy Fyler. No other boxes have more than three. I must say he is looking more and more like the spider at the centre of the web."

"An excellent point, Bill," agrees Shorty. "I think we are beginning to get a handle on what is going on and who is doing the manipulation. Let's concentrate our minds on Oliver Crump."

"There's another straw in the wind," I tell him, "I am sure Felicity Wright suspects some direct collaboration between Major Hunter and Oliver Crump."

"They don't seem likely shipmates," observes Shorty.

"No, indeed," I reply, "But Buster Crump tells me that Felicity has put the squeeze on him to keep a look out for any communication between his Dad and the Major."

"It would require a long and tenuous link to connect the Major and Oliver Crump on my chart," says Shorty. "And we need more than a reporter's hunch to justify it."

"I agree," I tell him, "But don't forget that the Major appears to have had Hangman's Copse surveyed so, again, I think we should assume that the jury is still out on whatever he might be up to."

"That's about as far as we can go with the chart this evening," says Shorty. "The old lady you met at the Copse is incidental and not a key player, so I am not adding her to the chart."

"You could paste a note at the bottom saying, *here be witches*, like they used to put *here be dragons* on old sea charts," I suggest, but Shorty ignores this as facetious.

"We'll keep it as simple as we can," he says. "There are bound to be more inter-connections as we gather more information."

"Your chart has already been a great help, Shorty," I tell him. "It is a stroke of genius on your part."

"We make a good team, Bill," he agrees, "You get the crazy ideas and I do the serious thinking. But it has been a long day and I think we deserve a proper night-cap."

I let the remark about crazy ideas slide, while he goes to his cupboard for a bottle of Scotch that he keeps for just such special occasions as this, and pours two generous tots.

"Here's to us," I say. "Investigators extraordinary."

"You are becoming hooked on all this, aren't you?" suggests Shorty.

"Yes," I agree, "I believe I am. I've got this garden fête tomorrow. I had originally intended to look in for half an hour and then leave because I disliked the thought of Felicity Wright threatening to cause problems if I didn't go."

"And now?" prompts Shorty, taking another sip of his whisky.

"And now, I am intrigued by all the possible interactions as you have so effectively charted, and I will stay in the game for as long as there is a chance of discovering some more leads."

We are in good spirits as we finish our drinks. Then Shorty says he must get home to Mary and I walk back to my own house. Barnacle's nose tells him that I am not bringing anything of interest as I enter the kitchen, so he doesn't bother to get out of his chair to greet me. I give him a pat on the head to show that I am in a good mood, and then go into the dining room to check on the dormice. At this time of the evening, they are busily running around their cage as though they are wondering why breakfast is so long in coming. I give them a handful of chopped nuts and some of the milled seeds that Diana had left for them, and they tuck into these offerings with uninhibited enthusiasm, as though they are afraid that winter might come upon them tomorrow and they won't get another meal until the spring. I watch them for a few minutes and then return to the kitchen.

I decide that television is again likely to prove a disappointment, so I make myself a coffee and a cheese sandwich and settle for a relatively early night.

"We'll have the workmen banging about at eight o'clock in the morning again," I tell Barnacle. "Best not to be too late for bed."

Barnacle opens one eye and gives a yawn that must have come close to unhinging his jaw.

"I'll take that as agreement," I say.

CHAPTER 25

The next morning, Kevin and Sean make their presence heard soon after eight o'clock. They are clattering their ladders, shouting loudly at each other and generally making an unnecessarily noisy start to their work in what, I am sure, is a ploy to attract my attention to their need for refreshment.

I am not taken in by such an obvious try-on. I bring the dormice into the kitchen and share a leisurely breakfast with them and Barnacle. Then I return the mice to the dining room and take my time shaving and showering.

It is nine-thirty by the time I go outside to see how the building work is progressing. To my surprise, I discover that they have actually done some useful brick-laying, but they stop work and hail me as soon as I set foot outside the door.

"Good morning, Guv," Kevin greets me from way up on the scaffolding. "That's great timing. We've just got enough of this batch of mortar left for another half dozen bricks and then we'll be ready for a break."

"I'll say," adds Sean.

"Alright," I tell them, holding up a hand with spread fingers. "Five minutes."

"You're a star, Guv," shouts Kevin.

"Right on," agrees Sean with a brevity that makes me wonder whether he has been infected by a bi-syllabic virus from the scaffolder, Fred.

I return to the kitchen to make their tea and count out their ration of standard biscuits and, by the time I take their refreshments out to them, they are already down from their platform and sitting, expectantly, on the tree-trunk.

"You've saved my life, Guv," says Kevin, as put my tray down between them.

"And mine," says Sean as he starts to spoon vast quantities of sugar into his mug.

Thinking back to what we had learned from Shorty's situation chart, I feel that I ought to take this opportunity to find out more about Oliver Crump. On the other hand, I remind myself that these guys, unlike the scaffolders, are working directly for him, so I need to tread carefully.

"I wasn't sure you would be here this morning, being Saturday," I begin.

"We are on overtime, right enough," says Kevin. "But Mr Crump wants us to get the new window in and make it all weather-tight before we knock-off for the weekend. That will just leave the roof to tidy up on Monday"

"It's good money," adds Sean.

"We ought to finish by the middle of the afternoon," explains Kevin. "By that time we'll have earned more than a normal day's pay. It's all a matter of pacing ourselves and getting the timing right. Mr Crump appreciates that."

"He seems a very understanding boss," I comment. "Have you been with him for him long?"

"A few years," says Kevin. "How many would you say, Sean?"

"A few," agrees Sean, which like many of his pronouncements, is not especially illuminating.

"He must be a good boss, then," I suggest.

"He expects us to work," says Kevin, in an aggrieved voice, as though this is a thoroughly unreasonable expectation on the part of his employer.

I wait for Sean's economical confirmation and I am relieved when it is relatively expansive.

"And he gives us a bit of stick if we don't," he complains.

"That sounds excessive," I commiserate, with my tongue wedged in my cheek. "Why do you put up with it.?"

"Most bosses are like that," explains Kevin, philosophically. "But Mr Crump is alright. You know where you are with him."

Sean, uncharacteristically, is at a loss for supportive words. Perhaps he doesn't do philosophy, I think to myself. It also strikes me that this is the first time I have heard anyone say a good word about Oliver Crump. I decide to check that I have understood Kevin correctly. "So he's a good bloke to work for, then?" I ask.

"Oh, yus,"chimes in Sean feeling, I suppose, that he has some conversational ground to make up. "He expects a lot, but he treats us fair."

"There's many worse," agrees Kevin, "And I've worked for a good few of them. He looks after us, does Mr Crump."

I jump on that statement. "You mean he'll give you a bonus if you do something special for him?" I ask.

Kevin looks uncomfortable. "Er, yes," he agrees. "That sort of thing."

"Did you earn a bonus yesterday afternoon, then, Kevin?" I ask.

"I dunno what you mean, Guv," he replies, but he doesn't meet my eyes and he shifts his feet nervously.

"Of course you don't Kevin," I say. "Just my joke. Anyhow, I am glad to hear that Mr, Crump treats you well, it means I can expect him, and you of course, to do a good job on repairing my house."

"You can rely on us, Guv," Kevin assures me, grasping at the opportunity to change the subject, but he has something else on his mind.

"Has Mr Crump said anything about coming to check our progress today?" he asks.

"Not to me," I tell him. "And I will be out myself after lunch. You should have an uninterrupted afternoon which will allow you to get a lot of work done."

"Don't we always," says Sean, re-joining a conversation in which he had, temporarily and very pointedly, lost interest, but Kevin looks at me warily, as though he detects a hint of sarcasm in my statement. I give him a half smile in return and then pick up their empty mugs, place them on the tray with the cleared biscuit plate and carry it back to the kitchen. They stand staring after me for a few seconds and then take the hint and begin to mix another batch of mortar.

I keep out of their way for the rest of the morning so as not to give them an excuse to stop work again. In fact, I am hoping to have a couple of hours to myself, but it is not long before the doorbell rings. When I answer it, I find Felicity Wright standing there, tablet in hand as always. I am not overly pleased to see her, but I don't want to leave her standing on the doorstep for an indefinite period of time.

"Come in, Felicity," I say. "And what brings you here?"

"That is not the most gracious of welcomes, Bill," she replies, cheerfully "And, since you are about to ask, yes, I would love a cup of coffee."

She fondles Barnacle who has come across to greet her, but he loses interest quickly when he realises that she has brought nothing of interest to a cat. I switch on the kettle and busy myself with mugs, instant coffee and a packet of plain biscuits. I am not about to overdo my show of hospitality.

"I thought it would be a good idea to drop in and remind you about the fête this afternoon," she says, as she takes a seat at the kitchen table.

"Well you can rest assured that I'll be there as promised," I tell her. "I agreed to go, and so I will."

"I never doubted it for a moment, Bill," she purrs, as I put mugs of the caffeine-rich refreshment on the table. "I am sure you are the embodiment of reliability."

"So, what is new since I last saw you?" I ask.

"Reporters don't go around giving individual people information," says Felicity. "We go around absorbing information from individuals, welding it into a coherent story, and then publishing it without fear or favour for the greater good of the public at large."

"Yes, of course," I say. "That's as likely as finding an iceberg in the Red Sea during August.

"You are awfully cynical for one so old," says Felicity.

"It's experience, not cynicism," I reply, and I have a flash of *déja vu* as I try to remember where I have recently been party to a similar exchange of words. Leaving that aside, I persist with my attempt to prise some information out of her.

"I was glad to see you at the Allotment Holder's meeting, yesterday evening," I say. "Does that mean you think there might be a plot to close the site and build apartments there?"

"Surely, 'plot' is too strong a word," protests Felicity. "To some people, it would make sense to build there. The town is short of good, affordable housing, but I haven't heard of there being a shortage of vegetables."

"That Wendy Fyler has been bending your ear," I accuse her. "Didn't you listen to the other speakers at the meeting?"

"Don't get steamed up about it, Bill," she grins. "I'm just pointing out that there are at least two sides to this matter, maybe more."

"Take a look out of the window," I tell her. "A multi-story block of flats on that site would be staring down into my back garden from point-blank range, and into similar gardens of a hundred houses around the block. It would be a monstrous development that would devastate a pleasant residential area."

"That is, literally, a 'not in my backyard' statement," Felicity admonishes, but I recognise from the look on her face that she is winding me up.

"Just because NIMBY's are the subject of derision, it doesn't mean we are not sometimes right," I tell her.

"Calm down, Bill," she says, "If it's any consolation to you and your friend Shorty Smith, my personal view is that the allotment's site is unsuitable for housing but, as a reporter, I have to take account of all the arguments."

"Fair enough," I say, "But have you been able to find anything more about Verdant Heritage and a possible connection with Oliver Crump's company?"

"Nothing more, as yet," she says, "But I haven't had much time to spare. I have to cover a lot of different stories, and there is always a deadline when you work for a newspaper."

"Well, Shorty and I think there is a possibility that Verdant Heritage are behind a move to build on the allotment's site as well as at Hangman's Copse. We have produced a 'Situation Chart' covering both sites and all the people involved, but Verdant Heritage is an outlier and we need to be able to tie them into the main network."

"I am intrigued," says Felicity. "Am I going to be invited to view this Chart?"

"Tomorrow, at lunchtime, would be possible," I tell her. "It's in Shorty's shed on the allotments. His is the plot on which nothing is allowed to grow, as given a special mention by Wendy Fyler yesterday evening."

"I'll be there," promises Felicity, making a note on her tablet.

"And what about the fête this afternoon?" I enquire. "Do you have a master plan for that?"

"We'll play it as it comes," says Felicity. "Keep well away from me so nobody associates you with the press, and just keep your ears open. I don't know exactly who will be there, but note any comments that might be made by anyone about Hangman's Copse or about ancient woodlands. You have met some of the major players, and I want to know who is talking to whom and about what. Anything that smells of conspiracy."

"Is that all?" I ask, ironically.

"No," she replies. "Don't forget that, as you are watching other people, I will be keeping an eye on you. I am still not sure about your role in all this, Bill Selsey, but I do pick up the impression that you have not told me everything you know."

"Like what?" I ask.

"Like the dormice, for example," she says.

"How do you know about the dormice?" I ask, startled.

"Diana Hunter is roping me in so I can photograph them and report their presence in Hangman's Copse," she tells me.

"Oh!" I say. "Well she had me sworn to secrecy. They are in my dining room if you would like to see them, but they will be fast asleep at this time of the day."

Felicity follows me into the dining room where I lift the cover off the cage and allow her to view the slumbering creatures."

"Pretty little things, aren't they?" I say.

"Ugh! I'm not mad about mice," confesses Felicity, pulling a face. "They are somewhere between spiders and snakes in my list of un-favourite animals."

It pleases me to hear that the formidable Felicity Wright has at least one weakness. It is like finding a vulnerable point in the armour plating of the battleship *Bismark*. I replace the cover and we leave the rodents to their rest.

"Well, good to talk to you, as always, Bill," she says. "I'll look forward to seeing you in the distance at the main event this afternoon, and you can report whatever you might discover when I visit Shorty's shed around midday tomorrow."

She picks up her bag, waves a cheerful goodbye, and cycles off to her next assignment.

I look at the clock, which confirms that it is nearly time for lunch, so I find a couple of yesterday's sandwiches in the back of the fridge. They are good enough for those two skivers, I think to myself as I take them out with a beer each for Kevin and Sean.

"Just leave them there," calls Kevin. "We'll be down for them in five minutes."

"Thanks, Guv," adds Sean. "You're the tops."

"You are welcome," I shout back. "Keep up the good work. I'll be out all the afternoon."

I return to the kitchen and bake myself a potato in the microwave. I fill it with tomato and melted cheese, and the thought of Kevin and Sean munching on stale sandwiches makes my lunch taste even better than usual.

Barnacle takes his usual place next to me at the table. Unfortunately, he doesn't like any of cheese, tomato or potato, but I open a can of his favourite cat-food and we enjoy a companionable meal.

"It's time for your afternoon nap, Barny," I tell him, as I put the dishes away and prepare to leave. I don't bother to check the dormice because I know they will carry on sleeping until the evening. I spend a few minutes sorting out some smart/casual clothes and take myself off for my afternoon at the fête.

CHAPTER 26

As I drive off, I recall the briefing that Felicity had given me about the fête. It is being organised by Mrs Emma Gooding in the garden of her home in Laburnum Avenue which is, to my mind, too close to Major Hunter's house for comfort. I remember that Mrs Gooding lives at number four but, when I make a ninety-degree turn into Laburnum Avenue, it is immediately apparent that I don't need to check the address. Above the double wrought iron gates that guard the access to her drive-way is an extravagant banner bearing the message, SAVE HANGMAN'S COPSE.

This is, evidently, a popular cause because cars are parked, bow to stern, solidly along the length of the Avenue and I have to drive two blocks before I can find a vacant space. This, I decide, is not a bad thing. The further I park my distinctive red Volvo from Major Hunter's place, the better.

I pass his house, and glance in, as I walk back to the fête. His green Landrover and Diana's bijou roadster are parked in the drive but, otherwise, there is no sign of life. I carry on to number four and, as I enter the garden, I am relieved of a fifty-pence entry fee by a jolly middle-aged lady, sitting at a table by the gates.

"Just the one?" she asks as she takes my money and drops it into a shoe-box by her side.

This strikes me as an odd question. It should be perfectly obvious that I am not two people, but I turn my head in case someone has crept up behind me, un-noticed. I decide to humour her.

"Yes," I confirm, "I am only one person."

"Ah!" she says, "In that case you might like to pay a pound to come in. Men don't spend as freely as women around the stalls at these kind of events and I am sure you want to support our cause."

I give her a pound coin, expecting her to return my fifty-pence piece, but she makes no move to do so. "I am sorry," she says, But we operate a one-way cash system. Once money has gone into the box, I am not allowed to take it out again. We charities have to be extremely careful, you understand, and we have to account properly for every penny we give away."

This policy is little short of banditry, I tell myself, but I know I would feel impossibly cheap and mean if I were to stand and argue with her. To give in, gracefully, is the only sensible course of action, but that doesn't mean without protest.

"I can see I'll have to keep tight hold on my wallet in this place," I complain.

"Not at all," she admonishes. "You should keep an open mind and an open pocket-book. We are all trying to preserve our countryside."

She is speaking with authority, and I wonder if she is our host for the day. "Tell me, are you Mrs Gooding?" I ask.

"Oh, no," she says, looking over her shoulder. "That is Emma Gooding coming down the steps now. Major Hunter arrived a few minutes ago and I believe he wants a word with her."

I look past her and see a serene lady, whose age I am too much of a gentleman to even guess at, making a Hollywood style entrance into the garden in the front of her house. Unhurriedly, she descends a flight of broad, stone steps from open French doors onto the small grassed area, where I now see that Major Hunter is waiting with an impatience he can barely contain. He is practically pawing the ground like a starving lion in an ancient Roman arena, desperate to meet up with his first Christian.

It seems to me that a promising scenario is developing at which I can usefully start to deploy my detecting skills. The unscrupulous toll-collector tells me that the stalls and the main action are to be found at the rear of the house, and she then turns her attention to fleecing a new arrival. Instead of following her advice, I take the opportunity to sidle off to a corner of the front garden, from where I can hear whatever conversation might develop between the lady of the house and her irate, military visitor.

I have my back to them as I make a pretence of admiring a stand of tall delphiniums, but my ears are doing their best to rotate so as to best pick up the sound coming from astern. As it turns out, the Major and Mrs Goodman are too pre-occupied with each other to pay any attention to me.

The Major attempts to get the exchange under way, but is too overcome with emotion to articulate recognisable words. This hands an immediate advantage to Emma Gooding, who uses it adroitly. "How nice of you to join us, this afternoon, Henry," she says. "I was afraid you might not wish to support this effort to preserve our ancient woodlands."

The Major clearly sees this statement as a pre-emptive assault on his position and, in the best traditions of the service he launches an immediate counter-attack.

"I am not here to support your ridiculous cause, dammit, Emma," he explodes. "I am here to tell you to stop meddling in other people's affairs."

"Now, now, Henry, we shouldn't allow ourselves to become too worked up at our time of life," warns Emma, soothingly. "In any case, you ought to be the first to agree that Hangman's Copse is an important part of the county environment and is worth preserving. It is part of our heritage."

"Hangman's Copse belongs to me," shouts the Major, as though he is rallying troops on the battlefield. "It's my heritage, not anyone else's and I'll do with it whatever I damned well please."

"That seems to me a very selfish attitude to take, Henry, dear," says Emma. "The Copse was there for many hundreds of years before you were born and it is right that it should be there for hundreds of years in the future. Why not look upon yourself as the guardian of an irreplaceable feature in the countryside rather than the owner of some insignificant piece of land that can be disposed of when it has served your purpose."

Emma's consistent good humour is sapping the strength of the Major's offensive, but he doesn't give up easily. "You have no right to form an association for protecting something that does not belong to you," he fumes. "It is like taking control of someone else's property. I expect there is a law against it."

"Why don't you ask the Clerk of the Court next time you are doing your magistrate thing?" suggests Emma with a smile. "He's bound to know."

"You'll all laugh on the other side of your faces by the time I've done with you," threatens the Major. "There could well be a more productive use for the Copse than to leave it in its present, decayed state. It is not much good to anyone as it is."

"Oh dear," says Emma. "Have you been listening to that Oliver Crump? I saw his Jaguar parked outside your house a few days ago."

"I can't stand the feller any more than you can, Emma," says the Major, but I notice he does not deny meeting Oliver Crump.

I risk turning my head slightly to take a peek at them. Emma is taking the Major by the arm and directing him towards the steps. "Why don't we go indoors? I think we need to talk about this over a gin and tonic, with plenty of ice and lemon. Just the thing for a warm day like this."

"Very well, Emma," agrees the Major, as they walk in through the French doors and out of earshot. "But don't think you have won me over. I am not a man to be trifled with."

I turn back to the delphiniums. "Well, that was an interesting few minutes," I tell them. "Could there be an unlikely love/hate relationship building up between the Major and Emma Gooding, do you think?"

A cat's paw of breeze catches the flower spikes so that some of them appear to be nodding and others shaking their flower heads. "You are being deliberately ambiguous, and putting on airs." I accuse them. "Just because you are delphiniums it doesn't mean you have to be Delphic."

I turn away and follow a wide path round the side of the house. The gardens to the rear are extensive, with a large, central, lawned area set out with bring-and buy stalls, a marquee where tea and scones are offered, and various amusements aimed at separating visitors from their money. In one corner is a bouncy castle where children of many shapes and sizes are noisily disporting themselves.

I feel I have made a good start in my investigative role by eavesdropping on the exchange between the Major and our hostess, and I survey the crowded scene to look for my next quarry. I have a worry in the back of my mind that what I am doing might not be entirely ethical and, as a consequence, I jump like a guilty grasshopper when a hand falls on my shoulder.

"My, we are on edge," says Diana in my ear. "What have you been up to that you shouldn't have, Bill Selsey?"

I relax when I see who has crept up behind me, "Oh, it's you, Diana," I croak.

"Who did you think it was?" She asks. "Old Nick, come to carry you off to Hades for all your misdeeds."

"I am here because I have decided that Hangman's Copse, and similar stands of ancient woodland are worth saving," I say, primly.

"Hmm. - So why didn't you just put a cheque in the post, then?" she asks. "I wouldn't have thought a fête like this was your scene at all."

At this point I spot Felicity Wright on the far side of the lawn. Our eyes meet, but she makes no acknowledgement and neither do I. Diana has noticed that I was momentarily distracted and surveys the crowd, but without identifying who or what caught my eye. She turns back to me.

"You are up to something, Bill Selsey," she accuses. "Are you going to come clean or do I have to shake it out of you?"

"You are entirely mistaken, Miss Hunter," I tell her, firmly. "I am here to support the cause and, as part of that, I want to check out the sort of people who are involved in this Association for Saving Hangman's Copse."

A sudden thought strikes her and she throws a worried expression my way. "Nothing has happened to the dormice, has it?"

"Certainly not," I assure her. "They are happy, well-fed little rodents and are, as we speak, enjoying a restorative sleep."

"Thank goodness for that," she says. "The whole future of Hangman's Copse rests on their little shoulders."

"Did you know that your father is here?" I ask, having decided that a change of subject would be desirable.

"Oh, yes," she replies, he has gone rushing off to berate Emma Gooding for having the temerity to chair an association for protecting his property."

"Do you not fear for her safety, then?" I ask. "He might have a shot-gun up his sleeve."

Diana laughs. "Emma Gooding is more than a match for Daddy," she assures me. "He'll start off at a gallop as though he is leading the charge of the Light Brigade but, in ten minutes, she'll have him trying to impress her with his old army stories."

This assessment confirms my own observation of recent events, but I don't mention this to Diana. In fact, my attention is attracted by a new development. Trotting across the centre of the lawn, and heading in our direction, is none other than Buster Crump.

"Your greatest admirer is heading this way," I whisper to Diana.

She turns to follow my gaze but, instead of her eyes softening at the approach of a hunky lover, they harden like chips of carborundum. "That worm," she cries, "He's the last person I want to see." And, with that statement, she darts away and I catch a last glimpse of her as she flits behind a stall selling home-made apple jelly. Seconds later, Buster pants to a halt by my side.

"I saw Diana with you," he says. "Where did she go?"

"I don't know," I tell him. "As soon as she saw you coming, she shot off as though the bailiffs were chasing her."

"I saw you speaking to her," he accuses, fixing me with a suspicious glare. "What were you talking about?"

"I was trying to persuade her that she should give you another chance," I tell him, "But she has it firmly in her mind that you deserted her in her hour of need, so I'm afraid you are still in her bad books."

I have to say that I am shocked at the slick way in which I came out with this glib, and totally untrue response. I am usually a reasonably truthful and reliable person, I think to myself. It must be the bad influence of those two devious girls I have been dealing with during the past few days. Meanwhile, Buster has absorbed the bad news I have given him, but he is not prepared to give up.

"I'll go and find her," he says. "If I could just talk to her for a few minutes, I am sure I would be able to make her see my point of view."

"The best of luck, then, Buster," I tell him. "But, if you take my advice, you would do better to let her cool down for a while. In due course, I am sure she will find that she needs you to help with one of her schemes, and that will be your best chance to cosy up to her again."

I can practically hear rusty cogs turning in what passes for Buster's brain as he considers my advice but, in the end, he rejects it.

"I can't wait that long," he decides. "I need to talk to her right now." And, with that, he canters off to search amongst the people and the stalls for the object of his affection.

Seeing no obvious targets for my own investigation, I wander past the stalls offering, not only cakes and chutney and other home-produced delights, but also tombola, lucky dip and a prize draw to entice those of us who are habitual gamblers. I resist the temptation to participate in these decadent activities, but then I come to a coconut shy.

This is a game of skill rather than chance, so I invest in half a dozen wooden balls and hurl them at the coconuts. More by luck than real expertise, I hit one of the coconuts square on, but it remains obstinately in its cup. It would be in keeping with the ambience of this fête if the coconuts are secured in place by a deposit of superglue, I tell myself, sourly. Of course, I understand that it is fund-raising for a good cause but, nevertheless, I don't like being taken for a ride.

I am about to remonstrate with the smiling old gentleman who is tending the coconut shy when my attention is caught by two figures marching purposefully around the perimeter of the lawn in my direction. It is Major Henry Hunter, accompanied by the police constable who was so keen to arrest me during the incident at the supermarket. True to the Major's name, they are in full hunting mode and projecting the concentrated menace of a wolf pack with the scent of a Russian peasant in their nostrils. I have no idea where they are bound, and I am fairly sure they do not have me in their sights, nevertheless, I turn away before they have a chance to recognise me.

I have no wish to meet either of these two characters independently, and the thought of having to deal with them both together is horrendous. One of them, as a policeman, has the power of arrest and the other, as a Justice of the Peace, can dish out sentences, - and what is more, they both dislike me. It is intolerable that they can band together like wolves to intimidate innocent citizens like me. There should be a law to prevent them even talking to each other. For the first time, I understand why the United States' constitution puts so much emphasis on keeping the executive and the judicial arms of government in separate compartments. I don't have time to think about the place of the legislature although I am sure they have good reason to worry about that too.

However, my priority right now is to look around for a quick escape route. I rapidly conclude that a substantial tent next to the coconut shy offers my best chance of avoiding the two-man wolf-pack. Outside the tent is a board making, what seems to me, an extravagant promise. I dive in without a second thought.

MADAME MERNOV.

INTERNATIONALLY FAMED

CLAIRVOYANT.

FORTUNES TOLD.

PROFESSIONAL AND SOCIAL

ADVICE.

It is quite dark inside, and it takes, perhaps a minute, for my eyes to become accustomed to the low light level. Then I make out Madame Mernov, herself, sitting at a table to the right of the entrance. She has her back to the light, so her face is in shadow, but I see that she has a brightly coloured scarf wound round her head in gipsy style and is wearing a heavily embroidered gown. Large gold (or at least gold coloured) ear-rings add to her Romany-style outfit. She is gazing intently into a crystal globe that she holds carefully between the palms of her hands, perhaps to prevent it being scratched because, on her fingers, she has more rings than the planet Saturn.

Without looking up she says to me, cheerfully, "Why, hello there, sailor. Take a seat and cross my palm with silver and we'll take a look to see if your future is properly ship-shape."

To say that I am startled by this knowledgeable greeting is the understatement of the year. "How did you know I was a sailor?" I gasp, as I take the chair opposite to her.

"I can see it in my crystal-ball, of course," she says, looking up for the first time. "What's more, you walk like a sailor. That rolling gait, you know. Unmistakable."

"It's a myth that sailors walk with a rolling gait," I tell her. "We walk the same way as everyone else."

"No you don't," she argues. "Sailors plant their feet further apart than other folk. It's so they don't keep lurching sideways when they are pacing the deck of a rolling ship."

I have to admit that this sounds logical and, with all that oil sloshing about under the deck, tankers can certainly roll heavily in a beam sea. On the other hand, she could hardly have analysed my walking style from the two steps it took me to enter the tent, which leaves her claim that she somehow saw my profession in her crystal ball. That is even more difficult for me to accept. I decide to find out what else she can come up with and, in any case, I need to allow plenty of time for Major Hunter and the policeman to clear the area before poking my nose out of the tent again.

"How much silver do you charge for a consultation?" I ask.

"Well," she explains, "Crossing my palm with silver is a traditional expression, but you wouldn't expect to get much from me for that. If you want a worthwhile session, you'll need to give me one of those rectangular pieces of crisp paper with the Queen's head on."

"You would think this fête is being run by the Mafia, with all this extortion going on," I grumble, as I fish in my wallet for a five-pound note and find that I have nothing less than a ten-pound note to give her.

"It's all for a good cause," she reminds me as she takes the money and stows it somewhere in the folds of her voluminous skirt. "Saving Hangman's Copse. I don't take a penny for myself you know, and it's against the rules to give change."

"So I've been told," I tell her, ruefully. "Now, what about this advice you are supposed to dispense in return for my hard-earned money?"

She loosens her scarf so that it falls on either side of the crystal ball while she leans forward and peers into its depths. As she does this, a greenish light brings a glow to the southern hemisphere of the ball. She lets out a dramatic sigh as the glow changes hue to blue and then yellow and, finally, red, which leads me to wonder whether she is controlling it with a foot-pedal.. "I can see a ship and the sea," she says. "The sea is calm and the sky is blue and, provided you steer a careful course and avoid the cross-currents that are generated by your enemies, you can win through to a happy and contented retirement."

"What sort of a ship do you see?" I ask, thinking that she is highly unlikely to come up with a tanker, but she neatly evades committing herself.

"It is not an actual ship I see," she explains. "It is concept of a ship. Like it is the concept of the Sun and the sea. It needs interpretation and there aren't many of us that can do that."

"Tell me more about the course I have to steer and the cross-currents I have to look out for, then," I demand. Having invested so extravagantly in her skills, I intend to get my money's worth.

She makes a great show of consulting her crystal ball again. "Venus and the Moon are in conjunction right now," she tells me, "So you need to avoid becoming too involved with women for the next few days unless you are seeking excitement or risk-taking."

That sounds like good advice whatever Venus and the Moon might be up to, I think to myself, but my reply is designed to lead her on rather than to question her performance. "What about those cross-currents?" I ask.

She frowns to herself as she wrestles with this one. "It looks to me as though your enemies might be controlled by Taurus or Scorpio, so you need to look out for a person who throws his weight around and tramples on your plans, or someone who lies in wait and springs out to attack you when you least expect it," she advises. Between them, those profiles could cover just about anyone, I muse. I decide that I have had enough of this mumbo-jumbo.

"So, Taurus and Scorpio, eh?" I say. "A load of bull or a painful sting! Is that it?"

She looks up at me, reprovingly. "There are matters you should not joke about, young man," she warns.

For some minutes, a number of cogs in my mind have been idling away without doing anything useful, like a car's gear-box in neutral. Madame Mernov's last pronouncement changes all that. The cogs mesh as though they have suddenly been shifted into gear, and they produce an illuminating result. I have heard that self-same sentence recently and I know exactly where I heard it. What is more, now that my eyes are accustomed to the gloom, I can see her face quite clearly.

"What has happened to the wart that was on the tip of your nose?" I ask her.

"What are you talking about, dearie?" she asks, sharply.

"I'm talking about Mernov being an anagram of Morven, amongst other things," I tell her.

To her credit, she does not attempt to deny anything.

"So, you have caught me out," she admits. "Well no harm in that. I'm like my 'familiar', you see. Not always the same person."

"You put on a great performance," I tell her, admiringly. "You were very convincing when you were playing the scary witch the other day. So what did happen to your wart?"

"I was convincing because I *was* a witch," she tells me. "And the warts disappear when I rub them with my magic toadstool cream." She reaches down to a basket by her side. "I've got some here if you want to try. It does wonders for your complexion, and you can have it for a special price, only two-pounds fifty."

I look at the jar of cream and then at her, curiously. "Aren't you afraid it will harm people's skin if they put that stuff on. You could be held responsible."

"Nah," she says, "They wouldn't stock it in supermarkets if it wasn't safe. I get it from those giant-size bottles of own-brand body cream they sell for next to nothing on the bottom shelves."

"And then you transfer it to small jars, put your own labels on, and sell it at inflated prices, I suppose," I say. "Don't you have a conscience about that?"

"Certainly not," she says. "If people expect it to work then, in nine cases out of ten, it will work. The placebo effect, that is. It's what all those fancy cosmetic companies depend on."

"So I understand," I say.

"Of course, it works the other way, too," she adds, slyly. "And that is 'specially useful when I happen to be a witch. If people think one of my potions will give them excruciating stomach pains, it very likely will."

"I feel safer when you are a business woman," I tell her. "Selling cheap skin cream at outrageous prices makes you a good business woman too. Do you have a special rig-out for that, when you aren't playing at being a witch or a gypsy fortune-teller? Smart black suit, severe hair-style, sensible shoes, brief case at the ready?"

"I can be who I like, when I like, dearie," she says, tartly, "And just now I am a Romany clairvoyant who is helping to raise funds for the protection of ancient woodland in general, and Hangman's Copse in particular. Do you have a problem with that?"

"None, whatsoever," I assure her, hastily. "In fact, I applaud you. You had me going for a moment when I first came in and you identified me as a sailor. And you were very quick with all that stuff about a sailor's gait. I remember now that I told you I was a sailor when I met you in your fancy-dress witch's outfit the other day."

"Think what you like," she tells me, "But, even if you hadn't told me, I'd have still known you were a sailor by the way you walk."

"I believe you," I say in that tolerant tone of voice that we sceptics use when we do nothing of the sort. "But let's not worry about that. It seems to me we are both on the same side and should be working together. I am here to help save Hangman's Copse from the bull-dozers and I am sure you are serious in wanting to do the same."

"Of course, I'm serious," she says. "I live next door to the Copse, remember, and I need it to collect all my raw materials."

"But you just told me you didn't use them in your creams and potions," I point out.

"True enough," she admits, "But I need them for window-dressing, don't I?" She leans down and lifts up a basket of shrivelled toadstools and wilting nettles. "I don't tell people what's in my preparations because they expect me to keep it secret, but they notice my herbs and fungi and make their own assumptions. It's their imagination that makes it all work."

"Some people might consider it misleading if you sell toadstool cream without any toadstools in it," I suggest, mildly.

"It's just a name," she says. "If you buy Sun cream you don't expect it to include any thermo-nuclear activity."

This doesn't sound to me like a remark a gipsy fortune-teller would come out with and I wonder if she is slipping into yet another of her library of characters. Perhaps an eccentric astro-physicist, - but I don't want to be side-tracked in that direction. I am beginning to think that we ought to be collaborating rather than sparring.

"Listen," I say to her. "My friend, Shorty, and I are investigating a suspected plot to develop Hangman's Copse and what we believe is a related conspiracy to build apartments on the allotments site to the rear of my house."

"And you want my help, do you?" she says, acutely. "Well, it doesn't come cheap."

"You have a quick wit and powers of observation like Sherlock Holmes on one of his better days," I point out. "And you are remarkably good at taking on different guises. You could be a great asset if you were to team up with us."

"I'll think about it," she promises, "But I don't have time to talk any more now. I'll have Emma Gooding chasing me if I don't fleece a few more customers before the afternoon is out. Why don't you bring your friend, Shorty, to my place tomorrow, around three o'clock? You can tell me what you have in mind."

"That's fine," I agree. "We'll fill you in with what we know and you can bring us up to date about any further activity in and around the Copse."

We part on good terms and, as I leave the tent, I come across two couples hovering at the entrance. "Do go in," I tell them, "She's absolutely marvellous. Take her advice and you could make a fortune at the betting shop or at the stock-broker's."

"Really?" they say.

"Absolutely," I assure them. "Best go for the betting shop, There are fewer scoundrels there than at the Stock Exchange. Ask her about the Ascot Gold-Cup."

Having done my bit to advertise Madame Mernov's services, I scan the horizon in all directions to make sure that neither the Major nor the young policeman are in the offing. There is no sign of either of them, so I make a rapid tour of the remaining stalls without feeling the least temptation to part with any more of my hard earned pension on the frivolities that are on offer. Home-made black-currant jam, hand embroidered table napkins and lovingly knitted teapot-cosies all fail to attract me. The toll-collecting lady at the gate was right about that, I tell myself. Men do tend to keep a tight hold of their money on such occasions.

Eventually, I come to the tea marquee which is abuzz with patrons sitting at tables and consuming cream teas which, apart from the beverage itself, appear to be composed of solid cholesterol. The tables and chairs are packed close together and everyone is talking loudly in an attempt to make themselves heard above the ear-numbing decibels of general hubbub. Just the place for eavesdropping on other people's conversations, I decide.

I see immediately that this is not a situation where a hesitant approach is likely to result in any useful progress, so I shoulder my way through the chattering throng until I find a vacant chair at a table for six. Four of its occupants are talking happily amongst themselves. The fifth is an oldish man who appears to be on his own, so I take the chair next to him.

"There is no waitress service," he tells me. "You have to go to the counter and serve yourself."

"Many thanks," I say. "Save this seat for me, would you please?"

I thread my way back through the tables to a long trestle where trays are set out with cups, saucers and plates of scones, pats of butter, jugs of cream and tiny pots of strawberry jam. I pick up a tray, whereupon a lady wearing a floral apron places a pot of tea on it and directs me to the cashier at the end of the table.

"Just the one?" she says. "That will be five pounds, sir."

I know the drill now. "And if I offer you this ten-pound note, you wouldn't be allowed to give me any change," I suggest.

She beams at me. "That is correct, sir," she agrees.

"Do you take cheques or credit cards?" I ask.

"No, I'm afraid not, sir," she says, patiently. "But if you give me the tenner you would be entitled to take two trays."

"It seems to me I am taking my life in my hands eating this single portion of pastry, cream and butter in one sitting as it is," I grumble, "And I certainly wouldn't risk doubling up."

At this point, she decides that the matter has been discussed for ling enough. She snatches the ten-pound note from my limp fingers and stows it away in the standard shoe-box. "Best bring a friend with you, next time, sir. Either that or make sure you have smaller denomination notes."

She turns away to serve another customer and I carry my tray back to the table where the elderly man is working his way through his second scone. "This place is one great extortion racket," I tell him. "They'd have the shirt off your back if you didn't keep the buttons done up."

He has a drooping mouth and long-suffering eyes, like a walrus with toothache. "You don't have much experience of fêtes and such like, do you?" he says, sadly. "My wife loves them, so I speak from long experience. It is standard practice for them to turn a bloke upside down and shake all the money out of his pockets."

"Why are you here on your own then?" I ask, curiously.

"Oh, I'm not on my own," he assures me with a worried glance towards the door of the marquee. "My wife is doing the rounds of all the stalls. Fortunately I have a gammy leg which invariably becomes acutely painful at events like this, so I can hole-up here and I am not expected to trail around all the other offerings."

"It sounds as though you have it all sorted," I suggest.

"The bring-and-buy sales are the worst," he muses. "We bring some old junk that has been cluttering up the house for years, but then the wife tours the stalls and usually buys more stuff than we came with. It defeats the whole purpose if you ask me. Sometimes, she even buys back the items we donated. How's that for crazy economics?"

I shake my head sympathetically, but I have in mind to steer our conversation towards a more relevant topic. "What do you feel about the object of this fête?" I ask him.

"I've really no idea what it's all in aid of," he says, apologetically, "And I don't believe the wife has, either. Something to do with saving something or other I seem to remember seeing on the banner."

Clearly, this chap and his wife are indiscriminate fête-goers, and small matters like the cause that is being supported or the destination of the funds raised, are of no interest. I make a show of concentrating on my cream tea while, at the same time, trying to tune my ears so as to pick up key words from the surrounding conversations. Almost all are of every-day topics, but I have spotted Emma Gooding with some friends two tables away and I try to home in on that. It seems that they may be discussing how to make the best use of the proceeds of the afternoon's shake-down, but it is too distant, and there is too much background noise, to make out more than the odd phrases. "Instruct lawyers." "Lobby the Council." "Save the wild-life." That kind of thing.

I finish my cream-laden scone and decide that there is little chance of learning anything useful in this environment, so I say farewell to my gloomy companion, who manages a wan smile as I leave him waiting, patiently, for his errant wife to return. Presumably that will be when she has spent the whole of the week's housekeeping money and bought nothing remotely useful.

By this time, it appears that the event is beginning to wind down and I decide that I might as well be amongst those punters who are already heading for the gate. As I wander in that direction, I pass a recess in a yew hedge and there, sitting on a bench and writing something on a pad, is Diana Hunter. When she sees me, she pats the bench by her side as an invitation to sit beside her. I take the offered place and she puts the pad away in her bag.

"I'm sorry I had to rush off earlier, before we had finished speaking," she begins, "But the last thing I needed was to have an embarrassing meeting with Buster Crump."

"You are lucky he didn't catch up with you," I say. "How did you manage to avoid him at a relatively small gathering like this?"

She attempts to look contrite, but it is not an expression that sits well in her repertoire. "Well, I ducked into the house where Daddy was sitting with Emma Gooding and mentioned that I had seen a suspicious looking character lurking behind the tents and that he had stared at me in a frightening way."

"You shopped poor Buster," I exclaim, horrified.

"Well, not by name, of course," she says. "I just gave Daddy a description that happened to fit Buster. Then Daddy got hold of his tame policeman and they charged off round the garden looking for the intruder."

"And Buster took fright and left the scene, I suppose," I say.

"We must presume so," she says, primly. "I haven't seen him since. That boy has the courage of a nervous rabbit."

This is a girl who will stop at nothing, I tell myself but, at least it explains why the Major and his faithful constable had been on the prowl, and I am relieved to have it confirmed that it was not me they were after.

"By the way," I say. "You might have let me know that you had told Felicity Wright about the dormice. She came to see me yesterday and practically accused me of being deceitful because I had kept their presence under my hat."

"Oh! Sorry about that," says Diana, airily. "There's so much on my mind, you know, and there just wasn't the opportunity."

"I must say, you don't give the impression of having more on your mind than you can cope with," I tell her. "In fact you seem to have plenty of spare capacity to manipulate other people's minds, like your father's and the policeman's and Buster's and probably mine as well."

"Oh! How could you possibly think such a thing?" she protests, with pretended confusion. "And me just a frail young woman in a man's world."

Yes, I think to myself, like a Portuguese man-of-war is a frail jellyfish, but one should keep clear of its spreading tentacles unless one wants to be seriously stung.

"There is something else I wanted to ask you," I say, "And I hope it won't send your delicate little female brain into a dither. Do you know if your father has had any contact with Oliver Crump? About Hangman's Copse, for example?"

Diana gives this question some consideration before she answers, "The impression I get it that they dislike each other intensely," she says, at length. "It is certainly an interesting notion that they might, secretly, get together but, as far as I know, it has not happened."

"It was just a thought," I tell her.

"Rather more than that," I suspect," says Diana. "Now what made you ask a thing like that, I wonder?"

I am too wary of her to give a direct answer. "Why don't you have a word with Mrs Gooding about it?" I suggest.

"Very well," agrees Diana. "Since you insist on being mysterious, I'll do just that."

I get to my feet with less alacrity than would have been the case thirty years ago, but without too much creaking of my joints. "If there is nothing else, I'll be getting along," I say.

"I'll look in on you tomorrow morning, if that is OK," says Diana. "I might pick up the dormice if I can get everything organised in time but, more probably, I'll have to leave them for another day."

"Try and make it tomorrow," I urge her. "The sooner I get those little beasts off my hands the better I'll be pleased."

Diana also rises to her feet. "I'll take your advice and have a chat with Emma while I have the opportunity," she says. "I'll see you tomorrow, Bill Selsey."

We part amicably and I walk the two blocks to pick up my car.

CHAPTER 27

I have plenty to occupy my mind as I drive home from the fête. By the time I arrive, Kevin and Sean have long gone and it is with a light heart that I enter my house. I am cheered by the thought that the dormice might soon be moving out.

My first indication of impending disaster becomes apparent as soon as I open the kitchen door. Instead of Barnacle strolling over to greet me, I see that he is cowering under his chair. His dilated eyes watch my every movement and I am sure that, beneath his thick fur, there lurks the frown of a deeply worried cat.

"What's wrong, Barney?" I ask him. "What have you been up to this time?"

Then it hits me. The dormice! Did I shut the dining room door properly after I had introduced the mice to Felicity before lunch? I rush to check and, sure enough, the door is ajar. One look inside the room is enough to confirm my worst fears. The cage has been nudged off the table and lies on its side on the floor. It must have fallen on a corner causing the bars to become buckled and bent, leaving plenty of space for the dormice to escape or, worse still, a cat to insert a paw.

I pick up the cage and turn it this way and that, hoping against hope that I might find a mouse or two still inside, but there is nothing. I look around the room, under chairs and behind furniture, searching in likely, unlikely and, finally, quite impossible places, but there is not a mouse to be seen. Not even a whisker.

I return to the kitchen where Barnacle clearly has no intention of leaving his defensive position. I can see no mouse remains which I would expect if he had eaten them, but that still seems to me the most likely outcome.

"Alright, Barney," I tell him, wearily, "You were just being a cat, and it was my fault for leaving the dining room door open, but don't go thinking that lets you off the hook completely."

Barnacle appears to relax slightly, but he stays where he feels safe. Meanwhile, I sit at the table with my head in my hands as I ponder the immediate future. It does not make pleasant pondering.

"Well, sitting here worrying is not going to help matters," I tell Barnacle. I look at the clock and note that it is just before five. If I am quick, I should be able to make the pet shop before it closes. I am not particularly anxious to meet up again with the young lady assistant there, but I recognise that a desperate situation calls for desperate measures.

I make a sprint for my car and surprise even myself by taking less than five minutes to arrive at the pet shop. I dash in, hoping that someone other than the young lady might be on duty but, in this, I am disappointed. She recognises me immediately.

"And what can I do for you this time, Sir?" she asks, suspiciously.

"Listen, this might sound strange," I begin, "But I need to buy some mice that are not actually dormice, but that, as nearly as possible, look like dormice."

"You will have to be more specific, sir," she says. "There are nearly thirty different species of dormice, and they all look different."

This puts me on the wrong foot at once, which I am sure is what she intended.

"I want proper British dormice," I tell her. "The ones you find in woodlands around the country."

"That would be hazel dormice, then," she says. "They are protected animals, as you well know."

"That's why I want unprotected pet mice that look like dormice but aren't," I explain. She wilfully continues to misunderstand me.

"Why do I get the impression that you are trying to buy some genuine dormice but you want me to tell you that they are perfectly legal pet mice?" she asks. "I really feel I should report you for attempting to traffic in an endangered species."

"I am *not* looking for actual dormice," I tell her, so forcibly that she backs away from the counter in fright. "I just need animals that look like dormice. What about gerbils or hamsters?"

"If you try to intimidate me, I will call the police," she warns. "And, for your information, no-one who knows the first thing about small mammals would mistake gerbils or hamsters for dormice. Nor would they be fooled by domestic mice for that matter. For one thing, dormice have furry tails."

I take a grip on myself. It is doing no good to become worked up by this annoying young woman. I take a deep breath and speak to her in a more conciliatory tone. "Look here," I say, quietly and reasonably. "Never mind about the exact pedigree. Will you please sell me half a dozen of the nearest small mammal you have to the hazel dormouse?"

She gives a half smile as she hands out the clincher. "As a matter of policy, we never keep live pets of any kind on the premises," she says. "We only stock pet-food and animal welfare products."

My new-found calm evaporates in a flash. "Why didn't you tell me that at the beginning, you daft girl?" I explode. "It would have saved your time and, more importantly, my time."

"I thought it would be best to keep you talking until the police arrive." She explains, with what can only be construed as a smirk.

I do not believe she has had the opportunity to call the police, unless she has some kind of a panic button under the counter. And that seems unlikely. She is serving in a pet-shop and not a bank. On the other hand, it doesn't seem wise to call her bluff, so I exit the shop smartly and am soon driving home with nothing but a black cloud of frustration to show for my excursion.

I park the car, and disperse a little of the black cloud by kicking the tyres. Then I walk around the back of my house so I can look over the allotments to see if there is any sign of life in Shorty's shed. As I expect, there is none. He is usually home with Mary at this time of the day. They will be enjoying a pre-dinner drink together and bringing each other up-to-date with happenings during the earlier part of the day when they had gone their separate ways. I am always reluctant to intrude upon them at this time, even with a phone call.

When I re-enter the kitchen, I find Barnacle is less uptight, but still watching me warily and not allowing me to approach closer than an arm's length. The thought of Shorty and Mary having a drink together suggests to me that it might help my own case. I reach up to my cupboard and decide that the situation is serious enough to require something special. I select a single malt whisky and pour myself a generous tot.

It is going to take a little while for this treatment to show any effect, I tell myself and, in the meantime, I feel a need to share my problems with someone understanding. Shorty is unavailable and Barnacle, however inappropriately for a feline, is in the dog-house. I fall to wondering who else I might confide in.

Then the telephone rings and I snatch at it, gratefully like a man-overboard welcoming a lifebelt thrown to him.

"Is that Mr Selsey?" comes a voice which I immediately recognise as Buster Crump's. Just my luck, I think to myself, when I had been hoping to speak to a rational human being.

"Yes, Buster." I admit, wearily. "Bill Selsey speaking."

"I still haven't been able to talk to Diana," he tells me. "She seemed to disappear completely at the fête, and I am desperate to make up with her."

"Well, I did advise you not to go chasing after her," I remind him.

"Yes, I know," he agrees. "I believe you really want to help, and Diana seems to trust you. I am on my bike and only a few streets away from your place. I would be very grateful for a chat. Could I take you out for a drink?"

Buster is not a person I would choose for a convivial chat over a beer or two but it occurs to me that, when Diana finds out about the demise of the dormice, I will be in as much trouble with her as Buster is. There is a need for alliances at such times and one cannot afford to be too picky with whom one forms them.

"Come round to my place, Buster," I tell him. "I don't feel like spending the evening in a pub, but I can find you a beer, or something stronger."

"That's great, Mr Selsey," he gushes. "I'll be with you in two minutes."

He rings off, and I can imagine him firing up his bike and scorching a path to my door. In fact it is not much longer than his two minute estimate before my door-bell rings and I find him standing on my doorstep. With his helmet under his arm and his collar turned up to hide most of his face, he looks like a headless spectre. At my invitation, he strides into the kitchen, takes a chair, and places his helmet carefully on the table. I check carefully to satisfy myself that his head is not still inside it and am relieved to find that it remains on his shoulders, although looking absurdly small compared to the bulk of his motor-cycling gear.

Barnacle is not enjoying a happy evening and the sight of the heavily built Buster storming into the kitchen in full biker gear is enough to send him scuttling under his chair again. I am not disposed to sympathise with him and I address myself to Buster.

"I'm on to whisky already," I tell him. "But I can do you a beer if you prefer, - or even a tomato juice if you want to feel safe driving the motorised monstrosity of yours."

"I ought to have the tomato juice, but I need the whisky," Buster tells me. "I am in such despair at the thought of losing Diana that I feel almost suicidal, and that is more dangerous for a biker than being over the alcohol limit."

I pour a generous glass of whisky for Buster and he takes a gulp before settling back in his chair and looking at me with the sad, but hopeful, eyes of a much put-upon spaniel.

"You have to help me, Mr Selsey," he pleads. "What can I do?"

Counselling lovelorn morons is not something of which I have had much experience, and my instinct for self-preservation is urging me towards caution. As I have mentioned before, Buster has the build of a bloke who sprinkles steroids on his breakfast cornflakes so it would not be wise to offer advice that might irritate him. I decide to tread carefully.

"There are a great many young women of your age in the world," I tell him. "Are you absolutely sure that Diana is the only one for you? She is not the easiest person to get along with."

"That's what makes her so special," enthuses Buster. "She has so many brilliant ideas. Exciting wheezes that I would never think of."

This is going completely against the folk-wisdom which holds that men are frightened of entering into relationships with more intelligent women. I can only conclude that Buster is too thick to be aware of the danger. It is looking like a hopeless case, but I give it another try.

"You are a well set-up young man," I tell Buster, "And you cut a glamorous figure roaring around the streets on your Harley-Davidson. You must have adventurous girls clamouring for a chance to ride on back of your bike. Surely you find a few of them attractive. Your life would be much simpler if you were to take up with someone like that."

"That's all very well, Mr Selsey," he says, "But I don't want a simple life. I want an exciting life, and Diana can give me that in bucketsfull. She is the only woman I could ever love. I must find out how to make her fond of me again. No-one else could possibly do."

We sit for a few minutes, staring into space and sipping our drinks as I realign my thoughts. Clearly, some major commitment is needed on Buster's part if he is going to regain Diana's favour. I ask him the same question as I had asked Diana.

"Do you know if your father has had any contact with Major Hunter recently? About Hangman's Copse, for example?"

Buster looks up with a start. "Felicity Wright asked me that," he says. "I told you about it, didn't I?"

"Yes, you did," I agree. "You told me that she had wanted you to keep a look-out for any evidence that they had corresponded. So, did you find any?"

"What has this to do with me and Diana?" he asks, with a puzzled expression.

"I think it might have," I assure him, as I top up his glass. "Just bear with me."

"Alright, I'll trust you, Mr Selsey, Well, I didn't find out much, but the Gov'nor did mention to me one evening that he was planning a new development and that he had even been able to reach an agreement with Henry Hunter. He was exceptionally pleased because they don't like each other, normally."

"Can you tell me more about it?" I ask. "Where the development was to take place, or who else might be involved?"

"Sorry," apologises Buster. "I should have paid more attention. The Gov'nor is always trying to get me interested in his work, but I've got into the habit of switching off once he starts on that subject. I am not turned on by all the wheeling and dealing that he gets into and I am sure I would not be very good at it."

"Listen, Buster" I say, "It seems to me that your father and Major Hunter are planning to flatten Hangman's Copse and develop the site for housing. If you are really serious in wanting to regain Diana's affection, you will have to help save the Copse, and that means working against your father's plans."

Buster absorbs this information. Then his brow creases into a painful frown as he considers the implications.

"The Gov'nor wouldn't like that," he pronounces, at length. "He is unhappy with me as it is, because I don't want to become involved in his company. He says I am work-shy and he's very reluctant to give me my allowance and to pay for my Harley Davidson. He would cut that off like a shot if I were to really upset him."

"I can see your difficulty," I tell him, sympathetically, "But it does seem to me that you may have to choose between Diana and your motor-bike."

There is another pause for thought as he wrestled with this dilemma. As a hot-headed young man, with more testosterone than sense, I expect him to protest his undying love for Diana and a willingness to consign the Harley to the scrap heap rather than lose Diana but he does not come up with this nor, indeed, any other conclusion.

"Hmm. Tricky one, that," he murmurs.

I look at him with a new respect. It seems that logical processes do sometimes occur in the grey gunge that occupies his cranium. At the same time, I can see that his careful weighing of the pros and cons in this particular case would not, if she knew about it, endear him to Diana.

"Sleep on it," I advise him. "Life is full of difficult decisions."

Instead of answering, Buster takes a gulp of whisky and slumps disconsolately in his chair. Barnacle observes this from his own hide-out and decides that, for the time being, Buster is less threatening than I am. He creeps across the carpet and rubs his head against Buster's leg while, at the same time, keeping safely out of my reach. Buster automatically lowers his hand and ruffles the fur on the cat's head, and Barnacle looks across at me as much as to say, well, at least somebody still loves me.

While this has been going on, I have been wondering whether to tell Buster about the absentee, and probably deceased, dormice. It seems sensible to tell as few people as possible, but I remind myself that he already knows about Diana lodging them in my house and there is just a chance that he might be able to help in some way. I take a swig of my drink.

"As a matter of fact, the need for another decision has arisen," I tell Buster. "You remember Diana gave me some dormice to look after?"

"Yes, of course," says Buster, arousing himself from his reverie. "How are the little creatures?"

"They aren't," I tell him. "There is an acute shortage of dormice on the premises, and Diana will be coming tomorrow morning to pick them up."

"She can't pick them up if they aren't here," points out Buster, arriving quickly at the nub of the problem.

"You've got it in one," I tell him.

"So, where are they?" asks Buster, "You must recover them before Diana arrives."

"I am not entirely sure where they are," I confess, "But I strongly suspect they are inside that cat you are fondling."

Buster removes his hand, smartly from the top of Barnacle's head and looks at him, aghast. "Is that right?" he demands.

Barnacle continues to rub his whiskers against Buster's trouser leg in his, 'What me? Of course not!' manner, but he receives no more stroking.

"Diana doesn't know about this, yet," I explain.

"Well I'm not going to tell her," says Buster. "I am unpopular enough with her already."

I hold up my hand. "No. No. Of course not," I reassure him. "I wouldn't think of asking you to do such a thing. On the other hand, I am not looking forward to telling her, myself."

"She'll go through the roof," predicts Buster, apprehensively. "It will be like launching a ballistic missile indoors."

We sit and contemplate this outcome, and then drain the rest of our whisky to steady our nerves. I replenish our glasses before speaking again.

"I am not sure exactly how it would work, Buster," I say, "But you might be able to turn this situation to your advantage. I shall have to take the blame for wrecking Diana's scheme for using the dormice but, if you can then come up with a way of recovering the situation, I am sure she would be enormously grateful to you. You would become her knight in shining leathers, no less."

Buster reverts to the agonised face he wears when he is thinking. "Do you really believe that, Mr Selsey?" he asks, eventually.

"Of course Buster," I reassure him. "It is classic psychology. The stuff of fairy tales. The hero riding to rescue the distressed heroine and slaying the dragon of despair."

His face lightens for a moment but then darkens again as he remembers that there is a condition to be fulfilled before this happy outcome can be achieved. "So you have lost the dormice," he says. "But how do I go about retrieving the situation? Diana needed those mice to show that Hangman's Copse is home to an endangered species."

"I haven't got that far, yet," I admit. "I am just setting out a possibility. It will need a bit of thought to work out the detail." I clap him on the back. "I am sure a young chap like you will come up with something."

"Well I'm not at all sure," complains Buster, as though I am putting an impossible load on his mental capabilities. "You have given me two things to think about now. I not only have to choose between Diana and my Harley, but I also have to think up an alternative to the dormice for protecting the Copse."

"You will have to make the first decision on your own," I explain. "But I'll be giving some thought to the second and I'm sure we'll come up with something between us."

"Well, at least I can see the problems a little clearer now," admits Buster, "Although you haven't actually solved anything for me."

"Give it time," I tell him. "The great gyro-compass engineer, Elmer Sperry, once said that ninety percent of any invention lies in a clear statement of the problem it is intended to address."

"I hope you are right, Mr Selsey," says Buster, uncertainly, as though he is wondering why I have brought gyroscopes into the conversation. "But time is something we don't have much of if Diana is expecting to pick up the dormice tomorrow morning."

"I'll tell you what," I say. "Give me a ring about nine-thirty in the morning and we can discuss whatever ideas you might have come up with overnight. Then, if we think we have hit the jack-pot you could come round while Diana is here and explain it all to her. She would be bound to look more kindly on you again."

Buster has taken to scratching an appreciative Barnacle again, but he eases him away as he stands up to leave. "Thanks for the drink and the chat, Mr Selsey," he says. "And don't be too hard on your cat. It's not his fault. Catching mice is hard-wired into his brain."

So, I think to myself, Buster is a big softy, after all. I rise to my feet to see him off the premises. "Yes, I agree he couldn't help it," I say. "It's genetic, like blokes are constitutionally incapable of remembering birthdays, and women have a built in compulsion to buy shoes. Don't worry, I'll have forgiven him by tomorrow, I promise."

Buster fastens his helmet as he walks down the path and mounts his gleaming Harley-Davidson. He brings the engine to life, revs up for effect, and then roars off along the road before the neighbours have time to open their windows and complain about the noise. I can easily see why he had been so torn between the alternatives of giving up his bike or giving up on Diana.

CHAPTER 28

I wander back into the kitchen where Barnacle, having lost his new friend and protector, is still not sure how safe he might be. I put some fresh food in his bowl and he approaches it with caution and sniffs suspiciously as though he suspects I might have slipped some arsenic into his chunky chicken pieces. He does, warily, eat some and, in so doing, reminds me that it is time for my own supper. I am not in the mood for cooking, but I find a ready-made curry-and-rice meal in the freezer and transfer it to the microwave. I make myself a mug of coffee, retrieve a jar of mango-chutney to complement my Rogan Josh and, in a few minutes, I am tucking into it. Of course, I am sad about the presumed fate of the dormice, but it is not going to make things any better if I starve myself.

On the other hand, I do feel responsible for their demise, and I decide that it would be heartless to spend the rest of the evening watching the occasionally amusing bilge that forms a normal evening of television entertainment. In any case, I need to do some serious thinking about how I am going to break the news to Diana tomorrow morning.

I know I have set this as one of the tasks Buster should be addressing, but I have no faith at all that he will come up with anything remotely useful. Buster's thinking seems to me like Samuel Johnson's dog walking on its hind legs. I do not expect it to be done well, and I will be surprised if it is done at all.

Having finished my supper and cleared the decks, I fall to wondering how best to deal with the disastrous loss of the dormice.

I make little progress and I again feel the need to talk to someone. My chat to Buster has thrown up a few items of interesting flotsam, but he is not the most stimulating of conversationalists. With Shorty off-limits for the evening, I begin to wonder about his earlier advice that my best option might be to leave the country or, at least, go to visit my sister in Barnstable until the whole business has blown over.

Either of these, I decide, would be cowardly actions and neither would be practical until Kevin and Sean, in their leisurely way, have completed the repairs to my house. But I could, perhaps, talk to my sister on the phone.

The reason I hesitate is because she is three years older than I am and, between the ages of four to sixteen, whatever I did was constrained by a bossy big-sister breathing down my neck. It is no wonder I ran away to sea before my seventeenth birthday. She has mellowed only marginally during the past sixty-plus years, so initiating a conversation with her is not something I enter into lightly. The reason I am considering calling her at all is because I remember she once kept hamsters and she does occasionally come up with innovative ideas. She might just be able to suggest something useful. I reach for the phone and punch in her number.

I immediately have second thoughts. Surely, this is like waking a sleeping dragon to get a light for your cigarette. I find myself hoping she will not answer, but no such luck. Her booming voice may have gone up a few semitones as she has aged, but I still have to hold the earpiece at arm's length as she demands to know who is calling her at this time of the evening.

I am tempted to ask whether she needs double glazing or a new kitchen so I can replace the receiver as soon as she gets under way with the wrathful reply she serves up to telephone salesmen but, having come this far, I decide that I might as well keep going.

"Hello Betty," I begin. "Bill here."

"Glory be, little brother," she says. "I am relieved you are safe. It has been such a long time since you called that I thought you'd been abducted by aliens. What trouble have you got yourself into now?"

I ignore the sarcasm, which is only to be expected from a big sister, but I defend myself against her assumption concerning the motive for my call.

"What makes you think I am in trouble?" I ask. "I just thought it would be nice to have a chat and find out how things are going for you."

"I wasn't born yesterday," she tells me, in what must be the understatement of the year. "Of course you are in trouble. It's the only time you ever want to talk to me. I suppose it is some female that has been leading you astray. You sailors are all too easily taken in by a scheming woman. That's why you were always broke by the second evening of your shore leave."

Betty has this knack of putting me on the back foot as soon as we start a conversation. I can imagine how she will be nodding knowingly to herself if I tell her about the way Felicity and Diana have been pressuring me, to say nothing of the threats from Wendy Fyler.

"Listen," I tell her. "This is not about women, it is about dormice and how I might go about finding some. Do you still keep hamsters by any chance?"

"I am a grown woman," she reminds me. "It's seventy years since I was of an age when it seemed an attractive idea to have little furry pets. So why do you suddenly want to share your house with dormice? I always thought you were mentally immature but this is really over the top. I am beginning to suspect that you need counselling?"

This reaction puts me into a near panic. When Betty talks about counselling she has herself in mind as the counsellor. The next thing is she will be bustling up from Barnstable to stay with me for a week or two so she can enjoy making an extensive analysis of my shortcomings, and attempt to bring some unpalatable order into my life. I am already wishing I had gone into my cold-calling salesman act when she first answered the phone.

"I don't need counselling or anything of that kind," I protest with all the force I can muster. "I need the dormice for a serious project, not as pets."

"I remember your serious projects, Bill" says Betty, grimly. "Uncle Fred told you that, if you hold a guinea-pig up by its tail its eyes will fall out, and you would have experimented with my hamsters if I hadn't stopped you."

"I was only five at the time." I remind her.

"And now you want to try the same thing with dormice," she accuses. "Don't you think you should have become a more responsible person after all this time."

This conversation is not going at all in the direction I had hoped. I try to explain that I need the dormice for an attempt to re-establish a viable colony in an area of ancient woodland, and that this is a properly devised, scientific project to help preserve an endangered species of small mammal in an environmentally important tract of woodland. I don't mention that it is intended to deceive the local Council into believing that dormice are indigenous to the site so that it cannot be developed for housing because I know she will misunderstand, and that will lead to further criticisms of my motives.

Of course, she misunderstands anyway.

"Does this scientific project involve holding dormice up by their tails?" she asks, suspiciously.

"Certainly not," I tell her. "We are simply trying to ensure that dormice have a secure future in their natural habitat. I am part of a dedicated team. The wild-life expert, Diana Hunter will release the creatures, and Felicity Wright, a professional journalist, will photograph them as they settle in. This is all about saving the creatures for posterity."

"Hah!" exclaims Betty, triumphantly. "I thought as much. You are involved with two women. No wonder you are out of your depth. I'll pack my bag and catch the train tomorrow. I'll let you know later what time you will need to meet me at the station."

This is turning into my worst nightmare. "No, Betty!" I scream. "You can't come."

I look around, desperately, for a reason as to why she can't come and my eye catches the scaffolding outside the window.

"A tree has fallen on my house," I tell her. "There is no way I could put you up until it is repaired."

Betty snorts with derision. "Really, Bill," she says, severely. "I know it irks you when I visit to try to bring some order into your haphazard lifestyle, but that is the most far-fetched and ridiculous excuse you have ever come up with."

"It is perfectly true," I protest. "The tree has been removed but there is still scaffolding on the side of the house, the wall is being rebuilt, a new window is being fitted and there is still some roofing to be done."

"Have it your own way," says Betty who, all too obviously, does not believe a word I am saying. "As it happens, it would be exceedingly inconvenient for me to come to check up on you tomorrow, so I will postpone my visit. But, don't imagine you are in the clear. I can tell you need help to sort out whatever pickle you have got yourself into, so be sure I will come as soon as I am free of my commitments in Barnstable. I can already see that the first thing that needs to be done is to send those two hussies packing."

A thought comes into my mind that it would be interesting to set Betty onto Wendy Fyler next time she comes knocking on my door, but there is no time to indulge in such fantasies.

"I am perfectly in control of my own affairs, Betty," I assure her. "There is absolutely no need for you to interrupt your peaceful life in Barnstable."

"So why did you phone me in such a panic?" asks Betty.

"I thought you might be able to help me locate some dormice, that's all," I explain. "Or, perhaps you could suggest some small mammals that are similar to dormice. You are so knowledgeable about such things, and I would greatly value your advice."

"You don't get around me with flattery, young Bill, as you should know by now," says Betty, "But, since you ask me, my advice is that you should forget the dormice and forget whatever this project might be, and avoid getting deeper into trouble than you already are."

This is just protective, big-sister talk, I think to myself, by someone who does not believe her younger brother is capable of tying his own shoe laces, let alone operating on his own in a complex world. It is time to take a stronger line with her.

"I am not in trouble," I tell her, "But I do want help to re-establish dormice in our local woodland. Some constructive assistance would be appreciated rather than simply telling me to put up the shutters and batten down the hatches."

"Are you sure you are telling me everything," she asks. "Why do I pick up the impression that you are holding something back?"

Betty's ability to spot when I am trying to hide something from her was a frequent embarrassment to me in my younger days, and in some of my older days as well, for that matter.

"Alright," I agree, and I explain that we are hoping that the presence of an endangered species in Hangman's Copse will cause the abandonment of Council plans to develop it. I expect this exegesis will be met with strong disapproval but, as is often the case, Betty surprises me.

"Twisting the tails of the ungodly, eh?" she says. "I am all for that but, if you are determined to put a toe into such muddy waters, be careful that you don't get out of your depth."

"I'll take care," I promise, "But, now that you have the whole picture, you will understand why I need the dormice."

"Never mind the dormice," she counsels. "There must be other approaches to saving the Copse. Think more widely about what might be done instead. Get Greenpeace and Friends of the Earth to adopt Hangman's copse as a campaign. Encourage activists to set up camp in the woods, perhaps in tree houses. Take the lead yourselves."

I point out that the movement to save the Copse is led by people like Emma Gooding and Diana Hunter, neither of whom are the type to camp out in a dark and muddy copse.

"You wouldn't catch me there either," I tell her. "It's probably malarial."

"Faint-hearted lot," pronounces Betty. "I'd be there myself if I were forty years younger. You need someone to put some backbone into your team."

I am alarmed by Betty's renewed threat to descend on me, and I decide it is time to bring our conversation to an end.

"Well, thanks for the advice, Betty," I tell her. "It has been good talking to you, as always."

"You should try it more often," she replies, sharply. "And don't think for a minute that I believe you are capable of coping with all this on your own."

"I spent nearly fifty years sailing the seven seas," I protest, "And I never once bumped into a reef or another ship. I have always been able to look after myself."

"You are clever enough," she concedes, "And lucky with it, but you have never had your full quota of common sense. I still have every intention of coming to straighten you out before too long."

"I might be going abroad," I mutter, remembering Shorty's advice.

"No you won't," she says. "You won't leave that spoiled cat of yours. Barnacle, isn't it? I don't approve of him in general but, at least, he has a steadying influence on you."

"I have no intention of spending the rest of the evening listening to Betty's views on my relationship with Barney. "Good-night, Betty," I say.

"And good-night to you, young Bill," she replies. "Just try and keep yourself out of trouble."

We ring off, and I am left to wonder whether there was any point in calling Betty in the first place. Probably not, I decide, but it has cured my craving for someone to talk to. A session with Betty is enough to satisfy a chap's need for conversing with anyone for a couple of decades.

It is with some relief that I turn to Barnacle. It is time to make it up with him. He has come out from under his chair but is not yet confident enough to approach me too closely. I reach out a hand and he steps carefully forward to allow me to scratch him behind his ears.

"That was your Auntie Betty on the phone," I tell him. "It was a mistake to ring her because she is now threatening to come to organise our way of life. If you remember, it took nearly a month for us to recover from her last visit, and she only stayed for a long weekend."

Barnacle relaxes as he realises that I am no longer dangerous to approach. He rolls over and offers his expansive waistline for my attention.

"Perhaps she was right, though," I add. "Maybe the dormice are not indispensable. There must be other ways in which we can prevent development of the Copse."

Barnacle begins to purr loudly, which I take as agreement. Then I take a beer from the fridge, retrieve a copy of Shorty's Situation Chart from my coat pocket, and settle down to spend the rest of the evening on some hard thinking.

From what Buster told me, I feel justified in adding a line linking Major Hunter and Oliver Crump. I also add a box for Emma Gooding with links to Diana Hunter, Major Hunter and Hangman's Copse. I wonder, for a while, whether to include a box for Peggy Morven (or should it be Madame Mernov?) to the chart, but I decide that she is a peripheral player in the overall game and that it would increase the complexity of the connections without adding much of value.

Then I put my mind to considering how the Copse might be saved now that the dormice are no longer in the equation. In this, I am unsuccessful but, by the time I have finished my second beer and a whiskey chaser, and I am preparing for bed, the problem does seem to have lost its urgency.

CHAPTER 29

The next morning, I am sitting at the breakfast table, with Barnacle on his chair at my right elbow. Mostly I restrict myself to muesli with an added handful of blueberries, and a marmalade or cheese-filled croissant if I am feeling extravagant. Full English breakfasts are a distant memory of the time when my digestive system and my appetite were much younger.

The present table contains little of interest to a cat, but I deploy the cheese-slicer to detach a thin sliver of Edam and offer it to him. He accepts, politely but without enthusiasm and then looks at me with his 'I'm sure you could do better than this' expression. I have just drained my first cup of coffee when the telephone rings. I glance at the clock . That will be Buster Crump, right on nine-thirty, I suspect. And so it proves.

"Mr Selsey," comes his excited voice through the ear-piece. "Is Diana with you yet?"

"No, Buster," I tell him. "She didn't say she would be here at a specific time. Why don't you try phoning later?"

"I think I've got it," says Buster, who is clearly in transmitting, rather than receiving, mode.

"What have you got, Buster?" I enquire, sourly. "You needn't come near me if it is contagious."

"No! No! There's nothing wrong with me," says Buster. A statement with which I am sure many people would disagree. "No! I have come up with a great idea about how we can make up for the lost dormice."

That Buster should actually produce a useful idea seems to me about as likely as coming across a vegetarian crocodile, but I feel it is only good manners to enquire as to what his idea might be.

"Tell me about it," I invite him.

"I'll explain everything when I come round," he promises. "I'd like Diana to be one of the first to hear it all."

I accept that, since his main motivation is to make a favourable impression on Diana, this is not an unreasonable suggestion.

"Alright, Buster," I tell him. "Why don't you come here at about ten-thirty. I expect she will have arrived by then, and I'll be glad enough to have you around to take her mind off the deficiency of dormice."

"That sounds good, Mr Selsey," he says, enthusiastically. "I can't wait to explain my plan."

Following this conversation with Buster, I sink a second cup of coffee and, as I clear the breakfast table and put things away, I begin to anticipate the interview with Diana that is going to take place in the very near future. It does not give me any cause for optimism. I am still not decided as to how I can gently break the news about the departure of the dormice.

I alternately sit despondently and pace the floor irritably, without coming to any conclusion until, just after ten o'clock, the doorbell rings. As I go to open it, I fall to wondering why I ever imagined that retirement ashore would be less stressful than my life at sea.

"Hello Bill," says Diana, brightly. "It's a beautiful morning."
I swallow hard. This is going to be difficult. "Yes, it is, sort of," I agree.

"You are always over-cautious," she says, as she follows me into the kitchen. "You need to cultivate a more carefree attitude to life."

"Not much chance of that today," I tell her, "I'm afraid I have some unwelcome news."

She is immediately alert, and looks at me appraisingly. "Go on," she says.

"It's, er, it's about the dormice," I stutter. "They appear to have gone missing."

"Gone missing?" she repeats, ominously. "Gone missing spontaneously in the sense that no-one else was involved in their disappearance, least of all you?"

"Well, I might have just left a door ajar while I was at the fête so that Barnacle could get into their room and pull their cage off the table."

"Are you suggesting that Barnacle is to blame?" she asks.

"Oh no," I say, hurriedly. "Certainly not. It was my fault, entirely."

"So where do you think they might have gone?" she enquires with an unnerving calm.

"I really don't know," I confess, "But my best guess is that they are somewhere in Barnacle's digestive system."

"You are not trying to blame that poor cat again, are you?" she demands. "If you allow cats and mice to run around together, what do you expect?"

"I didn't *allow* it." I protest. "It was an accident. Just one of those things."

"You show a worrying lack of common sense and responsibility, Bill Selsey," she tells me, echoing sister Betty's similar diagnosis of yesterday evening.

"So I've been told," I admit, "But we mustn't be dismayed by a minor set-back like this. In the regrettable absence of endangered rodents, there will obviously be other ways in which we can proceed with our campaign to save Hangman's Copse."

"Of course there will be," says Diana, coldly, "And I am sure you are now going to propose a few of these alternatives for me."

Well, there she has me, of course. I have been racking my brain for hours without coming up with a remotely practical plan. I doesn't seem a good move to bring Buster Crump into play at this point, - or at any other point for that matter, but I have nowhere else to go.

"Buster phoned me this morning, and he says he has a brilliant idea for saving the Copse despite having lost the dormice," I tell her.

Diana looks at me as though I have taken leave of my senses. "Brilliant ideas and Buster Crump do not inhabit the same universe," she tells me. "It's like matter and anti-matter. Completely incompatible."

This is an assessment with which I entirely agree, but I feel bound to argue Buster's corner. "You should really be kinder to Buster," I tell her. "I haven't heard his idea yet, but he has already conducted some useful espionage for us. He tells me that his father and your father have come to some kind of agreement concerning a proposed collaboration and, bearing in mind your Dad's ownership of Hangman's Copse, and Oliver's involvement in the planning application, it is not hard to speculate what that collaboration might be about."

I am pleased to see that this news takes much of the wind out of Diana's sails.

"Now that is a surprise," she says. "A double surprise in fact. I never thought that Daddy and Oliver Crump would ever agree on anything, and I am amazed that Buster had the bottle to find out about it. Perhaps I have been underestimating the boy."

It is on the tip of my tongue to suggest that it would be quite difficult to underestimate Buster, but I feel a duty to act in his best interests, and I am relieved that the topic has diverted Diana from her displeasure at my failure to protect her precious dormice. A pro-Buster policy seems the best one to continue with.

"I am sure Buster has hidden depths." I say.

"Remarkably well hidden, if you ask me," comments Diana, "But I am impressed that he has shown the initiative to discover at least one item of considerable interest. If Daddy and Oliver Crump are, indeed, in cahoots, then we only need a connection between one of them and the Verdant Heritage Company, and we'll have a good indication of what is going on."

I dust off my sage, grand-old-man expression that Shorty says makes me look like a drunken owl. "It's always a good policy to identify the enemy before you start a war." I say.

"A military expert now, are we?" says Diana, cynically. "You should get together with Daddy one evening. You can re-fight every major battle since Julius Caesar and he'll explain exactly where they messed up."

"What I am saying is that Buster has been helpful so far. He has discovered one crucial connection and he might well be able to find some others."

Diana looks thoughtful. "You may be right," she agrees. "Buster can be irritating but he means well and he is the best lead we have for discovering what Oliver is up to. I agree it is time to bring him back into the fold."

I consult my watch "No difficulty with that," I tell her. "He is due here any minute, and I am sure he will be bursting to tell us about this 'brilliant' idea he has come up with."

"An idea for a way forward now that you have carelessly misplaced the dormice, you say?" she frowns.

"Er. Yes. You could put it like that," I admit.

"And there was I thinking it wouldn't be a difficult thing to ask you to do," she sighs.

"Alright. Alright. I'm sorry," I say, as I wonder how it has come about that we have switched topics back to the dormice again. I am trying to work out how to nudge the conversation back to the less fraught subject of Buster when a peal of the doorbell solves the problem for me.

"I expect that will be Buster now," I say, in what I am sure is a relieved tone of voice.

I answer the door and find Buster standing there with his head under his arm as usual. For once, I usher him in as a welcome guest and Barnacle, perhaps remembering how well they got on yesterday evening, lopes over to greet him. But, elsewhere, there is ice to be broken. For an awkward moment, Buster and Diana eye each other across the kitchen table, with Buster especially ill at ease and unsure how to start.

"Hello, Buster," says Diana, as the moment passes. "I hear you have been doing some enterprising detective work and that you have a bright idea to share with us."

Buster is clearly overwhelmed by the realisation that this aptly named goddess is deigning to speak to him again. "Oh, definitely, Di," he stammers. "I've been thinking about you all the time, and how I might be able to help with your plan to save Hangman's Copse."

"You weren't much help at the protest meeting," she tells him, with what seems to me an unfeeling reminder of his ungallant role on that occasion.

"Buster has more than made up for that," I tell her. "And I suggest we move forward rather than dwell on the past. Let's sit round the table and consider the situation positively."

Buster treats me with one of his fawning, puppy-dog looks, while Barnacle jumps up onto a chair next to his new friend. Diana looks hard at Buster for a moment and then appears to decide that it is, perhaps, time to let him off the hook.

"Bill tells me you have discovered that our fathers are working together on some kind of project." She says. "Have you been able to find out any more about it?"

"I haven't had much time since I saw Mr Selsey yesterday evening," apologises Buster, "But I have remembered something else that might be useful."

"Go on then, Buster," she urges him. "Tell us about it."

"Well, you know the Gov'nor is always trying to get me interested in his business affairs. Like I told Mr Selsey," He glances at me in an invitation to corroborate this statement, and I nod, encouragingly. "I usually switch off as soon as he starts that kind of thing but, I've remembered that, the last time he tried it, he wanted me to become a director of one of his subsidiary companies."

He has the full attention of both of us, but it appears he has completed what he has to say.

"So, what is the name of the company?" Asks Diana, impatiently, whereupon Buster stares blankly at her and then at me.

"Try to remember the name of the company," I urge.

In an effort to stimulate his memory cells, Buster frowns and slaps the side of his head. From the twitching of Diana's hands, I can see that he has only just forestalled her from doing it for him. However that might be, the treatment does have some effect.

"I thought it sounded like an American company," he says. "What is that State right up in the north?"

"Alaska?" queries Diana.

"No! The other side," says Buster. "Begins with a V."

"Vermont," I suggest. "In New England."

"That's it," agrees Buster. "I'm not sure I want to go to Vermont. Not without Di, anyway."

"What else can you remember?" prompts Diana.

"I think it had something to do with witches, as well," offers Buster.

"New England was certainly associated with witches," I say. "That does make some sort of sense."

"No, it doesn't," objects Diana. "The famous witches were in Salem and that's Massachusetts, not Vermont."

"I expect they burnt a few in Vermont as well," I say. "All those pine trees. They'd have had plenty of fire-wood."

"They didn't burn the witches, they hanged them," Diana corrects me. "It was heretics that got burnt."

Buster startles us by bringing his fist down hard on the table. "Heretics!" he cries. "That's what the company was all about. Not witches at all. Vermont Heretics."

Diana and I exchange glances and celebrate with a 'high five' meeting of hands.

"Verdant Heritage!" we shout together.

"That's what I just said, isn't it?" says Buster.

"That's exactly what you said, Buster" I tell him.

"My hero," exclaims Diana, throwing dignity and decorum to the wind as she rewards Buster with an enthusiastic kiss.

Barnacle emits a warning growl, probably because he thinks his friend is under attack, but a comforting hand reassures him that all is well. Buster, himself, is more than somewhat bemused by this sudden change in his fortune, but he rallies quickly. "I've done well, haven't I?" he says, wonderingly.

"You have done famously, my poppet" agrees Diana, "And I am about to tell you how you can do even better."

"Anything, for you, Di," he says, giving her the full works with his devoted, spaniel eyes. "You know that, don't you?"

I must say, I am finding this excess of sentimentality hard to swallow, but I am not about to interfere with the developing drama.

"I am sure you would make a great company director, Buster," says Diana softly, as she gazes into his vulnerable canine eyes.

Heaven help the poor chap, I think to myself.

"It's not my scene, Di," objects Buster. "I'd be hopeless at it."

"But it could be your scene," coos Diana. "If you were on the Board of Verdant Heritage, you could influence company policy and you would earn a useful salary."

"It would be good if I didn't have to rely on the Gov'nor for hand-outs," agrees Buster, "But I am not sure I could contribute much to company policy, I'd be out of my depth."

"It would be like riding your bike," Diana assures him. "It's a matter of confidence. You just have to keep the right balance. Go like the clappers when the road is clear and proceed with caution or look for an alternative route when the traffic gets sticky."

"I can't believe it would be as easy as that," says Buster, doubtfully.

"Don't worry about it," advises Diana. "I'd be able to help you make useful contributions if you just let me know what goes on at meetings."

"You mean we could work together as a team?" says Buster.

"Wouldn't that be great?" breathes Diana, hitting him between the eyes with a smile warm enough to have melted a polar icecap.

"I'll tell the Gov'nor this afternoon," promises Buster. "He'll be as happy as a parrot in a pistachio tree. What do you think, Mr Selsey?"

I am impressed by Diana's scheme to infiltrate a spy into the web of Oliver Crump's business interests, although I do have reservations about Buster's ability to carry it off. Nevertheless, encouragement seems to be the order of the day.

"It is good to see you both working together again," I tell them. "That is the way to go, and we have already made some progress."
I shuffle the papers that are piled up on a working top and retrieve the document I am looking for. "For a start, we can update this Situation Chart."

I explain how the character coding defines the various functions of the boxes, and that the lines represent known connections. Buster frowns ferociously as though the concentration is torturing his brain. Surprisingly, he is the first to comment.

"I like the connection between me and Di," he says. "And I see you have already added a line joining her Dad to my Gov'nor."

"Thanks to you, Buster. That was a useful piece of information you came up with," I say.

"We also now have a direct line between Verdant Heritage and Buster' father," says Diana. "We don't have to rely on an indirect connection through the Development Proposal and the Planning Committee boxes.

"There will be a direct line from Verdant Heritage to me as well, when I'm on the board of the Company," observes Buster.

"And so there will, my little plutocrat," says Diana, squeezing his arm in a show of affection that sets my teeth on edge. They made better company when they didn't like each other much.

"So, where does this leave us?" I ask, sourly. "What's the next step?"

"Ah!" says Buster, excitedly. "That's where my brilliant idea comes in. I told you about it on the phone."

"You told me you had an amazing idea, but you didn't say what it was," I remind him.

"Tell us now, Buster," says Diana in the tones of one who has no expectation at all of hearing a sensible proposal.

"Well, our next move was supposed to be taking the dormice to Hangman's Copse and therefore saving the Copse from development because dormice are a protected species."

"And now Bill has lost the dormice," grumbles Diana, "And we are stuck."

"So what we need is another endangered species," points out Buster, "And we have one right here."

"What are you talking about?" I ask, irritably.

"I am talking about a wildcat," says Buster, reaching out and massaging Barnacle's scalp. "And here he is."

"You have really flipped this time, Buster," I protest. "Barney is not a wild cat by any stretch of the imagination. He is a great, soppy, highly domesticated cat."

"I know he's not a wild cat," agrees Buster, "But he could pass for a wildcat. He's the right size and his markings are not that different."

"You are quite mad, Buster," I say. "Forget the whole thing. There is no way we could pass Barney of as a wildcat. Tell him, Diana."

Diana has, meanwhile, been staring intently at Barnacle and, to my dismay, she gives me no support whatsoever. Quite the opposite, in fact.

"Oh, I don't know. It might just work." she pronounces. "Barney is the right build and roughly the right colouring, and he has the large, bushy tail of a wildcat."

"But his tail is barred, like a racoon," I point out. "That is why his breed is called a Maine Coon."

"That is a minor point," say Diana, firmly. "Once we have photographed him in Hangman's Copse it will be easy to sort out details of that kind with an air-brush."

"You haven't thought it through," I complain. "The Copse isn't large enough to support a viable group of wildcats, and, in any case there is no way they could have remained undetected all these years."

"A wildcat might have trotted down from Scotland," puts in Buster. "I saw a TV programme once and there are these wild-life corridors along motorway verges and railway embankments. Wild animals use them all the time."

"Yes, of course," I say. "And that's about as likely as if a wildcat bought a ticket at Inverness Airport and flew down."

"Well I think it's a marvellous wheeze," chimes in Diana. "It doesn't matter if it is far-fetched. A wildcat is much more newsworthy than a dormouse. We might make the national press and television news. Think of all the lovely publicity."

"I'm sorry, but it's just not practical," I tell them. "If we were to release Barnacle in Hangman's Copse there is no telling what he might do. You can't train a cat to come to heel like a dog. He might rush off to try to find his way home, or climb a tree, or hide in a rabbit hole. We'd never find him again."

"You could have him on a lead and then hide behind a tree while Felicity is taking the photographs. She could airbrush out anything that didn't look right. Changing the colour of his eyes or his coat would be a doddle."

"Will you please both see sense," I expostulate. "We would never get away with it. It is a completely crazy idea."

"I like crazy ideas," says Buster, happily. "Di has lots of them."

"Well, I wish you would keep them to yourselves," I grumble, "We are not all nut-cases."

"Come on, Bill. Where's your sense of adventure?" says Diana. "You must have had one when you were younger or you wouldn't have gone to sea in the first place."

I feel as though I am being boxed into a corner by these two lunatics, but I have one more card to play. "No-one has consulted Barnacle about any of this yet," I point out. "He would be most upset if I were to cart him off to some unfamiliar location amongst a lot of people he doesn't know. He is uncomfortable with strangers." In typical cat fashion, Barney is giving the lie to the bit about strangers. He is enjoying the attention he is receiving from Buster and purring loudly.

"He likes me, Mr Selsey," says Buster.

"It will be fun, Bill," adds Diana, persuasively. "It will take you out of yourself, and it will make a lovely break for Barney. All those delightful smells in the woodland, and small creatures hopping about whichever way he looks."

How is it that I get myself into these situations, I ask myself. I am supposed to be quietly retired with my faithful cat, and with a stroll to Shorty's shed for a chat as the most exciting part of my day. And here I am, caught up in the madcap schemes of people like these two maniacs.

Well, at least they have teamed up again and are working as a couple, even if it is just to inveigle me into participating unwisely in their crazy scheme. Also, I suppose, I do feel guilty about the demise of the dormice and, perhaps, Barnacle should also accept a little of the blame.

"Alright," I hear myself saying. "You have beaten me down. The whole idea is farcical but, if you don't mind making a laughing stock of yourselves, go right ahead."

"I knew you would see sense in the end," beams Diana. "Now we can start looking at practicalities."

"There aren't any practicalities," I grumble. "It's all fantasy. You are both madder than hatters in the week before the Ascot Races."

"Don't be such a wet blanket, Bill," says Diana. "We can make this work. At the very least we will draw public attention to our campaign."

"Di is marvellous at this kind of thing," says the faithful Buster.

"You could have fooled me," I say, morosely.

"I was planning to take the dormice to Hangman's Copse tomorrow morning," says Diana, "And I have arranged to meet Felicity Wright there at eleven o'clock. She will be geared up to take photographs and write up the story. I don't think we need to change any of that. I am sure she will delighted to have a wildcat as her news item instead of dormice."

"That's great thinking, Di," says Buster, admiringly, as though she has come up with the equivalent of the WWII battle plan for the invasion of Normandy.

"So, are you expecting me and Barnacle to make our way into the thick of Hangman's Copse by eleven o'clock tomorrow morning?" I ask.

"Well, you are, between you, responsible for losing the dormice, so I think it is the least you can do to make amends," says Diana.

"Fair's fair, Mr Selsey," adds Buster, siding unsurprisingly, with his newly reconciled idol.

"Alright, we'll be there," I agree. "But I still think you are crazy people."

"There's a gate that leads off the road into the Copse," says Diana. "Follow the track as far as you can and we'll meet there at eleven, sharp."

"I know the gate," I say. "But suppose your father takes it into his head to turn up there at the same time. I'm not prepared to allow Barnacle within range of his shot-gun."

"Don't worry about that, Bill," Diana assures me. "Emma Gooding has promised to divert Daddy' attention tomorrow morning. She will have no difficulty in arranging that."

"Di thinks of everything," says her admiring swain.

"We'll see you tomorrow then, Bill, and, in the meantime, try not to create any more disasters." says Diana. "Come along, Buster, you need to have a serious talk with your father, and I have to bring Emma and Felicity up to speed on the change of plan."

"Just so you know," I tell them, "I am going, with my friend Shorty, to see old Mrs Morven this afternoon. We think she might be able to tell us some more about what has been happening in the Copse recently. And we'll take the opportunity to check out the lie of the land."

Diana looks doubtful. "Well just be careful what you say to that woman," she warns. "She's a loner and too volatile for my liking. You never know where you are with her."

"I've managed to work that out for myself," I tell her. "But she is an astute person, whatever guise she adopts, and I am sure she could be a valuable ally."

"Well, the best of luck," says Diana, "But don't let anything distract you from our date tomorrow."

She goes over to Buster who is engrossed in making a fuss of Barnacle. "You will see Barney again tomorrow," she tells him, "In fact Barney will be the star of the show, but right now we both have work to do."

She takes Buster by the arm and leads him towards the door. "Goodbye, Mr Selsey," he says, over his shoulder, "And thanks for everything."

"Take care not to misplace Barnacle before tomorrow," says Diana, as a parting shot. "You do seem rather prone to losing animals."

"Get off the pair of you," I tell them, "Before I set my wildcat on you."

They walk out of the house, arm-in-arm. Then Diana drives off in her roadster with Buster tail-gating her on his bike.

"It is dangerous getting too close to that woman," I tell Barney, "But your friend, Buster, either doesn't know it, or he knows it and doesn't care."

CHAPTER 30

With Diana and Buster out of the way, I spend a little time catching up with some much neglected housework. Then I find the makings of a couple of sandwiches in the fridge and stow them in a bag with a few cans of cold beer. It is time to visit Shorty again.

True to form, he is relaxing in his chair and reading the paper when I enter his shed. "You are out of the news altogether in Saturday's paper," he tells me. "But there is an even-handed write-up of my Allotment Holders' Association meeting. A bit too even-handed if you ask me. I would have expected a local paper to give more support to us residents."

"You can take that up directly with Felicity Wright," I tell him. "She was extremely interested when I told her about your Situation Chart, so I invited her to come and see it."

"I hope you know what you are doing," cautions Shorty. "It is not usually wise to trust a reporter."

"Better to have the press on our side than working against us," I counsel. I walk across to the easel and inspect the chart. "I have a couple of additions I can make to this."

I explain to Shorty about Buster's revelations, the news that he is now reconciled with Diana, and her decision that he should accept his father's offer to join the Verdant Heritage Board. Then I mark in lines connecting Major Hunter and Oliver Crump, Oliver Crump and Verdant Heritage and the Allotments Site to Oliver Crump.

I also sketch in a box for Emma Gooding with connecting lines to Hangman's Copse, Major Hunter and Diana Hunter. Then we stand back and consider the enhanced Chart for a minute or two.

"It looks like Oliver Crump is extending his lead for the most connections," observes Shorty.

"But there are more links to Hangman's Copse than to the Allotments Site," I point out, "Although it does now have a direct link to Oliver Crump."

We are interrupted at this point by a knock on the door. I open it to find Felicity standing there, her tablet at the ready, as always.

"Come in, Felicity," I welcome her. "You met my friend, Shorty Smith, at the Allotment Holders' meeting on Friday, I believe."

"Hi, Shorty," says Felicity. "I hope you were happy with my write-up of the proceedings."

"A bit disappointed, to be honest," replies, Shorty. "I think you might have given us allotment holders more of a fair wind. I am surprised you took the views of those lubbers on the Council so uncritically."

"We have to be even-handed," explains Felicity. "And Wendy Tyler did make some valid points. What are you actually growing on your allotment, Shorty?"

"I am keeping it ship-shape and clear of weeds," says Shorty, "And that is more than can be said for some of the unkempt patches of Council land around the district. Many of them harbour illegal weeds like ragwort, thistles and flowering dock."

"Alright! Alright!" Protests Felicity, holding up a defensive hand. "I don't want to get into all that stuff. I'm just saying that the issue of the allotments' future is not entirely black and white. In any case, I am more interested in the future of Hangman's Copse. That is where I think there may be some real skulduggery."

"Shorty and I believe that the allotments and Hangman's Copse are not, in fact, separate issues," I explain. "If you look at Shorty's Situation Chart, I am sure you will agree."

Shorty picks up a bamboo cane which might have been used to support a tomato plant if he had ever got round to growing one. He points to the boxes on his chart and explains how they are coded by function. He then goes on to point out the connecting lines and I chime in to detail the evidence that justifies each connection. I am particularly proud of the direct connection between Oliver Crump and Verdant Heritage which Buster had provided for us, but Felicity takes the wind out of my sails by telling us it was something she had already discovered.

"I checked the Verdant Heritage website and spent some time on-line, but I could find nothing that led to any specific names," I tell her.

"You were starting with Verdant Heritage and trying to work back to who were the company's beneficial owners," she explains. "I started with Oliver Crump and checked with the registered interests of Town Council members. And there it was, tucked away amongst his many other business connections."

"All roads lead to Rome," says Shorty, ponderously, "And, in this case to Oliver Crump. Just look at how many links there are to him compared to anyone else on the chart."

"That's most impressive," agrees Felicity, "Although there might be even more links to me if you were to mark them in. In fact, your note says that I connect to almost everyone."

"Yours would be one-way connections," I point out. "If we were to include them, they should all have little arrows to indicate that you collect information but you don't hand it out."

"I am not cluttering up my chart with anything like that," says Shorty, decisively. "As it is, it clearly shows Oliver Crump is a key actor in this pantomime, and he is certainly not playing Prince Charming."

"What is more," I add, "He is equally entwined in the possible development of both Hangman's Copse and the allotments site."

"OK," says Felicity, "You have convinced me on that." She looks around the shed. "And you have the makings of an impressive incident room here."

A set of box files that Shorty has set up on his otherwise pristine potting bench catches her eye. "I see you are compiling dossiers of all the individuals that appear on your chart," she observes. "Do you mind if I have a look?"

Shorty and I exchange embarrassed glances. "Well, that is the intention," I tell her, "But there is still a bit of work to do on those."

"What Bill means is that the files are full of blank sheets of paper," explains Shorty. "We haven't started on them yet."

"That place with all the roads leading to it wasn't built in twenty-four hours, you were about to tell me," says Felicity, with a grin. "Well, I wouldn't get any sympathy from my editor if I were to try that one on him, when I was late with my copy."

"We don't need detailed dossiers," I point out. "We can see from the diagram that there is something going on and it gives us a pretty good idea of how people are involved."

"OK, it's all circumstantial, but let's see where it leads us," agrees Felicity. "You are suggesting that Major Hunter may be working with Oliver Crump with a view to developing Hangman's Copse as a housing site, perhaps through the company, Verdant Heritage, which Oliver controls."

"Of course, we don't know the detail," I concede. "The Major might have in mind to sell the Copse, or he might want to retain ownership so that Oliver can develop it on his behalf. What we do know is that someone has already spent significant money on having the site surveyed, and that suggests some serious intent."

"I have checked out Verdant Heritage on the internet," says Felicity. "There is no information about the ownership, but they claim to be an environmentally benign company that buys land to protect it from undesirable development. They say that they then manage the property in a way that controls road and house building, conserves natural features, safeguards wildlife, and best serves the need of the community."

"And it you believe that, you'll believe anything," comments Shorty, drily.

"It might be true for all we know," says Felicity. "But it is certainly the case that, if you 'manage' ancient woodland in that way, it no longer remains ancient woodland."

"Which means we are justified in opposing it." I say.

"More immediately, it means I need to interview Oliver Crump, as soon as I can catch up with him," says Felicity.

"He'll only tell you he has no interest in the Copse," I warn her.

"Doesn't matter," replies Felicity. "It will still give me my story. 'Councillor Crump denies any plans for his company, Verdant Heritage, to build on the ancient woodland of Hangman's Copse.' That sort of thing."

"You journalists have no conscience at all," I comment.

"Well, I do have one, but I can't afford to listen to it very often," explains Felicity. "We'd never sell a paper."

"What you are proposing would certainly stir things up," says Shorty. "What else do you suggest we might do?"

"We go ahead with Diana Hunter's plan A," responds Felicity. "We are all set to discover dormice in the Copse tomorrow morning."

"Ahem," I break in. "You haven't heard about the dormice, have you?"

"What about them?" asks Felicity, so I bring her up-to-date with the non-availability of the dormice and the existence of what I believe to be a completely crazy plan B involving Barnacle masquerading as a wildcat. I expect her to agree with my assessment and to refuse to have any involvement in such madness, but she disappoints me.

"Of course it's a ridiculous idea," she pronounces, "But it would be fun, wouldn't it. Cats and dogs always make for popular stories in local newspapers."

"But your story would be based on a lie," I protest. "Barney is never going to be convincing as a wildcat."

"OK. So he'll be an alleged wildcat," says Felicity. "Our readers can make up their own minds about whether he is real or not but, in the meantime, he will have disappeared into the undergrowth and no-one will know for certain."

While Felicity and I have been discussing dormice and wildcats, I have sensed that Shorty is becoming more and more impatient. Eventually, he bangs his hand on the table to call us to order.

"When you have finished talking about Hangman's Copse and its non-existent animal content, could we please move on to the subject of the allotments. These are important to some of us."

"Very well, Shorty," says Felicity. "So what does your excellent chart tell us about the allotments site?"

"It is back to Oliver Crump again," says Shorty. "We know his lawyers have been assessing the site, and we know that Oliver is seriously interested in buying Bill's house, which would enable him to build an access road."

"He is pressing me hard," I confirm. "Offering to find me a retirement flat and, I suspect, inventing defects in my property to make me more willing to sell."

"I have to admit that I am not filled with such a crusading spirit when it comes to the allotments site," admits Felicity, "But it is a green space in the middle of a built-up residential area and I agree it would be a pity to lose it."

"Can you help at all, then?" asks Shorty.

"I will certainly tackle Oliver Crump about it as soon as I can catch up with him for an interview," offers Felicity. "Otherwise, I suggest your Allotments Holders Committee should make a direct approach to the Council."

"We are organising a petition," says Shorty. "All the allotment holders will sign and I am sure most of the residents in the area will also support us."

"Just the thing," says Felicity, making a note on her tablet. "I'll report that in tomorrow's paper. The more publicity you can get for your petition the better."

"That would be enormously helpful, Felicity," says Shorty. "Now, can I offer you some refreshment? Coffee? Tea? Something more alcoholic? Beer? Whiskey? It's all a bit male orientated I'm afraid."

Felicity consults her watch. "Kind of you, Shorty, but I need to get on. Copy doesn't write itself, unfortunately."

"I hope you feel it was worthwhile to catch up with what we have been discovering," I say.

"Oh, most definitely," she agrees. "Shorty's chart is a work of art, and I am fully persuaded that we should put the squeeze on Oliver Crump for the sake of both Hangman's Copse and the allotments site."

"Just one more thing before you go," I say. "Do you know anything about Peggy Morven, the old woman who lives in the cottage near Hangman's Copse? I have a feeling she might be a useful ally, so Shorty and I are going to visit her this afternoon."

"Hmm. She is certainly a colourful local character," says Felicity. "In fact I have in mind to interview her one day when I am short of real news, so I can write a feature about her."

"A good person to have on our side, then," I suggest.

"I wouldn't be too sure about that," counsels Felicity. "From what I hear, she is a maverick. Don't put too much trust in her."

"Oddly enough, Oliver Crump warned me against trusting you in just the same way," I tell her.

"So, you have disregarded Oliver's advice about me," she says, "And I am sure you are going to disregard my advice about Peggy Morven just as readily."

"It's what comes of him being in tankers," explains Shorty. "He and his mates were left to find their own way from port to port. They set their own courses without the discipline of the designated routes and timetables that had to be followed by those of us in the liner trades."

"You had best follow your own course, now, then Bill Selsey," says Felicity, "And I must be off to follow mine. Try to keep him off the rocks, Shorty."

She gathers up her electronic tablet, stows it away in her bag and makes for the door. "I'll see you both in Hangman's Copse tomorrow," she says in parting. "And I expect to find Barnacle ready to play the part of his lifetime."

Shorty shuts the shed door as she makes off towards the road. "There is just time for a quick lunch before we take off to visit Peggy Morven," we agree.

CHAPTER 31

As we drive towards Peggy Morven's cottage, Shorty and I speculate as to what guise she is likely to adopt.

"I have seen her as a pantomime witch and a spoof Gypsy fortune teller," I say, "But I have no idea whether we will find her playing one of those two roles or whether she will appear as someone completely different."

"From what you tell me, it sounds as though she takes on the persona that fits best into her surroundings at a given time," says Shorty. "Like those octopuses that can change their shape and colour to blend in with whatever the background happens to be."

"Octopuses also have three hearts and a brain that's distributed around their anatomy." I point out.

"What's that got to do with anything?" demands Shorty.

"I dunno," I tell him. "Just something to bear in mind. If she is like an octopus in one way, she might be like one in other ways too."

"Yeah. Of course," says Shorty, soothingly. "So we had better check that she doesn't possess eight tentacles instead of the normal quota of four limbs like the rest of us. Sometimes I worry about your outlandish trains of thought, Bill."

"It's called lateral thinking," I tell him. "It is generally recognised as a valuable asset. A lot of remarkable people have it."

"Sure," agrees Shorty, "And most of them are locked up as a matter of public safety, or for their own protection."

"No wonder you enjoyed serving in Purple Funnel," I tell him. "Everything cut and dried and no call to do your own thinking, vertical, horizontal or even down the middle."

"And it's obvious why no respectable shipping company would employ you if you can't tell the difference between a human being and a cephalopod."

We exchange grins to signal a truce in our amiable bickering and I have to concentrate on my driving as I turn off the main highway and take the narrow road that eventually passes through Hangman's Copse. I point out the neglected state of the woodlands and the dilapidated barbed wire fencing that surrounds it. Then I bring the car to a halt as we reach the gate that stands across the track leading into the Copse. The gate is secured with its padlock and chain but there is little point in this because the fence on each side is in such bad repair that anyone could walk in.

"I can see why it's classed as ancient woodland," observes Shorty. "It is in need of some tender, loving care. It doesn't look as though anyone has done anything to it, ever."

"It certainly has a sad and neglected appearance," I agree, "But that is just what makes it so valuable. All the vegetable and animal organisms it hosts have achieved a balance and maintained it for hundreds of years. Once disturbed, it might be impossible to ever regain the same natural equilibrium amongst all the competing or cooperating inhabitants."

"It is only a dedicated environmentalist that would want to preserve it in this state," says Shorty. He sniffs derisively. "It smells horrible for one thing. All that rotting timber and stagnant water lying about."

"Nevertheless, we have a duty to leave it as a legacy for future generations," I tell him, as I release the hand-brake and start to pull away. "There might be life-forms that we don't know about in places like this, and it is important to maintain bio-diversity."

"You have the jargon off pat," grumbles Shorty. "You and that cat of yours spend too much time watching television. You should get yourselves proper lives."

It is only a few minutes before we are clear of the densely packed trees and approaching Peggy Morven's cottage. I turn into the paved parking area, and we march across to rap loudly on her heavy front door.

We have only a short wait before we are greeted by a smiling, middle-aged lady, and I have to perform a double –take to recognise that she is Peggy Morven in the guise of everyone's favourite aunt. She is dressed in sensible shoes, sensible skirt, sensible blouse and a sensible cardigan, set off by a necklace of amber beads that can only be described as – well, sensible. The only jarring note is Horror, the cat, who is glaring at us with his one malevolent eye from a safe distance further down the hallway.

"Good grief, Peggy! What have you done to yourself?" I exclaim. "You are looking like a normal human being."

"Margaret, please," she corrects me. "Maggie to my friends, but never Peggy."

"Very well," I say. "I would like to introduce my old friend, Shorty Smith. He is chairman of the local Allotment Holders Association, you know."

"Well, do come in," Maggie invites us, as she conducts us along an unremarkable hallway and then ushers us through a doorway on the left and into a small but comfortable sitting room. We take an easy chair each and admire the beamed ceiling, the rustic plastered walls and the mullioned windows. The floor is constructed of wide, pinewood boards, darkened by age and with its expanse broken by two or three floral patterned rugs. Above floor level, cottage-style ceramic ornaments are distributed, generously on all the available horizontal surfaces.

"The kettle has just boiled, and I am about to make a pot of tea," says Maggie, "If you can just talk amongst yourselves for a moment I will bring it to you."

"Hold on, Maggie," I cry, as she moves to leave the room. "Is this your infamous herb tea that you are proposing to offer us?"

"Certainly not," she says. "Since you are men, you will have my standard, Darjeeling tea. For my women friends, I would also offer

Assam or Green Wu Long, but I am sure such refined blends would only be wasted on you two."

"In Purple Funnel, we carried every Asian tea you could imagine, mostly consigned to Europe," reminisces Shorty. "It needed great care because it was highly susceptible to tainting if other aromatic cargoes were stowed in the same hold. We would not even have allowed it in a hold that had recently been used for oranges unless the tea was for an Earl Grey blend, and then we might have got away with it."

"I wasn't expecting an expert," says a surprised Maggie. "Should I reconsider?"

"Ordinary black tea will be fine," I break in, to prevent Shorty launching into the niceties of cargo stowage in the Far Eastern trade before containerisation took all the fun out of it. "I was just checking that it will not be brewed from the nettles that grow around those rancid pools in Hangman's Copse."

"The very idea!" says Maggie, apparently affronted by my suggestion, as one would expect from a universal aunt.

She departs in what I presume is the direction of her kitchen and, left to ourselves, Shorty and I exchange grimaces.

"I thought we were meeting up with a make-believe witch," says Shorty.

"She plays many parts," I tell him, "And she plays them for all she is worth."

"Perhaps she was an actress in her younger days," suggests Shorty.

"She can certainly put on a convincing performance, now," I agree.

"All the world's a stage for some people," pronounces Shorty, ponderously.

"And William Shakespeare scooped up all the best lines before anyone else got into the game," I add.

"What is all this about the Stratford wordsmith?" asks Maggie as she re-enters the room carrying a tray set out with the makings of a formal afternoon tea.

"We were wondering if you were once an actress," explains Shorty.

Maggie put the tray down carefully on a low table before she replies. "I might have been, or, then again, I might not have been."

"Well, thanks for clearing that up," I say.

"I prefer not to think too much about what I once was," she tells us. "The past is just that. It has passed. I am happier concentrating on the here and now, with an occasional thought about the future."

"Bill and I talk a lot about the past. Mostly our old sailoring days," says Shorty. "It adds richness to our lives. Of course, my stories are much more interesting than his. I was in Purple Funnel ships you know."

"You had mentioned it," acknowledges Maggie with a smile.

"Never ask a merchant seaman what company he served with," I explain. "If he was with Purple Funnel, he'll tell you and, if he was not, it is unkind to embarrass him by asking. At least that's the way Shorty and his equally deluded shipmates think."

"At your ages, you do well to remember so much about your old times at sea," says, Maggie. "And long may your recollections continue."

"Oh, we don't worry about that," I tell her. "It is true that, as we grow older, we forget some of the things that happened in the past, but that is more than compensated by the fact that we can now, with perfect clarity, remember things that never happened at all."

"Dreamed them, p'raps. Or maybe they should have happened but didn't. Can't tell the difference now, anyway," Shorty says, cheerfully.

"You don't know how lucky you are to enjoy such happy memories, real or imagined, and to have each other to share them with," says Maggie, with a sadness in her voice that hints of things best left unspoken. "But now, if you don't mind, I would like to talk about the present."

She pours the tea and passes us each a small plate. "Help yourselves to milk and sugar, and do have a toasted tea-cake." She catches me looking suspiciously at a small pot of jam. "It's perfectly safe, Bill. Women's Institute approved strawberry conserve."

"I never doubted it for a moment," I protest as Shorty and I arrange minute serviettes over our gnarled old men's knees and attempt to balance the plates upon them. Having achieved that near-impossible feat, we do our best to eat and drink in a civilized manner, even remembering not to speak with our mouths full of tea-cake.

"When we met at the fête, you suggested that it might be useful if we were to work together to prevent the development of Hangman's Copse." Maggie reminds me. "Now that we have more time, perhaps you could tell me what you know about the threat."

"We were beginning to wonder if you would ever ask," says Shorty, fishing a much folded copy of his Situation Chart from his pocket. He leans forward, pushes the tea-tray aside, and spreads the chart out on the table.

"Goodness, you have been busy," enthuses Maggie. "Talk me through it, if you please, Shorty."

Shorty needs no encouragement to explain the coding system he has used for the chart and then goes on to provide a justification for each of the links that we had established between the various boxes.

"So," he concludes, "We think there is evidence of a concerted effort to develop Hangman's Copse for housing and to redevelop the allotments site for a similar purpose, both of which would have unfortunate effects on the local environment."

"More specifically," I add, "The chart clearly shows that Oliver Crump is a key player in both these matters. We suspect it is his surveyors that you have seen in the Copse, and we know he has been negotiating with Major Hunter, the owner. As for the allotments, we have a report of his solicitors inspecting the site, and he is keen to buy my house which would allow a road access to the site."

"So where does the Verdant Heritage company come into this?" asks Maggie.

"Verdant Heritage appears to be a private firm, controlled by Oliver Crump," I explain. "They are behind an application for outline planning permission to develop the Copse and it seems likely that

Oliver Crump could smooth the way to it being approved through his chairmanship of the Council's Planning Committee."

"His name does seem to be popping up everywhere," comments Maggie, "And I certainly would not like to see the Copse destroyed."

"It is officially classed as ancient woodland," points out Shorty, "So it should have some legal protection."

"Not much," I say. "The Council can override that, and Verdant Heritage are likely to offer to protect selected pockets of woodland while the rest is 'tastefully' managed with green space between the houses. I've seen their website and what they have done in other areas."

"Very well," says Maggie, "I can see that any such development would alter the whole character of the area, and I like it just as it is. I chose a remote spot because I wanted to live in a remote spot, and I don't want to be urbanised out of it. How do you suggest I could help?"

"We are hoping to find an endangered species or two in the Copse," I tell her. "An animal or plant with protected status. You probably know more than anyone else about the wildlife there."

"Ah." She says. "As you will remember, my *alter ego*, Peggy Morven, has thoughts about the bats, reptiles and toadstools that live in the Copse, but hers are more dangerous than endangered." She adopts the screeching tone and style of her witch's character. "They bats will get you if you disturb their secret places. One scratch and you'll die screamin' from rabies afore the next full moon. An' don't even ask what my toadstool toxins will do to you."

Shorty flinches, despite himself. "I don't know if you'll put the frighteners on Oliver Crump," he says, "But you scare the daylights out of me."

"Perhaps," agrees Maggie resuming her kind old auntie voice and manner. "But I have to say Peggy's incantations work more effectively on individuals than on property companies."

"Alright," I say, "We'll leave Peggy Morven out of it for the time being. What can you tell us about the woodland wildlife in your present manifestation as Margaret Morven?"

"It's not Morven, I'm Margaret Millard," she corrects me.
I look at her in surprise. "You can't be," I object. "Millard isn't an anagram like your Morven/Mernov characters."

"Well, let that be a lesson to you, young Bill," she tells me, like an aunt explaining the way the world works to a callow nephew. "Just because two related attributes follow a pattern, you should not assume that a third will do the same. Nothing is certain in this life as Werner Heisenberg could have told you in the nineteen-twenties."

"That's it," I cry. "I suspected you were a physicist in disguise when you talked about nuclear reactions in the Sun, and now I am sure of it."

"There you go again," she warns. "Leaping to a conclusion on the flimsiest of evidence."

"OK, OK," I say. "I get it. You might once have been a physicist or, there again, you might never have been."

"You are learning," she smiles, but Shorty, who has been following our exchange with a bemused expression on his face, breaks in.

"We are wandering from the point," he complains. "Bill is always doing that. It comes from being a tanker man. They often spend only twenty-four hours loading or discharging in port, so most of his time was spent at sea on long, lonely watches where his mind, all too easily, drifted off into dreamland."

I smile as sheepishly as a newly shorn merino, because I accept that I am not a world champion at keeping my thoughts into a single channel. "Alright," I agree, "Let's get back to the subject of Hangman's Copse." I turn to Maggie. "Can you tell us anything about vulnerable wildlife there?"

Maggie shrugs. "As a matter of principle, I never venture into the woods as Margaret Millard, it would be out of character and it might confuse people. I always go as Peggy Morven, and her interests lean more towards sorcery than science. "

"So you can't be much help on that topic," says Shorty.

We sit, quietly for a few minutes as we finish our tea and tea-cake. Then Maggie has a suggestion. "The best thing might be if I take you into the Copse now. Then you can see for yourselves what is growing there. We might even sight a few animals too."

Shorty and I agree that this would be a useful next step, and Maggie takes herself upstairs, as she says, to de-beautify herself and to change into her black witch-of-the-woods outfit. Left alone, we discuss how far we should let Maggie into our confidence and we conclude that she is shaping up well to become one of the team and that we should, accordingly, trust her with our plans for tomorrow.

Although we know what to expect, it is none-the-less a shock as she bursts, dramatically into the room in her Peggy Morven guise. The prominent wart has reappeared on her nose, together with its satellites on her chin and forehead. Indeed, her nose seems to have lengthened and acquired a twist, although I realise this can only be due to the clever application of make-up. Her hunched shoulders and shuffling gait complete her transformation from a handsome, middle aged matron into a menacing old crone. As a final touch, Horror, the cat, having disappeared during the tea-party, is following closely on her heels.

"Come with me into the dark woods if you dare, young fellows," she cackles.

"Hell's bells," shrieks Shorty, stepping back sharply, "It's the witch of Endor. No wonder they used to hang people like you from the nearest tree."

"Don't ee worry my pretty," says Peggy, stroking Shorty's hair. "I don't eat sailors or oysters unless there's an 'r' in the month."

"Come on, you two," I tell them, "We've got a job to do. It will save time if I drive you to the Copse."

"You are not invited this time, Horror," says Peggy, "You can stay in your own room."

I peep over her shoulder as she pushes open a door leading off the hall. I glimpse a crude, deal table and what looks like a stuffed stoat, baring its fangs from a shelf on the far wall.

Her birch-broom leans against a cupboard in the corner of the room. Horror leaps up and disappears into the dark space at the top of the cupboard from which vantage point his seemingly disembodied eye fixes me with a malignant glare.

"You just be a bad cat while I'm out," she admonishes him. "And don't let me find that you ain't been up to some wickedness when I come back."

She lets out a disgusting, gurgling snigger as she turns back to Shorty and me. "Let's get on with it, then," she leers.

As I drive the short distance, we explain to Peggy that, together with Diana and Felicity, we are planning to 'discover' a wildcat in the Copse, with Barnacle playing the leading role.

"Of course, there might really be wildcats there for all we know," says Shorty. "So it is not, necessarily a hoax."

"There are tales of big cats attacking sheep all over the county." Says Peggy, "But I don't give those much credence. It's easier to believe in my demonic bats and toads."

"So what do you think of our idea?" I ask. "If there is evidence of protected animals in the Copse, it could put a stop to any kind of development."

"I like the general idea," says Peggy, "But I think a wildcat is a mite ambitious. Couldn't you find something smaller, - like a mouse?"

We explain that we are right out of endangered mice, and Peggy accepts that our plan to go with a wildcat is the best we can do.

"It's a pity Horror is missing some significant parts of his anatomy or we could arrange to 'discover' a pair of wildcats," she observes.

I leave the car off the road, where I had parked it on Thursday, and we walk together to the gate. We are surprised to see that the padlock has been removed and the gate is standing wide open. What look like fresh tyre marks have left their imprint in the muddy track. We pause for a moment, uncertain about our next move, and Peggy is the first one to speak.

"It might be the Major," she says, "But, most times, he don't take his Range-Rover into the woods, he leaves it at the gate and prowls around on foot with his gun."

"Perhaps he had a reason for taking the car into the Copse today," I suggest. "Whoever it was must have had a key because the padlock and chain haven't been damaged."

"It would be useful to find out what is going on," comments Shorty, "But we need to be careful. We shouldn't go blundering into unknown waters without a pilot."

"You have a pilot," Peggy tells him. "I could take you anywhere in these woods with my eyes shut. I knows all the paths used by the deer and the foxes, and where the slime is so deep it would swallow you up if you was to step into it."

"Lead on, then Peggy," I say. "We'll be right behind you."

"I reckon it's best if you two stay here, while I wander in with my basket. No-one will take any notice of me. I'm allus poking about in the woods."

This seems a sensible suggestion but, at that moment, we hear the sound of a motor approaching from within the Copse and Peggy urges us to hide behind a clump of bushes while she accosts whoever might be driving.

It turns out to be Oliver Crump and Buster in a four-by-four pick-up van with 'Verdant Heritage' painted on the side. When it heaves into sight, Peggy starts to hobble towards it down the middle of the track so it is forced to stop.

Buster is driving the van, but it is Oliver who puts his head out of the window and addresses Peggy. "What are you coming in here for?" he demands. "Can't you read? That notice on the gate says 'Danger Keep Out' and it means what it says."

"Ah. That don't apply to me," Peggy informs him. "And I can tell you, I'm more dangerous than anything in they woods, 'specially when people are rude to me."

From our hiding place, we hear her treat Oliver to a shrill and unnerving cackle.

"Get out of our way, you crazy old woman," shouts Oliver. "And take yourself back home. This is private property, and you are trespassing."

"No I ain't," says Peggy. "The Major and me, we has an understanding. He lets me gather herbs and toadstools from his copse, and I don't interfere with all his huntin' and shootin' like I could if I wanted."

"Well Major Hunter isn't here and there's more going on today than hunting and shooting, so just keep out."

"An' just what is going on?" asks Peggy.

"It's none of your business, you nosey old hag," yells Oliver, angrily. "Just clear off or you'll regret it."

"I'm the one that makes threats around here," says Peggy, mildly. She turns her head to address Buster who is clearly embarrassed by the way the exchange is heading. She has noticed the family likeness as she notices everything. "You shouldn't let your old dad get so worked up. Insulting people who have the 'gift' could be bad for his health. Look at his little red face. His blood pressure has gone up already."

"Look, er, Mrs, er," says Buster as Oliver is temporarily rendered speechless. "Would you mind stepping aside to allow us to pass? There is some sampling work going on in the Copse, so it would be best if you could keep away for now."

"That I will, since you ask me nicely," says Peggy. She takes something black and squidgy from her basket and uses it to make a hieroglyph in the form of an arrowhead on the windscreen in front of Oliver. Then she moves around to Buster's side of the van. "I've taken a likin' to you, young man. A modicum of respect goes a long way. Oh, and that runic symbol I have just cast on the windscreen will make your dad either cool down or become more heated. One or the other. I'm a bit rusty on my runes these days."

"Silly old bag," mutters Oliver as Peggy stands aside and a much relieved Buster drives the van out of the gate and away down the road.

As the sound of their exhaust fades, Shorty and I emerge from behind the bush. "That was a brilliant performance, if I may say so, Peggy." I tell her. "And your final touch was masterly. You can claim the credit whatever happens to Oliver."

"Still as cynical as ever, young Bill," says Peggy. "You'll get a surprise one day."

"Never mind about the magic," breaks in Shorty. "Let's find out what Buster means by 'sampling work'. I vote we all follow the track together. Whatever is going on could be happening deep in amongst the trees."

Peggy and I agree that this is a sensible suggestion and we off at a brisk pace. As we walk, I bring Peggy up-to-date with the news that Diana had urged Buster to join the Verdant Heritage Board.

"The fact that he and Oliver are cosying up together in a Verdant Heritage vehicle suggest that he has wasted no time in complying," I explain. "She can be a persuasive girl, Diana Hunter."

Very soon, we begin to hear noises in the distance, and these grow rapidly louder as we progress further and further into the Copse. Initially, we hear banging and slashing sounds, and raised voices. Then, as we approach more cautiously, there comes the high-pitched buzz of a chain-saw being fired up. The track ends in a small clearing, by which time the noise from the chain saw has become deafening. We pause to survey the scene for a moment and then, as we continue into the open space, we notice a builder's truck on one side and two men operating a chain-saw on a sender beech tree on the other.

"Timber!" they shout as they see us, and the tree starts to fall in our direction. It topples slowly at first, but with increasing speed. We have barely time to dash sideways amongst the standing trees surrounding the glade before it crashes down with a cracking of twigs and a splintering of the larger branches.

The two men, wearing hard hats and ear defenders, come galloping across the clearing with expressions of concern on their faces, until they realise we are unharmed. Then they relax into smiles as they recognise me.

"Hello, Guv," says Kevin. "Have you come all this way to bring us our tea and biscuits?"

"Thirsty work, this is," confirms Sean.

I introduce them to Peggy and Shorty. "Mrs Morven is taking my friend, Shorty and me for a stroll through the woods," I explain. "We didn't expect to find trees falling on us."

"Mr Crump told us there wouldn't be anyone coming into the woods," explains Kevin.

"He said it was private property," adds Sean.

"Yes, it is," I agree, "But Mrs Morven has dispensation to come into the Copse whenever she likes, and she happens to have brought us with her."

"You just missed Mr Crump and his son," volunteers Kevin. "I'm surprised you didn't meet them when they were driving back to the road."

"Oh, A pity that," I say. "But I'm sure I will see them again before too long."

"Tomorrow, I expect," says Kevin. "We'll be back working on your roof in the morning and Mr Crump might drop in to see how we are getting on."

This is useful information, I think to myself. It means that we can expect to be undisturbed when we meet in the Copse for our wildcat expedition tomorrow.

"So, what are you doing in the woods today?" I ask.

"We're earning double pay," says Sean, "Cos it's Sunday."

"Good for you," I tell them. "But you are both skilled workmen in the building trade, and I am surprised to find you here felling trees."

"We are versatile lads," explains Kevin.

"What's more, we can do lots of different things," adds Sean.

"Have you got much to do here?" asks Shorty, who probably feels he has been excluded from the conversation for too long.

"Two or three hours should finish it," replies Kevin. "Mr Crump wants us to cut down some samples. One each of a dozen different sorts of tree. See where he has marked them with white paint."

"It shouldn't take you more than a few minutes for each tree with that thing," comments Shorty, with a nod towards the chain-saw.

"It doesn't do to hurry things," says Sean. "Not when we are on double time."

"Accidents happen if you are in too much of a rush," agrees Kevin. "You saw for yourselves what a dangerous job this is."

"I am sure you are right to be careful," I assure them. "Do you know what Mr Crump needs the samples for?"

Kevin scratches his head. "I think it's so he can decide whether the trees are worth anything or whether he should just clear the whole site before he starts building."

This news gives us all a jolt. We had not suspected that Oliver's planning had gone this far.

"Well, good talking to you both," I say to Kevin and Sean. "We mustn't keep you from your lumberjacking. I'll see you at my place tomorrow morning."

"Right, Guv." Says Kevin, "Enjoy your walk, but best if you give us a wide berth for the rest of the afternoon."

"It's hazardous work," agrees Sean. "We ought'a get three times our normal pay, not just twice."

Peggy, Shorty and I turn away and retrace out steps along the track towards the road.

"Things are moving more quickly than we expected," I say.

"And, as far as we know, Oliver Crump's Planning Committee has not considered the application by Verdant Heritage, yet," points out Shorty. "What is your take on this, Peggy? You kept very quiet when we were talking to those two workmen."

"I like to deal with the king frog rather than his tadpoles," she snorts. "But you are right. Oliver Crump must be confident that the planning application will get passed if he is already spending money on sampling the trees. And it is ten to one that he is also behind all that surveying work that has been taking place."

"I wonder if he has actually bought the Copse from Major Hunter, yet," I muse. "Or whether it is just a firm understanding."

"There are lots of such details that we are not yet sure about," warns Shorty.

"But we now have an insider who can provide us with all those missing links," I point out.

"Buster Crump," says Shorty.

"But can you trust him?" ask Peggy. "Spies have a nasty habit of becoming double agents. Now he has got his legs under the Board-

Room table, he could well see everything from a different perspective."

"You could be right," I agree, "But I feel sure we can rely on Diana to keep him on our side."

By this time, we have reached the road. We continue to my car and I drive to Peggy's cottage, where I drop her off. "You'll be joining us in the Copse tomorrow morning, I hope."

"I wouldn't miss it for the world," says Peggy.

"From what we have heard this afternoon, it is just as well we are poised for action," adds Shorty.

We take our leave from Peggy, and we decide that it is sufficiently late that Shorty can expect to be welcomed into his own home. Accordingly, I drive him there and then continue to my own place where I pour myself a beer and tell Barney about our adventures of the afternoon.

Barnacle listens attentively because he knows his patience will be rewarded by a fresh packet of cat-food when I have said my piece. As I am serving it, I notice that it is six o'clock and I decide it would be useful to bring Diana up-to-speed with the day's happenings. I call her mobile number and explain that events are moving more quickly than we expected in Hangman's Copse, which means that pre-emptive action on our part is becoming urgent. I also tell her about Buster's and Oliver's presence in the Copse, which seems to suggest that Buster has wasted no time in cosying up to his father.

"Thanks for letting me know, Bill," she says. "As a matter of fact, I am meeting up with Buster at the George and Dragon this evening for a drink and a pub-supper. It would be a good idea if you were to join us."

"I'm not sure Buster will agree it is such a good idea to have me playing gooseberry at your *tête á tête*," I warn. "I fancy he would like you to himself."

"That's too bad," she says, briskly, "But the fact is that you have some new information and I am hoping the Buster will also have picked up some bits and pieces this afternoon. My feeling is that we should put it all together as soon as possible."

"Fine by me," I tell her, and we agree that I will meet them at the pub at seven o'clock.

Meanwhile, having cleared his plate, Barnacle is washing his whiskers prior to settling down for a comfortable sleep.

"Things are happening, Barney," I tell him, "And you are going to share in the excitement tomorrow."

He yawns, with studied indifference, and closes his eyes.

CHAPTER 32

At seven, precisely, I enter the busy George and Dragon, and find Diana and Buster already ensconced at a table in a cosy alcove. Buster has a beer in his hand and Diana is sipping a glass of sparkling white wine. If Buster is not pleased to see me, he hides it well, and I receive a welcoming smile from both parties.

"Hello, Mr Selsey," says Buster. "What will you have to drink?"

"What you are drinking looks good," I say. "I'd like a glass of the same."

"I'm glad you could come, Bill," says Diana, as Buster elbows his way to the bar to place his order. "If we put our heads together, I am sure we can build a more complete picture of what is going on."

I explain how Peggy Morven, in her role of a creepy witch, had met Buster and his father driving out of Hangman's Copse in a Verdant Heritage van, while Shorty and I had lurked behind some bushes. Then Buster returns with my beer and we all revert to studying the menu and deciding what we would like to eat. Buster and I choose a steak pie each, and Diana goes for chicken and chips. While we wait to be served, we get down to business.

"So, my clever secret agent," says Diana to Buster, "Are you a paid up member of the Verdant Heritage Board of Directors?"

"Not quite yet," replies Buster, with a grin. "But the Gov'nor is going to arrange the formalities over the next few days. I am to be the Operations Director, apparently."

"Well, congratulations, Buster," I say. "But it seems from your presence at the Hangman's Copse site this afternoon that you are already settling into the job."

Buster looks startled and asks how I know where he was during the afternoon, and I explain that Shorty and I had been there, conducting a reconnaissance with Peggy Morven.

"Dad can't stand her," says Buster, "But I quite like her. I think she's funny."

"She does have a sense of humour in her own weird way," I agree.

"So, what was the object of your visit to the Copse, Buster?" asks Diana.

"Well, the Gov'nor set me the task of making an assessment as to whether it was suitable for building houses," says Buster, "He showed me a report from a surveying firm that has been working in the Copse for a couple of weeks, and then we went to look at it on the ground."

"Your father must be very confident that he can go ahead with this work if he is spending so much time and money on it," I comment. "Has he already bought the site from Diana's father?"

"Not yet," says Buster, "But he has an option to buy. That means he has the right to buy it at an already agreed price if he decides to go ahead."

"Thank you for explaining that for the benefit of those of us who are not property speculators," says Diana.

"This stuff is more interesting than I thought it would be," Buster tells her. "It's like you said, a kind of balancing act, and I am not at all convinced that the balance is in our favour in the case of Hangman's Copse."

"Who are you talking about when you say *our* favour?" demands Diana.

Buster looks anxious. "I suppose I mean Verdant Heritage," he says. "The whole site is waterlogged and it could easily cost too much to establish a proper drainage system and stabilise the soil."

245

"Buster," Diana reprimands him, "You are already starting to identify with the wrong team. 'Our side' is *opposed* to the development of the Copse, remember?"

"Oh, yes," says Buster, hurriedly. "In that case, it is in *our* favour that the site might be too expensive to be worth developing."

"That is, actually, rather good news," I say. "It means that we might only need a little extra hassle in the planning procedures and it could be enough to tip the balance in our direction. A legal inquiry involving the protection of an endangered species could be a long and expensive process, and more than enough to make the development un-economic."

"So it's all go for tomorrow, then," says Diana. She raises her glass. "Here's to Barnacle, the wildest cat south of the border."

As we replace our glasses, I turn to Buster. "When we looked into the Copse this afternoon, we found a couple of your father's workmen cutting down trees all over the place like hyper-active lumberjacks. What was that all about?"

"They were simply taking samples to discover what kind of timber is in the woods, and what condition it is in." explains, Buster. "If any of it is worth extraction, it could help with our finances."

He catches Diana looking at him appraisingly and corrects himself, hurriedly. "Or should I say, help with Verdant Heritage expenses. From *our* point of view, of course, it will be best if we find the timber to be worthless."

"Don't go forgetting which side you are on," Diana warns him.

But, I feel that Buster is doing remarkably well. "You have given us a great deal of useful background information," I tell him. "You have been able to confirm several of the questions we were not sure about, like whether the Copse had actually been sold, and whether it was your father who commissioned the survey."

"I'm glad I could be of help," says Buster.

"Just one more question then, if you don't mind," I say. "Have you heard about any plans that your father or Verdant Heritage might have for taking over the allotments site?"

"No, nothing at all," says Buster, "But that doesn't mean there aren't any plans. I've only been taking an interest in all this stuff for one afternoon so far, you know."

At this point, the waiter arrives with our food and we concentrate our attention and our conversation on this for the next twenty minutes. It is when we have cleared our plates and ordered coffee that I return to the subject of copse-saving.

"One thing that puzzles me," I tell them. "Why has this remained a purely local matter? Why have you not sought assistance from some of the heavyweights in the environmental movement? Greenpeace, Friends of the Earth, the Woodlands Trust. Organisations like that?"

"Some members of Emma Gooding's 'Save Hangman's Copse Action Group' have suggested that, but it was agreed to keep it a local initiative.," says Diana.

"So, why was that?" I ask.

"Well, it *is* Daddy that owns the Copse," she replies. "And he's really a great softy under his grumpy exterior. I wouldn't like to see him hounded by powerful national organisations if we can nudge him into doing the right thing by some low-key local actions."

"You are a greatly talented young lady," I tell her, "But I am surprised that you were able to sway the whole Action Group to your way of thinking."

"Oh, it wasn't just me," explains Diana. "As you have already noticed, Emma Gooding has a soft spot for Daddy too. "She can twist him around her little finger, but she wouldn't like anyone else to give him a hard time. And she is chairman of the Group."

"Your 'Save Hangman's Copse Working Group' is like the Strait of Gibraltar," I suggest. "There are currents on the surface but, hidden from sight, there are also powerful undercurrents. Well, thanks for explaining that, Diana. Now, perhaps we should return to more immediate matters."

"I am concerned about all the activity that was going on in the Copse, yesterday," she says. "We don't want to be disturbed while we are 'discovering' a wildcat in the woods. I've made sure Daddy will not make an appearance, but what about Mr Crump and his workmen?"

"The two would-be lumberjacks won't be there," I tell her, "So we won't need to worry about trees being chopped down all around us. They told me they would be back to finish the repairs to my house, tomorrow."

"I don't think my Gov'nor will be there," says Buster. "In fact, I don't think I will be there either. He wants me to go with him to look at a possible development site way up near Watermill Creek on the other side of town."

"We'll be sorry to miss you, poppet," says Diana, "But your presence in the Copse isn't essential. If you can take your father off to some distant location, that would be the most useful contribution you could make."

"He's keen to get me involved in the Verdant Heritage projects," explains Buster, "And this one really does seem to be promising. It is a market garden property that the Gov'nor says is ripe for development."

"I wouldn't be too happy about using productive agricultural land for house building," I say.

"It has become uneconomic," explains Buster. "Wages are rising, even for East European workers, and vegetable prices are flat. What is more, there is a pressing need for new housing in this area."

"You are absorbing your father's way of thinking very quickly," says Diana, with something approaching approval in her voice. "And, at least, that development would not destroy ancient woodland or displace endangered creatures."

For a moment, I entertain the unpleasant thought that she might be about to pat him on the head, but, thankfully, she takes a sip of coffee instead.

"So, it looks as though we should have a clear field for our expedition tomorrow," I say, cheerfully. "I think we have had a useful chat, and I'll leave you two to finish your coffee while I go home to tell Barney what is in store for him."

We say our farewells, and I am treated to a kiss on the cheek from Diana. As I drive home, I decide that an early night is called for. It is going to be a busy, and perhaps stressful, day tomorrow.

CHAPTER 33

Monday morning starts early with Kevin and Sean making their presence known by the clattering of aluminium ladders against scaffold poles and unnecessarily loud shouts to each other from various parts of the garden. I ignore these reminders that they are about to start work. They will get their tea and biscuits when I am good and ready.

Nevertheless, I am showered, shaved and dressed in good time, and I enjoy a leisurely breakfast which, as always, I share with Barnacle.

"It is your big day, today, Barney," I tell him, as I bend down to engage the lock on his cat-flap. I don't want him running off, which I am sure he will attempt to do as soon as I bring his carrying basket out of the store cupboard. He associates its appearance with visits to the vet where he has, in the past, endured several undignified treatments. There is no need for the basket yet, though. I consult the kitchen clock. Nine-thirty, so an hour before we need to leave.

I make two mugs of tea, find some biscuits, and take a tray out to the 'workers'.

"Cor. Thanks, Guv," says Kevin. "We were beginning to think you'd forgotten us this morning."

"We was just getting on with the job, quietly in case we woke you up," explains Sean.

"Yeah. Right," I say, "Well you can start making as much noise as you like, now,"

I place the tray on the tree-trunk and they scramble down from their platform like squirrels that have dropped a load of nuts."

"We've just got the roof to do, now," says Kevin, as they ladle vast quantities of sugar into their mugs of tea.

"Most people would have to strip all the tiles off and redo the whole roof," says Sean.

"But skilled blokes like us can slot the new tiles into place without disturbing the rest of the roof," explains Kevin.

"How long will it take you?" I ask.

Kevin takes a gulp of his tea as he considers this question. "We'll finish late this afternoon," he says, eventually. "And then there will be some clearing up to do."

Sean's face is too full of biscuit for him to add his comment, but I am satisfied that they have plenty to keep themselves occupied so there is no chance that they will move to Hangman's Copse to resume their tree-felling.

"OK, guys," I say. "I am going to have to go out shortly, but I'll leave you a thermos flask of tea and I'll make a couple of sandwiches for your lunch if you like."

"That'll be great, Guv," says Sean, having swallowed his biscuit. "Do you mind if I use your toilet?"

"You're giving us five star service," Kevin tells me as Sean goes into the house on his mission. "We'll make sure we leave everything neat and tidy for you."

"Like taking this tree with you?" I ask.

Kevin looks at the fallen tree and gives it an exploratory kick. "A good piece of oak there, Guv," he says. "It ought'a be worth something, even if it's just logs for someone's wood-fired stove. I've got a mate who might come and cart it away for nothin'. Shall I have a word with him?"

"Please do, Kevin," I tell him. "I'll be glad to be able to get at my garden again."

"OK. But don't let on to Mr Crump," says Kevin. "I've a feeling he'd like it to stay, cluttering up the place until you agree to sell him your house."

"Not a word, Kevin," I assure him. "This is just between you and me." We break off as Sean returns.

"I'll let you guys get on, then," I say, as I make my way back to the kitchen but, as usual, they linger over their refreshment and show no sense of urgency in returning to their building activity.

It is only the work of a few minutes to put a couple of sandwiches together and make the promised thermos of tea. Then I turn my attention to Barnacle. He is already looking at me anxiously, his sixth sense having detected that something unusual is being planned and that it is likely to involve his participation. He shrinks away as I go to pick him up, but I am expecting that and I soon have him tucked securely under my arm. With my free hand, I open the cupboard and take out his carrying basket and a leather harness.

By this time, he is thoroughly alarmed but, with a mixture of firmness and fair words, I manage to strap the harness around his shoulders and stow him securely in his basket. He peers at me sadly with that 'how could you do this to me' look in his eyes.

"This is no time to be faint-hearted," I tell him. "You have an important engagement this morning. The future of a tract of English Countryside depends on you."

I sneak Barnacle out of the kitchen door and load him onto the backseat of my car which I have parked at the side of the house, out of sight from Kevin and Sean. I return to place their lunch in a cardboard box which I leave by the foot of their ladder.

"Have fun," I call up to them. "I'm going off now, and I'm not sure what time I'll be back."

It is just ten-thirty as I drive away. Comfortable time to pick up Shorty and find our way to our assignation at Hangman's Copse.

We stop off at Margaret Millard's cottage and find that she is about to leave and is already dressed in her Peggy Morven, witch-of-the-woods regalia. She sits in the back of the car and attempts to engage Barnacle in conversation, but he clearly implicates her in the plot that is disturbing the pleasurable routine of his day and he responds with a cold stare.

Arriving at the track into the Copse, we find that the gate is unlocked, so we turn off and follow the track until we arrive at the clearing where we had, yesterday, encountered Kevin and Sean cutting down trees. Diana's roadster is already parked, and she and Felicity, are sitting in it to await our coming. I leave Barnacle in my car and we walk across to greet them.

"Well met, old friends," says Diana, stepping out of her roadster. I notice that she is looking, with some suspicion, at Peggy, but she addresses me. "I suppose you have remembered to bring Barnacle."

"He's waiting for us in the car," I say. "But I must tell you that he is as doubtful as I am about the wisdom of this charade."

"Nonsense," says Felicity, coming round from the far side of the roadster, "He'll have a great time. Animals always steal the show when there are photographs to be taken."

"So, how do you suggest we play this?" asks Shorty, always practical. "This area doesn't look very promising with all the truck tyre marks and murdered trees. We need to elect someone to take charge. A kind of director, since we are filming."

"I know Shorty well enough to suspect that he is angling to be elected himself but, if that is the case, he is disappointed.

"Felicity is doing the photography, so she should be the one to direct operations," says Diana, decisively. "We are going to need some convincing shots."

"I'm happy with that," says Felicity. "So the first thing is to find a more suitable site. I can cope with low light levels, but we need Barnacle in amongst quite dense vegetation, preferably in stalking mode and with his teeth bared in a scary snarl."

"I can show you just the place," offers Peggy. "It's easy to get to, if you knows the way, but you'd soon be up to your arm-pits in mud if you tried to find it on your own."

"A secret place. Untrodden by human foot since sixteen hundred," says Diana, enthusiastically. "Exactly what we need."

"Your Daddy ain't never been there for his shootin'," says Peggy, "He don't stray far from firm ground. O'course I go there for my toadstools, but my feet ain't properly human so they don't leave footprints."

No-one feels it is worth questioning this improbable statement, and it is left to our newly appointed director to get the show on the road.

"Let's give it a whirl, then," decides Felicity, adjusting the strap of her capacious shoulder bag. "Diana and I will follow Peggy and you two old matelots can bring up the rear with Barnacle."

I stroll over to my car to fetch Barnacle in his basket feeling, for the first time, that the day might, after all, be rewarding. If Felicity can get away with calling an old Purple Funnel shipmaster a matelot, who knows what other wonders might occur."

Despite his efforts to maintain an indifference to the proceedings, even Barnacle can't hide his interest in the constant movement of the light and shadow, the snapping of twigs and the rustle of leaves as we swing in line ahead through the trees following in Peggy's wake. He has eyes everywhere, like a late-season potato.

It is all too obvious how necessary it is to have Peggy as a pilot. There are patches of firm ground where it has been consolidated by a close network of tree roots but, in between, there is rank, algae-covered water or sickly green moss over squelchy mud. No-where is it possible to walk in a straight line for more than a few metres.

Peggy leads the column confidently, and the rest of us follow as best we may. We progress steadily and, in my imagination, we become a patrol of soldiers, wending our way in single file through a minefield with the comfortable knowledge among those of us in the rear, that, provided the leader does not come to a sticky end, we will also be safe.

It is a good tactic, but not fool-proof and, when Diana puts a foot out of line, she leaves her Wellington boot stuck firmly in a puddle of glutinous mud. Shorty gallantly offers her a shoulder to lean on as she waits, one legged, while I place Barney's basket against a tree and attempt to retrieve the boot. In response to my steady heave, it disengages from its gungy trap with a guttural squelch and the release of bubbles of foul smelling marsh gas.

"There's no need to be so disgusting," I tell the puddle, severely.

"Are you speaking to that mud?" asks Felicity, looking at me oddly.

"He's always talking to inanimate objects," says Shorty. "It's because he served for too many years in tankers. He and his shipmates spent so little time in port and so much time on lonely watches at sea, they were always chatting to binnacles or conversing with windlasses. We used to call it tankeritis."

"Nothin' wrong with that," says Peggy. "Once a month, when these pools reflect the full Moon, I come out here and sings to them."

A final bubble slurps to the surface and burst with a horrible 'gloop'.

"No wonder they have indigestion, then," says Shorty.

"Just you keep a civil tongue in your head," snaps Peggy. "You would all look silly if I was to leave you here to find your own way out of the Copse."

"Do you mind?" breaks in Diana. "When you have quite finished this fascinating discussion I'd be grateful if you could give me my boot back."

She leans down to take the boot from my hands but, as she does so, her mobile phone slides out of her top pocket and disappears into a particularly murky pool with an absence of splash that would have delighted an Olympic diver. I make a despairing grab, but have nothing to show for it but a muddy hand and sleeve.

"That's gone for ever," Peggy tells Diana. "There's deep silt in the bottom of that pool."

"Well, that's a nuisance," says Diana, calmly, "But it doesn't matter too much. The thing was nearly a year old and I had already decided I needed a smarter one."

"Just as well," says Shorty. "It looks as though it is taking the short route to Australia."

"Let that be a lesson to you all," Peggy warns us. "And watch carefully where I put my feet from now on."

"Perhaps we should all be roped together, like rock climbers, to make sure we don't lose anyone in those cess-pits," I say, as I help manoeuvre Diana's foot into the boot.

"We should have brought life-jackets, if you ask me," grumbles Shorty.

"Just concentrate and follow my footsteps exactly, and you will be fine," orders Peggy. She looks fiercely at Shorty. "And I don't want no more smart remarks."

Fortunately, we only need to walk for another ten minutes before she heaves to, and we let out a collective sigh of relief, especially heartfelt in my case because Barnacle is no lightweight and I am no spring-chicken. I rest his basket on a tree-stump and massage my shoulder.

"Will this do you, dearie?" says Peggy to Felicity.

We have come to a small glade, surrounded by trees and bushes that appear to be in healthier condition than most of the Copse, perhaps because it is slightly elevated and, therefore, better drained. In the centre, there is plenty of space for us to move around without falling into a mud-hole and the lush vegetation provides an attractive backdrop for Barnacle to strut his stuff as a feral feline.

"Excellent," says Felicity. "Let me try a few shots in different directions and we can decide where Barney can best take the stage."

She makes a careful survey around the perimeter of the glade and, finally, takes up station by a lichen-covered rock which she can use to steady herself. She gestures towards some bushes under which there is a wind-blown cluster of dead leaves, with sparse, fern-like plants providing most of the ground-cover elsewhere.

"Can you please deploy Barnacle over there, Bill?" she asks. "That makes a dramatic setting of light and shadows. I want him lurking in there like an angry tiger."

Barnacle already has his harness strapped on and so, while Shorty holds the lid of his basket open, I reach inside and clip a long lead onto the ring of his harness. "OK, Barney," I invite him. "You can come out now."

Barnacle, in typical cat fashion, declines to cooperate and stays exactly where he is. The only acknowledgement he gives me is a bored yawn. I reach into my pocket and produce a packet of his favourite cat treats. He inspects them from a distance and then, unhurriedly, he steps out of his basket and accepts them from my hand.

"Come along, Barney," I urge him. "It's time for you to earn your keep."

He looks, with mild interest at the unfamiliar surroundings and I allow plenty of slack on his lead because I expect his natural curiosity will encourage him to set off on a fact-finding tour. Instead of that, he strolls over to Felicity, sniffs the tablet she is holding at the ready, and then rolls over on his back in a blatant invitation for her to massage his tummy."

"You've got it all wrong, Barney," she tells him. "You are supposed to be playing the part of a fierce and hungry predator." But she does ruffle his fur all the same.

I haul away on his lead, which annoys him, and he does, for a moment, look cross enough to pass as a reasonably wild cat, - but it doesn't last. Then, he spots a movement, or perhaps hears a rustle, amongst the dead leaves under one of the bushes, but his natural laziness trumps his hunting instinct and so, instead of rushing to investigate it, he lies down where he is and watches the place intently.

"Patience is the game, when photographing wildlife," says Felicity, so we all make ourselves as comfortable as we can and wait for developments.

They are a long time coming. Barnacle stays perfectly still with his eyes focussed on the pile of leaves but, after a while, his eyelids start to droop, and he is clearly losing concentration.

"That cat is going to sleep," grumbles Shorty.

"Let's have some action, Barney," says Diana. "We didn't bring you here for a snooze."

"Wake up," Felicity orders. "You are supposed to be looking dangerous."

"I knew I should have brought my Horror," says Peggy. "He has a dangerous look about him even when he is asleep. He'd frighten anyone when he's awake."

"We are all wasting our time," says Shorty. "Nothing is going to happen. No-one is ever going to believe that dozy animal is a wildcat."

As if to give a lie to Shorty's statement, Barnacle spots another slight movement amongst the leaves but, instead of making the lethal leap expected of a hunting feline, he rises to his feet in a leisurely fashion and ambles across to investigate.

Felicity has her tablet focussed on him as he noses cautiously under the bush and then there is a sudden, frenzied movement among the fallen leaves that takes us all by surprise, not least Barnacle, who springs back in alarm.

We catch a glimpse of a lizard-like animal that darts away in the direction of the nearest pool and dives into it with hardly a splash. Meanwhile, Barnacle stays frozen to the spot with a startled look on his face.

"What on Earth was that?" asks Shorty who, even when astonished, remains sufficiently old-fashioned that he doesn't use sailor language in front of ladies.

"It had legs," says Diana, "But I couldn't see much else. It was too fast."

"There's strange creatures in these woods," says Peggy, darkly. "You don't want to mess with them."

I notice that Felicity is manipulating her tablet. "Did you catch it on your screen?" I ask.

"I've got something here," she replies. "I'm just trying to zoom in. Yes. Here it is." And she shows us a picture of a creature, like a stretched version of a frog, frozen in time as it had scuttled across a patch of bare mud on its way to the pool."

"It looks like a lizard to me," I say, "But I hardly know anything about reptiles."

I am interrupted by Diana, who is peering over my shoulder. She takes hold of the tablet so she can study the picture more closely.

"That is not a reptile, it's an amphibian," she pronounces. "What is more, it is a Great Crested Newt."

"Just a long frog, then," says Shorty. "What's so exciting about that?"

"Even I know that," says Felicity, with a congratulatory nod to Diana. "Our nature correspondent filed a feature on them last year. They are a highly protected species. It is a criminal offence to disturb Great Crested Newts or to damage their breeding sites. Barnacle could be sent to prison for six months for what he has just done."

Barnacle is still sitting with his puzzled, 'what was that and where did it go' expression. He doesn't realise that his presence in the Copse has suddenly become redundant. Nevertheless, his part in the proceedings is properly recognised.

Diana bends down and fondles his head. "What a clever cat you are Barney," she says. "I think you may have saved the Copse at a stroke by finding that newt."

"Is it going to be enough?" asks Shorty.

"Oh, I should say so." Felicity assures him. "We have photographic evidence and five reliable witnesses. It will be headline news in my paper tomorrow."

"But that might be the only Great Crested Newt in the whole Copse," warns Shorty. "If wildlife experts come to verify our sighting, they might find none at all."

"There's plenty of they things in the Copse alright," says Peggy. "I'm allus coming across them when I'm collecting herbs in the woods, and Horror sometimes brings one home and leaves it by the kitchen door. I reckon he wants me to cook it up for his breakfast."

"That's terrible," gasps Diana. "You could find yourselves in deep trouble, killing endangered animals."

"Only if we gets found out," retorts Peggy. "An' we didn't know there was anything special about them."

"That's all by the way," I break in. "The main thing is that we now know there are many Great Crested Newts in the Copse and we have photographic evidence and witnesses to back it up. Our mission here has been highly successful, although not in quite the way we expected. I would like to take Barney home now and I propose we should all return to base and consolidate our thinking."

This suggestion meets with general approval, so I pick Barnacle up, detach the lead from his harness, give him a pat on the head, and return him to his basket. Then, with Peggy again acting as our pilot, we begin to thread our way back through the swampy woodland.

We are in good spirits, but not so carried away that we become careless about where we are putting our feet. In due course, we arrive, without mishap, at the clearing where we had left our cars. We find an unwelcome surprise waiting for us.

A third vehicle has arrived while we have been away and there is no doubt as to who it belongs to. It is a van with 'Verdant Heritage Co' marked on the sides. Standing in front of it, with his hands on his hips is Oliver Crump, and peering over his shoulder is a seriously worried Buster.

"So." Says Oliver, aggressively. "What a motley cast of characters to find in this dark and dismal wood. Miss Hunter, the hyper-active protester, Miss Wright the radical hack reporter, Mrs Morven the amateur witch, Mr Smith the allotments champion, and Mr Selsey the immoveable home owner. Who is going to tell me what mischief you are engaged in?"

"I ain't no amateur," growls Peggy. "So you'd best watch your tongue when you are talking to me."

Diana, from daily contact with the Major, is also immune to men with overbearing manners.

"This copse is owned by my father," she says, coldly. "I am perfectly entitled to take a walk with my friends whenever I wish. You, on the other hand, are an interloper. So you can take yourself off right now."

"I have an option to buy this land," says Oliver, "And I don't want it trampled on by you or anyone else."

"An option you have not, yet, exercised," says Diana. "And when you have heard what we have to say, you might decide not to exercise it at all."

To my surprise, Buster emerges from behind Oliver, stands by his side, and addresses Diana directly. "I've already told Dad that I think this site is unlikely to be viable for house-building. I can see too many problems. Are you going to tell us that there are more, Di?"

I have the impression that Buster's initiative is as much a surprise to Oliver as it is to me and, perhaps, that he is even a little pleased by it.

"I'm afraid so, Buster," says Diana. "It happened when Peggy, here, was kindly taking us for a stroll through the woods. We accidentally disturbed a Great Crested Newt and that, as you may know, is a species that is protected by law."

"I managed to photograph it," says Felicity, waving her tablet.

"And we all got a good view of it," adds Shorty.

"Perhaps it was a single, isolated individual," says Oliver.

"No, there's lots of them in the Copse," says Peggy.

"Is this serious, Dad?" asks Buster.

"It is if it's true," replies Oliver, "But I don't trust this bunch of agitators. There's something fishy going on." He turns to me. "Why have you brought that cat of yours, Bill Selsey? It is not normal to carry a cat in a basket when going for a ramble in the country."

I think fast and, again, I am worried by the newly acquired glibness with which I come up with a dubious story. "I'm training him to hunt truffles in the woods," I say.

"I thought it was only pigs and dogs that could do that," says Oliver.

"Yes. Well, perhaps that's why he's not very good at it," I say. "He didn't find any for us."

"Oliver frowns. "You are trouble makers, the lot of you," he accuses us. "I don't know why I should believe anything you tell me."

"The Great Crested Newt will be headline news tomorrow," Felicity tells him. "You will have to believe it then. We never print anything that isn't true," she adds, virtuously.

Oliver turns to Buster. "Great Crested Newts are bad news for developers, son," he says. "If they really are in the Copse and we decide to fight it, the legal costs could be huge, and with no guarantee of success. It wouldn't just be these clowns we would be up against." He takes us all in with a dismissive sweep of his arm.

"We should talk about it this evening, Dad," says Buster. "But you already know my feelings about this site."

As they move away towards their van, Buster turns his head and treats Diana to an enormous wink. Oliver, meanwhile, can't resist a parting shot at Diana.

"If we don't go ahead with the purchase of Hangman's Copse, your father is going to be greatly disappointed," he warns her. "I understand he has been making some very unwise investments lately."

"I wonder what he meant by that," muses Diana, as we watch the van disappearing along the track.

"Don't worry, Di," counsels Felicity. "He's just trying to get at you."

"He's a bad loser," suggests Shorty, "But we'll keep an eye on him."

"Forget Oliver Crump, we ought to be celebrating," I say.

"Come back to my place, then," offers Peggy. "I can rustle up all kinds of drinks and nibbles."

"Er. I've got to take Barney home, right now," I say.

"And I must get back to the allotments," says Shorty, looking at his watch.

"And I have a lot of work to do on this story if I am to make the deadline for tomorrow's paper," says Felicity.

"But we ought to meet again soon," says Diana, "To make sure we are all telling the same story and to build up a momentum for saving the Copse."

"Tomorrow afternoon at my shed, then," suggests Shorty. "What about two-thirty?"

Everyone is in agreement, and I arrange to drive out to pick up Peggy in good time for the meeting.

Diana and Felicity drive off in their roadster, while I follow on with Peggy, Shorty and Barnacle. We drop Peggy off at her cottage, and then take Barnacle back to his home where we see him settled in his kitchen, glad to be out of the confines of his basket, and ready to compose himself for a restorative sleep after the excitement of the day.

Kevin and Sean have already finished their sandwiches and are putting the finishing touches to the repair to my roof. They wave, cheerfully, and call down that they expect to finish the job by about 4 o'clock. I find rolls, some cheese and a couple of beers in the fridge, and then walk with Shorty to his shed, where we enjoy a late lunch and discuss the implications of our morning's adventure. The outlook for Hangman's Copse is looking good, we decide, but, despite having obtained some useful new information, we come to no useful conclusions that would help our case for protecting the allotments.

"All this concentrated thought is getting us nowhere," says Shorty, at last. "What we need to do is to clear our minds completely so that our subconscious can work on the problem, and then come back to it later."

"Let's give it a try, then," I agree. "We need some entirely unrelated activity to divert us."

"A shanty or two, perhaps," he suggests.

So, we launch into a discordant rendering of some dubious, and half remembered sea songs.

A roving, a roving,
Since roving's been our ru-i-in,
We'll no more go a roving
With you, fair maid.

This exercise has the useful effect of making us thirsty, so we return to our beer with relish. On the other hand, our subconscious minds have entirely failed to recognise what was expected of them, and we have come up with no new ideas for saving the allotments. We pore over the Situation Chart and add a few connecting lines to it but, by the time Shorty has to make his way home for his evening meal, we have made no break-through and have thought of no new actions that we might pursue.

I walk back to my own house, and see that Kevin and Sean have, indeed finished their work and have been long gone. Then I remember that the stock in my fridge has become depleted, so I set off in the car to buy provisions at the little mini-market. As is often the case, when I am not in a mood for cooking, I stop off at

Charley's fish and chip shop on my way home. This time, I buy two pieces of haddock so that Barney can have one to himself rather than having a share of mine.

When we finally sit down for supper together, I explain that the bonus is because he is such a marvellous animal but, of course, being a cat, he already knows that.

"It has been a highly satisfactory day," I tell him, "And we have both earned a quiet and self-indulgent evening."

But Barney is far too polite to reply with his mouth full.

CHAPTER 34

That night, I sleep better than I have for several days, and I am not even bothered too much when the clanging of scaffold poles wakes me up at eight-thirty in the morning. I throw on a few clothes and saunter round to the side of my house to find out what is going on. I see that the roof repair, despite Kevin's and Sean's unhurried approach to the job, looks like good quality work. The scaffolders, Chris and Fred are busy dismantling the edifice they had erected in Friday. Unlike Kevin and Sean, they obviously have some incentive to move quickly because they politely decline my offer of refreshment.

"We've got another job on this morning," explains Chris, "And we'll earn a bonus if we can finish it by lunch-time."

"All go," adds Fred, true to his bi-syllabic style.

I return to the kitchen for a leisurely breakfast with an attentive Barnacle who, I can tell, is wondering if yesterday's supper signalled the start of larger portions of luxury food at every meal. He is disappointed when I open a sachet of cat-food for him, but he eats it all the same.

Dismantling the scaffolding turns out to be a much faster process that setting it up and so, by the time we have finished breakfast and I have showered and shaved, Chris and Fred have loaded up their lorry and are ready to leave. I go out to give them a tenner each for a drink and, as I stand by the gate to wave them off, a battered truck pulls up by the kerb-side. There is a hydraulic lifting davit attached to the cab, and it is towing a heavy-duty wood chipper-cum-shredder unit.

A scruffy, but cheerful bloke in well-worn jeans, winds down a window and calls out to me. "Mr Selsey, is it?" he asks.

"The same," I tell him. "How can I help you?"

He opens the door and walks across to me. "I'm Colin Sawyer. My mate, Kevin Slater, tells me you have an oak tree you want to get rid of."

"Yes, indeed," I reply. "That's it, lying across my front garden."

Colin walks over to the tree and gives it an exploratory kick, just as Kevin had done. It must be some kind of a superstition among woodmen, I think to myself, like sailors don't whistle in case it brings on a storm of wind.

"I'll be straight with you, Mr Selsey," says Colin, which immediately starts alarm bells in my head because those words are a classic preliminary to a scam.

"Go on," I say, suspiciously.

"That is a good piece of oak," continues Colin. "I can take it away for you, and leave your garden neat and tidy, and still make a bit for myself, but I can't give you anything for it."

"That's fine, Colin," I say, with some relief, because I thought he was building-up to charging me an exorbitant fee for removing the tree.

"It's a deal then," says Colin, offering his hand. "I'll be back this afternoon with a chain-saw and a couple of mates, if that's alright."

We shake hands, and I assure him that the sooner he removes the offending tree from my garden, the better I will be pleased.

I stand by the gate for a while after Colin has driven off, thinking about this and that, and I am about to return to my kitchen when I hear the sound of a motor-bike approaching. It's going to be another of those mornings, I think to myself, as I recognise the rider. Buster comes to a halt by the roadside, revs up his engine to a crescendo before switching off, and dismounting.

"Hello, Mr Selsey," he calls. "I am looking for Di, and I wondered whether she might be at your place."

"No, she isn't, Buster," I say, "But I'd like a word with you, and I don't think it's a good idea to talk in the street. Can you come inside for a few minutes?"

"Just for a few minutes then," agrees Buster, removing his helmet as he follows me into the house. "I do want to get on with finding Di."

"Tea? Coffee?" I offer as we enter the kitchen.

"No thanks, Mr Selsey," says Buster. "I want to get on with searching for Di. I've tried phoning her, but there is no reply, and I've been to her place and she is not at home."

"I can tell you about her mobile phone," I say. "It's at the bottom of one of those muddy pools in Hangman's Copse. She lost it there yesterday."

"But you don't know where she is now?" asks Buster, anxiously.

"No, I don't," I tell him, "But I think she might have gone to see Emma Gooding this morning to tell her about the Great Crested Newt we found in the Copse."

"I thought you were going to pretend that Barnacle was a wildcat," says Buster. "Did you take a newt in with you instead?"

"No. That was genuine." I tell him. "We really did find that newt when Barney was sniffing around in the undergrowth."

"Looking for truffles, you told us," says Buster. "Well the newt was a very lucky find, then."

"Er, yes," I agree. "But it wasn't so lucky for your father and his company, Verdant Heritage, was it?"

"Well, yes, I think it was," says Buster. "The Gov'nor is a good bloke, but he gets too emotionally involved in his projects sometimes. Once he sets his mind on something, he likes to push it through at all costs, and that is not always good business."

"That is a very mature assessment," I say, "You surprise me, Buster."

"Don't you remember Di telling me that being a director is like riding a bike," explains Buster. "Well some of my biker friends set themselves challenges and won't give up even when they become obviously impossible. They either come to their senses in hospital or they don't come to their senses at all. I've always known where to draw the line"

I reflect that this ability to make a rational decision, and not be carried away by the excitement of the moment, explains Buster's cautious behaviour at the Town Hall demonstration, which had put him temporarily out of favour with Diana. However, I do not intend to bring this up.

"So you think that your Dad was wrong to have kept pushing ahead with developing Hangman's Copse, then," I say.

"I'm sure it would have been unprofitable even before you found the newt, and it certainly is now," says Buster. "As a matter of fact, I have a feeling that the Gov'nor is secretly pleased that I am putting my foot down. It gives him an acceptable get-out."

"There is more to you than meets the eye, Buster," I tell him. "And what are your views about building a block of retirement apartments on the allotments site?"

"I don't like that much, either," says Buster. "To my mind, that is a brownfield site, and they are always tricky to develop. It's like buying a bike that has been in an accident. The repairs cost a fortune and, however much you spend, it never really comes right."

"You are amazingly knowledgeable about these things," I say. "You can't have picked it all up in a couple of days."

"Well, I suppose I must have absorbed some of the stuff that the Guv'nor has been telling me about for years although, at the time, I wasn't really interested," explains Buster.

"So, are you going to oppose the allotments site project then?" I ask.

"It's sort of, so, so," says Buster. "But the Gov'nor is set on going ahead with it and, given a bit of luck, it could make some useful money, Of course, it would help if you would agree to sell your house."

"Don't hold your breath on that one, Buster," I tell him.

"That's between you and my Gov'nor," says Buster. He consults his watch. "Look, I must get off to Emma Gooding's place to try to catch up with Di. Nice talking to you, Mr Selsey."

"Just one more thing before you go," I say. "How come you and your Dad turned up at Hangman's Copse yesterday? I thought you said you were going to be miles away, looking at land near Watermill Creek."

"We did go there," explains Buster, but the Gov'nor became uneasy. He gets these twinges, you know, like rheumatism."

"In that case, it probably is rheumatism," I suggest.

"Maybe," agrees Buster, "But, whatever the case, after we'd been on site for about ten minutes, he suddenly upped and said we should drop everything and head back for Hangman's Copse. He reckons it's a kind of sixth sense that warns him of trouble."

"Or rheumatism," I murmur.

"I'll see you later, Mr Selsey," says Buster. "Thanks for helping me find Di."

He ruffles Barnacle's fur and then sets off at a trot back to his bike. He dons his helmet, starts the engine, revs up to his trademark roar, waves a gloved hand, and hurtles off along the road to continue his search.

"I'm thinking we have been under-estimating young Master Crump all this time," I say to Barnacle. "He might well have the makings of a successful business man, and he will certainly need to be, if he is serious about hitching up with Diana Hunter. She strikes me as a young woman who is likely to have expensive hobbies."

If Barney has an opinion on the matter, he keeps it to himself.

CHAPTER 35

I spend some time cleaning the kitchen and tackling some much needed housework and then, at about twelve-thirty, I whizz out to the local mini-market where I buy a quiche, a case of beer and an apple pie. By one o'clock, I am knocking on the door of Shorty's shed with the lunch offerings in a basket. Shorty, as always, well almost always, is sitting reading the morning paper.

"Felicity has done us proud today," he greets me. "Listen to this, 'GREAT CRESTED NEWTS FOUND IN HANGMAN'S COPSE.' That's the headline," he explains.

"Go on then," I encourage him. "What else does she say?"

Shorty frowns. "There's a lot of it, but I'll read you a few snippets. 'Protected species in protected ancient woodland.' 'EU and UK laws apply.' 'Offence to disturb, capture, injure or kill.' How's that to be going on with?"

"Brilliant," I say. "I think we can claim total victory." And I tell him about Buster's view that any proposal for building houses on the Hangman's Copse site is dead in the water..

He passes me the paper and takes the lunch basket in return. There is a good half page about the discovery, including the photograph that Felicity took of the newt and a general picture of Hangman's copse as a whole. By the time I have finished reading, Shorty has cut the quiche into wedges and opened two cans of beer.

"I think we can nearly close the file on Hangman's Copse," suggests Shorty, "But that still leaves the allotments site under threat. Perhaps we can concentrate on that now,"

"The allotments could be more of a problem," I say, and I tell him about my conversation with Buster. "So he thinks it might be a viable proposition for Verdant Heritage to build there," I conclude.

"We must talk to Diana when she comes at two-thirty," says Shorty. "If she is on our side, it won't take her long to straighten Buster out."

"I'm not so sure about that," I tell him. "This is a new Buster we are dealing with. A couple of days ago, he wouldn't have said boo to his father, but now he is looking on Oliver as a bloke with suspect judgement who is in need of firm guidance."

"Felicity Wright has said she will support us, but she is a bit half-hearted," adds Shorty, gloomily,

"What about your petition?" I ask. "How is that coming along?"

Shorty brightens. "Oh, that is doing well," he says. "Felicity's piece in the paper helped spread the word and we have a lot of signatures. Ben Stamping, one of the Committee members is organising that. As a lawyer he knows how these things should be presented."

"That is promising, then," I say, encouragingly. "I am not sure what else we can do at the present time, but perhaps some of the others will come up with a suggestion when they arrive for our meeting."

We finish our sandwiches, and I check my watch. "There's just time to share that apple pie and then I must go off to collect Peggy Morven – or perhaps it will be Margaret Millard, or even Madame Mernov."

"Like I've always said, you never know where you are with women," grins Shorty. "You might even find she has reverted to being that astro-physicist you suspected she once was."

As it turns out, it is Margaret Millard who welcomes me when I knock on the door of her cottage. I am pleased about this because Maggie is the least embarrassing of the portfolio of characters she is able to assume."

"Do come in, Bill," she smiles. "I'm nearly ready. I just need to make sure that Horror has everything he needs."

True to her promise, we are soon on our way back to the allotments site. She is in sparkling form, and she keeps me entertained by telling me about some of the customers she had to deal with at Emma Gooding's fête.

It is just after two-thirty when we arrive at Shorty's shed, where we find that the other parties to the meeting have already made themselves at home. Apart from the easy chairs that are normally reserved for Shorty and me, he has pressed into service two folding chairs that we use for sitting outside on sunny days. Otherwise, there are sitting opportunities on two, low potting benches that have never been asked to support a pot in their lives. Diana and Felicity, I expected to see, but I am surprised that Buster has also found time to attend. He and Diana are sharing a bench designed to accommodate a couple of seed trays, and he is enjoying the proximity that this requires.

Maggie and I find places to perch and Shorty, as the host, calls the meeting to order. He begins by congratulating Felicity on her write-up of our discovery in the Copse. The Great Crested Newt is such a heavily protected species, he suggests, that it has become virtually impossible for the site to be developed.

"Absolutely right," confirms Buster. "Verdant Heritage has spent some money on this project, partly to pay Di's father for an option to purchase the Copse, and partly to have it surveyed and some of the trees sampled. Unfortunately, once my Gov'nor has invested money in something, he normally becomes determined to see it through, even when it is obviously running into problems."

"He is surely not going to fight over the Copse," I say.

"Not while I'm Operations Director of Verdant Heritage," declares Buster. "In fact, he has already backed down. He knows he will lose if I put the case to the Board."

"You are so forceful, Buster, dear," says Diana, giving him a hug.

"So the Verdant Heritage Company has no further interest in Hangman's Copse?" queries Felicity. "Can I quote you on that?"

"Not quite," says Buster. "I have in mind to put it to the Board that we might sponsor protective measures for the Copse. Repair the fencing and mark footpaths so the public can enjoy them. That kind of thing. It would provide Verdant Heritage with some fine green credentials for very little money. We might even adopt the Great Crested Newt as our logo."

"Ha! An environmentally sound and commercially attractive business proposal. Place an advertisement in my paper when the time comes and I'll write a feature for your company," offers Felicity.

"When you two have finished your mutual back-scratching, can I just say that I think the Copse should be left as it is," breaks in Maggie. "It needs preserving so it can continue to support all the plants and animals that have lived in it for generations. The last thing it needs is tarting up."

"Well, there is no fear of that now that the sale is off," says Diana. "Daddy confessed to me last night that he had made some unwise investments and that, without the money from the Copse, we will only have his army pension to live on. He'll have to sell our house and everything, and he certainly won't have any money to spend on the Copse."

"I am really sorry for you and the Major," comments Maggie, "But I am sure it is good news for all the creatures that live in the Copse."

"I don't believe I will enjoy being poor," laments Diana. "I expect I will have to sell my roadster."

"Join the paupers' club," says Felicity. "You could borrow my bicycle when I'm not using it."

"Or you could ride my Harley," offers Buster. "I'll have the use of the Company van."

"That would be marginally better," says Diana. "But what would I do if it rains, or in the winter?"

"Stay at home and read a book," suggests Shorty, unfeelingly.

"You should think about becoming independent and taking up a profession," advises Maggie, in her best wise-old-aunt manner. "There are always vacancies for nuns and, if you are looking for more fun, I'm sure Peggy Morven would take you on as an apprentice witch."

Diana manages a half-smile. "I suppose it has all been worth it," she says.

"Don't worry, Di," says Buster, putting a protective arm around her shoulders. "My director's fee is very healthy. I am sure we can work something out."

"Let's look on the bright side," says Shorty. "Thanks to the efforts and, in some cases, the sacrifices, of all concerned, Hangman's Copse has definitely been saved from development. That is a great achievement. Now we can concentrate our efforts on saving the allotments site."

There is an inspection of finger-nails and a shuffling of feet for an awkward few seconds. This topic is clearly not going to arouse so much enthusiasm as the ancient woodland. But I certainly do not want a block of apartments looming over my back fence.

"Come on," I rally them. "The proposal to build on the allotments site is not acceptable on either environmental or social grounds. It would constitute a monstrous overbuilding in the heart of what is, at present, a pleasant and well-balanced residential area."

"Allotments don't have the same emotional pull for my readers as the unspoilt countryside and endangered animals," says Felicity, "But you have made a fair case, and I'll support you however I can."

"Everyone agrees that new housing is needed," points out Buster, "But no-one wants it on their own doorstep, and no-one thinks we should build on green-field sites."

"It's a tough life for you property developers, isn't it?" says Shorty, sardonically.

"The allotments aren't a bad compromise" says Buster. "The site is an awkward shape, and we would need to demolish Mr Selsey's house, or a similar one, to provide access, but it might just be viable a business proposition in a town that is desperately short of retirement accommodation."

"Would you make enough money to be able to sell your Harley and buy a Ferrari?" asks Diana. "I wouldn't mind borrowing that."

"We'd be lucky to do much more than break even," says Buster, "But my Gov'nor is keen to go ahead with it."

"Whose side are you two on?" demands an exasperated Shorty. "What about the loss of amenities and the wrecking of the neighbourhood?"

"I am sure we will all support you when it comes down to it," says Maggie, "But you have to face the fact that there is a significant counter-argument."

"That is fair enough," I say, "And I certainly have no intention of selling my house to Buster's father or to anyone else. We are grateful for everyone's support in preserving the allotments, but I am wondering if you have any ideas about how we might proceed in practice."

"I don't see there is much more we can do," says Felicity. "Your best hope is to lobby the Council and then hit them with a heavily subscribed petition, and your Allotments Holders' Association has both of those actions in hand."

"I'm not mad about building on the allotments site," says Buster, "But I can't argue against the Gov'nor on business grounds. Of course he might find it impossible to push it through the Council's Planning Committee if the other members are influenced by your petition."

"I could talk to Emma Gooding," suggests Diana, "But I don't believe this is something that would fire her up into campaigning mode."

"We need to up our game, somehow," Shorty begins, but he is interrupted by a knock on the door of his shed. He breaks off and goes to open it. A tall, graceful woman, who I recognise as his Allotment Holders' Committee colleague Eileen Mulcher, is standing there. She has a bothered expression on her face.

"Oh, Shorty," she apologises, "I didn't realise you were entertaining. I'll come back later."

"No need for that, Eileen," says Shorty. "Please come in and meet my friends. We are discussing how we might save the allotments from redevelopment, and you are most welcome to join us."

"Hi, everybody," says Eileen, brightly, but she pauses just inside the door to show Shorty the contents of a bag she is carrying. "You remember I told you that something was eating my raspberries before they were properly ripe," she continues. "Well, Ben Stamping thought it might be mice and suggested I should set a trap."

"Ben is usually reliable on garden pests," says Shorty.

"Yes," agrees Eileen. "He was right as usual. I hate ordinary spring-loaded mouse-traps because I think they are cruel, so I bought one of those 'humane' traps, like a sort of cage with a one-way flap. The mice can get in, but they can't get out again. I left one by my raspberries overnight."

"And now I see you have caught two of the little thieves, and I suppose you don't know what to do with them," says Shorty.

"They are such sweet, cuddlesome little darlings," says Eileen. "I couldn't possibly kill them. Look, they have even got furry tails."

"What!" cry Diana and I, simultaneously. We rush over to the door to inspect the captives. "They are dormice," declares Diana.

"They must be two of the ones I had in my dining room," I exclaim. "So Barnacle didn't eat them after all. He just knocked their cage off the table and allowed them to escape. They will have found fat pickings on the allotments ...." I break off as I feel someone kick me in the shins.

"Not so fast, Bill," interrupts Diana. "I suspect your imagination is running away with you again. Fancy thinking you ever had any dormice in your home. And on your dining table. Were you proposing to have them for dinner?" She looks me straight in the eye and winks meaningfully.

"Oh dear. Have I been hallucinating again?" I smite my brow as I remember Laurence Olivier doing many years ago when over-playing a crazed King Lear at the Old Vic Theatre. "Of course there were never any mice in my house. I have a cat, you know," I explain to Eileen.

"But no mice?" she asks.

"My sister kept hamsters," I tell her, in the hope that, if I say something that is true it might, somehow, atone for the lie that preceded it.

"Take no notice, Eileen," Shorty comforts her. "I'll explain about Bill, later. His trains of thought go off onto more sidelines than Thomas the Tank-engine. It's all to do with his deprived life at sea. These dormice must have been established on the allotments for years without us suspecting."

"But what am I to do with the little things right now, Shorty?" asks Eileen. "It doesn't matter what they are called."

"Actually, it does matter a great deal," says Diana. "Dormice are an endangered species and highly protected. You weren't to know, of course, but you have already committed a criminal offence just by trapping them. You are not allowed even to handle them without a licence."

"I won't be sent to prison, will I?" asks a worried Eileen.

"Of course not," Shorty reassures her. "We can all vouch for the fact that you caught them accidentally and that they have been released without harm."

"But I have still got them in this cage," wails Eileen.

"Here, let me have them," says Diana, removing the cage from Eileen's shaking hand. "Come on, the rest of you, we must release these creatures as soon as possible. Be ready for some more photo-shots, Felicity."

"We must let them free in exactly the same place that you caught them, so they will know their way home," explains Diana to Eileen. "Please lead the way and we will all follow."

With Shorty and Eileen at our head and Diana immediately behind them, we proceed in a ragged column to Eileen's plot. This has been well cultivated and makes a striking contrast to Shorty's barren patch.

At one end is a thicket of raspberry canes. It is covered by close-mesh netting to protect the fruit from birds, but mice could easily crawl underneath. Eileen points to a small clear area, just inside the netting, and Diana sets the cage down carefully. While we had been walking, she had located the catch which would release the flap and allow the mice to escape.

"Which way do you think they will run?" asks Felicity, taking her tablet out of her bag and setting it up for photography.

We all look around, but the answer seems fairly obvious. Eileen's plot is right next to the uncultivated area where Shorty and I had sat in the Sun to enjoy our lunch on Saturday. Its trees and bushes could provide cover for a family of elephants.

"They'll go that way," indicates Shorty, confidently. "I am sure they have been living amongst those trees for ages."

"Stand by then," says Diana. "I'll release the catch on the count of three. One-two-three."

Nothing happens for a few, long, seconds as the dormice take in the fact that they are free to depart. Then they streak across the path, over a grass bank and up the silvery-grey trunk of the walnut tree before disappearing into a knot-hole, perhaps four metres above the ground.

"Did you get them, Felicity?" asks Diana.

Felicity makes a few adjustments to her tablet. "Yes," she says. "I have them as a movie, all the way."

"They will be back for my raspberries tomorrow," complains Eileen.

"I certainly hope so," says Shorty. "No-one will be able to interfere with the allotments while we have a colony of dormice in residence."

"Well that will definitely be worth a few raspberries," says Eileen.

"We'll all have to set aside ten-percent of our plots for growing food that dormice like," says Shorty. "I'll put it to our Committee tomorrow. I'll even grow sunflowers on my own plot. The seeds will ripen at just the right time to fatten up the little beauties for their winter hibernation."

Peggy and Buster had been interested onlookers for a while but now she gives him a nudge. "What is your take on all this, then, Buster? Do the dormice really mean the end to any possibility of building here?"

"We'll need to have their presence on the site confirmed by independent wildlife experts," says Buster, "But, yes, I am sure if dormice are established here, Verdant Heritage won't be evicting them."

"And that doesn't bother you, does it?" says Peggy.

"Not at all," replies Buster. "Even before the mice were found, I thought we could invest more profitably in that worked out market garden at Watermill Creek. The access is good, the site is already cleared, it is much larger scale and, better still, no-one is likely to object to its development."

"That is great news, Buster," I tell him. "It means I can get on with my life without anyone pressurising me to sell my house."

"Larger scale and more profitable, eh," Diana muses. "Are we talking Ferrari money this time?"

Buster grins. "Watch this space," he says. "And that reminds me, I am supposed to be meeting the Gov'nor in half an hour. I'll just have time to run you home if we go right away, Di."

"I wanted to see Emma Gooding first," says Diana. "I need to bring her up-to-date with everything."

"You take yourself off, Buster," I urge. "You mustn't keep your father waiting. I am going to drive Maggie home, so I can easily drop Diana at Emma Gooding's place on the way."

Buster hurries away and then the rest of us say our goodbyes in a more leisurely fashion.

I walk back to my own house with Maggie and Diana in tow. We check that all is well with Barnacle who opens a sleepy eye as we enter the kitchen, and closes it again when he realises we are not intending to stay with him. I load them into my red Volvo and we set off to carry our good tidings to Emma Gooding.

CHAPTER 36

Emma welcomes us warmly. "Hello, Diana," she says. "And you too, Maggie. Nice to see you playing yourself for once"

I file this piece of information in my memory cells for future use. If Margaret Millard is her real name, I can Google it when I get home and, perhaps, find out whether she was once an actress or a physicist. I bring my attention back to what is going on in time to hear Diana introducing me.

"And this chap with the absent look on his face is Bill Selsey. He has helped enormously in our campaign to save Hangman's Copse from the developers."

"With considerable success, I understand," smiles Emma.

"Not only that, but we have managed to scupper the plans that were being hatched for building on the allotments site," I tell her. And then Diana takes up the story and explains how we discovered what is probably a colony of dormice, which, effectively, blocks any development of the site.

"Well, that is excellent news," says Emma, "But do come in, all of you. Diana's father, Henry, is in the lounge, and we have some news of our own to tell you about."

We follow Emma into a large, sunny, sitting room, where Major Hunter is standing with his back to the window and wearing a somewhat bemused expression on his face.

"I think you have met everyone, Henry," says Emma. The Major manages to recognise his daughter but, perhaps fortunately, he is obviously not able to recall where he has seen me before and, understandably, he makes no connection between the placid Maggie and the witch-like Peggy who frequents his woodland.

"Hrrrmph. Pleased to see you again," he says, accepting a peck on the cheek from Diana and shaking hands cautiously with Maggie and me.

"The thing is," says Emma, "I have at last persuaded Henry to propose to me and I have, just this minute, graciously accepted."

Diana moves quickly to give her a hug. "That's great news, Emma, but are you sure you know what you are taking on?"

"Oh, certainly, my dear," says Emma. "He needs someone to look after him. Ex-soldiers are so easily taken in by unscrupulous business-men when they leave the army."

"I met the fella at my golf-club," protests the Major. "How was I to know he was a wrong-un. Turns out he wasn't even a member."

"The 'fella' was an ex-patriot Greek whose registered office was a PO box in the Cayman Islands, and who was selling the deeds for a gold-mine in Aberdeenshire," Emma tells us.

"Can't trust anyone these days," complains the Major. "Would you believe, that Oliver Crump has pulled out of what I thought was a done-deal and left me in an untenable position. But then I never liked the chap. I didn't meet him in the golf-club, of course, we would never have accepted him as a member.

"It's good news about finding Great Crested Newts in Hangman's Copse, though," says Maggie. "You aren't allowed to shoot unscrupulous business men, but you will still be able to go there to let off steam with your shot gun. So long as you don't hit the newts, of course."

"I have in mind to appoint a part-time ranger to keep an eye on the Copse. Just to make sure nothing compromises its status as ancient woodland," muses Emma. "Would you like to take that on, Maggie?"

"That's just up my street," says Maggie. "I am in the woods at least three days a week as it is."

"I am sure Buster Crump would love to sponsor whatever costs are involved," I suggest. "It would look good on the Verdant Heritage website."

"I'll talk that over with Buster," promises Emma. And it occurs to me that that the future of the Major and the future of the Copse, are both equally secure in her capable hands.

"So, what about practical matters?" asks Diana, excitedly. "We aren't going to need two houses now, are we?"

"There's plenty of room for you and Henry to move in with me, once we are married," says Emma. "And I am sure we can find space in the garage for your little roadster."

"I say Emma," cuts in the Major. "Now we've got these people here, shouldn't we be offering them a celebratory drink?"

"Of course, Henry. I'll go and open a bottle of Bollinger at once," says Emma and, in an aside to us, "Isn't it lovely to have a masterful man about the house?"

CHAPTER 37

I limit myself to one glass of Emma Gooding's champagne, so I am in reasonable shape for driving Maggie Millard to her cottage. She is entertaining company, and we chat comfortably on the way about the happenings of the day. She is a fine looking woman when she is being herself, full of life and highly intelligent, I reflect, and I wonder why she lives in such an isolated situation and why she has no partner.

When we arrive at her cottage, she is in no hurry to leave the car. "So, what about you and me, Bill Selsey?" she says, at last. "Is this the end of our journey, or are you going to take me any further?"

"I'd very much like us to stay good friends," I tell her, "But, I think we are both much too independent to become closer. In any case, our cats wouldn't get on together."

She smiles and leans across to kiss my cheek. "I'm happy to settle for that," she says.

I drive home in a mellow mood. At last, my world seems to be settling down into a peaceful and satisfactory state again. Felicity has a great follow-up story for tomorrow. Diana looks set to keep her roadster and Buster looks set to keep Diana. Shorty's allotment and Maggie's Copse are looking safe. Even the Major can look forward to a comfortably regimented future under the benign colonelship of Emma Gooding. As for me, my house has been put into good shape and no-one is going to continue badgering me to sell it. I look forward to being master of my own ship again.

When I arrive home, I am amazed to find that Kevin's friend, Chris Sawyer has been as good as his word and in much less time than I expected. The fallen tree has completely disappeared, the debris has been removed and, apart from some damage to shrubs and plants and a few holes in my lawn, the garden has been left neat and tidy.

"Even the garden is ship-shape again," I tell Barnacle, as I let myself into the kitchen. "I think we have all earned a drink, don't you?"

I pour him a saucer of milk and I take down my bottle of single-malt whisky. "I am having this drink because I deserve it, not because I need it. There's a huge difference," I explain. Barnacle doesn't understand the words, but he senses that I have relaxation in mind, and this is something cats have a talent for. As soon as I have poured my drink, he jumps onto my lap and I tell him about my afternoon adventures. In particular, I apologise to him for suspecting that he had eaten the dormice.

"So, at last, we can settle back into our old, comfortable routine without having to worry about what the next interruption will bring," I tell him, which I should have known was tempting fate. The telephone rings immediately. I reach out to pick it up and, as I put it to my ear, I am not at all pleased to recognise the deep, brown voice of Oliver Crump.

"Hello Bill," he says. "I hope this isn't an inconvenient time. There are a couple of things I'd like to talk to you about."

"Hello Oliver," I reply, "What can I do for you? You don't still want to buy my house, do you?"

"Well, no," says Oliver, "In fact, that was one of the things I wanted to let you know about. As I am sure you understand, circumstances have changed and I'm no longer in the market for it."

"All that dry rot and rising damp, I suppose," I say, drily.

"Ah, well, I do get carried away when I am determined to have something," apologises Oliver, "But, all the same, I would have given you a fair price for it. No hard feelings, I hope."

"None at all, Oliver," I say.

"The other thing I wanted to talk about is the way you have helped my son, Boswell."

Good grief, I think to myself. Boswell! Poor chap. No wonder everyone calls him Buster.

"Hello Bill. Are you still there?" asks Oliver.

"Yes, of course, Oliver," I say. "It's just that I didn't recognise your son's name as Boswell."

"I know he likes to be called Buster, for some reason," says Oliver. "Anyhow, he thinks a lot of you, Bill. He tells me you have been a good friend to him over the past few days and I would like to thank you for that. He is a changed lad. I had almost given up trying to interest him in my business and now he has suddenly become, not just interested, but enthusiastic."

"He has achieved a remarkable grasp of the essentials in an incredibly short time," I agree.

"He has a more analytical approach than I do," admits Oliver. "I've always made my decisions on a gut feeling, which has mostly worked well enough, although there have been times when it has got me up to my neck in alligators."

"He still has a lot to learn," I warn.

"I understand that," says Oliver, "But the motivation is there now, and I am sure much of it is down to the support you have given him. I can't say how grateful I am."

"I don't believe I have done much at all," I tell Oliver, with perfect truth. "But I am glad for both you and – er – Boswell."

"Look here," says Oliver. "I'll drop round to your place tomorrow to check that the repairs to your house are satisfactory, and I'm sure I will, after all, be able to arrange for that tree to be cleared away from your garden."

"That's kind of you Oliver," I say, but I don't tell him that the tree has already been dealt with. He will be surprised, tomorrow, to find that it has completely gone, but I feel it is nice for people like Oliver to be surprised sometimes. I am just sorry that I can't think of a more scary one to spring on him.

"Good talking to you, Bill," says Oliver.

"Thanks for the call, Oliver," I reply.

I replace the phone and pick up my glass. Barnacle is sitting, patiently, in the chair next to mine and wondering how much longer it will be before I stop talking and offer him one of his cat treats.

"That has to be the last of the loose ends tied up," I tell him as I reach for the plastic box containing his favourite crunchies. "You and I have each played vital parts in resolving some highly complex challenges, and we have every right to feel self-satisfied."

I offer him a handful of crunchies and he wastes no time in burying his face in them.

"It is great to be able to resume our peaceful lives with no fear of further interruptions," I say, incautiously, and, right on cue, there is an urgent ringing of the door-bell. I pause, just long enough for Barnacle to finish his treats, and then go to find out who our visitor might be.

To my dismay, it is my big sister, Betty. Beyond her intimidating figure, I see a taxi-driver struggling up the garden path with a huge suitcase in each hand.

"I don't see any fallen trees . I can't think why you make up these stories, Bill," she says as she brushes me aside and strides into the kitchen.

Her eyes take in the whisky bottle and my empty glass. "Drinking the hard-stuff, and before supper, too. It looks as though I have got here just in time," she declares.

Barnacle has taken refuge under his chair and is peering out with wide, frightened eyes, and I have an almost irresistible compulsion to join him.

"Well don't just stand there with your mouth open. Go and take my bags and pay the driver," she orders. "I can see I'll have to start straightening you out right away. There's no time to lose. I can only stay here with you for a month."

Printed in Great Britain
by Amazon.co.uk, Ltd.,
Marston Gate.